SCOOBY-DOO

YOU MEDDLING KIDS!

WRITTEN BY:
CHRIS DUFFY
TERRANCE GRIEP
SAM HENDERSON
BARBARA SLATE
DAN SLOTT

ILLUSTRATED BY:
IVAN BRUNETTI
ERNIE COLÓN
GARY FIELDS
TIM HARKINS
ANDREW PEPOY
BOB SMITH
NED SONNTAG
JOE STATON

COLORED BY:
PATRICIA MULVIHILL

LETTERED BY:
ALBERT DEGUZMAN
PHIL FELIX
GASPAR
TIM HARKINS
KEN LOPEZ

SCOOBY-DOO VOL. 1: YOU MEDDLING KIDS!
Published by DC Comics. Cover and compilation copyright © 2003 Hanna-Barbera.
All Rights Reserved. Originally published in single magazine form as SCOOBY-DOO
1-5. Copyright © 1997 Hanna-Barbera. All Rights Reserved. SCOOBY-DOO and all
related characters and elements depicted herein are trademarks of Hanna-Barbera.
The DC Bullet is a trademark of DC Comics. The stories, characters and incidents
featured in this publication are entirely fictional. DC Comics does not read or
accept unsolicited submissions of ideas, stories or artwork.

CARTOON NETWORK and its logo are trademarks of Cartoon Network.

DC Comics, 1700 Broadway, New York, NY 10019
A Warner Bros. Entertainment Company.
Printed in Canada. First Printing.
ISBN: 1-40120-177-6
Cover illustration by Glenn Barr.

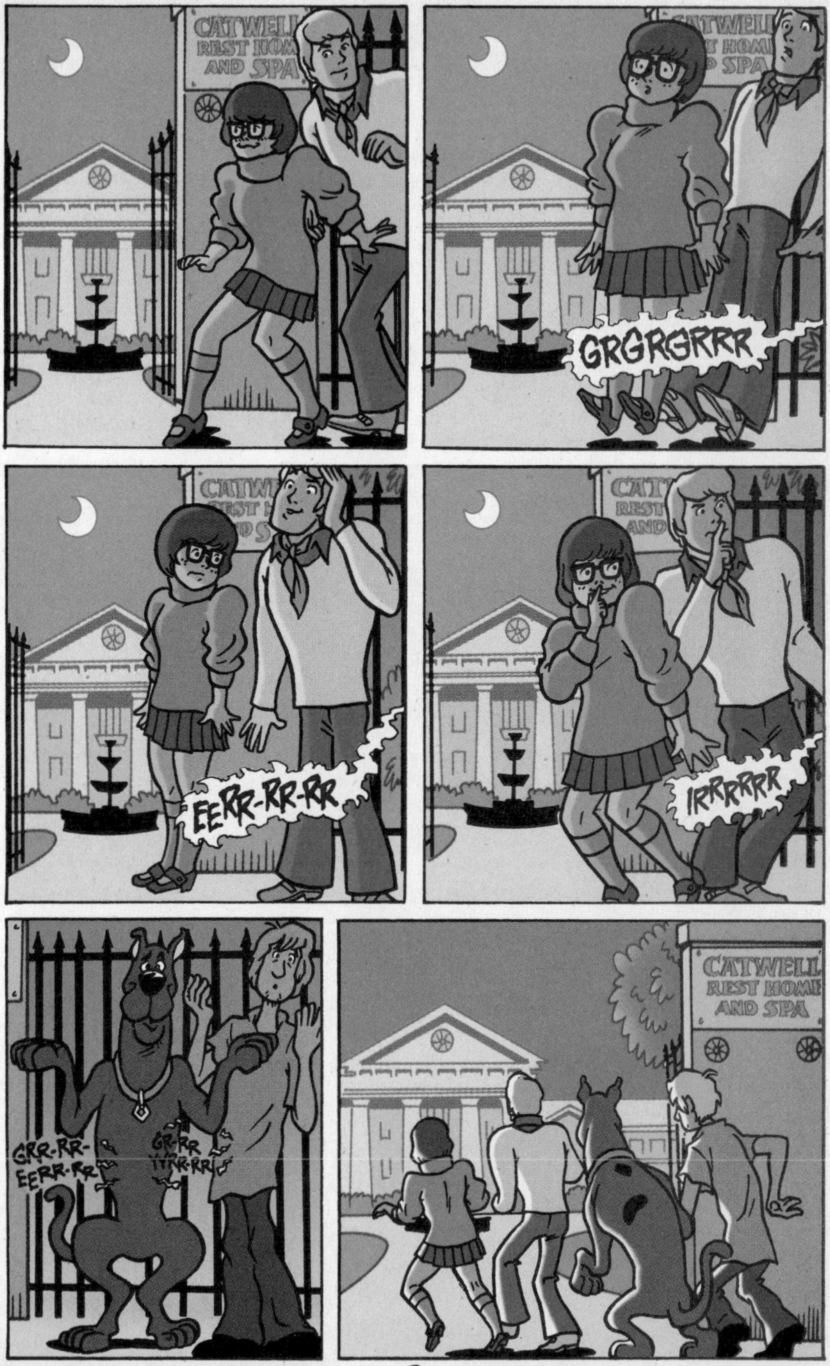
CATWELL
REST HOM
AND SPA
GRGRGRRR
EERR-RR-RR
IRRRRRR
GRR-RR-
EERR-RR
GR-RR
YYRR-RR
CATWELL
REST HOME
AND SPA

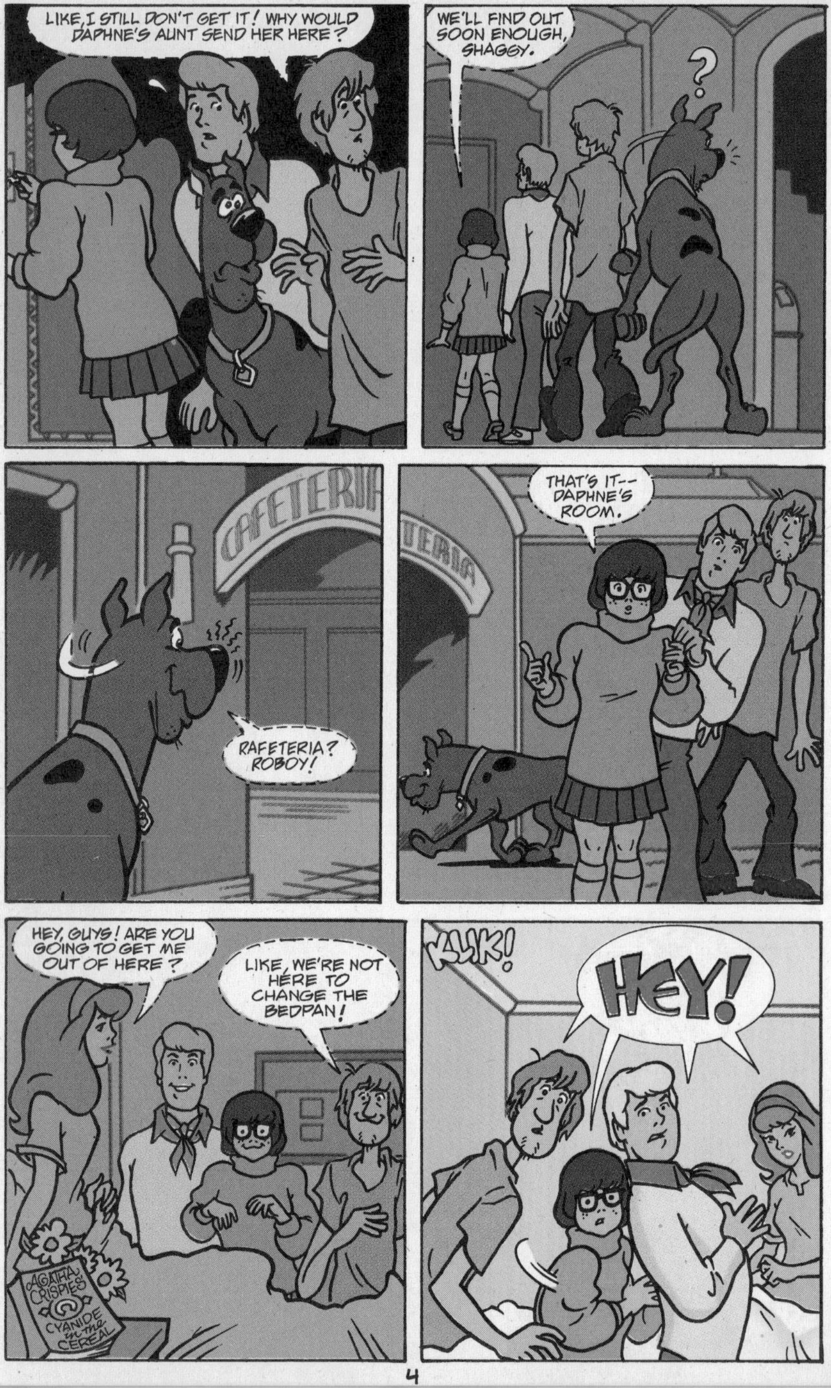
LIKE, I STILL DON'T GET IT! WHY WOULD DAPHNE'S AUNT SEND HER HERE?
WE'LL FIND OUT SOON ENOUGH, SHAGGY.
?
CAFETERIA
RAFETERIA? ROBOY!
TERIA
THAT'S IT-- DAPHNE'S ROOM.
HEY, GUYS! ARE YOU GOING TO GET ME OUT OF HERE?
LIKE, WE'RE NOT HERE TO CHANGE THE BEDPAN!
AGATHA CRISPIES
CYANIDE in the CEREAL
KLIK!
HEY!

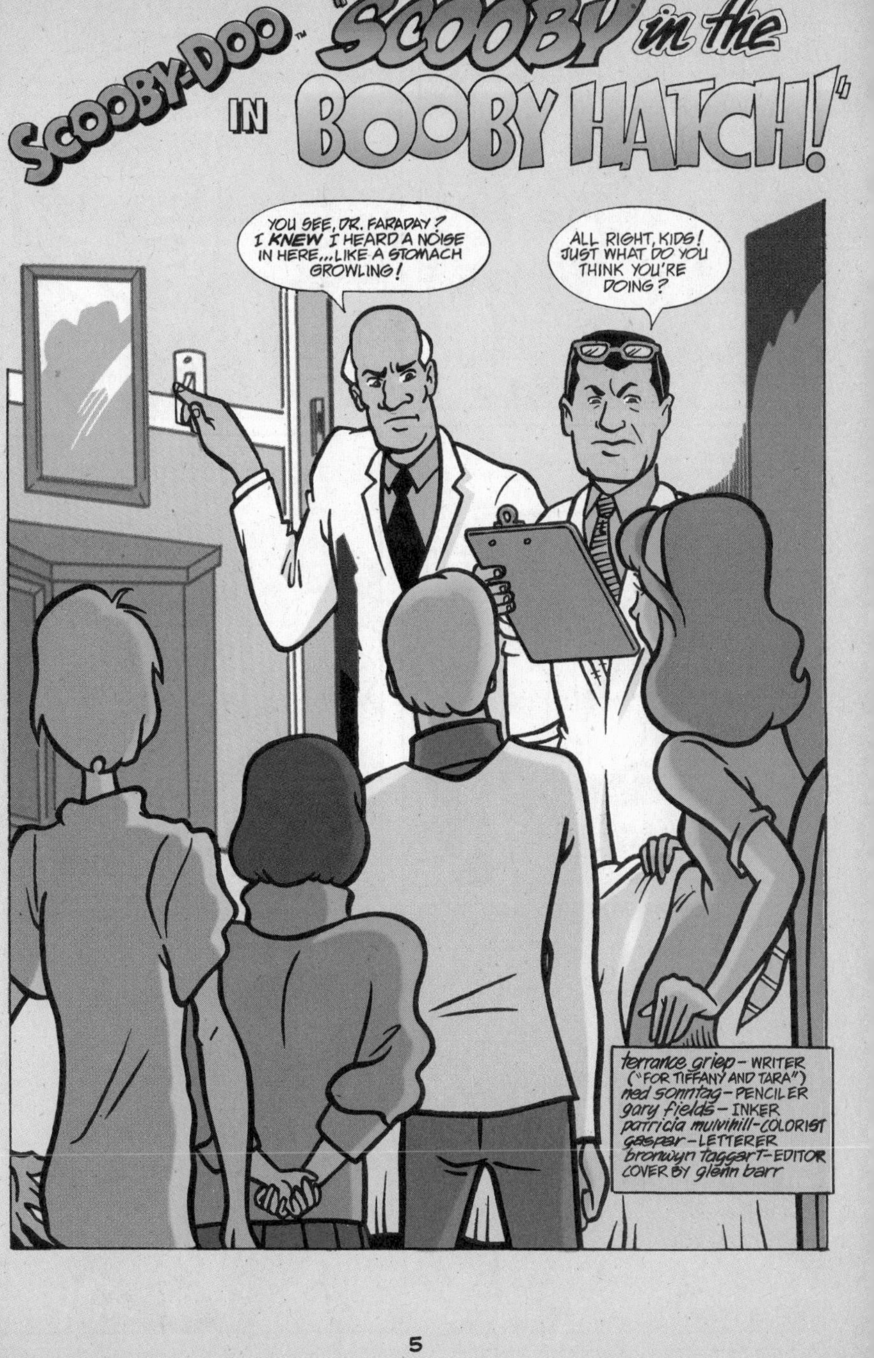
SCOOBY-DOO™ IN "SCOOBY in the BOOBY HATCH!"
YOU SEE, DR. FARADAY? I KNEW I HEARD A NOISE IN HERE...LIKE A STOMACH GROWLING!
ALL RIGHT, KIDS! JUST WHAT DO YOU THINK YOU'RE DOING?
terrance griep - WRITER ("FOR TIFFANY AND TARA") ned sonntag - PENCILER gary fields - INKER patricia mulvihill - COLORIST gaspar - LETTERER bronwyn taggart - EDITOR COVER BY glenn barr

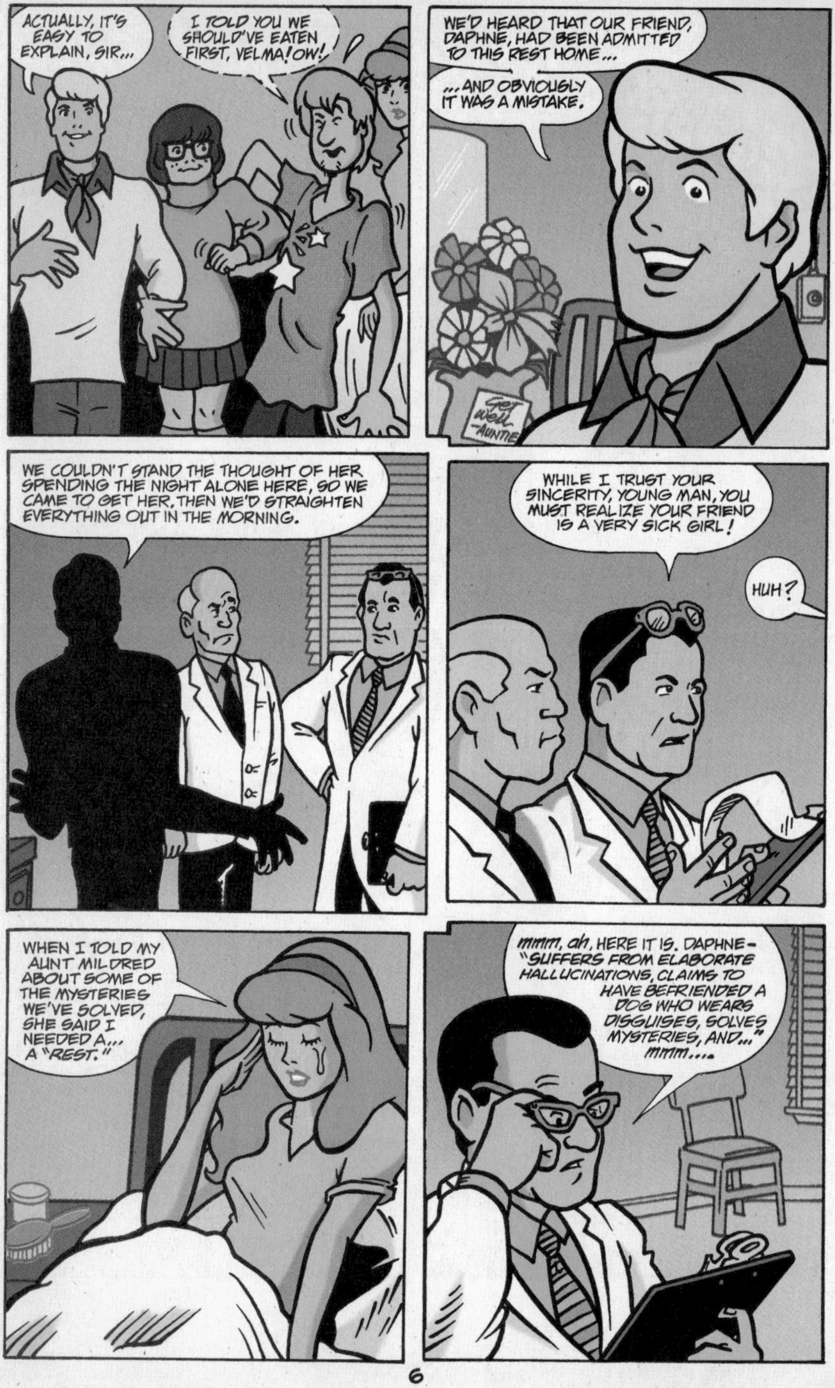

ACTUALLY, IT'S EASY TO EXPLAIN, SIR...
I TOLD YOU WE SHOULD'VE EATEN FIRST, VELMA! OW!
WE'D HEARD THAT OUR FRIEND, DAPHNE, HAD BEEN ADMITTED TO THIS REST HOME...
...AND OBVIOUSLY IT WAS A MISTAKE.
GET WELL -AUNTIE
WE COULDN'T STAND THE THOUGHT OF HER SPENDING THE NIGHT ALONE HERE, SO WE CAME TO GET HER, THEN WE'D STRAIGHTEN EVERYTHING OUT IN THE MORNING.
WHILE I TRUST YOUR SINCERITY, YOUNG MAN, YOU MUST REALIZE YOUR FRIEND IS A VERY SICK GIRL!
HUH?
WHEN I TOLD MY AUNT MILDRED ABOUT SOME OF THE MYSTERIES WE'VE SOLVED, SHE SAID I NEEDED A... A "REST."
mmm, ah, HERE IT IS. DAPHNE- "SUFFERS FROM ELABORATE HALLUCINATIONS, CLAIMS TO HAVE BEFRIENDED A DOG WHO WEARS DISGUISES, SOLVES MYSTERIES, AND..." mmm....

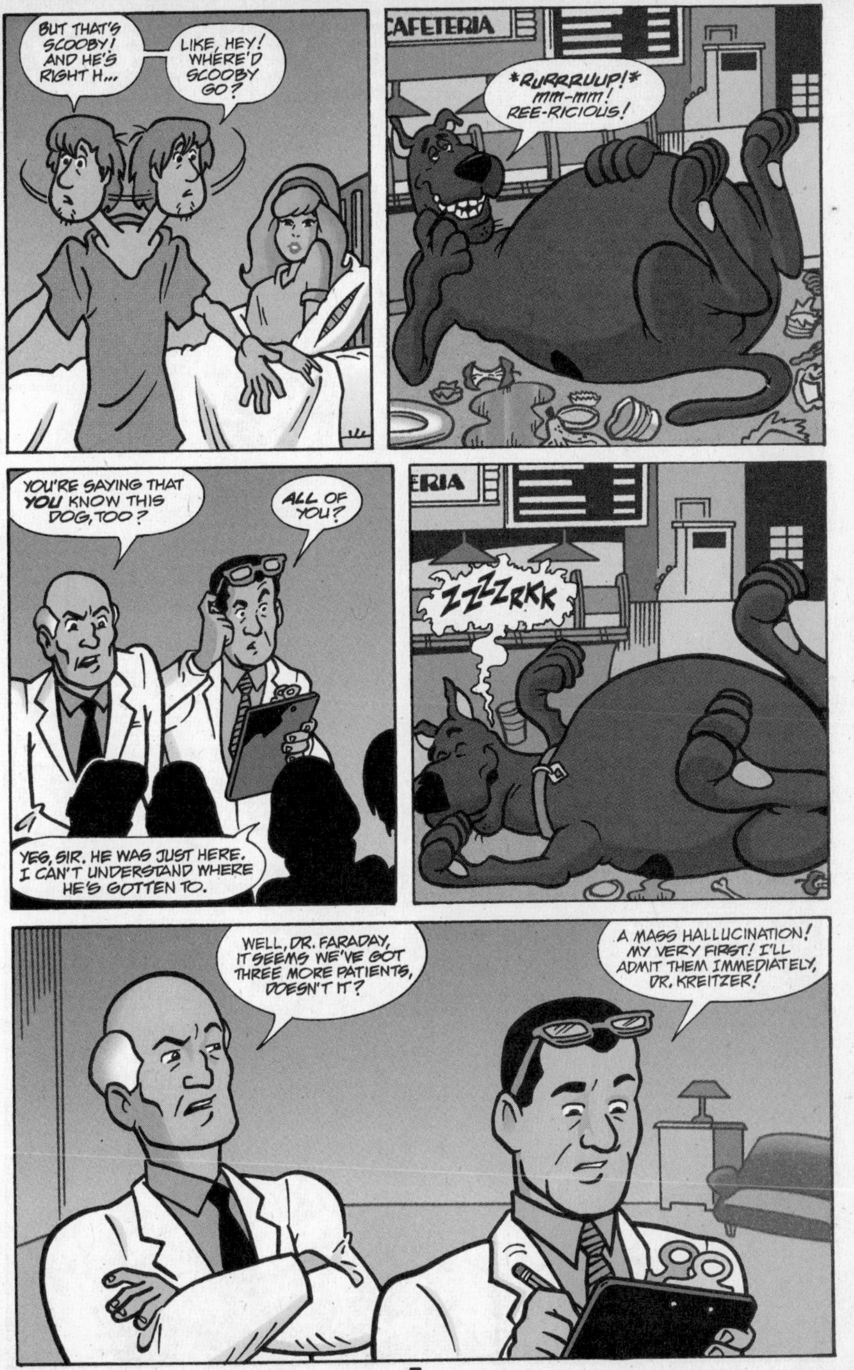
BUT THAT'S SCOOBY! AND HE'S RIGHT H...
LIKE, HEY! WHERE'D SCOOBY GO?
CAFETERIA
RURRRUUP! mm-mm! REE-RICIOUS!
YOU'RE SAYING THAT YOU KNOW THIS DOG, TOO?
ALL OF YOU?
YES, SIR. HE WAS JUST HERE. I CAN'T UNDERSTAND WHERE HE'S GOTTEN TO.
ERIA
ZZZZRKK
WELL, DR. FARADAY, IT SEEMS WE'VE GOT THREE MORE PATIENTS, DOESN'T IT?
A MASS HALLUCINATION! MY VERY FIRST! I'LL ADMIT THEM IMMEDIATELY, DR. KREITZER!

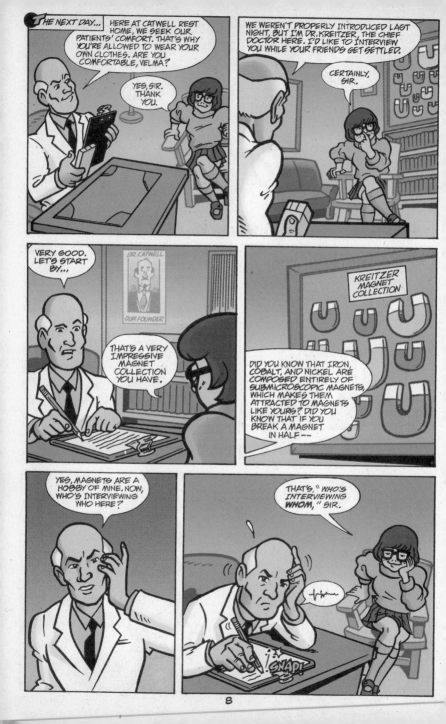

THE NEXT DAY... HERE AT CATWELL REST HOME, WE SEEK OUR PATIENTS' COMFORT. THAT'S WHY YOU'RE ALLOWED TO WEAR YOUR OWN CLOTHES. ARE YOU COMFORTABLE, VELMA?

YES, SIR. THANK YOU.

WE WEREN'T PROPERLY INTRODUCED LAST NIGHT, BUT I'M DR. KREITZER, THE CHIEF DOCTOR HERE. I'D LIKE TO INTERVIEW YOU WHILE YOUR FRIENDS GET SETTLED.

CERTAINLY, SIR.

VERY GOOD. LET'S START BY...

DR. CATWELL

OUR FOUNDER

THAT'S A VERY IMPRESSIVE MAGNET COLLECTION YOU HAVE.

KREITZER MAGNET COLLECTION

DID YOU KNOW THAT IRON, COBALT, AND NICKEL ARE COMPOSED ENTIRELY OF SUBMICROSCOPIC MAGNETS, WHICH MAKES THEM ATTRACTED TO MAGNETS LIKE YOURS? DID YOU KNOW THAT IF YOU BREAK A MAGNET IN HALF --

YES, MAGNETS ARE A HOBBY OF MINE. NOW, WHO'S INTERVIEWING WHO HERE?

THAT'S, "WHO'S INTERVIEWING WHOM," SIR.

SNAP!

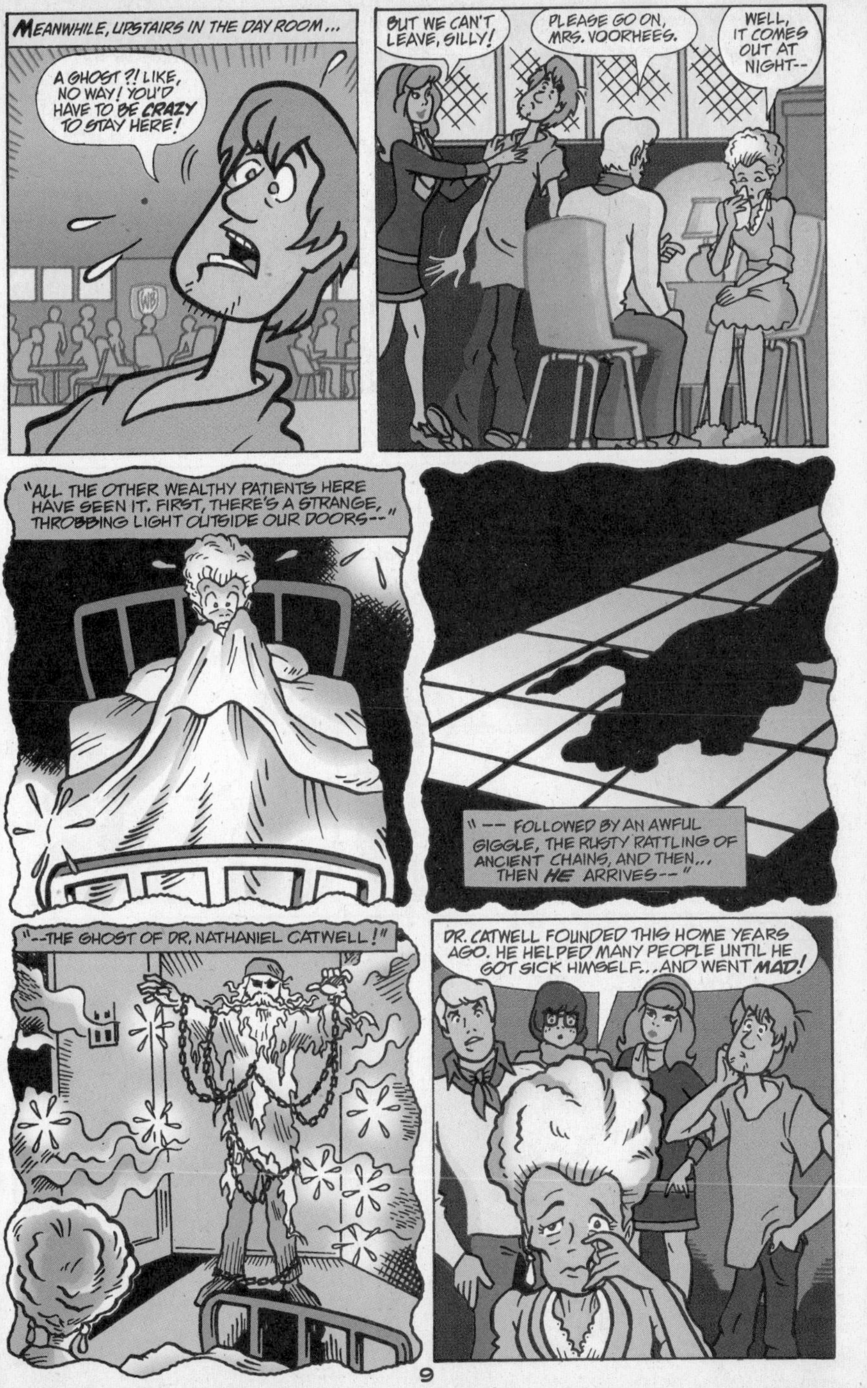
MEANWHILE, UPSTAIRS IN THE DAY ROOM...
A GHOST?! LIKE, NO WAY! YOU'D HAVE TO BE CRAZY TO STAY HERE!
BUT WE CAN'T LEAVE, SILLY!
PLEASE GO ON, MRS. VOORHEES.
WELL, IT COMES OUT AT NIGHT--
"ALL THE OTHER WEALTHY PATIENTS HERE HAVE SEEN IT. FIRST, THERE'S A STRANGE, THROBBING LIGHT OUTSIDE OUR DOORS--"
"-- FOLLOWED BY AN AWFUL GIGGLE, THE RUSTY RATTLING OF ANCIENT CHAINS, AND THEN... THEN HE ARRIVES--"
"--THE GHOST OF DR. NATHANIEL CATWELL!"
DR. CATWELL FOUNDED THIS HOME YEARS AGO. HE HELPED MANY PEOPLE UNTIL HE GOT SICK HIMSELF... AND WENT MAD!

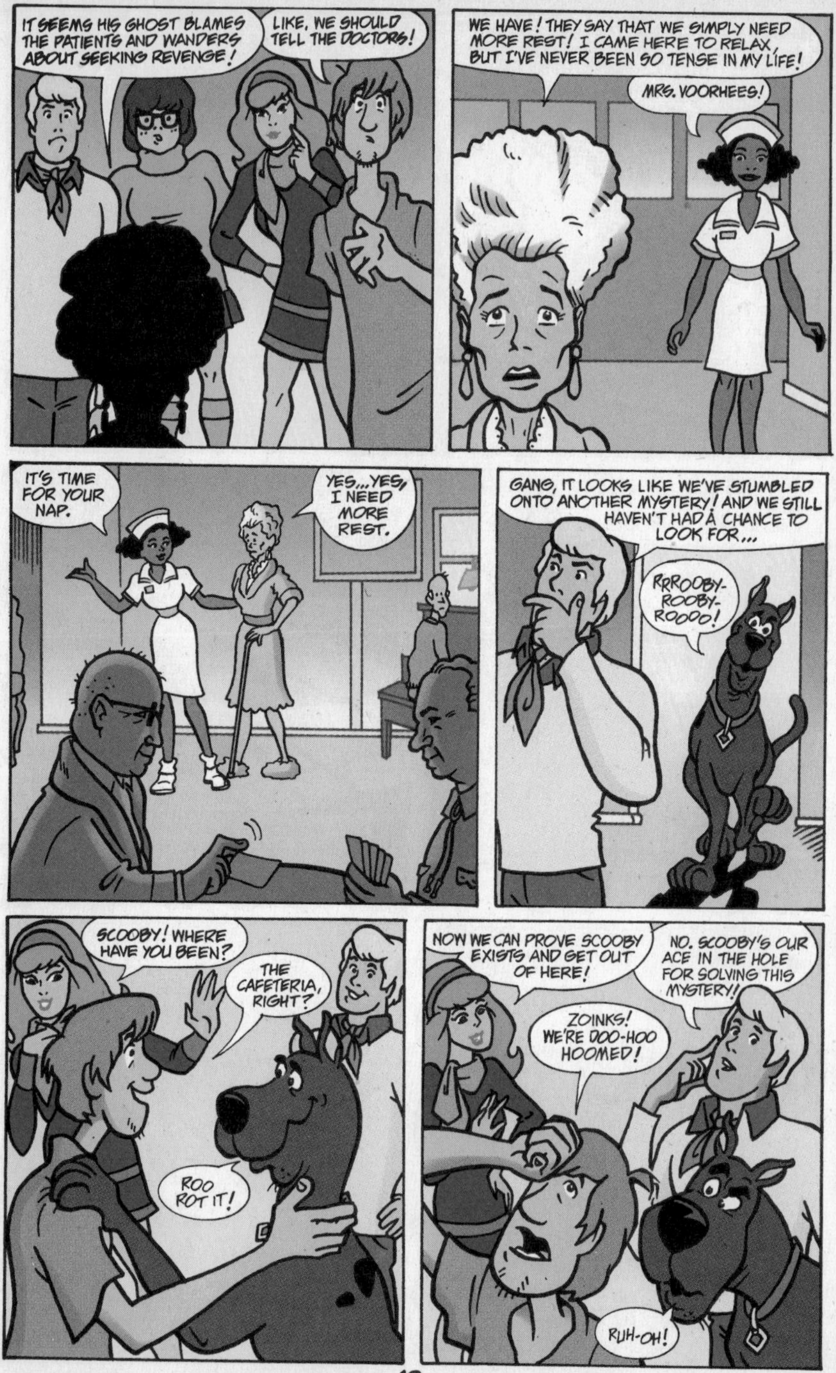
IT SEEMS HIS GHOST BLAMES THE PATIENTS AND WANDERS ABOUT SEEKING REVENGE!
LIKE, WE SHOULD TELL THE DOCTORS!
WE HAVE! THEY SAY THAT WE SIMPLY NEED MORE REST! I CAME HERE TO RELAX, BUT I'VE NEVER BEEN SO TENSE IN MY LIFE!
MRS. VOORHEES!
IT'S TIME FOR YOUR NAP.
YES...YES, I NEED MORE REST.
GANG, IT LOOKS LIKE WE'VE STUMBLED ONTO ANOTHER MYSTERY! AND WE STILL HAVEN'T HAD A CHANCE TO LOOK FOR...
RRROOBY-ROOBY-ROOOO!
SCOOBY! WHERE HAVE YOU BEEN?
THE CAFETERIA, RIGHT?
ROO ROT IT!
NOW WE CAN PROVE SCOOBY EXISTS AND GET OUT OF HERE!
NO. SCOOBY'S OUR ACE IN THE HOLE FOR SOLVING THIS MYSTERY!!
ZOINKS! WE'RE DOO-HOO HOOMED!
RUH-OH!

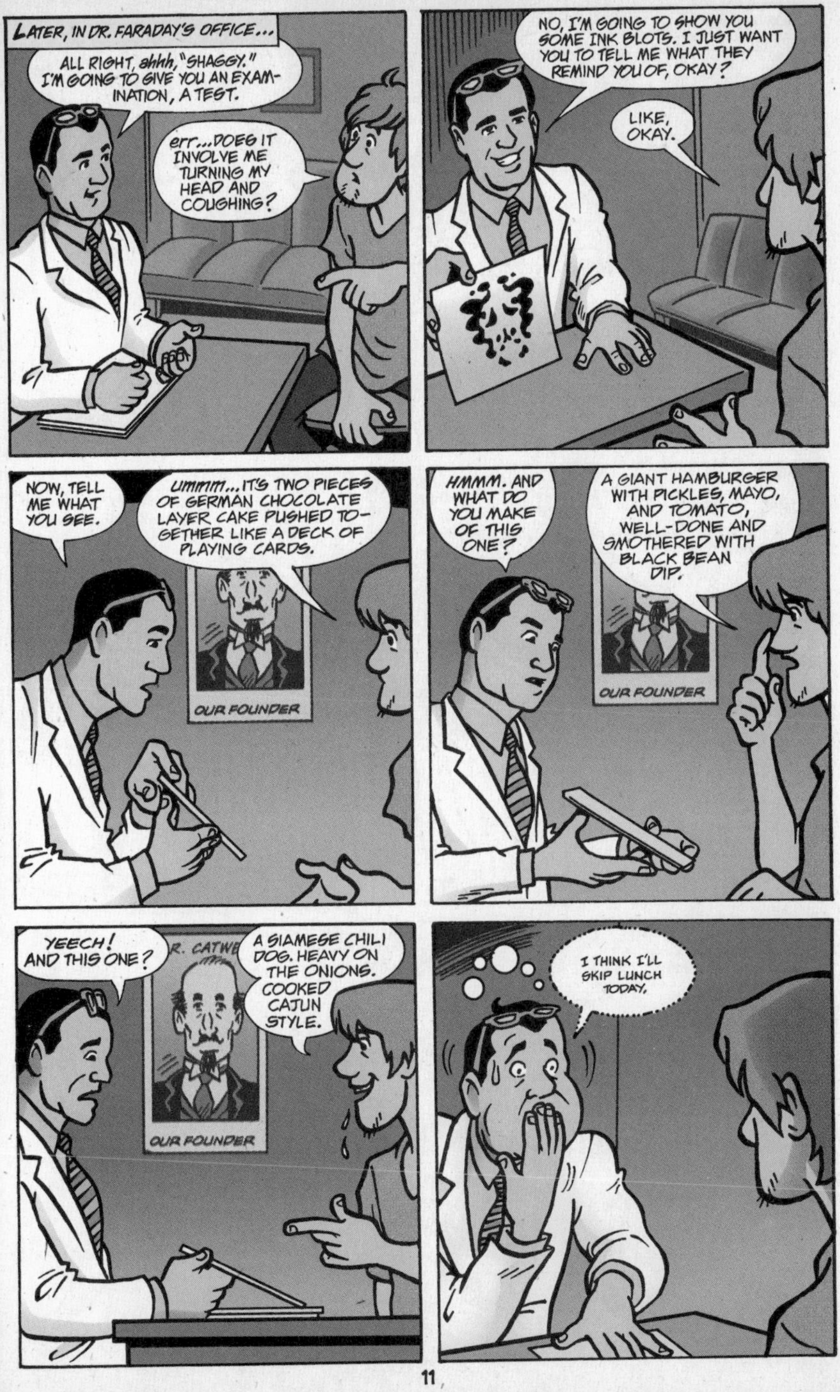
LATER, IN DR. FARADAY'S OFFICE...
ALL RIGHT, shhh, "SHAGGY." I'M GOING TO GIVE YOU AN EXAMINATION, A TEST.
err...DOES IT INVOLVE ME TURNING MY HEAD AND COUGHING?
NO, I'M GOING TO SHOW YOU SOME INK BLOTS. I JUST WANT YOU TO TELL ME WHAT THEY REMIND YOU OF, OKAY?
LIKE, OKAY.
NOW, TELL ME WHAT YOU SEE.
UMMMM... IT'S TWO PIECES OF GERMAN CHOCOLATE LAYER CAKE PUSHED TOGETHER LIKE A DECK OF PLAYING CARDS.
OUR FOUNDER
HMMM. AND WHAT DO YOU MAKE OF THIS ONE?
A GIANT HAMBURGER WITH PICKLES, MAYO, AND TOMATO, WELL-DONE AND SMOTHERED WITH BLACK BEAN DIP.
OUR FOUNDER
YEECH! AND THIS ONE?
R. CATWE
A SIAMESE CHILI DOG. HEAVY ON THE ONIONS. COOKED CAJUN STYLE.
OUR FOUNDER
I THINK I'LL SKIP LUNCH TODAY.

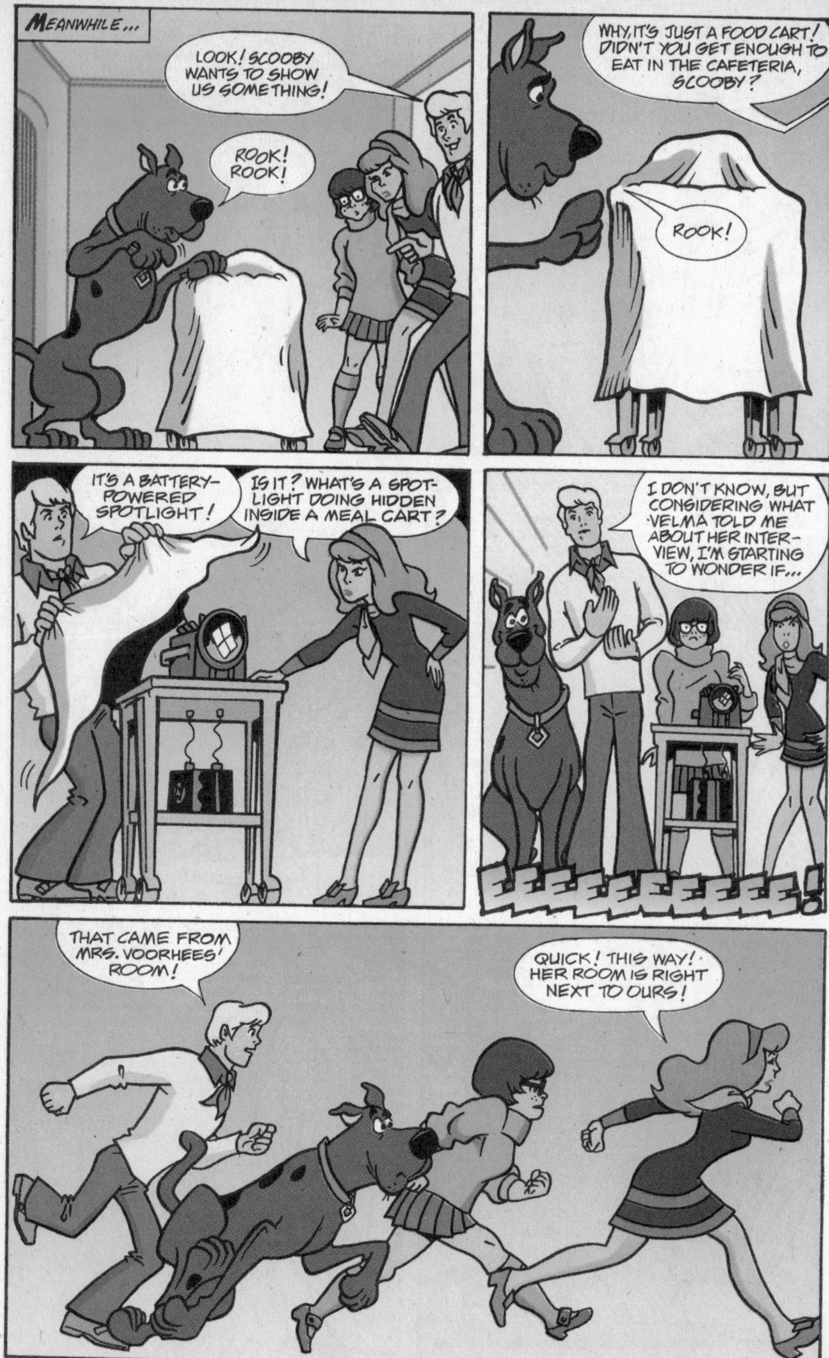
MEANWHILE...
LOOK! SCOOBY WANTS TO SHOW US SOMETHING!
ROOK! ROOK!
WHY, IT'S JUST A FOOD CART! DIDN'T YOU GET ENOUGH TO EAT IN THE CAFETERIA, SCOOBY?
ROOK!
IT'S A BATTERY-POWERED SPOTLIGHT!
IS IT? WHAT'S A SPOT-LIGHT DOING HIDDEN INSIDE A MEAL CART?
I DON'T KNOW, BUT CONSIDERING WHAT VELMA TOLD ME ABOUT HER INTER-VIEW, I'M STARTING TO WONDER IF...
EEEEEEEEEEE!
THAT CAME FROM MRS. VOORHEES' ROOM!
QUICK! THIS WAY! HER ROOM IS RIGHT NEXT TO OURS!

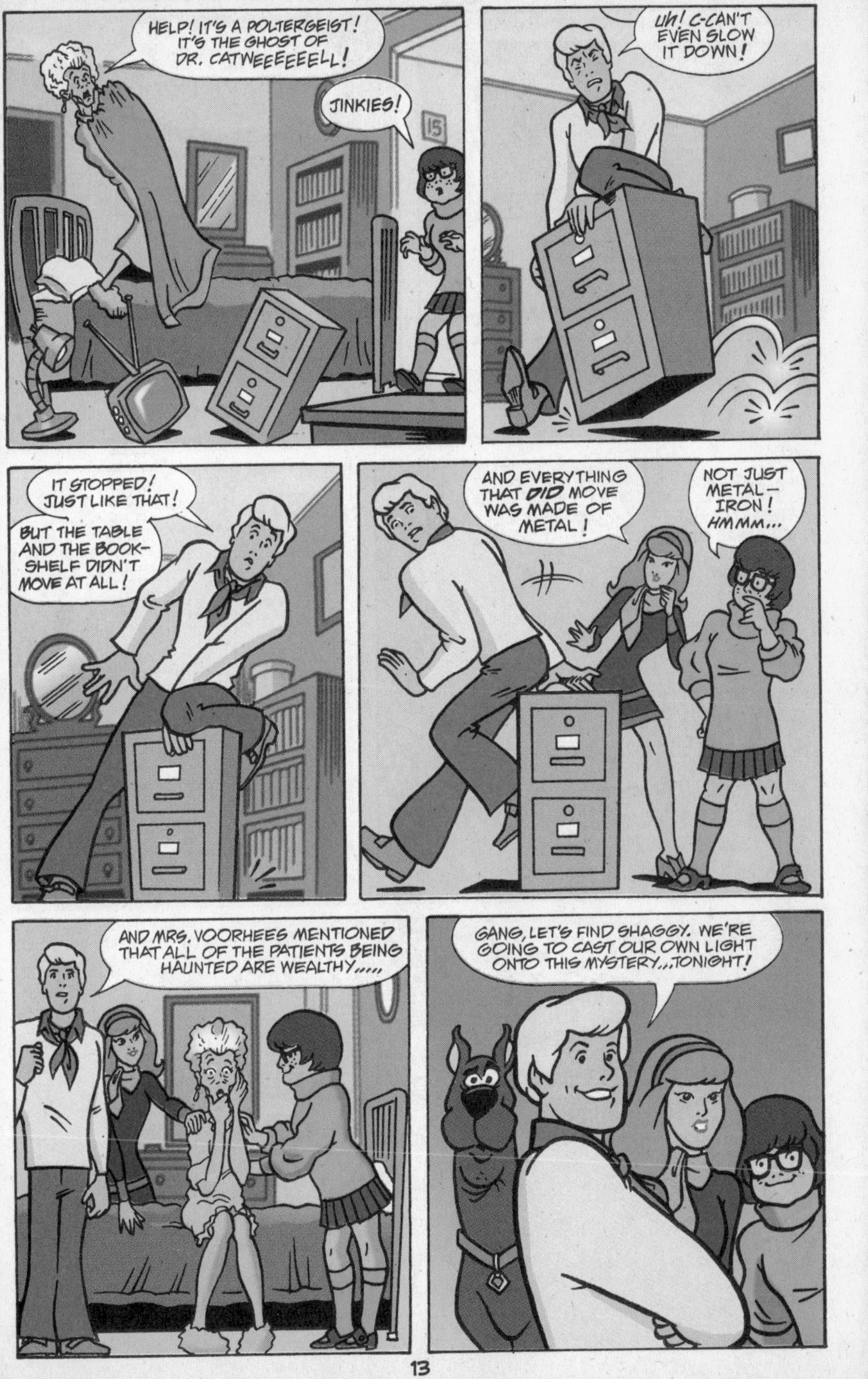
HELP! IT'S A POLTERGEIST! IT'S THE GHOST OF DR. CATWEEEEEEELL!
JINKIES!
UH! C-CAN'T EVEN SLOW IT DOWN!
IT STOPPED! JUST LIKE THAT!
BUT THE TABLE AND THE BOOK-SHELF DIDN'T MOVE AT ALL!
AND EVERYTHING THAT DID MOVE WAS MADE OF METAL!
NOT JUST METAL— IRON! HMMM...
AND MRS. VOORHEES MENTIONED THAT ALL OF THE PATIENTS BEING HAUNTED ARE WEALTHY.....
GANG, LET'S FIND SHAGGY. WE'RE GOING TO CAST OUR OWN LIGHT ONTO THIS MYSTERY...TONIGHT!

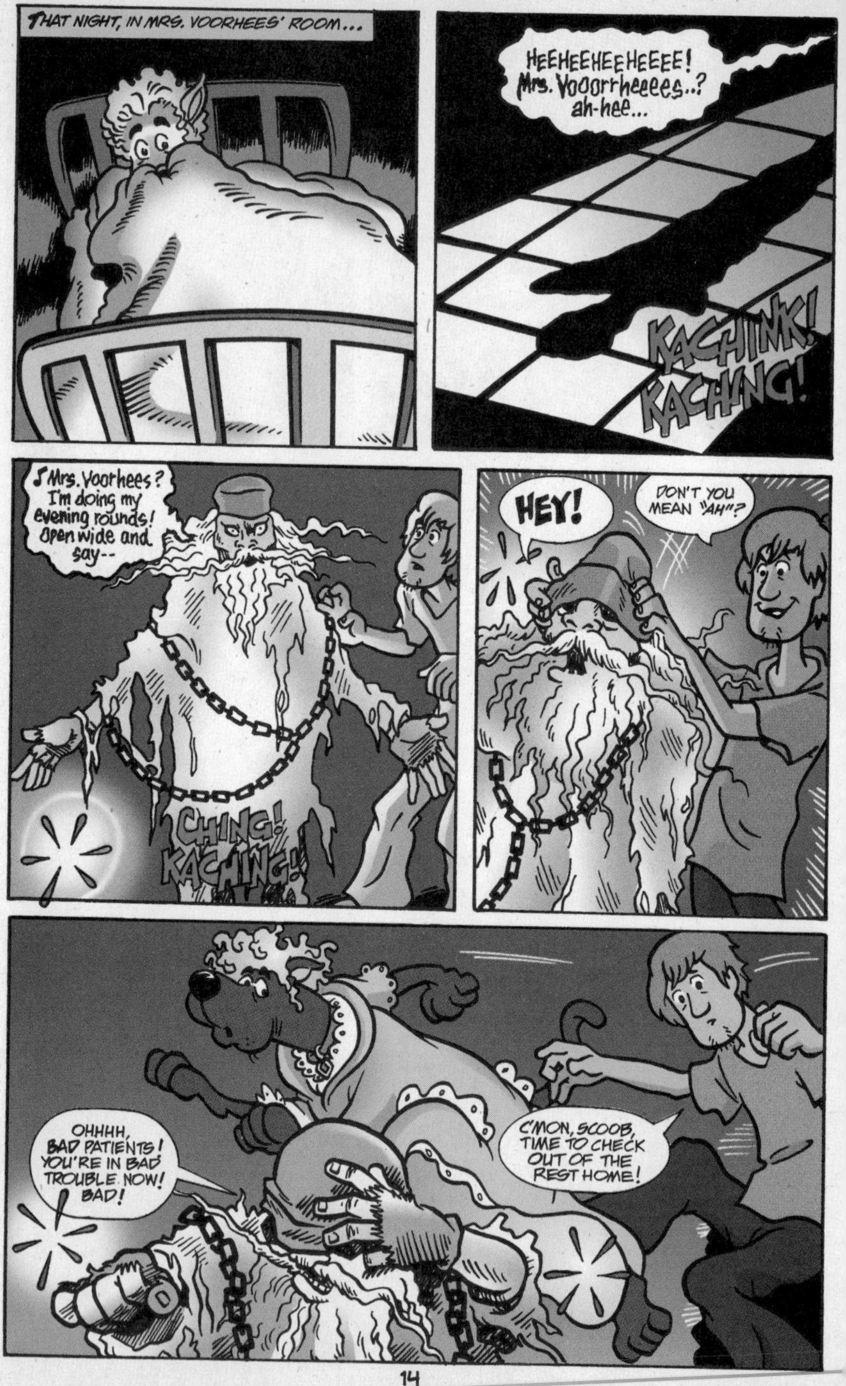
THAT NIGHT, IN MRS. VOORHEES' ROOM...
HEEHEEHEEHEEEE! Mrs. Vooorrheeees..? ah-hee...
KACHINK! KACHING!
♪ Mrs. Voorhees? I'm doing my evening rounds! Open wide and say--
CHING! KACHING!
HEY!
DON'T YOU MEAN "AH"?
OHHHH, BAD PATIENTS! YOU'RE IN BAD TROUBLE NOW! BAD!
C'MON, SCOOB, TIME TO CHECK OUT OF THE REST HOME!

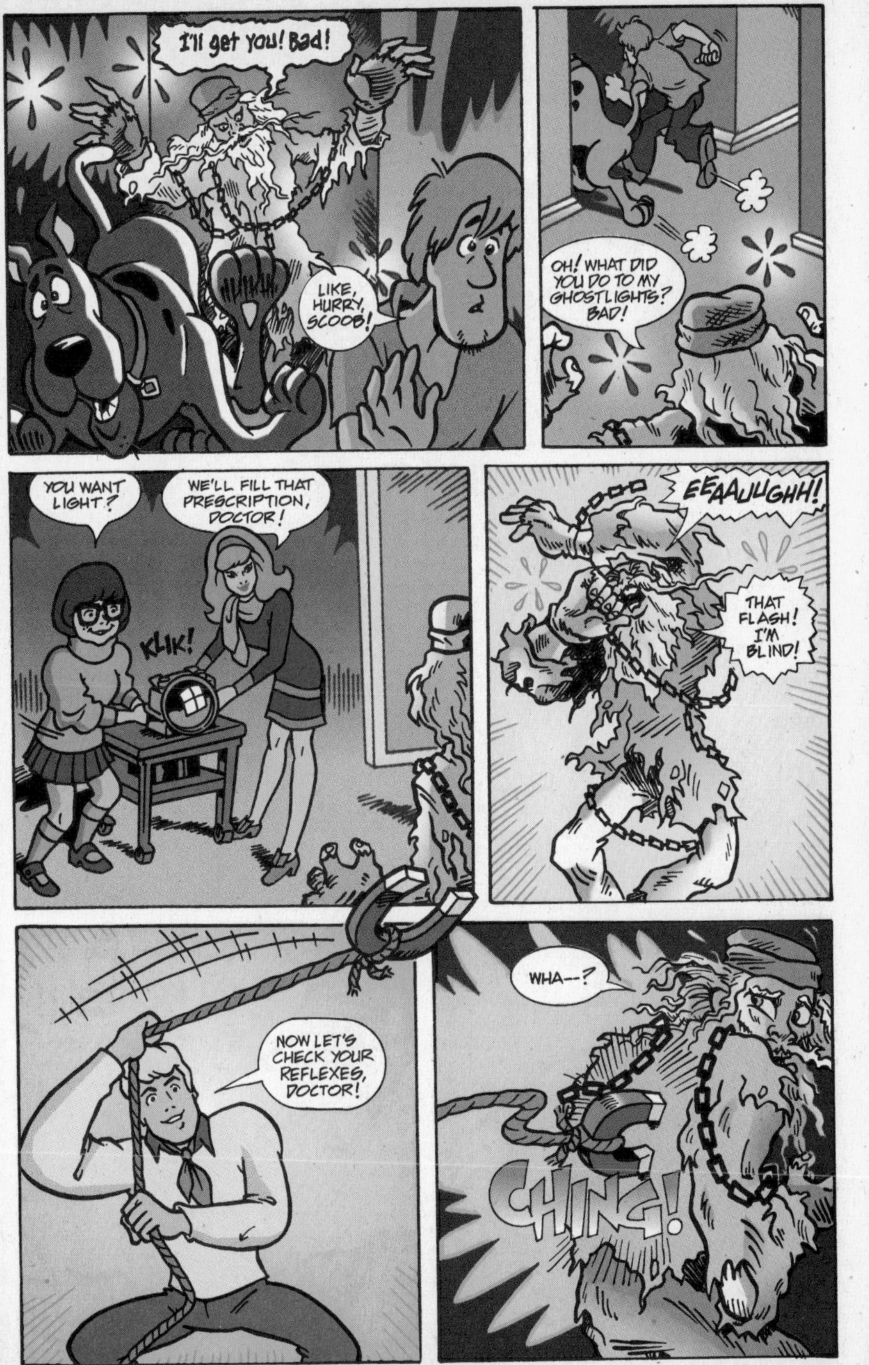
I'll get you! Bad!
LIKE, HURRY, SCOOB!
OH! WHAT DID YOU DO TO MY GHOSTLIGHTS? BAD!
YOU WANT LIGHT?
WE'LL FILL THAT PRESCRIPTION, DOCTOR!
KLIK!
EEAAUUGHH!
THAT FLASH! I'M BLIND!
NOW LET'S CHECK YOUR REFLEXES, DOCTOR!
WHA--?
CHING!

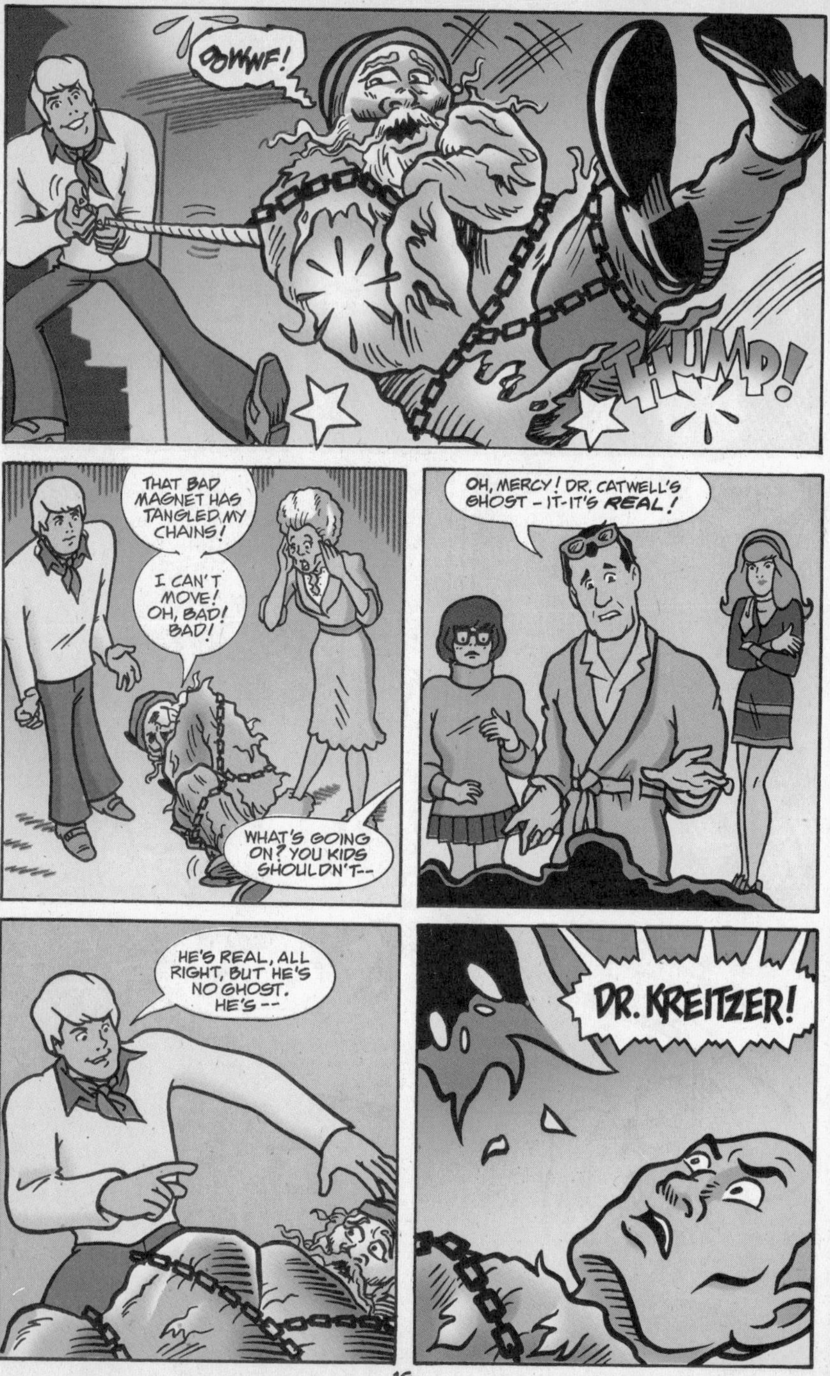
OOWWNF!
THUMP!
THAT BAD MAGNET HAS TANGLED MY CHAINS!
I CAN'T MOVE! OH, BAD! BAD!
WHAT'S GOING ON? YOU KIDS SHOULDN'T--
OH, MERCY! DR. CATWELL'S GHOST - IT-IT'S REAL!
HE'S REAL, ALL RIGHT, BUT HE'S NO GHOST. HE'S --
DR. KREITZER!

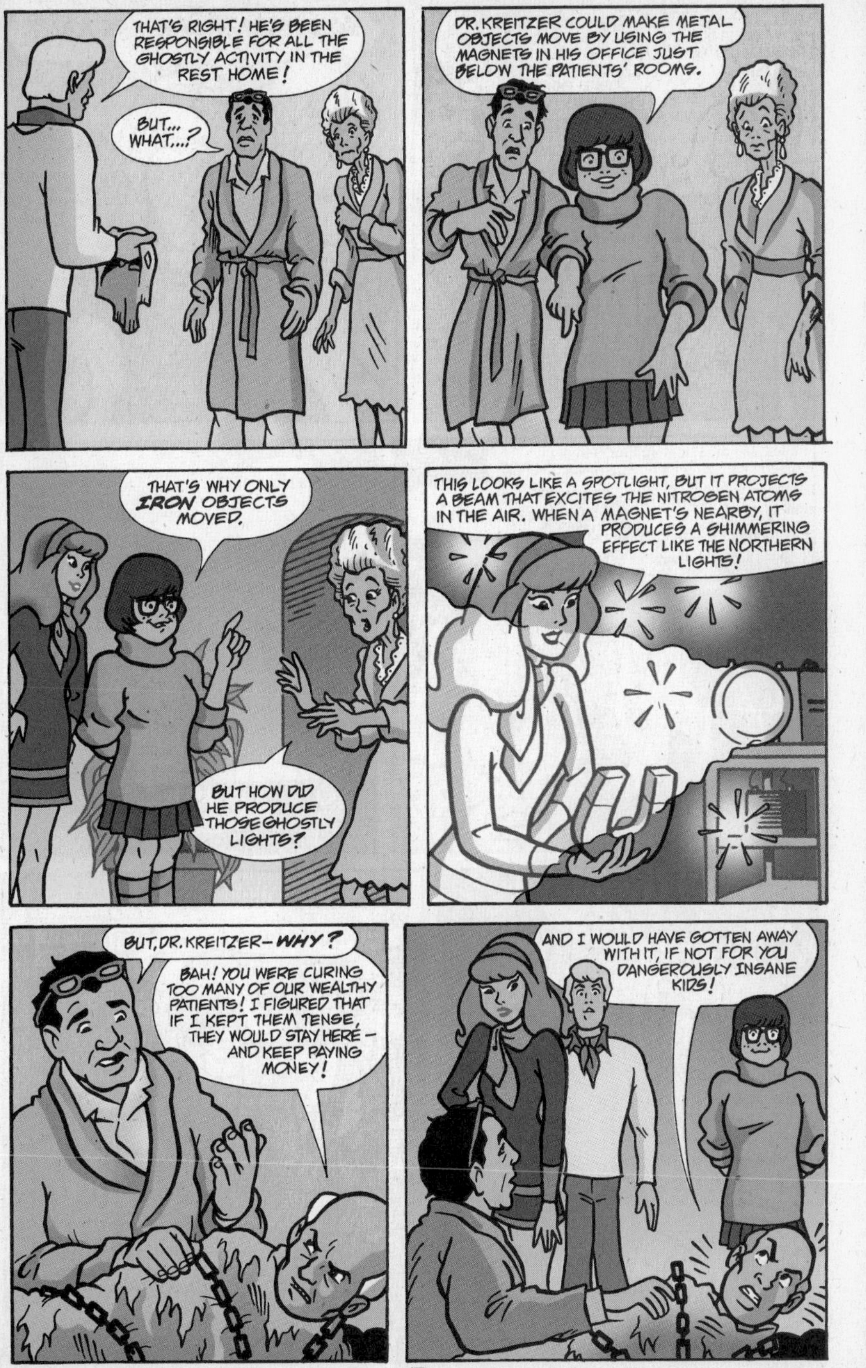
THAT'S RIGHT! HE'S BEEN RESPONSIBLE FOR ALL THE GHOSTLY ACTIVITY IN THE REST HOME!
BUT... WHAT...?
DR. KREITZER COULD MAKE METAL OBJECTS MOVE BY USING THE MAGNETS IN HIS OFFICE JUST BELOW THE PATIENTS' ROOMS.
THAT'S WHY ONLY IRON OBJECTS MOVED.
BUT HOW DID HE PRODUCE THOSE GHOSTLY LIGHTS?
THIS LOOKS LIKE A SPOTLIGHT, BUT IT PROJECTS A BEAM THAT EXCITES THE NITROGEN ATOMS IN THE AIR. WHEN A MAGNET'S NEARBY, IT PRODUCES A SHIMMERING EFFECT LIKE THE NORTHERN LIGHTS!
BUT, DR. KREITZER— WHY?
BAH! YOU WERE CURING TOO MANY OF OUR WEALTHY PATIENTS! I FIGURED THAT IF I KEPT THEM TENSE, THEY WOULD STAY HERE — AND KEEP PAYING MONEY!
AND I WOULD HAVE GOTTEN AWAY WITH IT, IF NOT FOR YOU DANGEROUSLY INSANE KIDS!

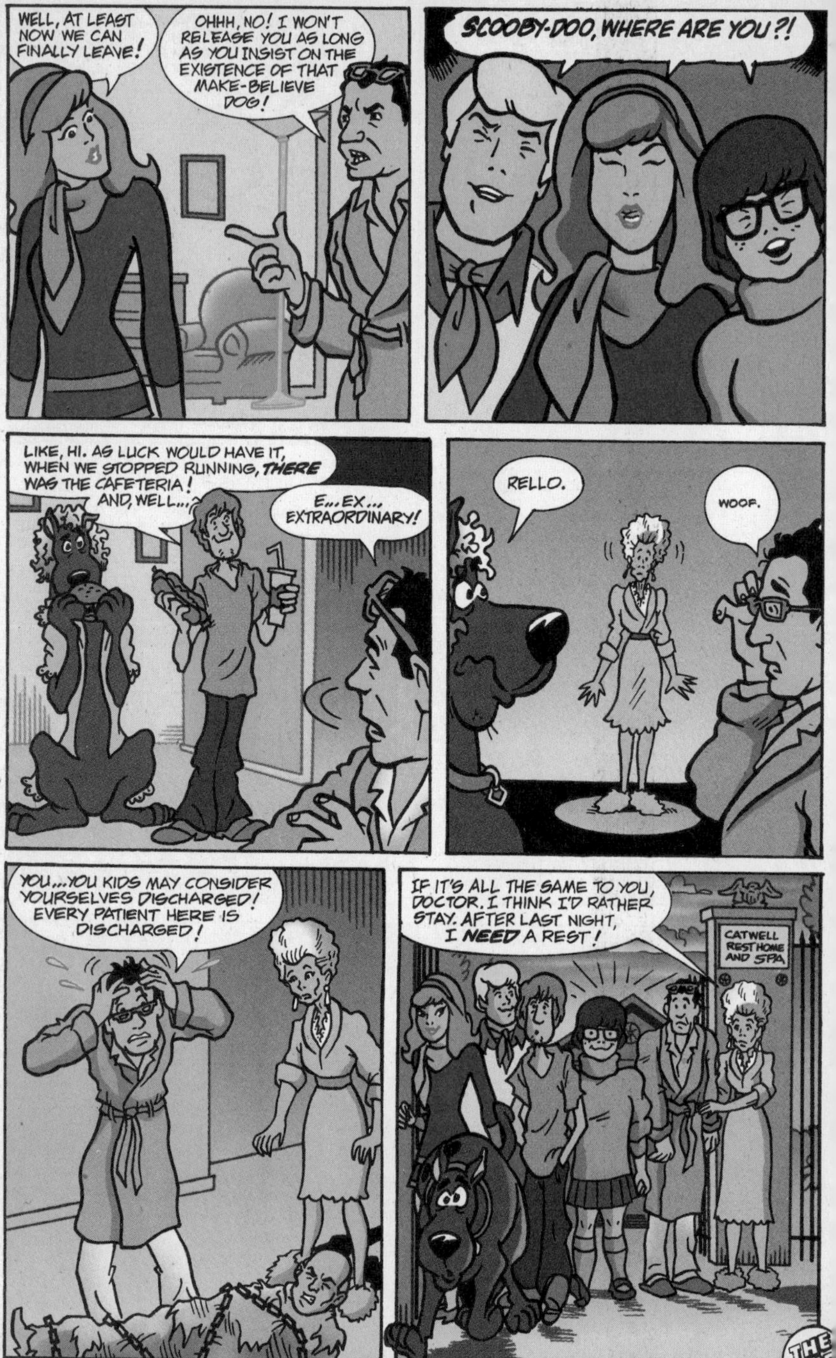
WELL, AT LEAST NOW WE CAN FINALLY LEAVE!
OHHH, NO! I WON'T RELEASE YOU AS LONG AS YOU INSIST ON THE EXISTENCE OF THAT MAKE-BELIEVE DOG!
SCOOBY-DOO, WHERE ARE YOU?!
LIKE, HI. AS LUCK WOULD HAVE IT, WHEN WE STOPPED RUNNING, THERE WAS THE CAFETERIA! AND, WELL...
E... EX... EXTRAORDINARY!
RELLO.
WOOF.
YOU... YOU KIDS MAY CONSIDER YOURSELVES DISCHARGED! EVERY PATIENT HERE IS DISCHARGED!
IF IT'S ALL THE SAME TO YOU, DOCTOR. I THINK I'D RATHER STAY. AFTER LAST NIGHT, I NEED A REST!
CATWELL REST HOME AND SPA
THE END

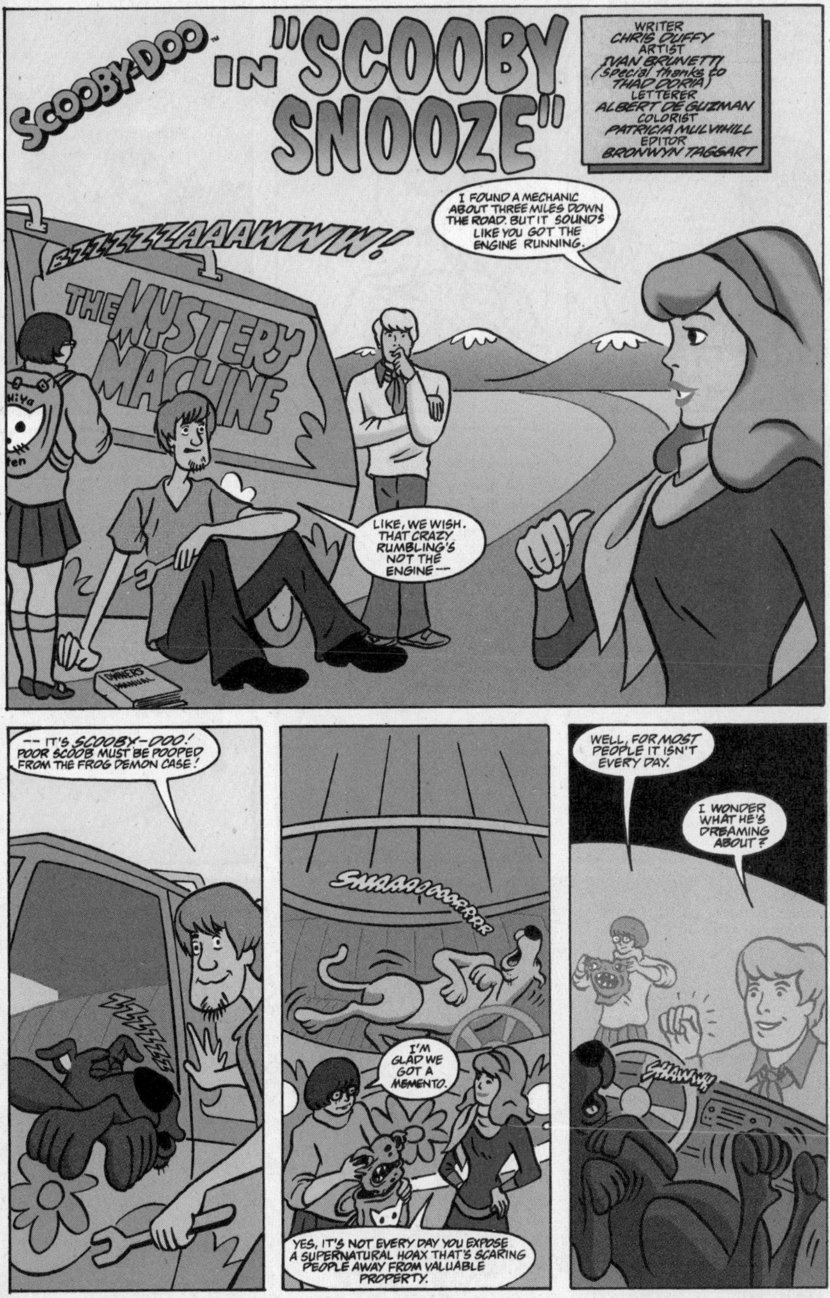
SCOOBY-DOO™ IN "SCOOBY SNOOZE"
WRITER CHRIS DUFFY
ARTIST IVAN BRUNETTI (Special thanks to THAD DORIA)
LETTERER ALBERT DE GUZMAN
COLORIST PATRICIA MULVIHILL
EDITOR BRONWYN TAGGART
THE MYSTERY MACHINE
I FOUND A MECHANIC ABOUT THREE MILES DOWN THE ROAD. BUT IT SOUNDS LIKE YOU GOT THE ENGINE RUNNING.
LIKE, WE WISH. THAT CRAZY RUMBLING'S NOT THE ENGINE--
OWNERS MANUAL
-- IT'S SCOOBY-DOO! POOR SCOOB MUST BE POOPED FROM THE FROG DEMON CASE!
I'M GLAD WE GOT A MEMENTO.
YES, IT'S NOT EVERY DAY YOU EXPOSE A SUPERNATURAL HOAX THAT'S SCARING PEOPLE AWAY FROM VALUABLE PROPERTY.
WELL, FOR MOST PEOPLE IT ISN'T EVERY DAY.
I WONDER WHAT HE'S DREAMING ABOUT?

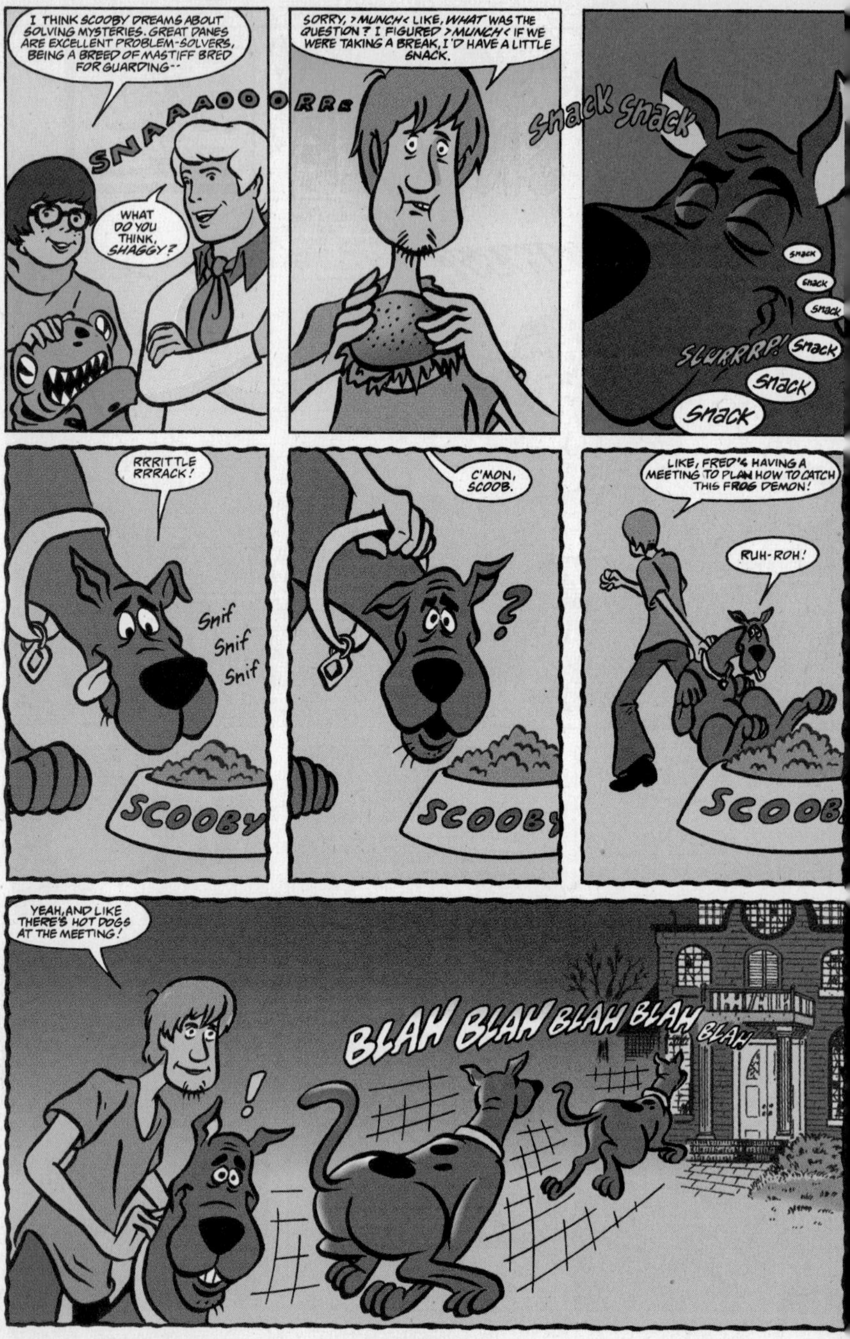

I THINK SCOOBY DREAMS ABOUT SOLVING MYSTERIES. GREAT DANES ARE EXCELLENT PROBLEM-SOLVERS, BEING A BREED OF MASTIFF BRED FOR GUARDING--
SNAAAAOOOORRR
WHAT DO YOU THINK, SHAGGY?
SORRY, >MUNCH< LIKE, WHAT WAS THE QUESTION? I FIGURED >MUNCH< IF WE WERE TAKING A BREAK, I'D HAVE A LITTLE SNACK.
SNACK SNACK
SNACK
SNACK
SNACK
SLURRRP!
SNACK
SNACK
SNACK
RRRITTLE RRRACK!
SNIF
SNIF
SNIF
SCOOBY
C'MON, SCOOB.
?
SCOOBY
LIKE, FRED'S HAVING A MEETING TO PLAN HOW TO CATCH THIS FROG DEMON!
RUH-ROH!
SCOOB
YEAH, AND LIKE THERE'S HOT DOGS AT THE MEETING!
!
BLAH BLAH BLAH BLAH BLAH

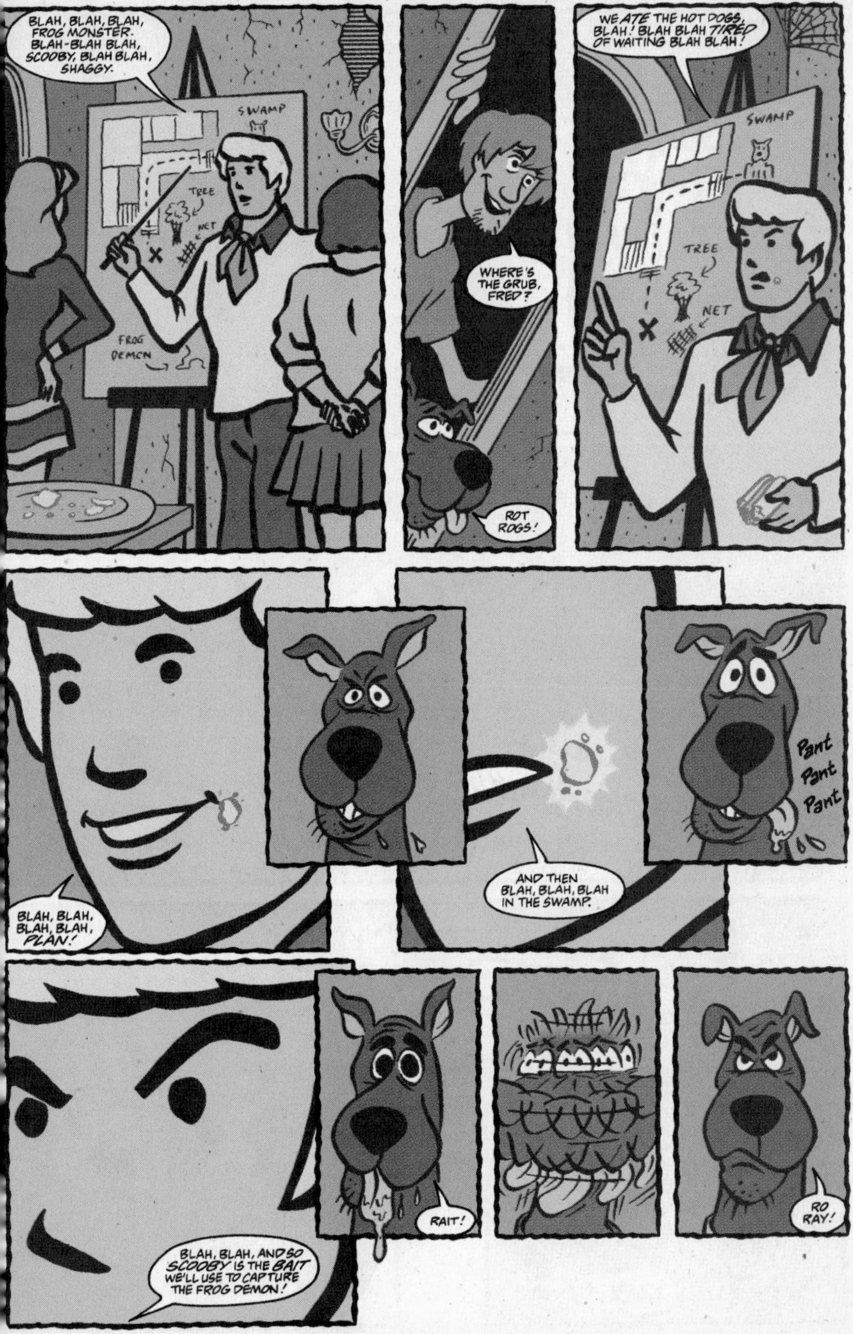

BLAH, BLAH, BLAH, FROG MONSTER. BLAH-BLAH BLAH, SCOOBY, BLAH BLAH, SHAGGY.
SWAMP
TREE
NET
FROG DEMON
WHERE'S THE GRUB, FRED?
ROT ROGS!
WE ATE THE HOT DOGS, BLAH! BLAH BLAH TIRED OF WAITING BLAH BLAH!
SWAMP
TREE
NET
BLAH, BLAH, BLAH, BLAH, PLAN!
AND THEN BLAH, BLAH, BLAH IN THE SWAMP.
Pant Pant Pant
BLAH, BLAH, AND SO SCOOBY IS THE BAIT WE'LL USE TO CAPTURE THE FROG DEMON!
RAIT!
RO RAY!

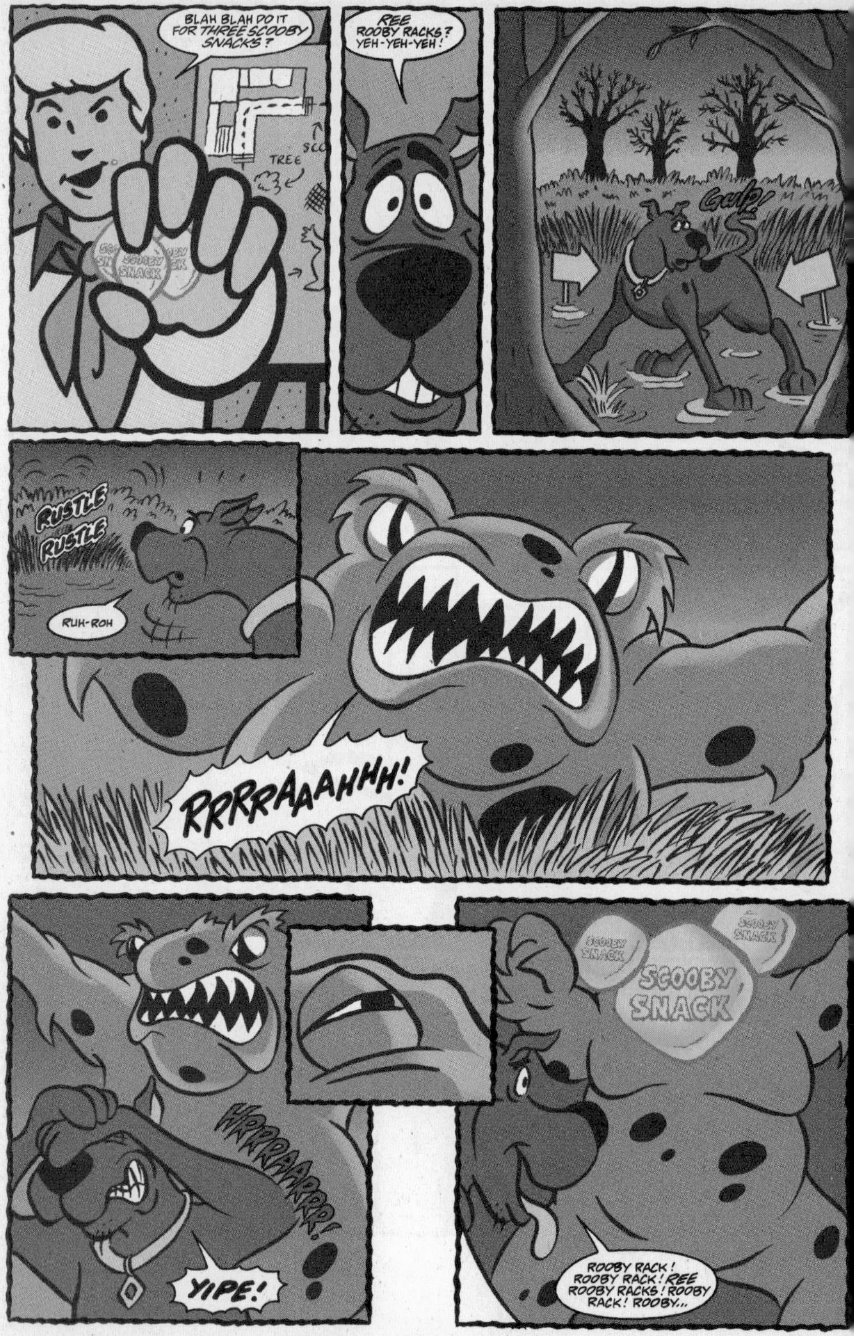
BLAH BLAH DO IT FOR THREE SCOOBY SNACKS?
TREE
SCOOBY SNACK
REE ROOBY RACKS? YEH-YEH-YEH!
Gulp!
RUSTLE
RUSTLE
RUH-ROH
RRRRAAAHHH!
HRRRAARRR!
YIPE!
SCOOBY SNACK
SCOOBY SNACK
SCOOBY SNACK
ROOBY RACK! ROOBY RACK! REE ROOBY RACKS! ROOBY RACK! ROOBY...

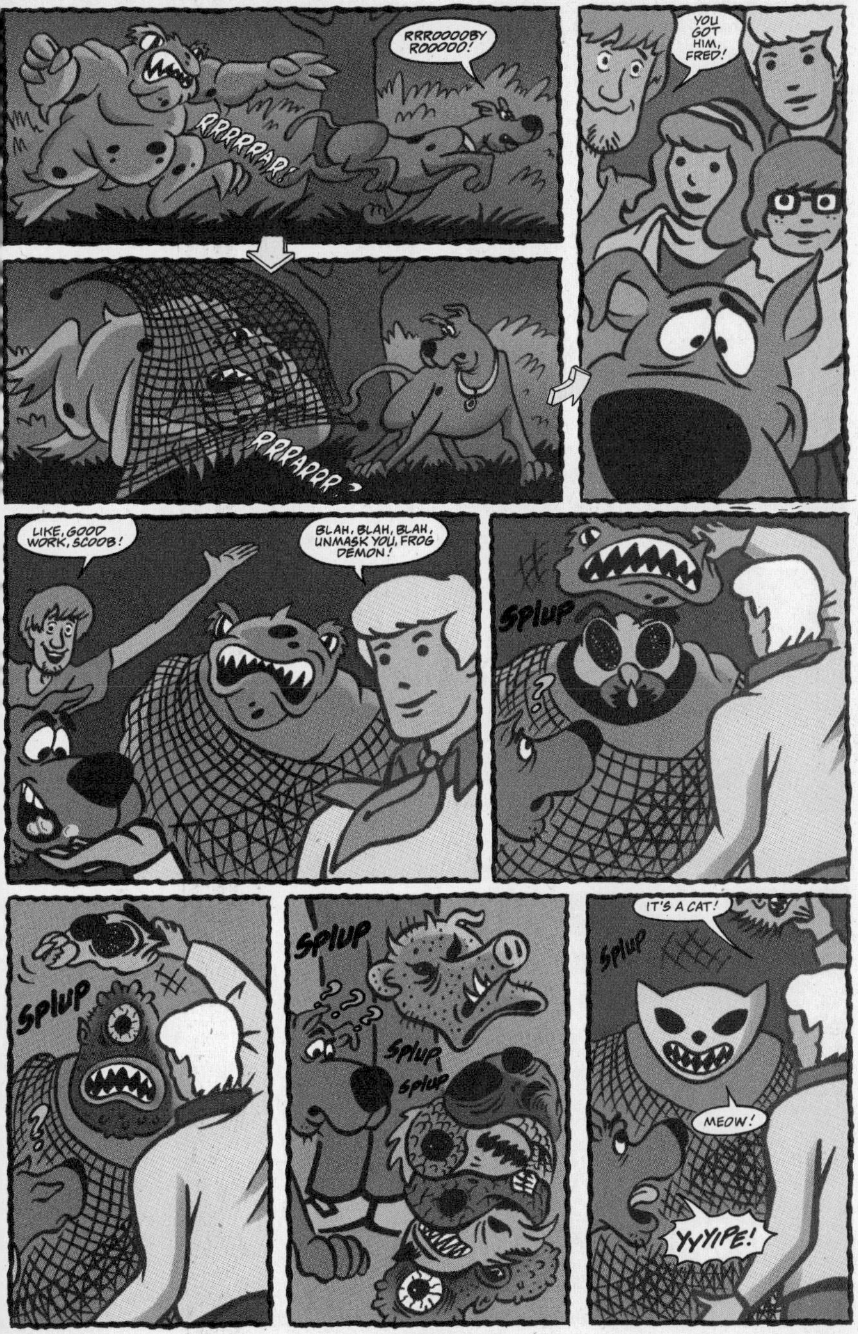
RRRROOOOBY ROOOOO!
RRRRRRAR!
RRRRAPRRR
YOU GOT HIM, FRED!
LIKE, GOOD WORK, SCOOB!
BLAH, BLAH, BLAH, UNMASK YOU, FROG DEMON!
SPLUP
SPLUP
SPLUP
SPLUP
SPLUP
SPLUP
IT'S A CAT!
MEOW!
YYYIPE!

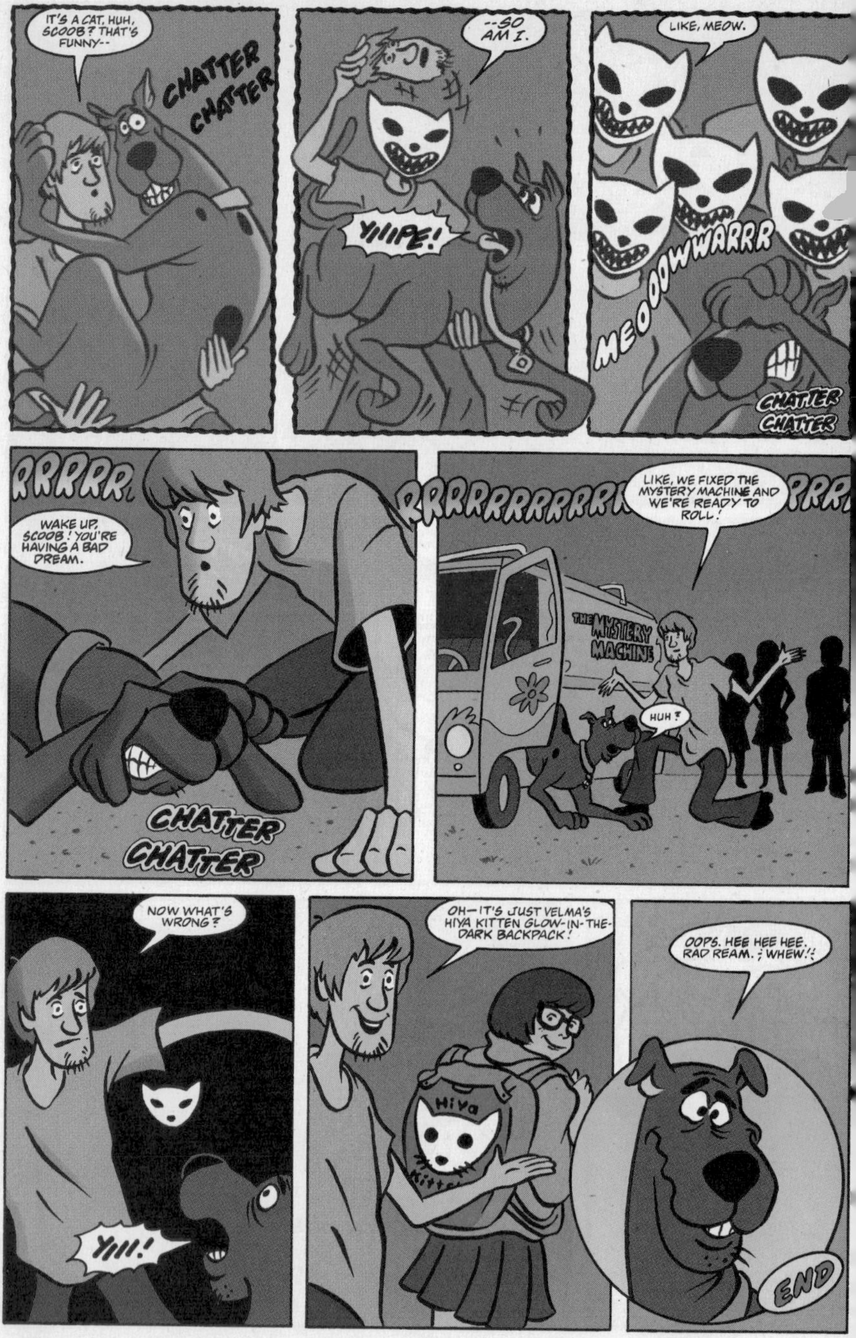
IT'S A CAT, HUH, SCOOB? THAT'S FUNNY--
CHATTER CHATTER
--SO AM I.
YIIIPE!
LIKE, MEOW.
MEOOOWWARRR
CHATTER CHATTER
RRRRR
WAKE UP, SCOOB! YOU'RE HAVING A BAD DREAM.
CHATTER CHATTER
RRRRRRRRRRR
LIKE, WE FIXED THE MYSTERY MACHINE AND WE'RE READY TO ROLL!
PRR
THE MYSTERY MACHINE
HUH?
NOW WHAT'S WRONG?
YIII!
OH—IT'S JUST VELMA'S HIYA KITTEN GLOW-IN-THE-DARK BACKPACK!
Hiya
OOPS. HEE HEE HEE. RAD REAM. ; WHEW!
END

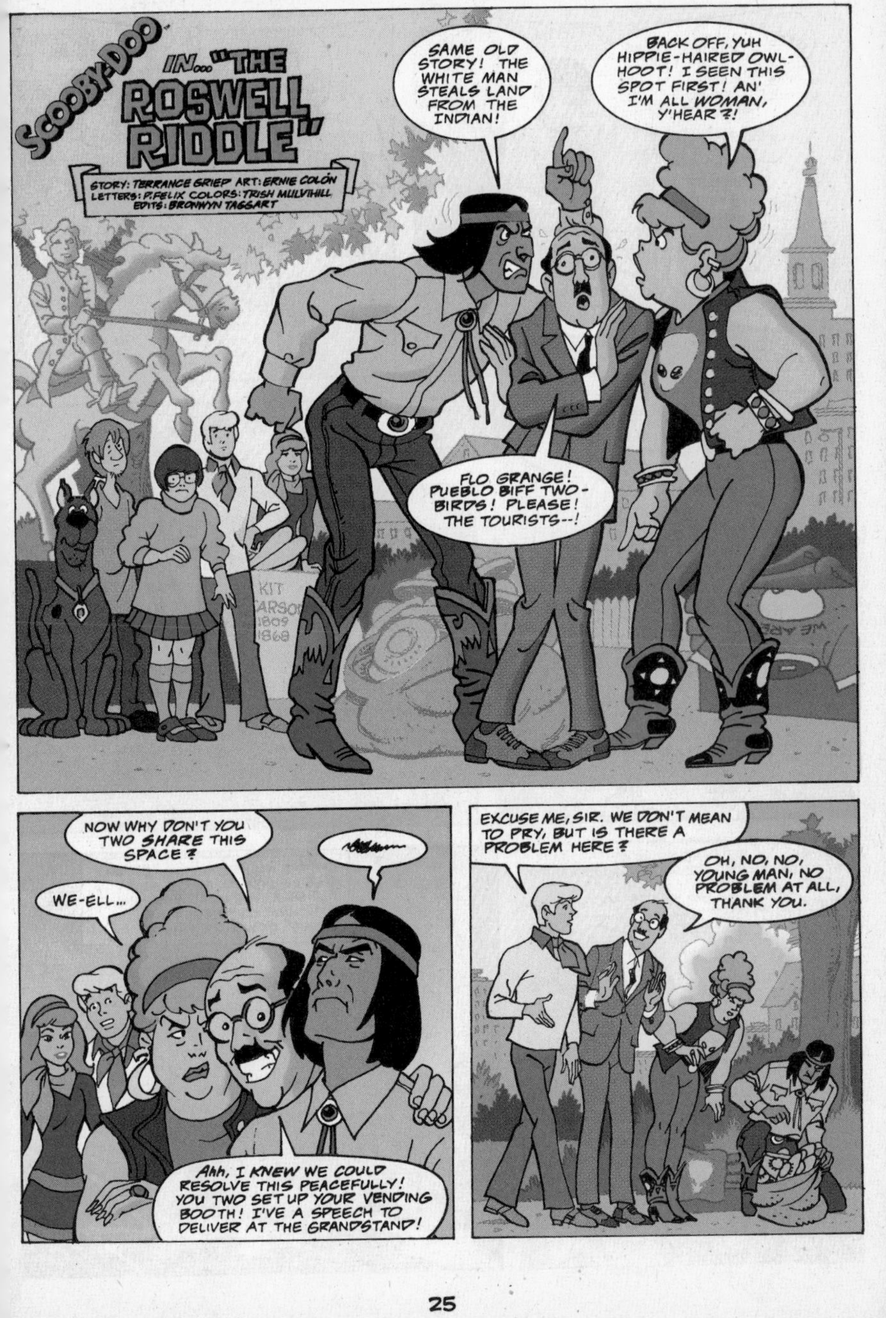
SCOOBY-DOO™ IN... "THE ROSWELL RIDDLE"
STORY: TERRANCE GRIEP ART: ERNIE COLÓN
LETTERS: P. FELIX COLORS: TRISH MULVIHILL
EDITS: BRONWYN TAGGART
SAME OLD STORY! THE WHITE MAN STEALS LAND FROM THE INDIAN!
BACK OFF, YUH HIPPIE-HAIRED OWL-HOOT! I SEEN THIS SPOT FIRST! AN' I'M ALL WOMAN, Y'HEAR?!
FLO GRANGE! PUEBLO BIFF TWO-BIRDS! PLEASE! THE TOURISTS--!
NOW WHY DON'T YOU TWO SHARE THIS SPACE?
WE-ELL...
Ahh, I KNEW WE COULD RESOLVE THIS PEACEFULLY! YOU TWO SET UP YOUR VENDING BOOTH! I'VE A SPEECH TO DELIVER AT THE GRANDSTAND!
EXCUSE ME, SIR. WE DON'T MEAN TO PRY, BUT IS THERE A PROBLEM HERE?
OH, NO, NO, YOUNG MAN, NO PROBLEM AT ALL, THANK YOU.

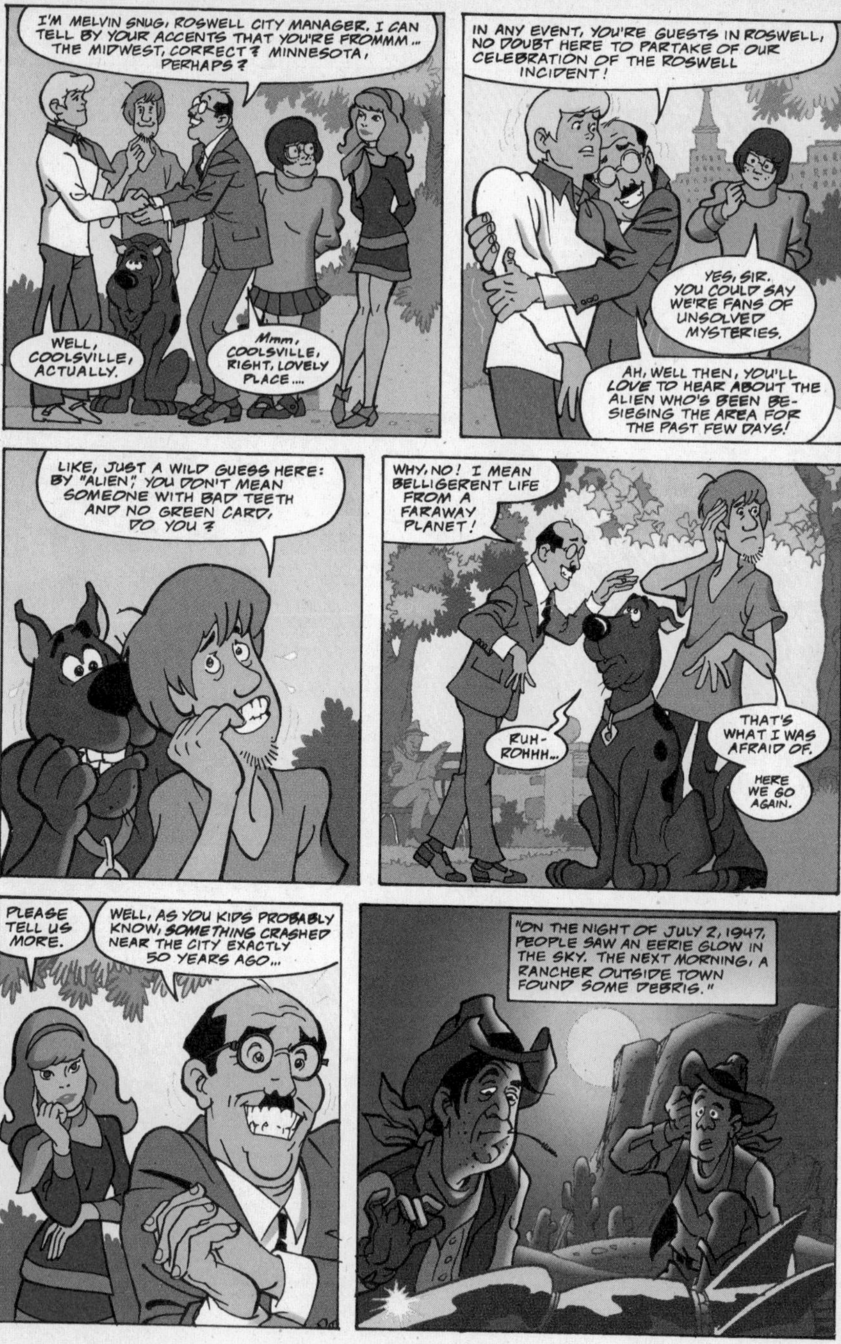
I'M MELVIN SNUG, ROSWELL CITY MANAGER. I CAN TELL BY YOUR ACCENTS THAT YOU'RE FROMMM... THE MIDWEST, CORRECT? MINNESOTA, PERHAPS?
WELL, COOLSVILLE, ACTUALLY.
Mmm, COOLSVILLE, RIGHT, LOVELY PLACE....
IN ANY EVENT, YOU'RE GUESTS IN ROSWELL, NO DOUBT HERE TO PARTAKE OF OUR CELEBRATION OF THE ROSWELL INCIDENT!
YES, SIR. YOU COULD SAY WE'RE FANS OF UNSOLVED MYSTERIES.
AH, WELL THEN, YOU'LL LOVE TO HEAR ABOUT THE ALIEN WHO'S BEEN BESIEGING THE AREA FOR THE PAST FEW DAYS!
LIKE, JUST A WILD GUESS HERE: BY "ALIEN," YOU DON'T MEAN SOMEONE WITH BAD TEETH AND NO GREEN CARD, DO YOU?
WHY, NO! I MEAN BELLIGERENT LIFE FROM A FARAWAY PLANET!
RUH-ROHHH...
THAT'S WHAT I WAS AFRAID OF.
HERE WE GO AGAIN.
PLEASE TELL US MORE.
WELL, AS YOU KIDS PROBABLY KNOW, SOMETHING CRASHED NEAR THE CITY EXACTLY 50 YEARS AGO...
"ON THE NIGHT OF JULY 2, 1947, PEOPLE SAW AN EERIE GLOW IN THE SKY. THE NEXT MORNING, A RANCHER OUTSIDE TOWN FOUND SOME DEBRIS."

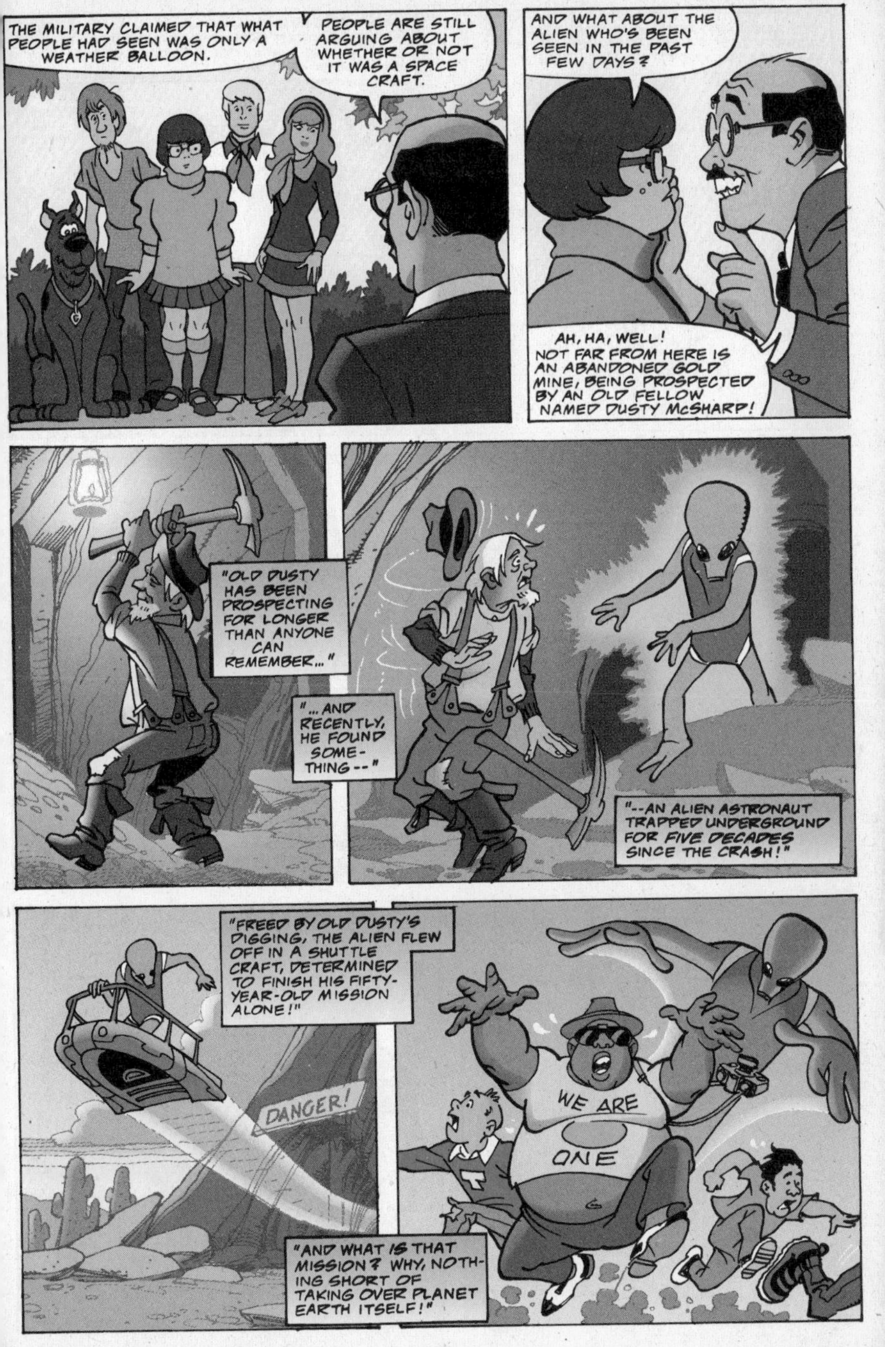
THE MILITARY CLAIMED THAT WHAT PEOPLE HAD SEEN WAS ONLY A WEATHER BALLOON.
PEOPLE ARE STILL ARGUING ABOUT WHETHER OR NOT IT WAS A SPACE CRAFT.
AND WHAT ABOUT THE ALIEN WHO'S BEEN SEEN IN THE PAST FEW DAYS?
AH, HA, WELL! NOT FAR FROM HERE IS AN ABANDONED GOLD MINE, BEING PROSPECTED BY AN OLD FELLOW NAMED DUSTY McSHARP!
"OLD DUSTY HAS BEEN PROSPECTING FOR LONGER THAN ANYONE CAN REMEMBER..."
"...AND RECENTLY, HE FOUND SOME-THING--"
"--AN ALIEN ASTRONAUT TRAPPED UNDERGROUND FOR FIVE DECADES SINCE THE CRASH!"
"FREED BY OLD DUSTY'S DIGGING, THE ALIEN FLEW OFF IN A SHUTTLE CRAFT, DETERMINED TO FINISH HIS FIFTY-YEAR-OLD MISSION ALONE!"
DANGER!
WE ARE ONE
"AND WHAT IS THAT MISSION? WHY, NOTHING SHORT OF TAKING OVER PLANET EARTH ITSELF!"

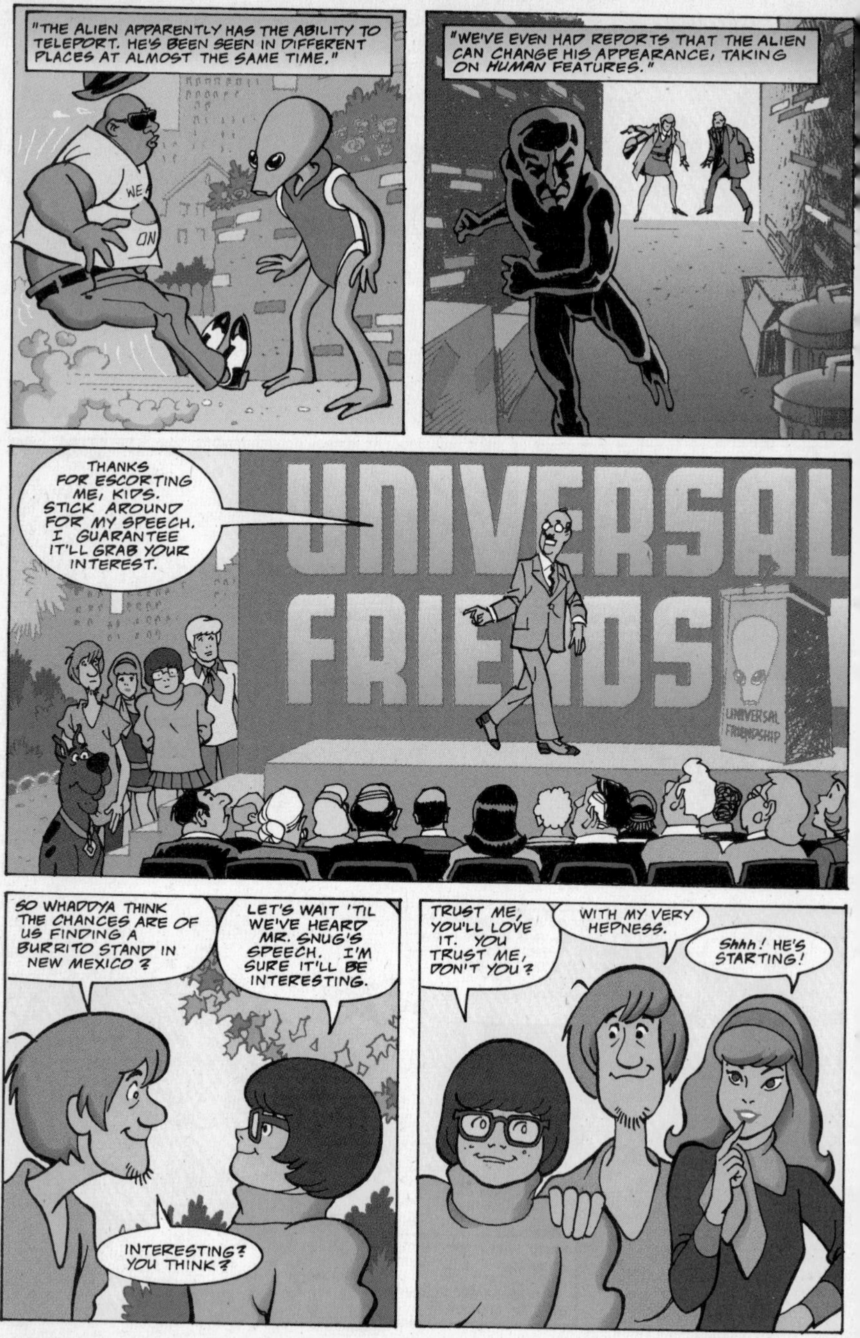
"THE ALIEN APPARENTLY HAS THE ABILITY TO TELEPORT. HE'S BEEN SEEN IN DIFFERENT PLACES AT ALMOST THE SAME TIME."
"WE'VE EVEN HAD REPORTS THAT THE ALIEN CAN CHANGE HIS APPEARANCE, TAKING ON *HUMAN* FEATURES."
THANKS FOR ESCORTING ME, KIDS. STICK AROUND FOR MY SPEECH. I GUARANTEE IT'LL GRAB YOUR INTEREST.
UNIVERSAL FRIENDS
UNIVERSAL FRIENDSHIP
SO WHADDYA THINK THE CHANCES ARE OF US FINDING A BURRITO STAND IN NEW MEXICO?
LET'S WAIT 'TIL WE'VE HEARD MR. SNUG'S SPEECH. I'M SURE IT'LL BE INTERESTING.
INTERESTING? YOU THINK?
TRUST ME, YOU'LL LOVE IT. YOU TRUST ME, DON'T YOU?
WITH MY VERY HEPNESS.
Shhh! HE'S STARTING!

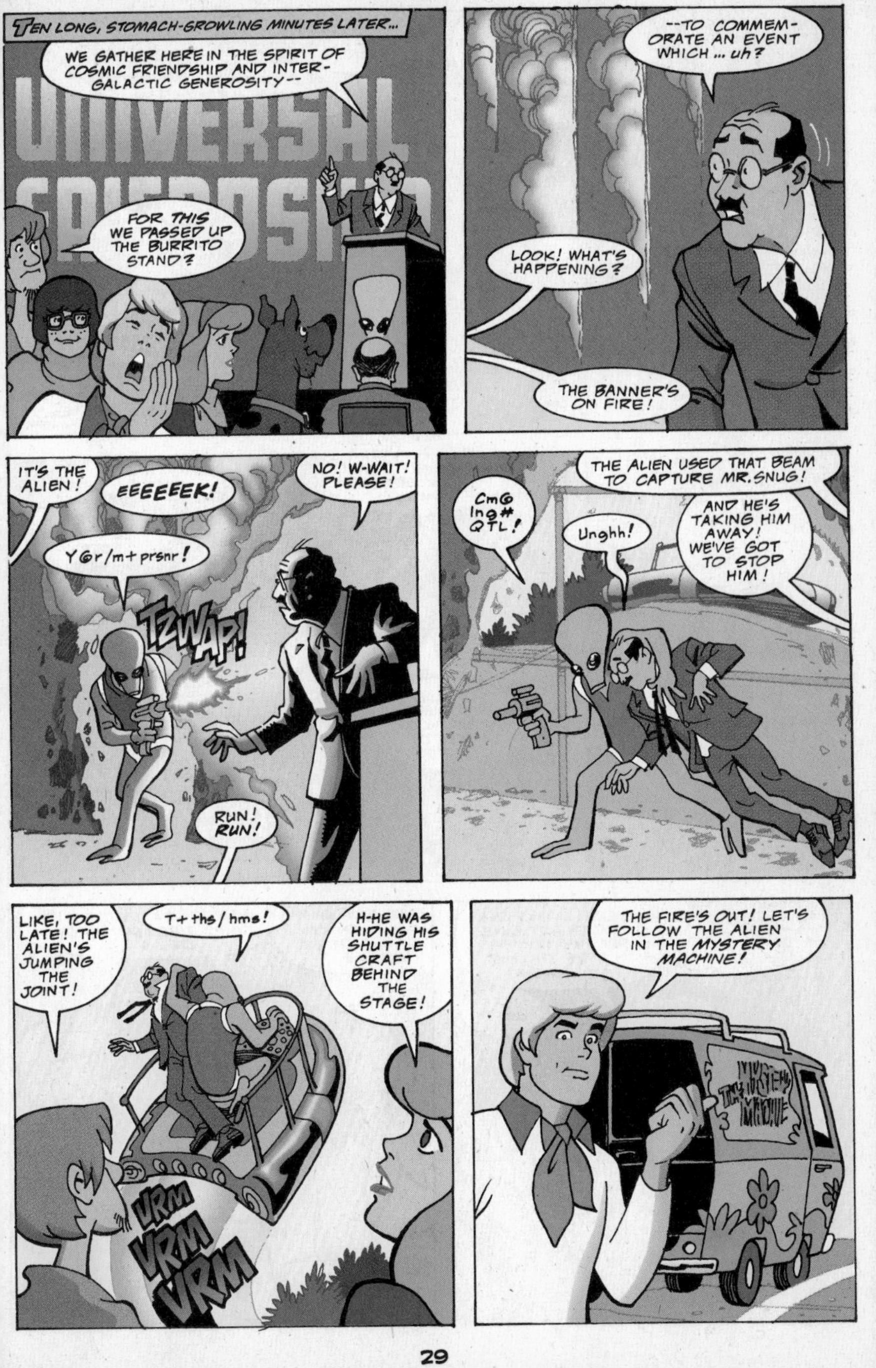
TEN LONG, STOMACH-GROWLING MINUTES LATER...
WE GATHER HERE IN THE SPIRIT OF COSMIC FRIENDSHIP AND INTER-GALACTIC GENEROSITY--
UNIVERSAL FRIENDSHIP
FOR THIS WE PASSED UP THE BURRITO STAND?
--TO COMMEMORATE AN EVENT WHICH ... uh?
LOOK! WHAT'S HAPPENING?
THE BANNER'S ON FIRE!
IT'S THE ALIEN!
EEEEEEK!
NO! W-WAIT! PLEASE!
Y©r/m+prsnr!
TZWAP!
RUN! RUN!
THE ALIEN USED THAT BEAM TO CAPTURE MR. SNUG!
Cm© Ing# QTL!
Unghh!
AND HE'S TAKING HIM AWAY! WE'VE GOT TO STOP HIM!
LIKE, TOO LATE! THE ALIEN'S JUMPING THE JOINT!
T+ths/hms!
H-HE WAS HIDING HIS SHUTTLE CRAFT BEHIND THE STAGE!
VRM VRM VRM
THE FIRE'S OUT! LET'S FOLLOW THE ALIEN IN THE MYSTERY MACHINE!

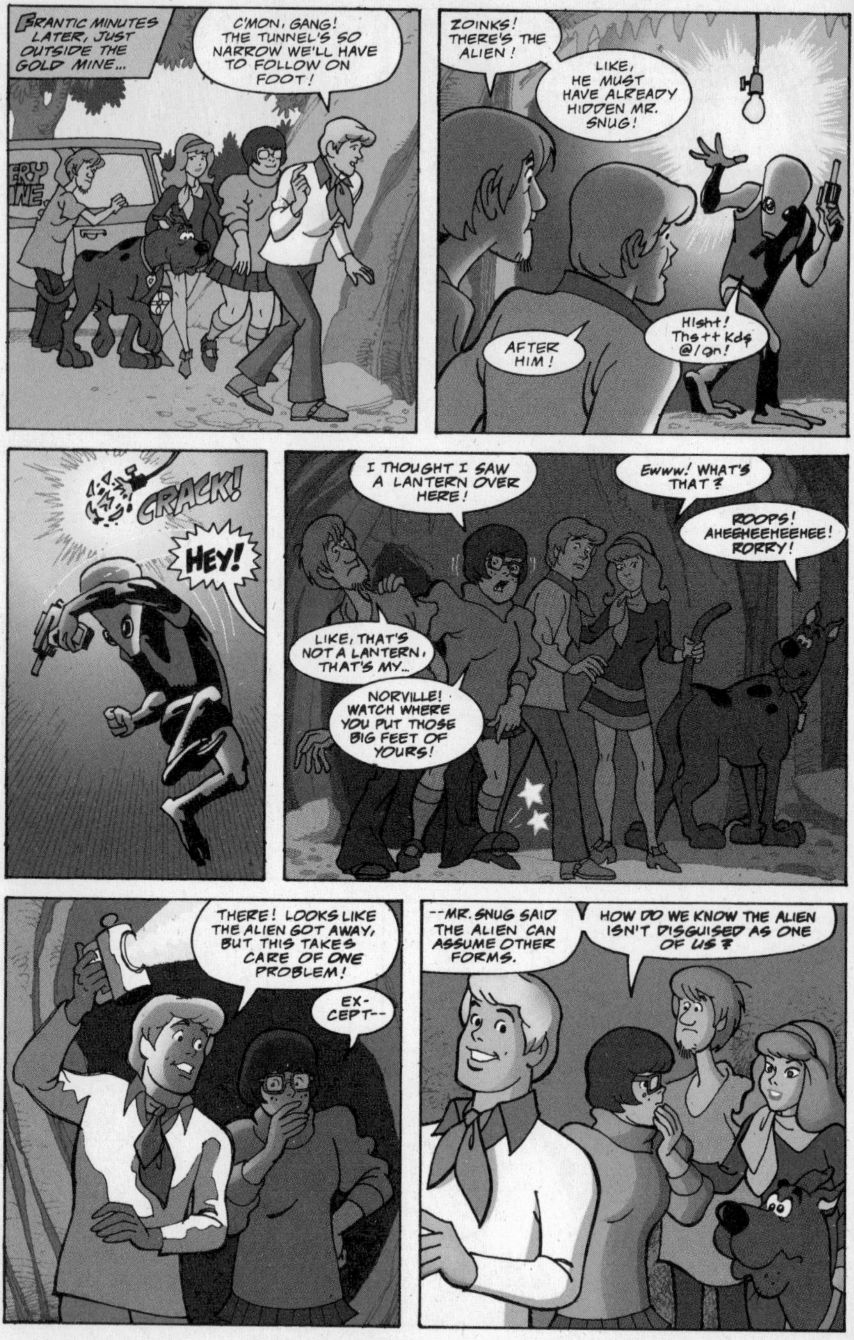
FRANTIC MINUTES LATER, JUST OUTSIDE THE GOLD MINE...
C'MON, GANG! THE TUNNEL'S SO NARROW WE'LL HAVE TO FOLLOW ON FOOT!
ZOINKS! THERE'S THE ALIEN!
LIKE, HE MUST HAVE ALREADY HIDDEN MR. SNUG!
AFTER HIM!
HIsht! Ths++ Kds @/gn!
CRACK!
HEY!
I THOUGHT I SAW A LANTERN OVER HERE!
EWWW! WHAT'S THAT?
ROOPS! AHEEHEEHEEHEE! RORRY!
LIKE, THAT'S NOT A LANTERN, THAT'S MY...
NORVILLE! WATCH WHERE YOU PUT THOSE BIG FEET OF YOURS!
THERE! LOOKS LIKE THE ALIEN GOT AWAY, BUT THIS TAKES CARE OF ONE PROBLEM!
EX-CEPT--
--MR. SNUG SAID THE ALIEN CAN ASSUME OTHER FORMS.
HOW DO WE KNOW THE ALIEN ISN'T DISGUISED AS ONE OF US?

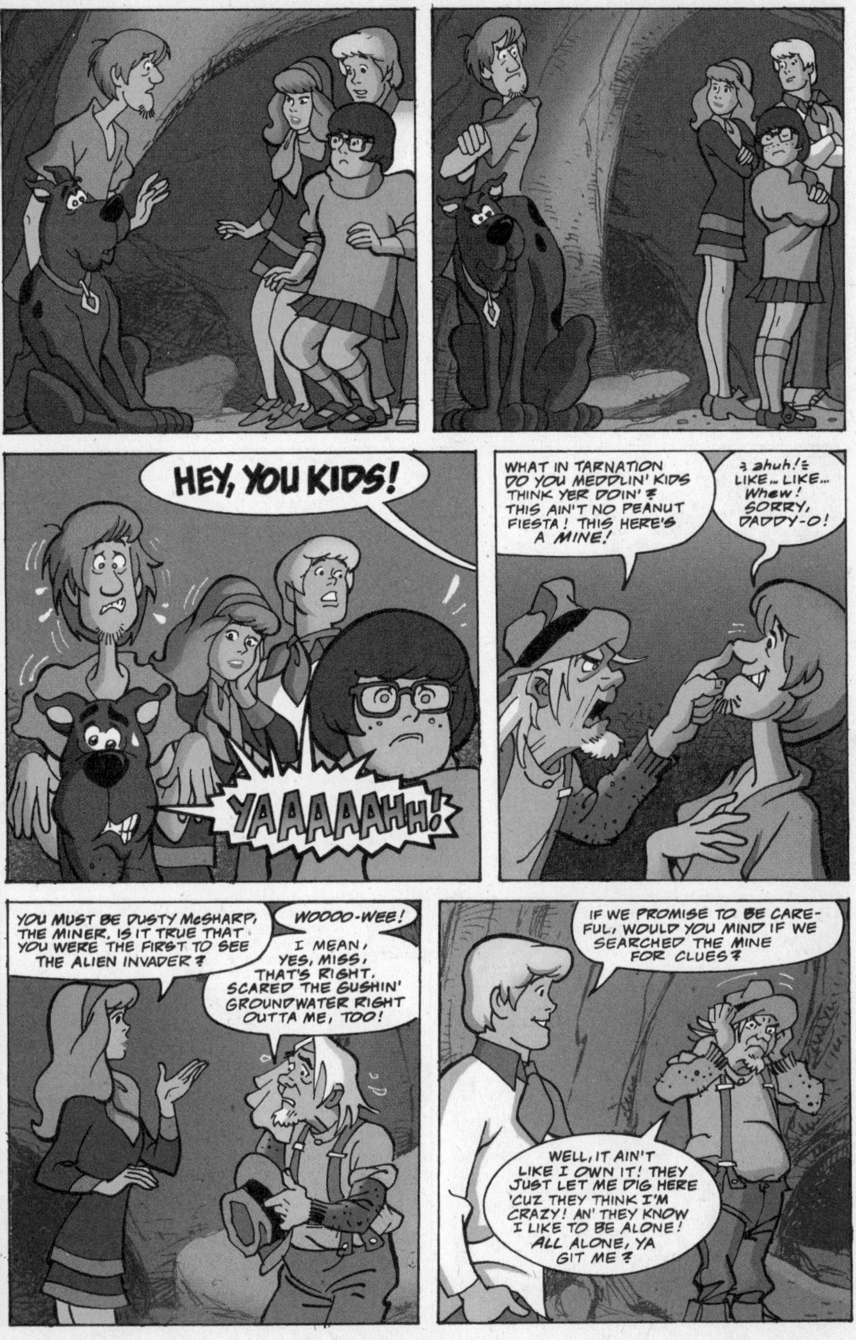
HEY, YOU KIDS!
YAAAAAHH!
WHAT IN TARNATION DO YOU MEDDLIN' KIDS THINK YER DOIN'? THIS AIN'T NO PEANUT FIESTA! THIS HERE'S A MINE!
ahuh! LIKE... LIKE... Whew! SORRY, DADDY-O!
YOU MUST BE DUSTY McSHARP, THE MINER. IS IT TRUE THAT YOU WERE THE FIRST TO SEE THE ALIEN INVADER?
WOOOO-WEE!
I MEAN, YES, MISS, THAT'S RIGHT. SCARED THE GUSHIN' GROUNDWATER RIGHT OUTTA ME, TOO!
IF WE PROMISE TO BE CAREFUL, WOULD YOU MIND IF WE SEARCHED THE MINE FOR CLUES?
WELL, IT AIN'T LIKE I OWN IT! THEY JUST LET ME DIG HERE 'CUZ THEY THINK I'M CRAZY! AN' THEY KNOW I LIKE TO BE ALONE! ALL ALONE, YA GIT ME?

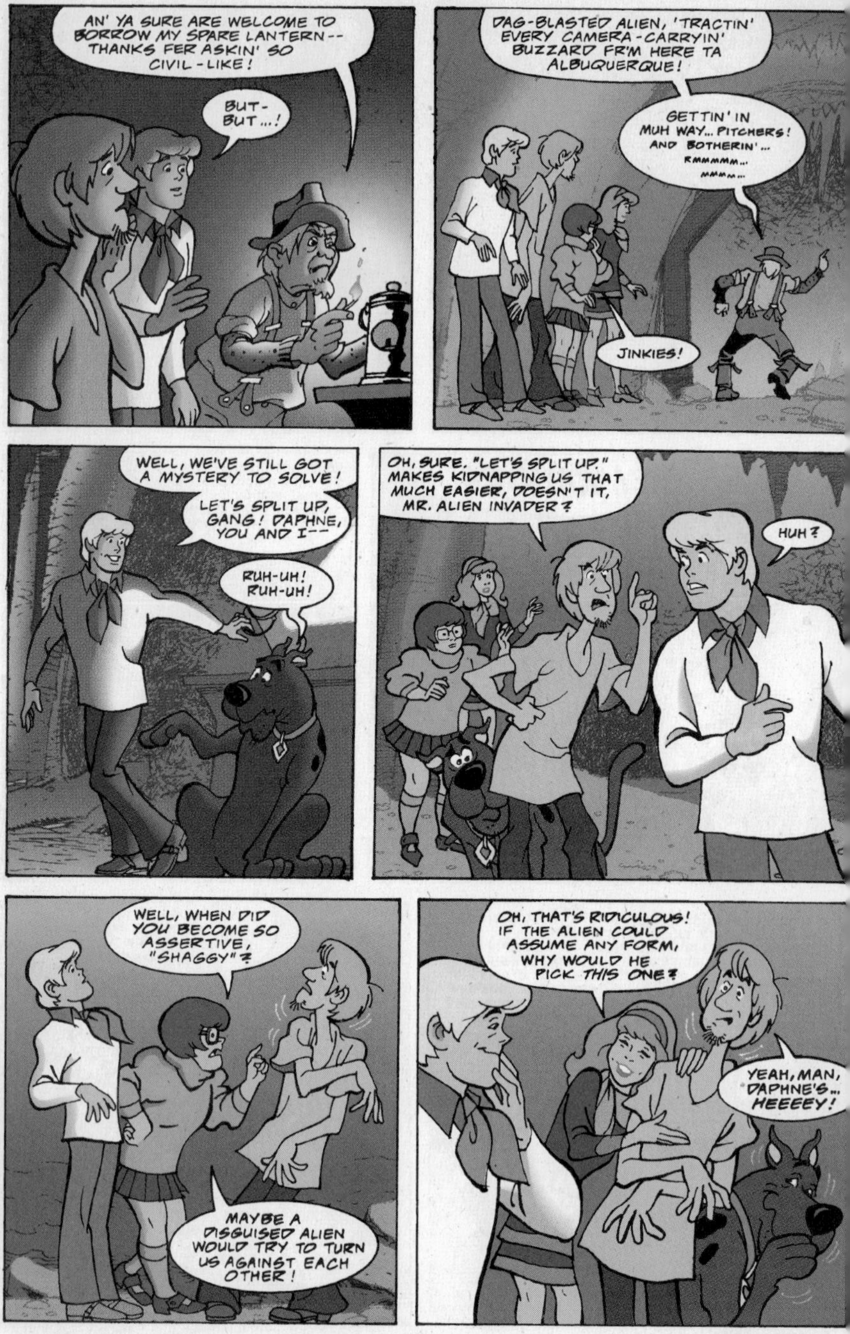
AN' YA SURE ARE WELCOME TO BORROW MY SPARE LANTERN-- THANKS FER ASKIN' SO CIVIL-LIKE!
BUT- BUT...!
DAG-BLASTED ALIEN, 'TRACTIN' EVERY CAMERA-CARRYIN' BUZZARD FR'M HERE TA ALBUQUERQUE!
GETTIN' IN MUH WAY... PITCHERS! AND BOTHERIN'... RMMMMM... MMMM...
JINKIES!
WELL, WE'VE STILL GOT A MYSTERY TO SOLVE!
LET'S SPLIT UP, GANG! DAPHNE, YOU AND I--
RUH-UH! RUH-UH!
OH, SURE. "LET'S SPLIT UP." MAKES KIDNAPPING US THAT MUCH EASIER, DOESN'T IT, MR. ALIEN INVADER?
HUH?
WELL, WHEN DID YOU BECOME SO ASSERTIVE, "SHAGGY"?
MAYBE A DISGUISED ALIEN WOULD TRY TO TURN US AGAINST EACH OTHER!
OH, THAT'S RIDICULOUS! IF THE ALIEN COULD ASSUME ANY FORM, WHY WOULD HE PICK THIS ONE?
YEAH, MAN, DAPHNE'S... HEEEEY!

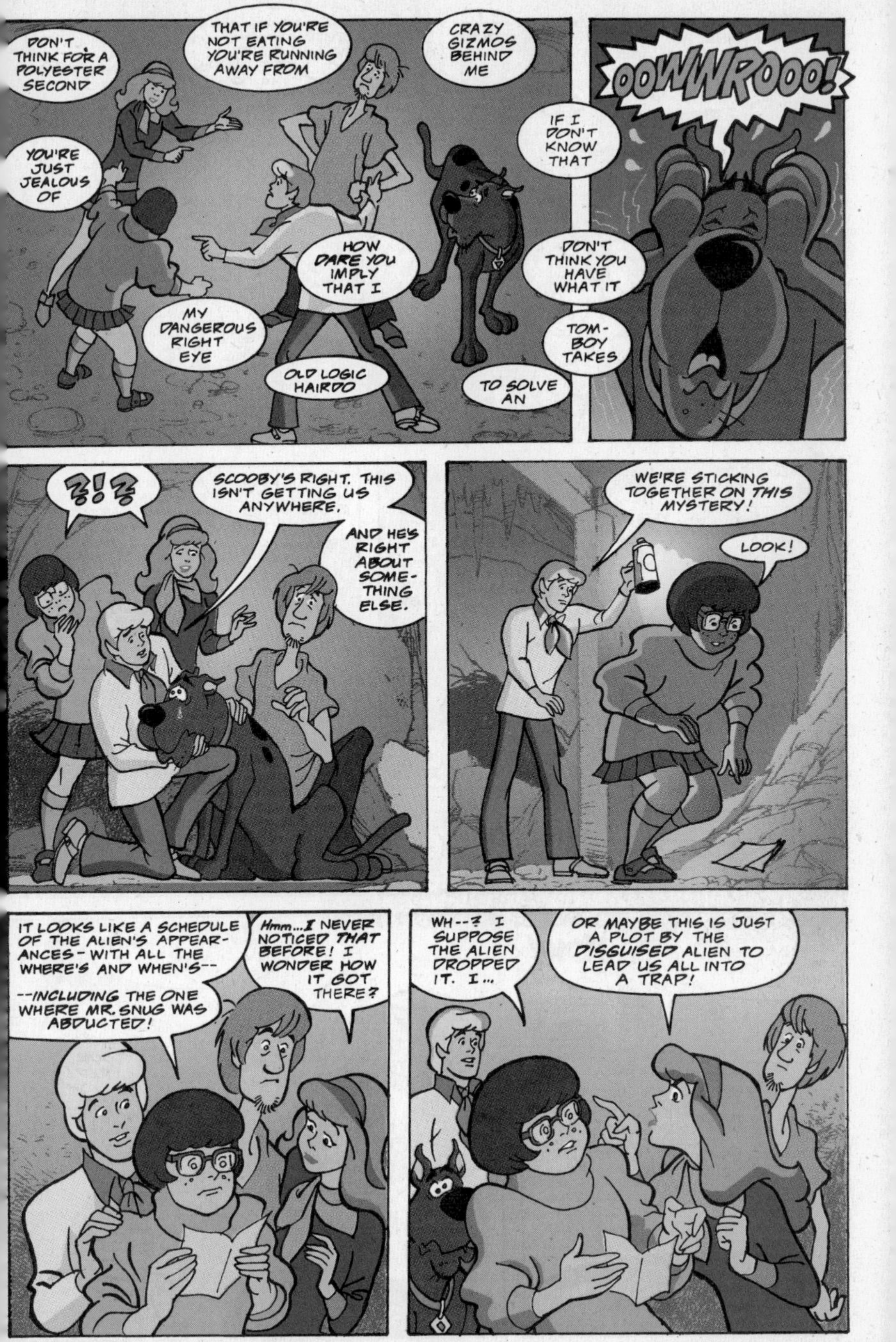
DON'T THINK FOR A POLYESTER SECOND
THAT IF YOU'RE NOT EATING YOU'RE RUNNING AWAY FROM
CRAZY GIZMOS BEHIND ME
YOU'RE JUST JEALOUS OF
HOW DARE YOU IMPLY THAT I
IF I DON'T KNOW THAT
DON'T THINK YOU HAVE WHAT IT
MY DANGEROUS RIGHT EYE
OLD LOGIC HAIRDO
TOM-BOY TAKES
TO SOLVE AN
OOWWROOO!
?!?
SCOOBY'S RIGHT. THIS ISN'T GETTING US ANYWHERE.
AND HE'S RIGHT ABOUT SOMETHING ELSE.
WE'RE STICKING TOGETHER ON THIS MYSTERY!
LOOK!
IT LOOKS LIKE A SCHEDULE OF THE ALIEN'S APPEARANCES-- WITH ALL THE WHERE'S AND WHEN'S--
--INCLUDING THE ONE WHERE MR. SNUG WAS ABDUCTED!
Hmm... I NEVER NOTICED THAT BEFORE! I WONDER HOW IT GOT THERE?
WH--? I SUPPOSE THE ALIEN DROPPED IT. I...
OR MAYBE THIS IS JUST A PLOT BY THE DISGUISED ALIEN TO LEAD US ALL INTO A TRAP!

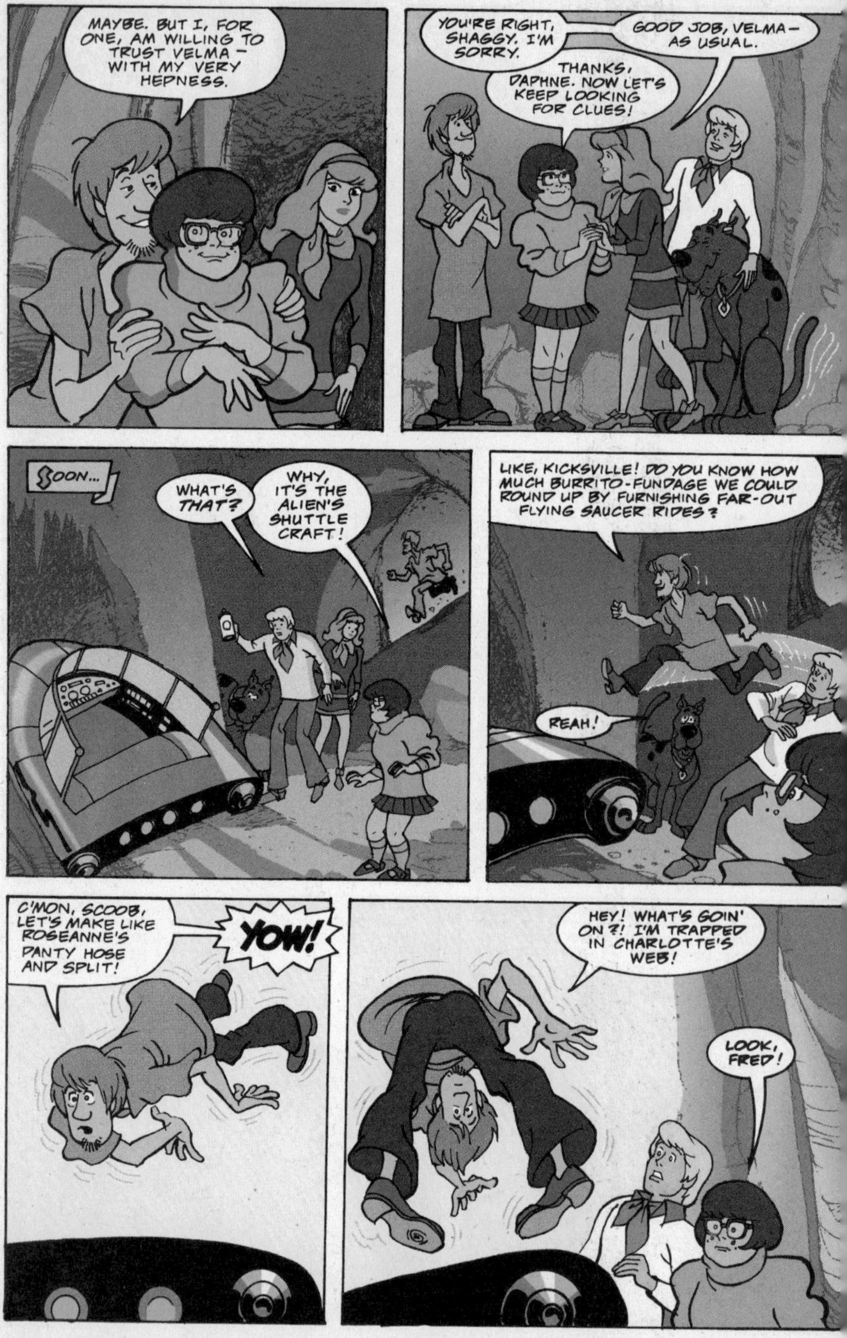
MAYBE. BUT I, FOR ONE, AM WILLING TO TRUST VELMA — WITH MY VERY HEPNESS.
YOU'RE RIGHT, SHAGGY. I'M SORRY.
GOOD JOB, VELMA — AS USUAL.
THANKS, DAPHNE. NOW LET'S KEEP LOOKING FOR CLUES!
SOON...
WHAT'S THAT?
WHY, IT'S THE ALIEN'S SHUTTLE CRAFT!
LIKE, KICKSVILLE! DO YOU KNOW HOW MUCH BURRITO-FUNDAGE WE COULD ROUND UP BY FURNISHING FAR-OUT FLYING SAUCER RIDES?
REAH!
C'MON, SCOOB, LET'S MAKE LIKE ROSEANNE'S PANTY HOSE AND SPLIT!
YOW!
HEY! WHAT'S GOIN' ON?! I'M TRAPPED IN CHARLOTTE'S WEB!
LOOK, FRED!

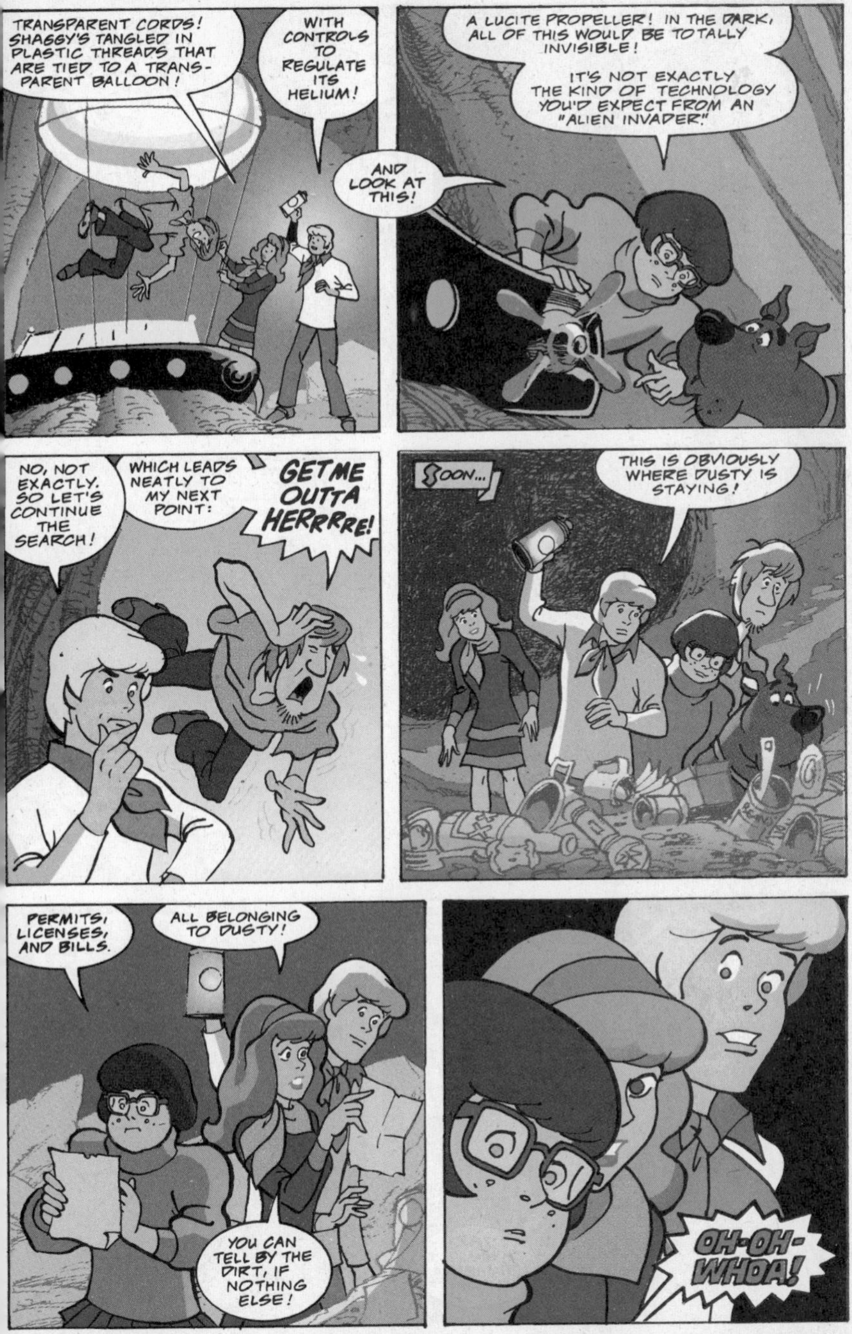
TRANSPARENT CORDS! SHAGGY'S TANGLED IN PLASTIC THREADS THAT ARE TIED TO A TRANS-PARENT BALLOON!
WITH CONTROLS TO REGULATE ITS HELIUM!
AND LOOK AT THIS!
A LUCITE PROPELLER! IN THE DARK, ALL OF THIS WOULD BE TOTALLY INVISIBLE!
IT'S NOT EXACTLY THE KIND OF TECHNOLOGY YOU'D EXPECT FROM AN "ALIEN INVADER."
NO, NOT EXACTLY. SO LET'S CONTINUE THE SEARCH!
WHICH LEADS NEATLY TO MY NEXT POINT:
GET ME OUTTA HERRRRRE!
SOON...
THIS IS OBVIOUSLY WHERE DUSTY IS STAYING!
PERMITS, LICENSES, AND BILLS.
ALL BELONGING TO DUSTY!
YOU CAN TELL BY THE DIRT, IF NOTHING ELSE!
OH-OH-WHOA!

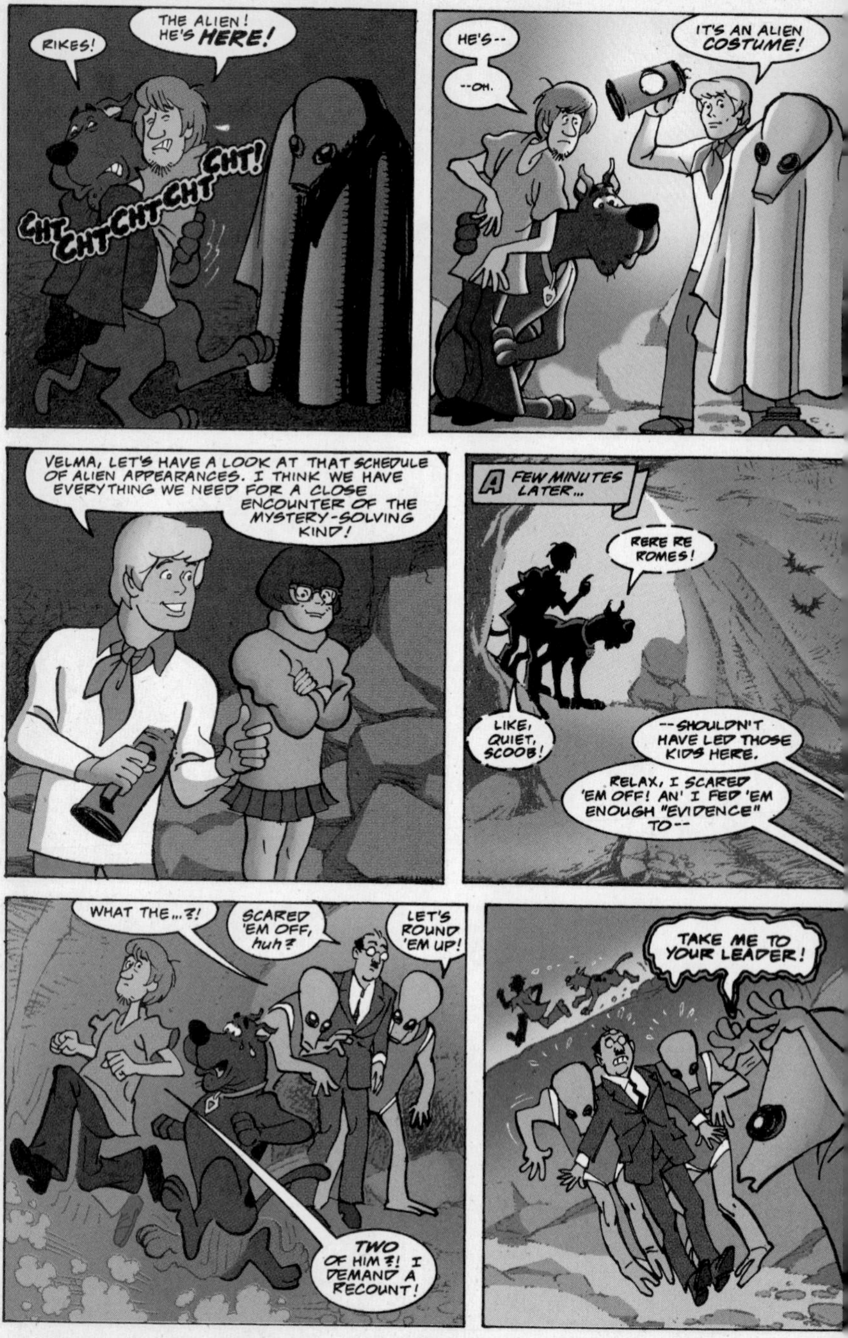
RIKES!
THE ALIEN! HE'S HERE!
CHT CHT CHT CHT CHT CHT!
HE'S--
--OH.
IT'S AN ALIEN COSTUME!
VELMA, LET'S HAVE A LOOK AT THAT SCHEDULE OF ALIEN APPEARANCES. I THINK WE HAVE EVERYTHING WE NEED FOR A CLOSE ENCOUNTER OF THE MYSTERY-SOLVING KIND!
A FEW MINUTES LATER...
RERE RE ROMES!
LIKE, QUIET, SCOOB!
--SHOULDN'T HAVE LED THOSE KIDS HERE.
RELAX, I SCARED 'EM OFF! AN' I FED 'EM ENOUGH "EVIDENCE" TO--
WHAT THE...?!
SCARED 'EM OFF, huh?
LET'S ROUND 'EM UP!
TWO OF HIM?! I DEMAND A RECOUNT!
TAKE ME TO YOUR LEADER!

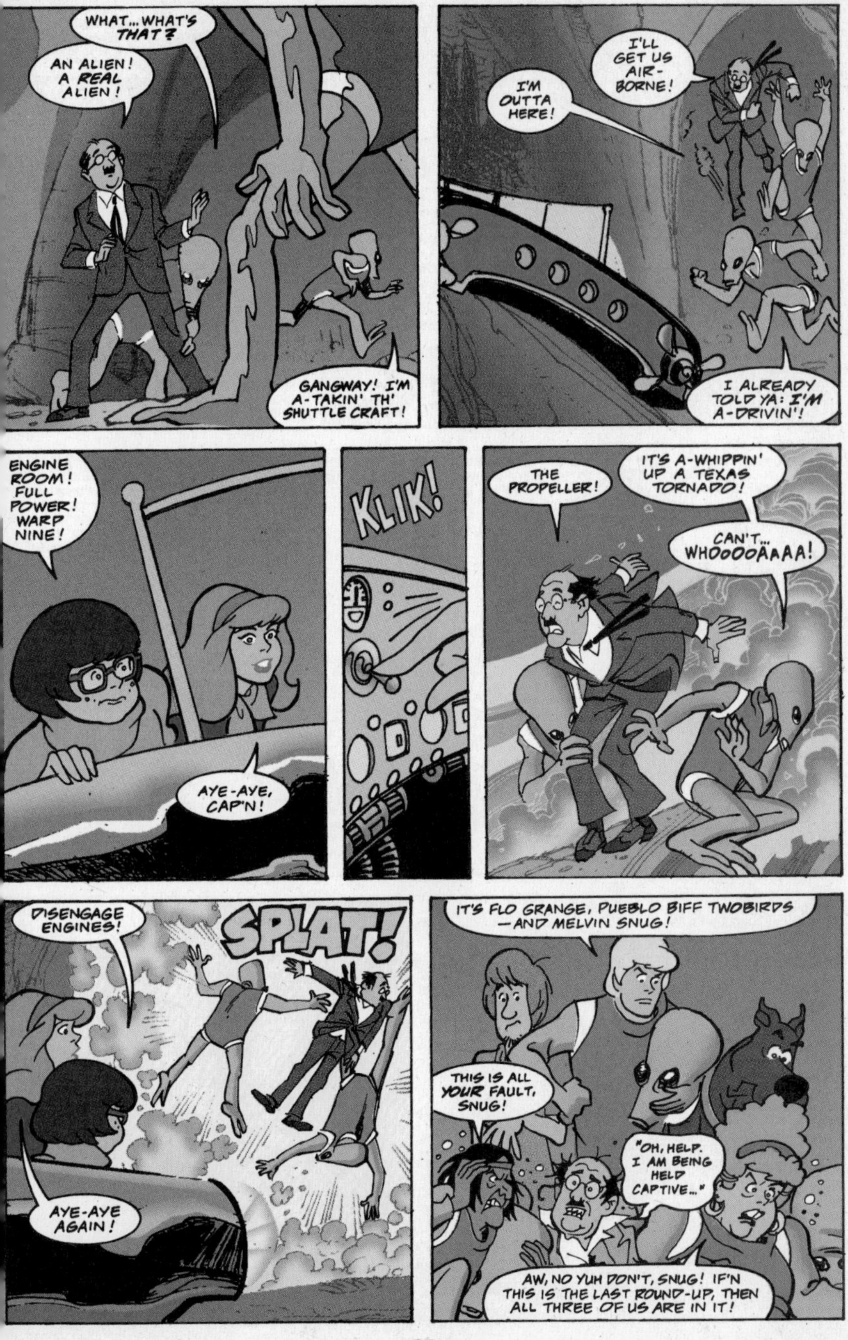
WHAT... WHAT'S THAT?
AN ALIEN! A REAL ALIEN!
GANGWAY! I'M A-TAKIN' TH' SHUTTLE CRAFT!
I'LL GET US AIR-BORNE!
I'M OUTTA HERE!
I ALREADY TOLD YA: I'M A-DRIVIN'!
ENGINE ROOM! FULL POWER! WARP NINE!
AYE-AYE, CAP'N!
KLIK!
THE PROPELLER!
IT'S A-WHIPPIN' UP A TEXAS TORNADO!
CAN'T... WHOOOOAAAA!
DISENGAGE ENGINES!
SPLAT!
AYE-AYE AGAIN!
IT'S FLO GRANGE, PUEBLO BIFF TWOBIRDS —AND MELVIN SNUG!
THIS IS ALL YOUR FAULT, SNUG!
"OH, HELP. I AM BEING HELD CAPTIVE..."
AW, NO YUH DON'T, SNUG! IF'N THIS IS THE LAST ROUND-UP, THEN ALL THREE OF US ARE IN IT!

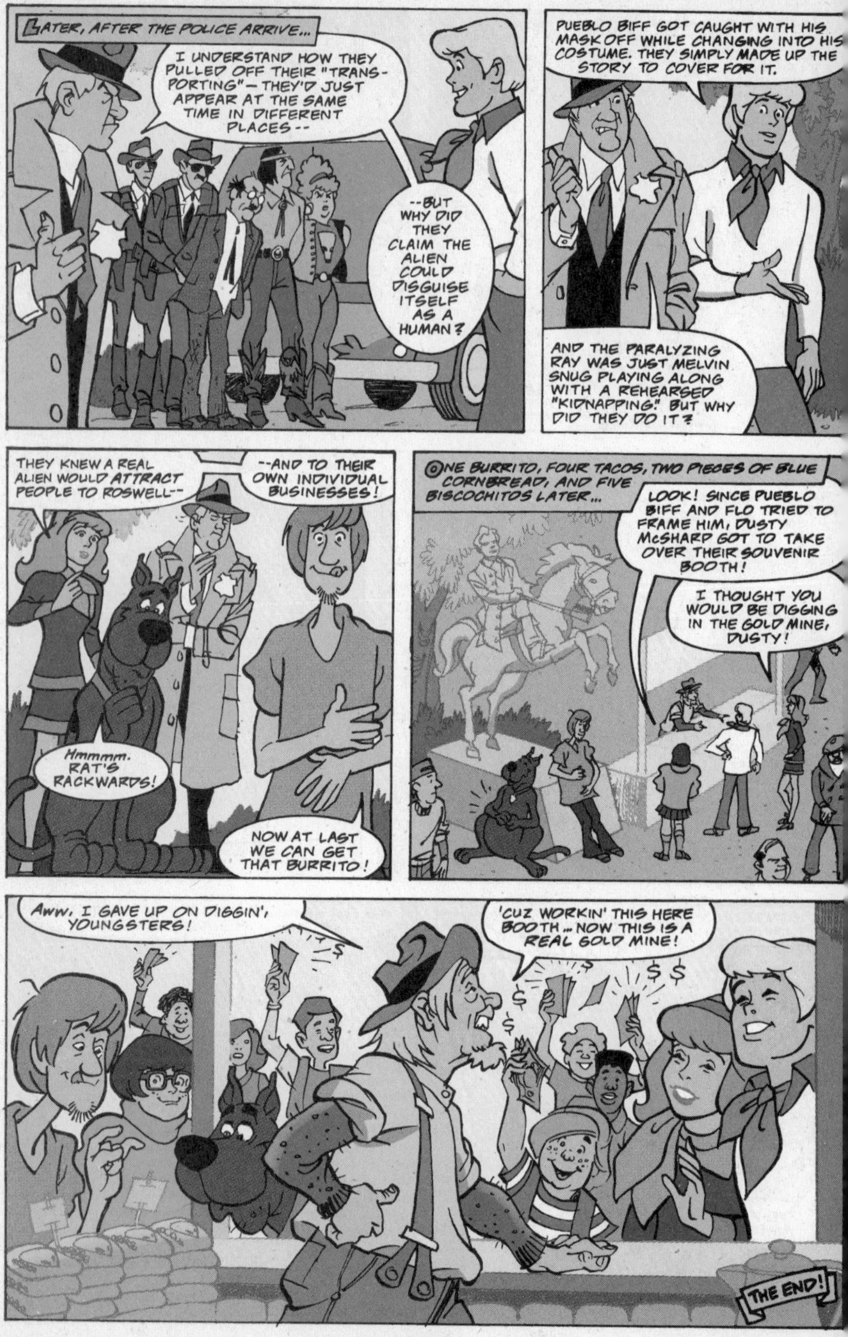
LATER, AFTER THE POLICE ARRIVE...
I UNDERSTAND HOW THEY PULLED OFF THEIR "TRANS-PORTING"—THEY'D JUST APPEAR AT THE SAME TIME IN DIFFERENT PLACES --
--BUT WHY DID THEY CLAIM THE ALIEN COULD DISGUISE ITSELF AS A HUMAN?
PUEBLO BIFF GOT CAUGHT WITH HIS MASK OFF WHILE CHANGING INTO HIS COSTUME. THEY SIMPLY MADE UP THE STORY TO COVER FOR IT.
AND THE PARALYZING RAY WAS JUST MELVIN SNUG PLAYING ALONG WITH A REHEARSED "KIDNAPPING." BUT WHY DID THEY DO IT?
THEY KNEW A REAL ALIEN WOULD ATTRACT PEOPLE TO ROSWELL--
--AND TO THEIR OWN INDIVIDUAL BUSINESSES!
Hmmmm. RAT'S RACKWARDS!
NOW AT LAST WE CAN GET THAT BURRITO!
ONE BURRITO, FOUR TACOS, TWO PIECES OF BLUE CORNBREAD, AND FIVE BISCOCHITOS LATER...
LOOK! SINCE PUEBLO BIFF AND FLO TRIED TO FRAME HIM, DUSTY McSHARP GOT TO TAKE OVER THEIR SOUVENIR BOOTH!
I THOUGHT YOU WOULD BE DIGGING IN THE GOLD MINE, DUSTY!
AWW, I GAVE UP ON DIGGIN', YOUNGSTERS!
'CUZ WORKIN' THIS HERE BOOTH ... NOW THIS IS A REAL GOLD MINE!
THE END!

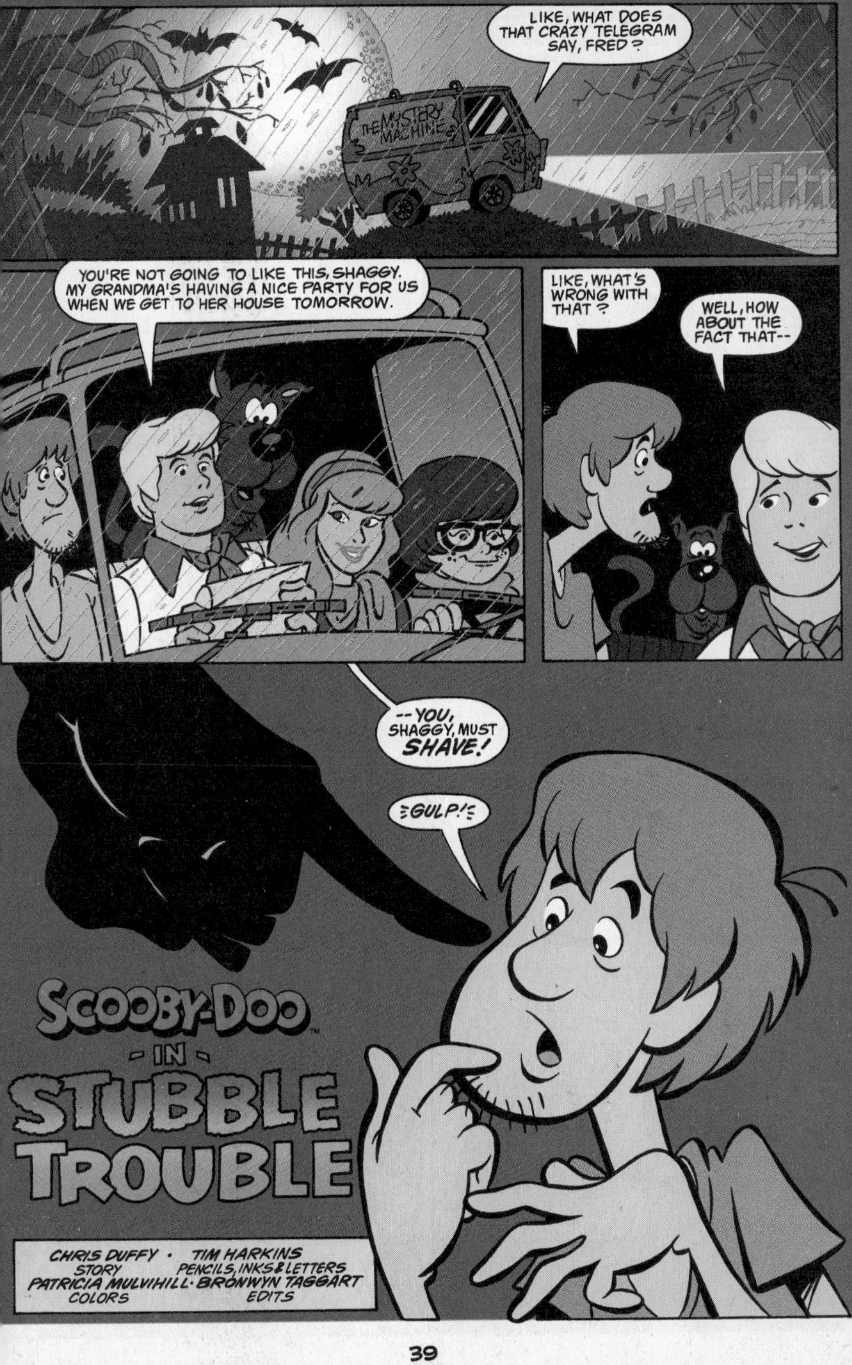
LIKE, WHAT DOES THAT CRAZY TELEGRAM SAY, FRED?
THE MYSTERY MACHINE
YOU'RE NOT GOING TO LIKE THIS, SHAGGY. MY GRANDMA'S HAVING A NICE PARTY FOR US WHEN WE GET TO HER HOUSE TOMORROW.
LIKE, WHAT'S WRONG WITH THAT?
WELL, HOW ABOUT THE FACT THAT--
--YOU, SHAGGY, MUST SHAVE!
GULP!
SCOOBY-DOO™
IN
STUBBLE TROUBLE
CHRIS DUFFY · TIM HARKINS
STORY PENCILS, INKS & LETTERS
PATRICIA MULVIHILL · BRONWYN TAGGART
COLORS EDITS

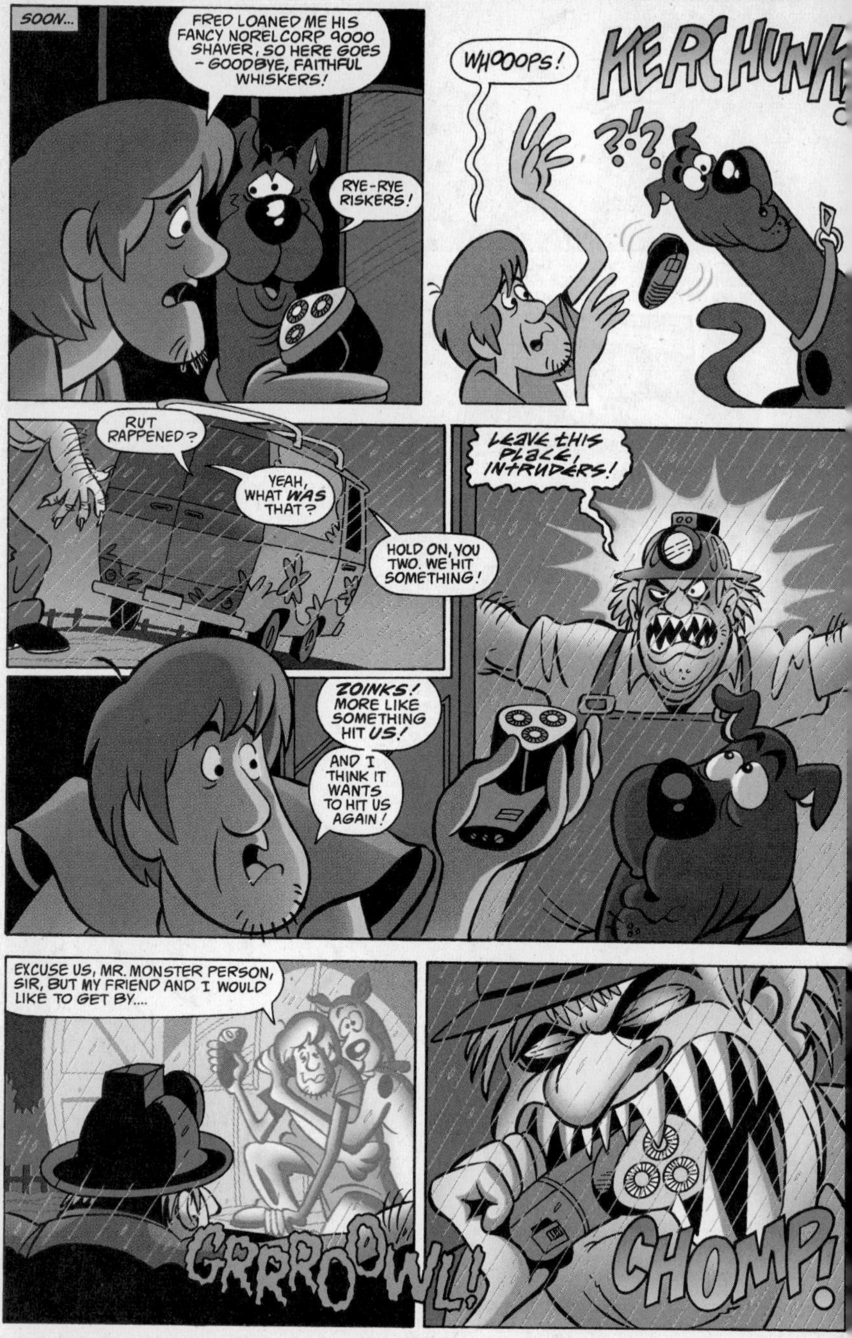
SOON...
FRED LOANED ME HIS FANCY NORELCORP 9000 SHAVER, SO HERE GOES - GOODBYE, FAITHFUL WHISKERS!
RYE-RYE RISKERS!
WHOOOPS!
KERCHUNK!
?!?
RUT RAPPENED?
YEAH, WHAT WAS THAT?
HOLD ON, YOU TWO. WE HIT SOMETHING!
LEAVE THIS PLACE, INTRUDERS!
ZOINKS! MORE LIKE SOMETHING HIT US!
AND I THINK IT WANTS TO HIT US AGAIN!
EXCUSE US, MR. MONSTER PERSON, SIR, BUT MY FRIEND AND I WOULD LIKE TO GET BY....
GRRROOWL!
CHOMP!

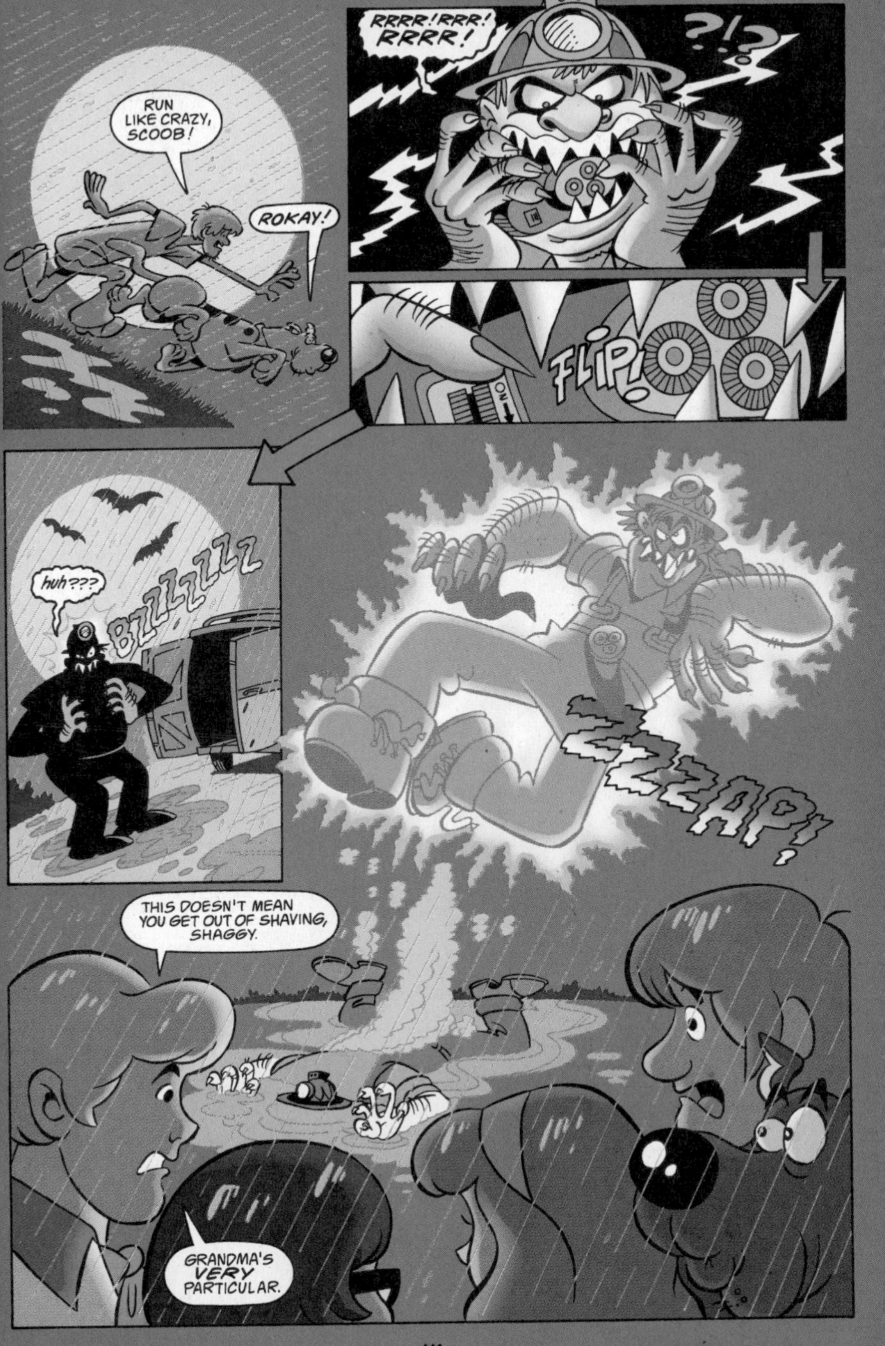
RUN LIKE CRAZY, SCOOB!
ROKAY!
RRRR! RRR! RRRR!
?!?
FLIP!
huh???
BZZZZZZZ
ZZZZAP!!
THIS DOESN'T MEAN YOU GET OUT OF SHAVING, SHAGGY.
GRANDMA'S VERY PARTICULAR.

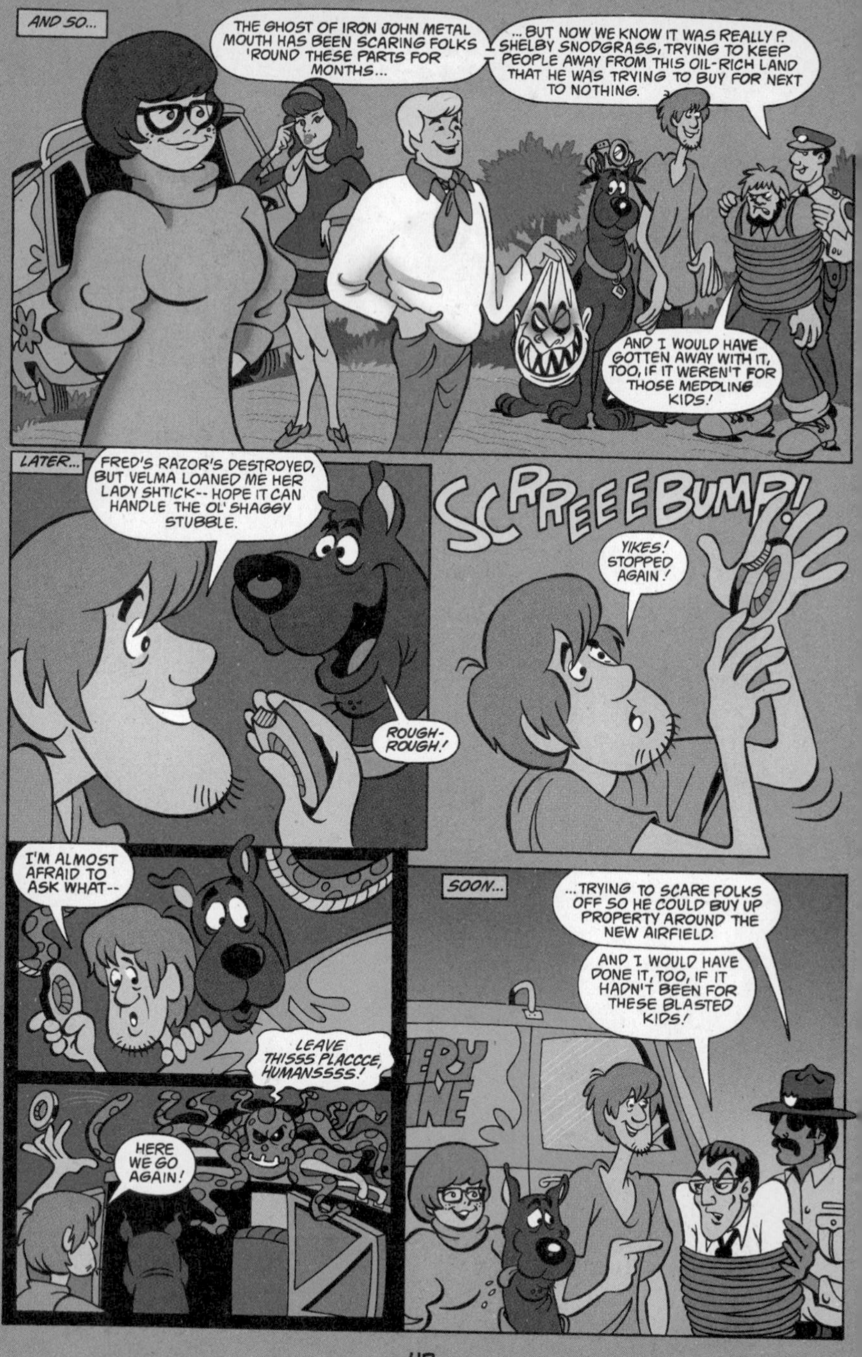

AND SO...
THE GHOST OF IRON JOHN METAL MOUTH HAS BEEN SCARING FOLKS 'ROUND THESE PARTS FOR MONTHS...
...BUT NOW WE KNOW IT WAS REALLY P. SHELBY SNODGRASS, TRYING TO KEEP PEOPLE AWAY FROM THIS OIL-RICH LAND THAT HE WAS TRYING TO BUY FOR NEXT TO NOTHING.
AND I WOULD HAVE GOTTEN AWAY WITH IT, TOO, IF IT WEREN'T FOR THOSE MEDDLING KIDS!
LATER...
FRED'S RAZOR'S DESTROYED, BUT VELMA LOANED ME HER LADY SHTICK-- HOPE IT CAN HANDLE THE OL' SHAGGY STUBBLE.
ROUGH-ROUGH!
SCRREEEEBUMP!
YIKES! STOPPED AGAIN!
I'M ALMOST AFRAID TO ASK WHAT--
LEAVE THISSS PLACCCE, HUMANSSSS!
HERE WE GO AGAIN!
SOON...
...TRYING TO SCARE FOLKS OFF SO HE COULD BUY UP PROPERTY AROUND THE NEW AIRFIELD.
AND I WOULD HAVE DONE IT, TOO, IF IT HADN'T BEEN FOR THESE BLASTED KIDS!

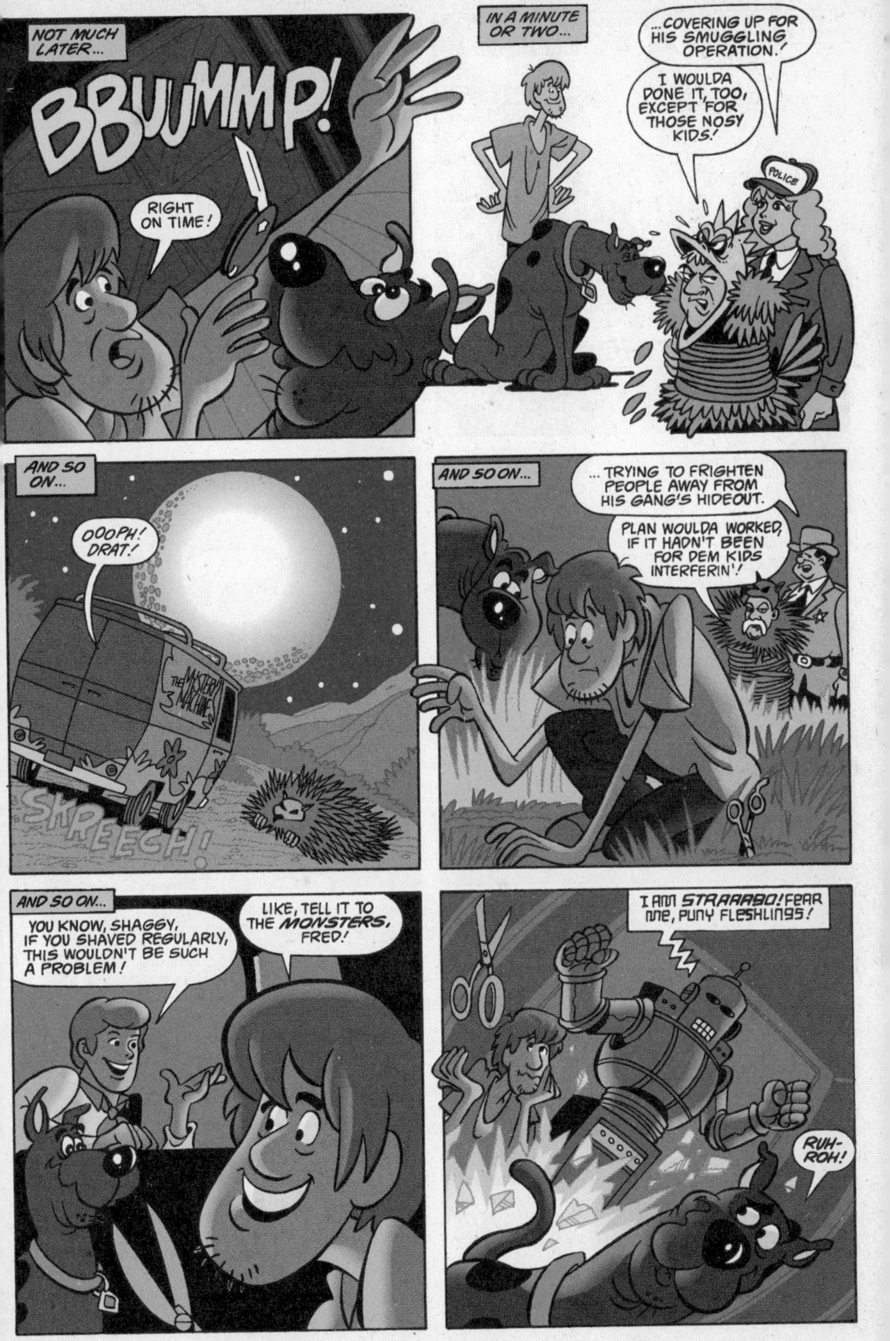
NOT MUCH LATER...
BBUUMMP!
RIGHT ON TIME!
IN A MINUTE OR TWO...
...COVERING UP FOR HIS SMUGGLING OPERATION.!
I WOULDA DONE IT, TOO, EXCEPT FOR THOSE NOSY KIDS!
POLICE
AND SO ON...
OOOPH! DRAT!
THE MYSTERY MACHINE
SKREECH!
AND SO ON...
... TRYING TO FRIGHTEN PEOPLE AWAY FROM HIS GANG'S HIDEOUT.
PLAN WOULDA WORKED, IF IT HADN'T BEEN FOR DEM KIDS INTERFERIN'!
AND SO ON...
YOU KNOW, SHAGGY, IF YOU SHAVED REGULARLY, THIS WOULDN'T BE SUCH A PROBLEM!
LIKE, TELL IT TO THE MONSTERS, FRED!
I AM STRAAAGO! FEAR ME, PUNY FLESHLINGS!
RUH-ROH!

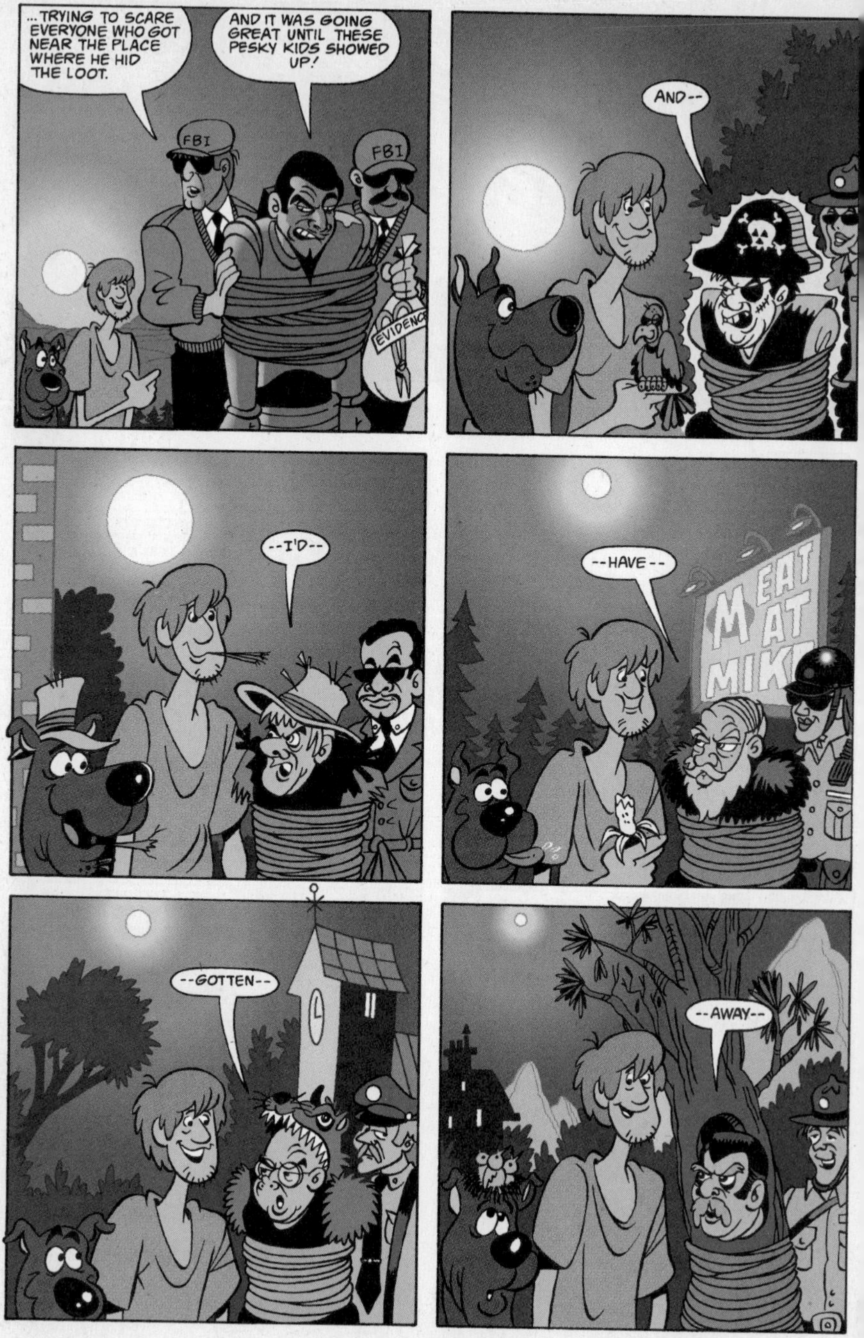
...TRYING TO SCARE EVERYONE WHO GOT NEAR THE PLACE WHERE HE HID THE LOOT.
AND IT WAS GOING GREAT UNTIL THESE PESKY KIDS SHOWED UP!
FBI
FBI
EVIDENCE
AND--
--I'D--
--HAVE--
MEAT AT MIK
--GOTTEN--
--AWAY--

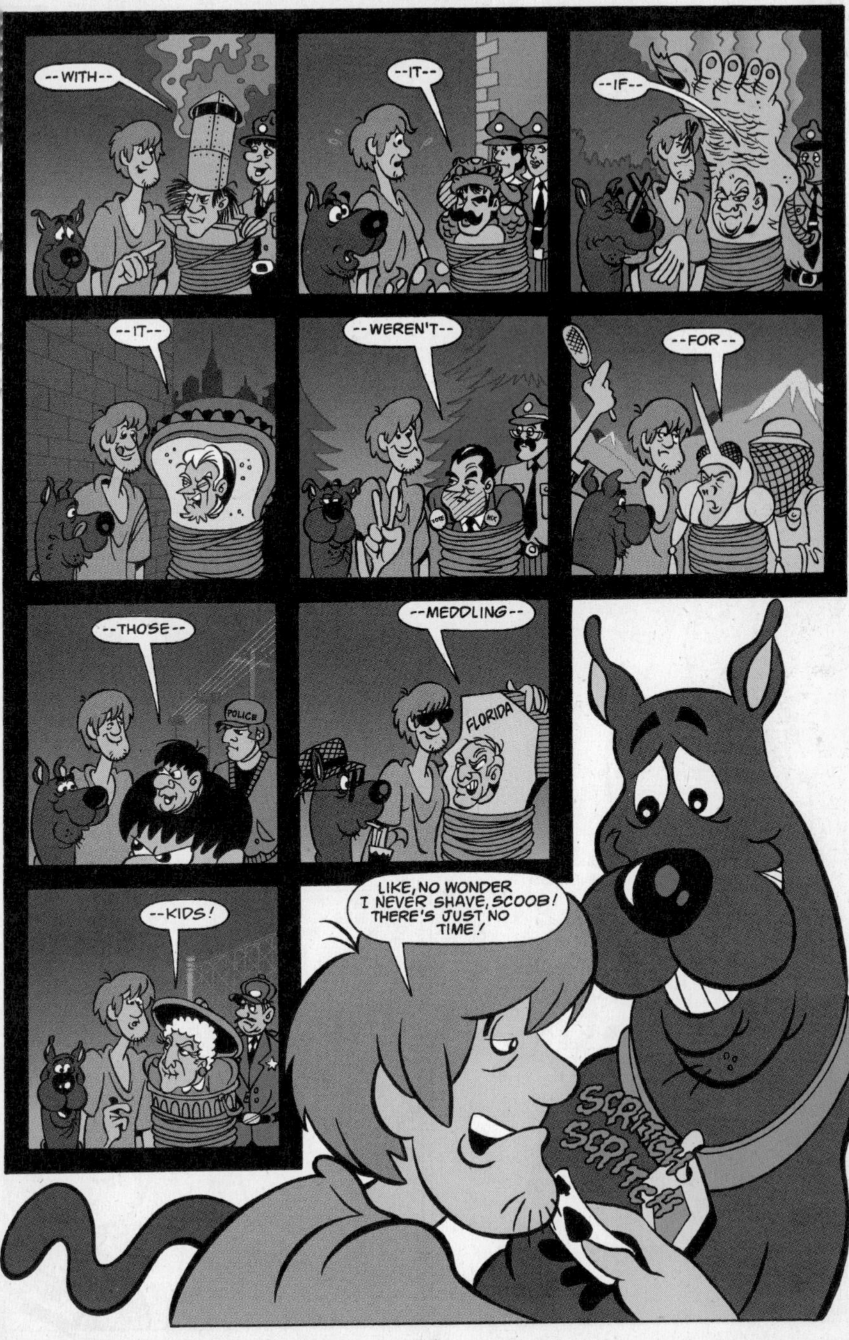
--WITH--
--IT--
--IF--
--IT--
--WEREN'T--
--FOR--
--THOSE--
POLICE
--MEDDLING--
FLORIDA
--KIDS!
LIKE, NO WONDER I NEVER SHAVE, SCOOB! THERE'S JUST NO TIME!
SCRITCH! SCRITCH!

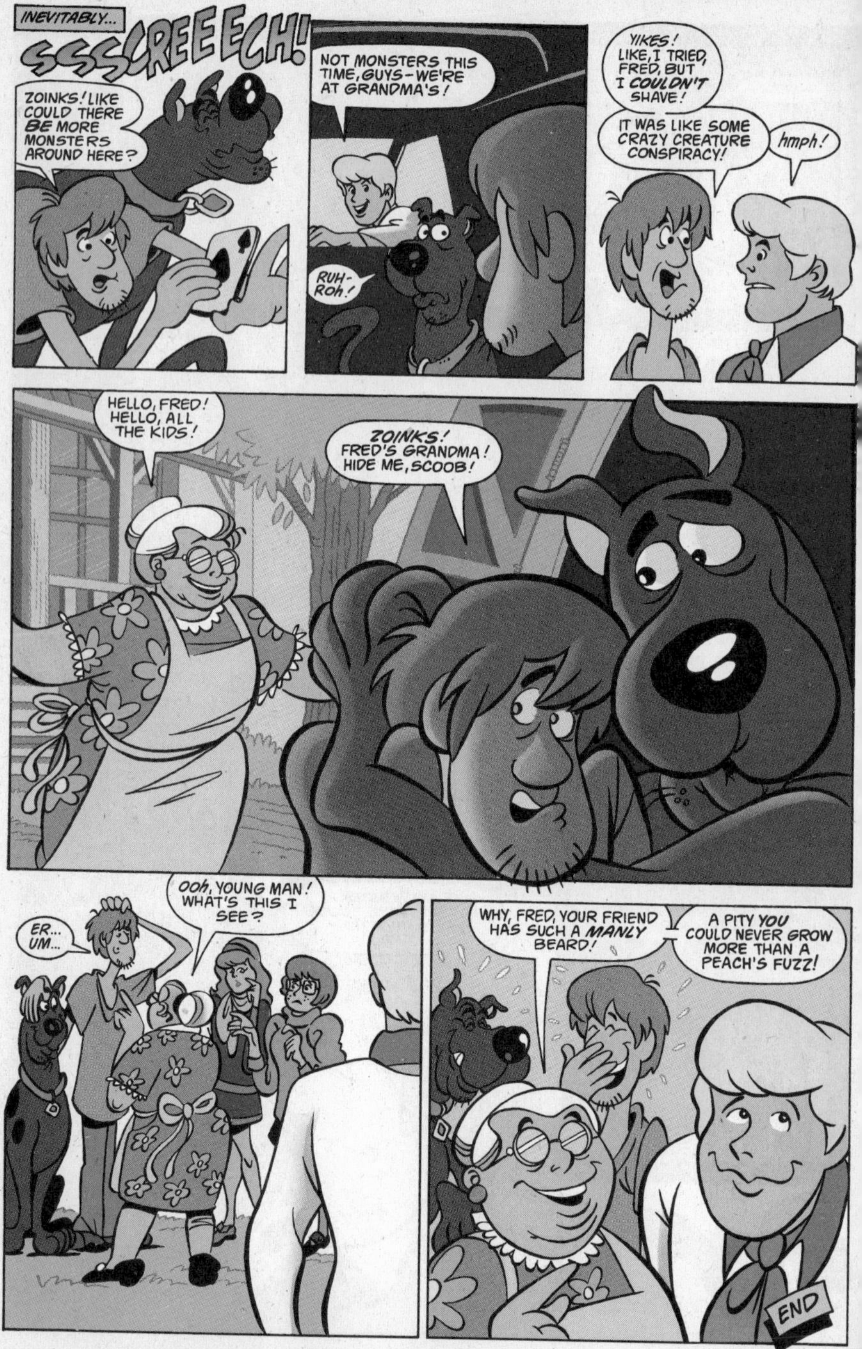
INEVITABLY...
SSSCREEECH!
ZOINKS! LIKE COULD THERE BE MORE MONSTERS AROUND HERE?
NOT MONSTERS THIS TIME, GUYS—WE'RE AT GRANDMA'S!
RUH-ROH!
YIKES! LIKE, I TRIED, FRED, BUT I COULDN'T SHAVE!
IT WAS LIKE SOME CRAZY CREATURE CONSPIRACY!
hmph!
HELLO, FRED! HELLO, ALL THE KIDS!
ZOINKS! FRED'S GRANDMA! HIDE ME, SCOOB!
ER... UM...
OOH, YOUNG MAN! WHAT'S THIS I SEE?
WHY, FRED, YOUR FRIEND HAS SUCH A MANLY BEARD!
A PITY YOU COULD NEVER GROW MORE THAN A PEACH'S FUZZ!
END

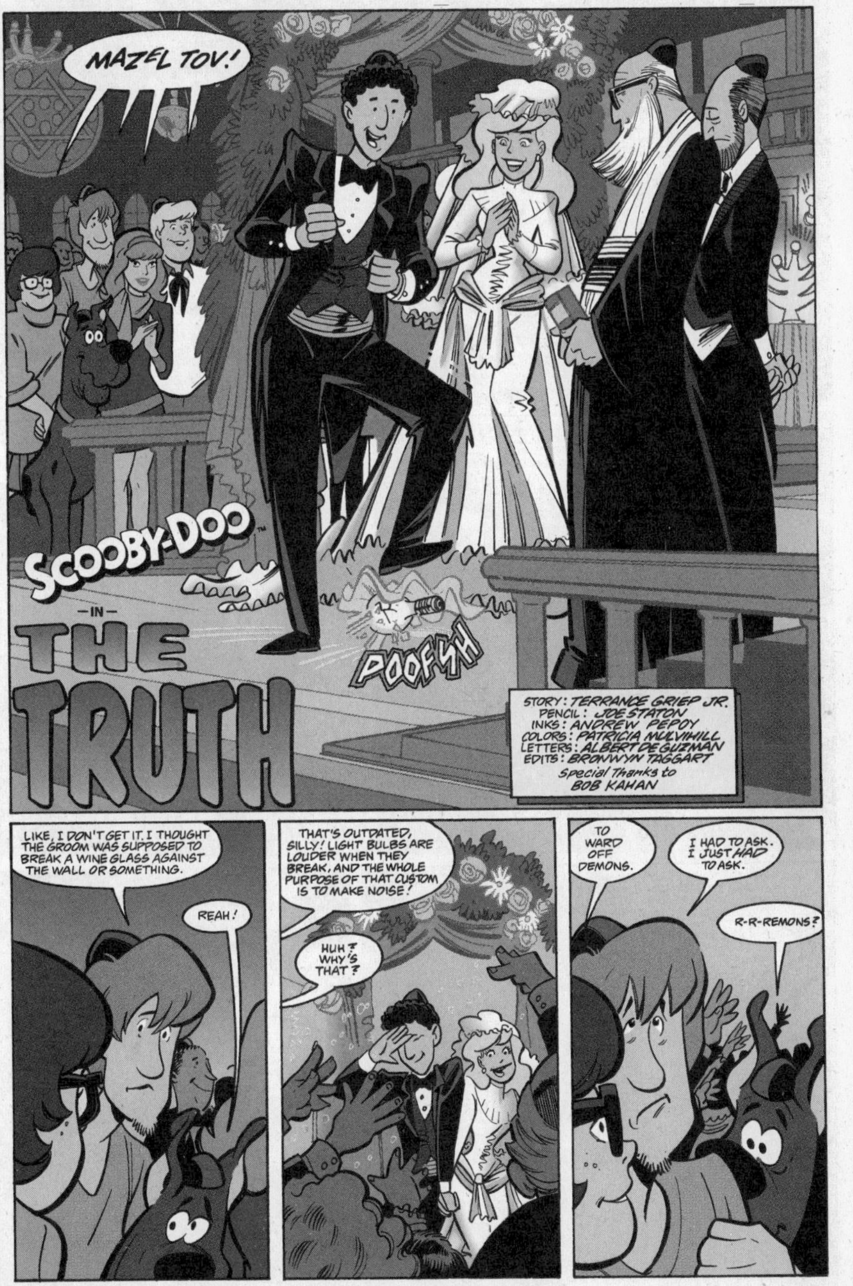
MAZEL TOV!
SCOOBY-DOO
-IN-
THE TRUTH
POOFSH
STORY: TERRANCE GRIEP JR.
PENCIL: JOE STATON
INKS: ANDREW PEPOY
COLORS: PATRICIA MULVIHILL
LETTERS: ALBERT DE GUZMAN
EDITS: BRONWYN TAGGART
Special Thanks to BOB KAHAN
LIKE, I DON'T GET IT. I THOUGHT THE GROOM WAS SUPPOSED TO BREAK A WINE GLASS AGAINST THE WALL OR SOMETHING.
REAH!
THAT'S OUTDATED, SILLY! LIGHT BULBS ARE LOUDER WHEN THEY BREAK, AND THE WHOLE PURPOSE OF THAT CUSTOM IS TO MAKE NOISE!
HUH? WHY'S THAT?
TO WARD OFF DEMONS.
I HAD TO ASK. I JUST HAD TO ASK.
R-R-REMONS?

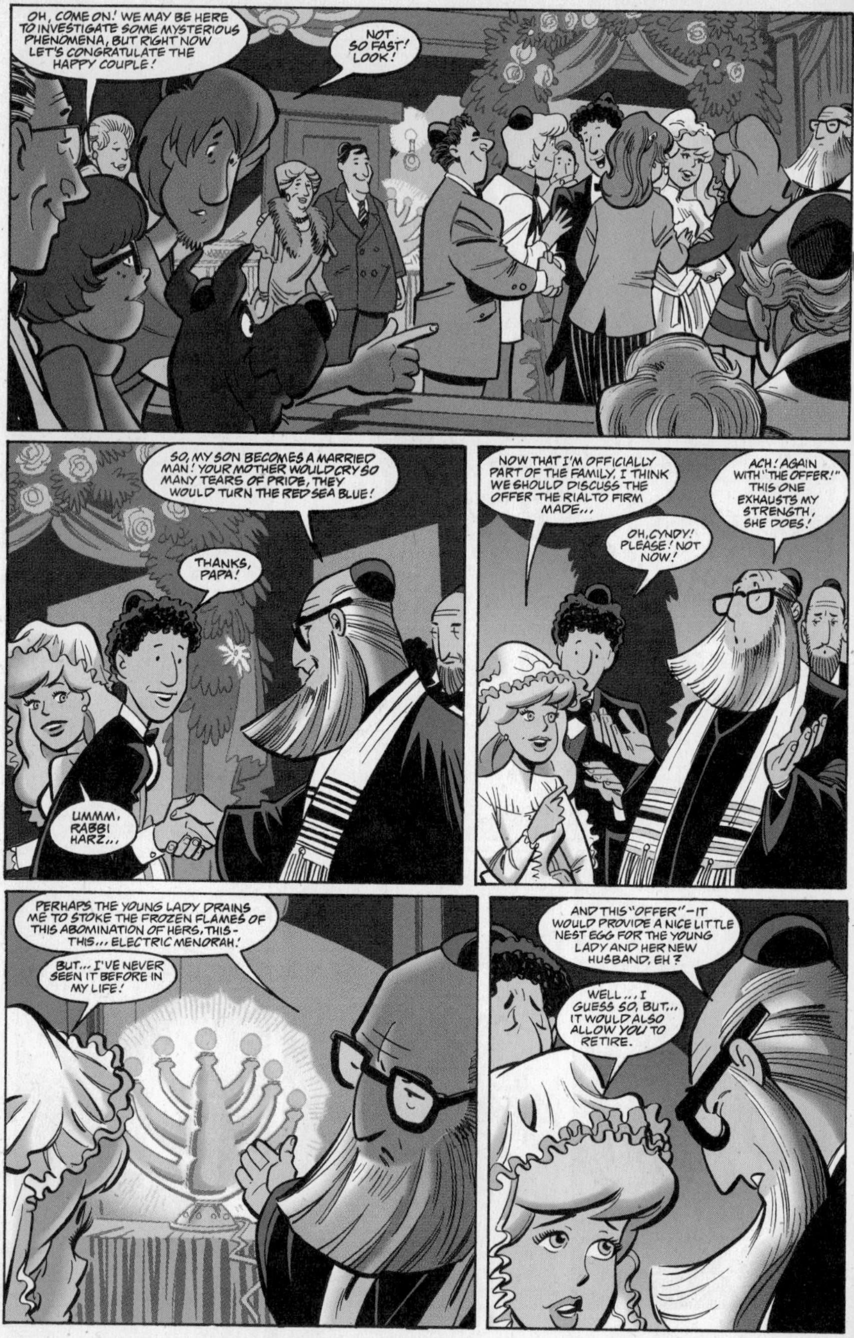
OH, COME ON! WE MAY BE HERE TO INVESTIGATE SOME MYSTERIOUS PHENOMENA, BUT RIGHT NOW LET'S CONGRATULATE THE HAPPY COUPLE!
NOT SO FAST! LOOK!
SO, MY SON BECOMES A MARRIED MAN! YOUR MOTHER WOULD CRY SO MANY TEARS OF PRIDE, THEY WOULD TURN THE RED SEA BLUE!
THANKS, PAPA!
UMMM, RABBI HARZ...
NOW THAT I'M OFFICIALLY PART OF THE FAMILY, I THINK WE SHOULD DISCUSS THE OFFER THE RIALTO FIRM MADE...
OH, CYNDY! PLEASE! NOT NOW!
ACH! AGAIN WITH "THE OFFER!" THIS ONE EXHAUSTS MY STRENGTH, SHE DOES!
PERHAPS THE YOUNG LADY DRAINS ME TO STOKE THE FROZEN FLAMES OF THIS ABOMINATION OF HERS, THIS-- THIS... ELECTRIC MENORAH!
BUT... I'VE NEVER SEEN IT BEFORE IN MY LIFE!
AND THIS "OFFER"--IT WOULD PROVIDE A NICE LITTLE NEST EGG FOR THE YOUNG LADY AND HER NEW HUSBAND, EH?
WELL... I GUESS SO, BUT... IT WOULD ALSO ALLOW YOU TO RETIRE.

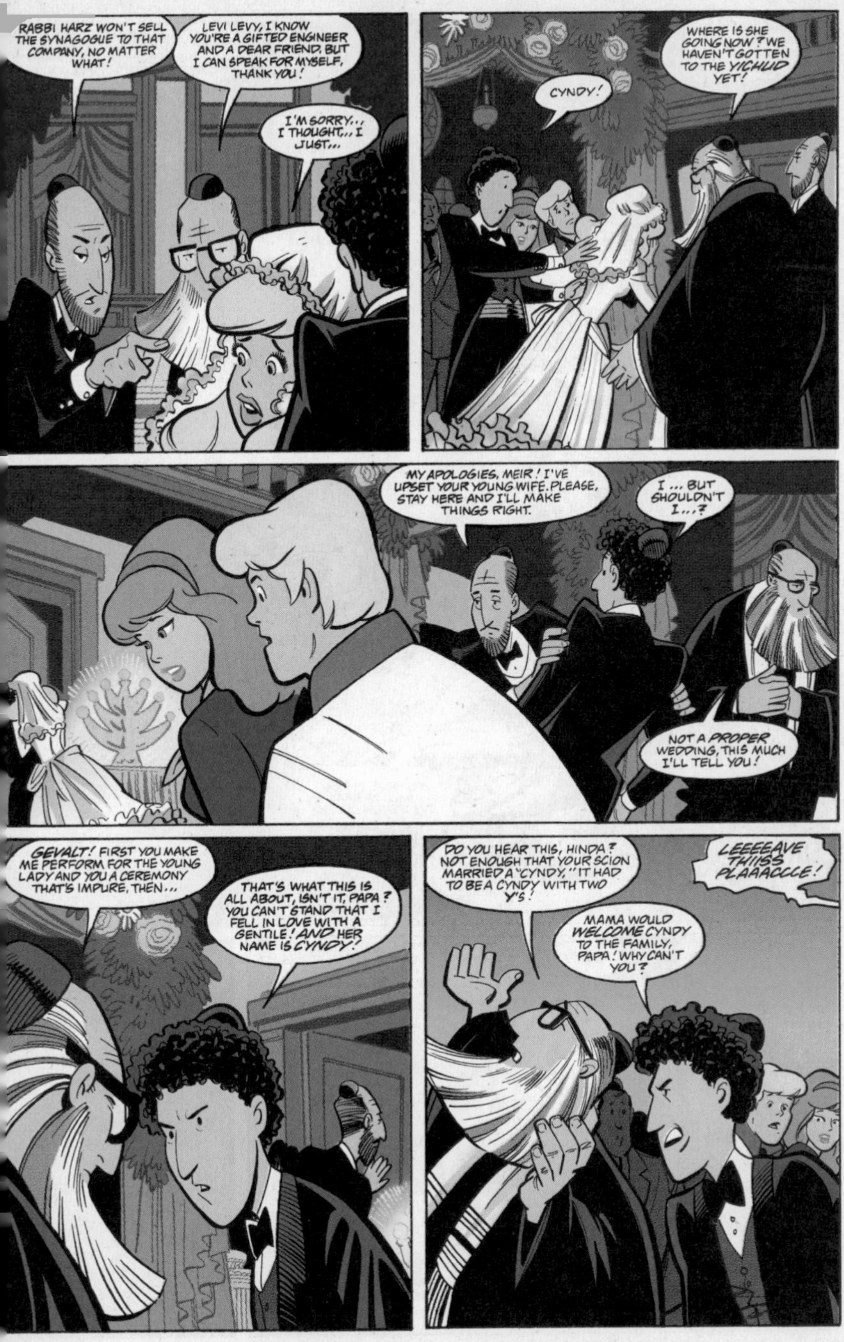

RABBI HARZ WON'T SELL THE SYNAGOGUE TO THAT COMPANY, NO MATTER WHAT!
LEVI LEVY, I KNOW YOU'RE A GIFTED ENGINEER AND A DEAR FRIEND, BUT I CAN SPEAK FOR MYSELF, THANK YOU!
I'M SORRY... I THOUGHT... I JUST...
CYNDY!
WHERE IS SHE GOING NOW? WE HAVEN'T GOTTEN TO THE YICHUD YET!
MY APOLOGIES, MEIR! I'VE UPSET YOUR YOUNG WIFE. PLEASE, STAY HERE AND I'LL MAKE THINGS RIGHT.
I ... BUT SHOULDN'T I...?
NOT A PROPER WEDDING, THIS MUCH I'LL TELL YOU!
GEVALT! FIRST YOU MAKE ME PERFORM FOR THE YOUNG LADY AND YOU A CEREMONY THAT'S IMPURE, THEN...
THAT'S WHAT THIS IS ALL ABOUT, ISN'T IT, PAPA? YOU CAN'T STAND THAT I FELL IN LOVE WITH A GENTILE! AND HER NAME IS CYNDY!
DO YOU HEAR THIS, HINDA? NOT ENOUGH THAT YOUR SCION MARRIED A "CYNDY," IT HAD TO BE A CYNDY WITH TWO Y'S!
MAMA WOULD WELCOME CYNDY TO THE FAMILY, PAPA! WHY CAN'T YOU?
LEEEEAVE THIISS PLAAACCCE!

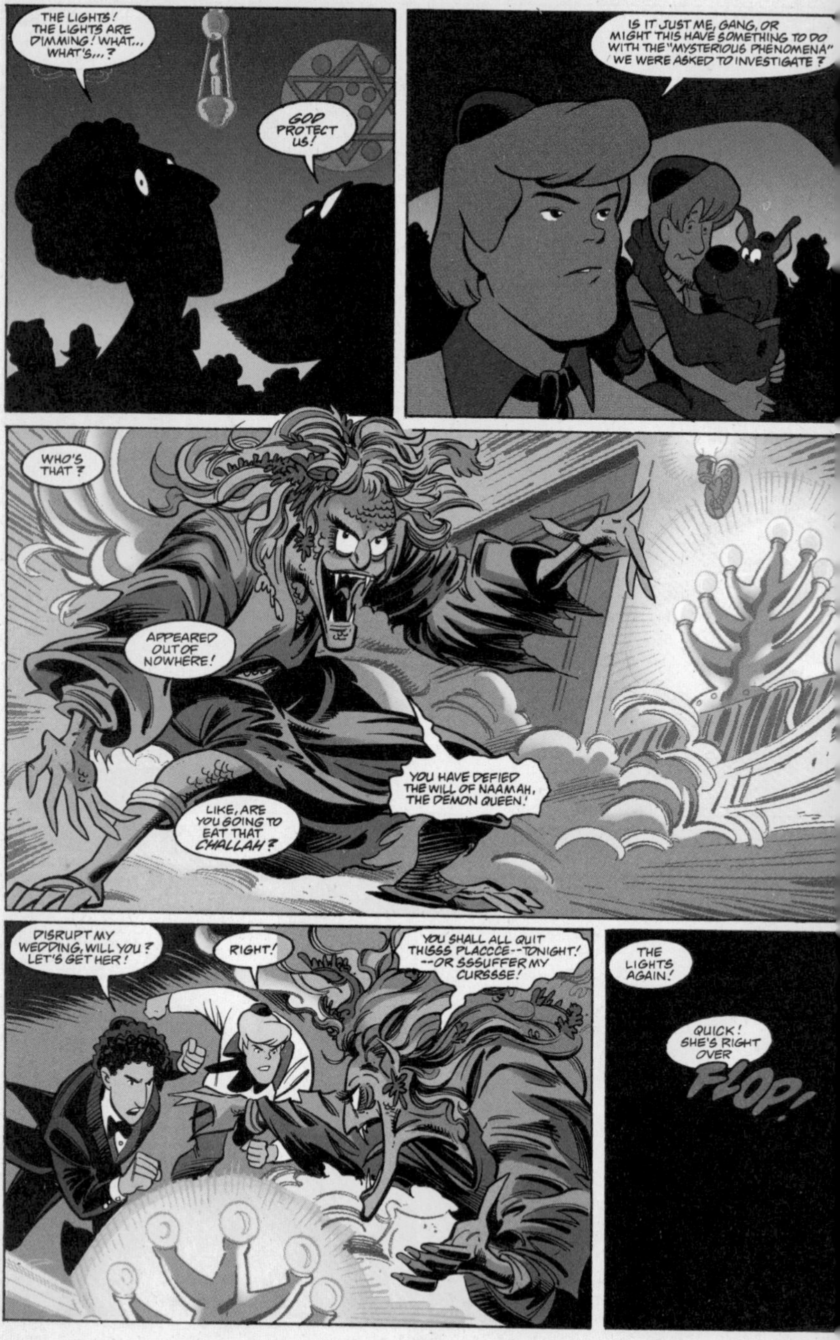
THE LIGHTS! THE LIGHTS ARE DIMMING! WHAT... WHAT'S...?
GOD PROTECT US!
IS IT JUST ME, GANG, OR MIGHT THIS HAVE SOMETHING TO DO WITH THE "MYSTERIOUS PHENOMENA" WE WERE ASKED TO INVESTIGATE?
WHO'S THAT?
APPEARED OUT OF NOWHERE!
YOU HAVE DEFIED THE WILL OF NAAMAH, THE DEMON QUEEN!
LIKE, ARE YOU GOING TO EAT THAT CHALLAH?
DISRUPT MY WEDDING, WILL YOU? LET'S GET HER!
RIGHT!
YOU SHALL ALL QUIT THISSS PLACCCE--TONIGHT! --OR SSSUFFER MY CURSSSE!
THE LIGHTS AGAIN!
QUICK! SHE'S RIGHT OVER
FLOP!

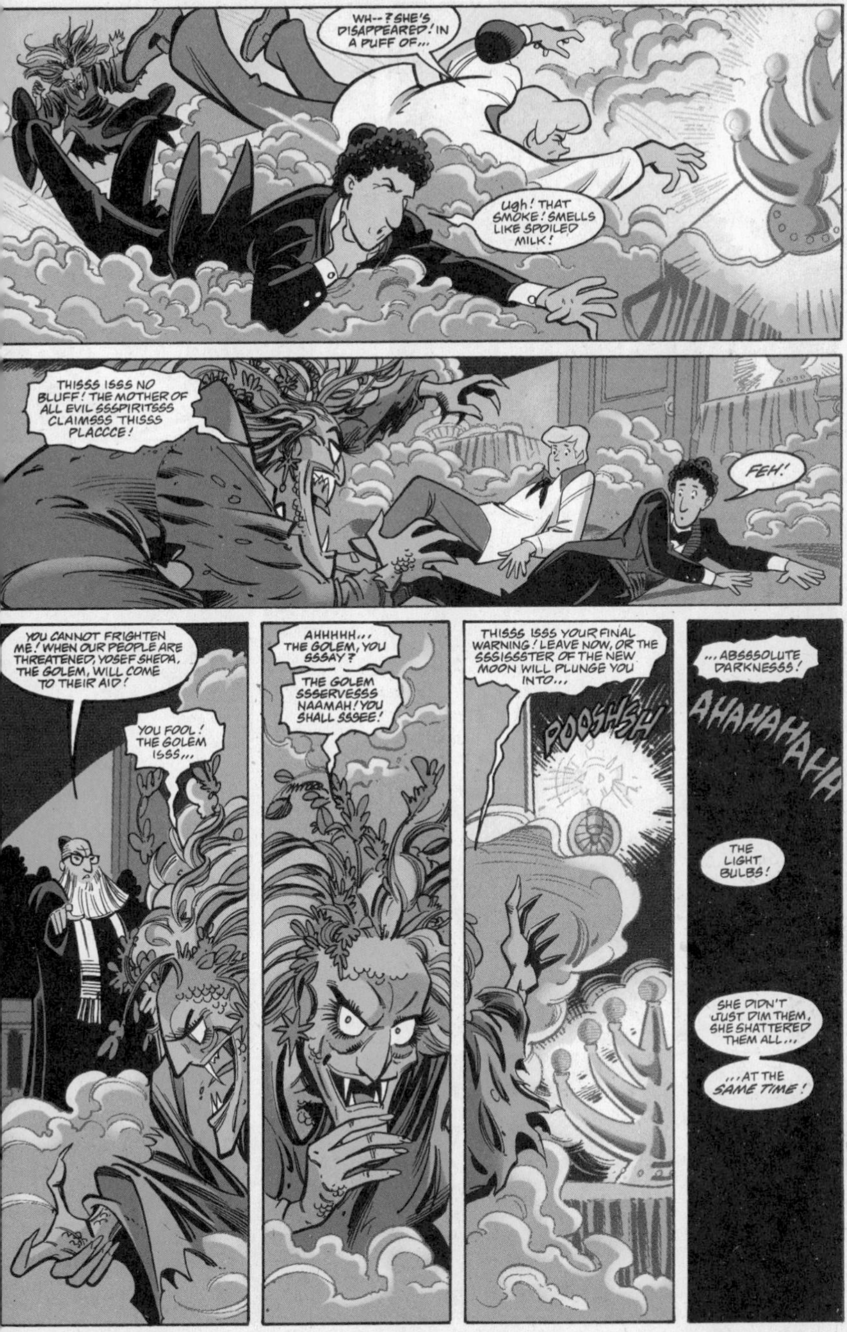
WH--? SHE'S DISAPPEARED! IN A PUFF OF...
UGH! THAT SMOKE! SMELLS LIKE SPOILED MILK!
THISSS ISSS NO BLUFF! THE MOTHER OF ALL EVIL SSSPIRITSSS CLAIMSSS THISSS PLACCCE!
FEH!
YOU CANNOT FRIGHTEN ME! WHEN OUR PEOPLE ARE THREATENED, YOSEF SHEDA, THE GOLEM, WILL COME TO THEIR AID!
YOU FOOL! THE GOLEM ISSS...
AHHHHH... THE GOLEM, YOU SSSAY?
THE GOLEM SSSERVESSS NAAMAH! YOU SHALL SSSEE!
THISSS ISSS YOUR FINAL WARNING! LEAVE NOW, OR THE SSSISSSTER OF THE NEW MOON WILL PLUNGE YOU INTO...
POOSHSH
...ABSSSOLUTE DARKNESSS!
AHAHAHAHAHH
THE LIGHT BULBS!
SHE DIDN'T JUST DIM THEM, SHE SHATTERED THEM ALL...
...AT THE SAME TIME!

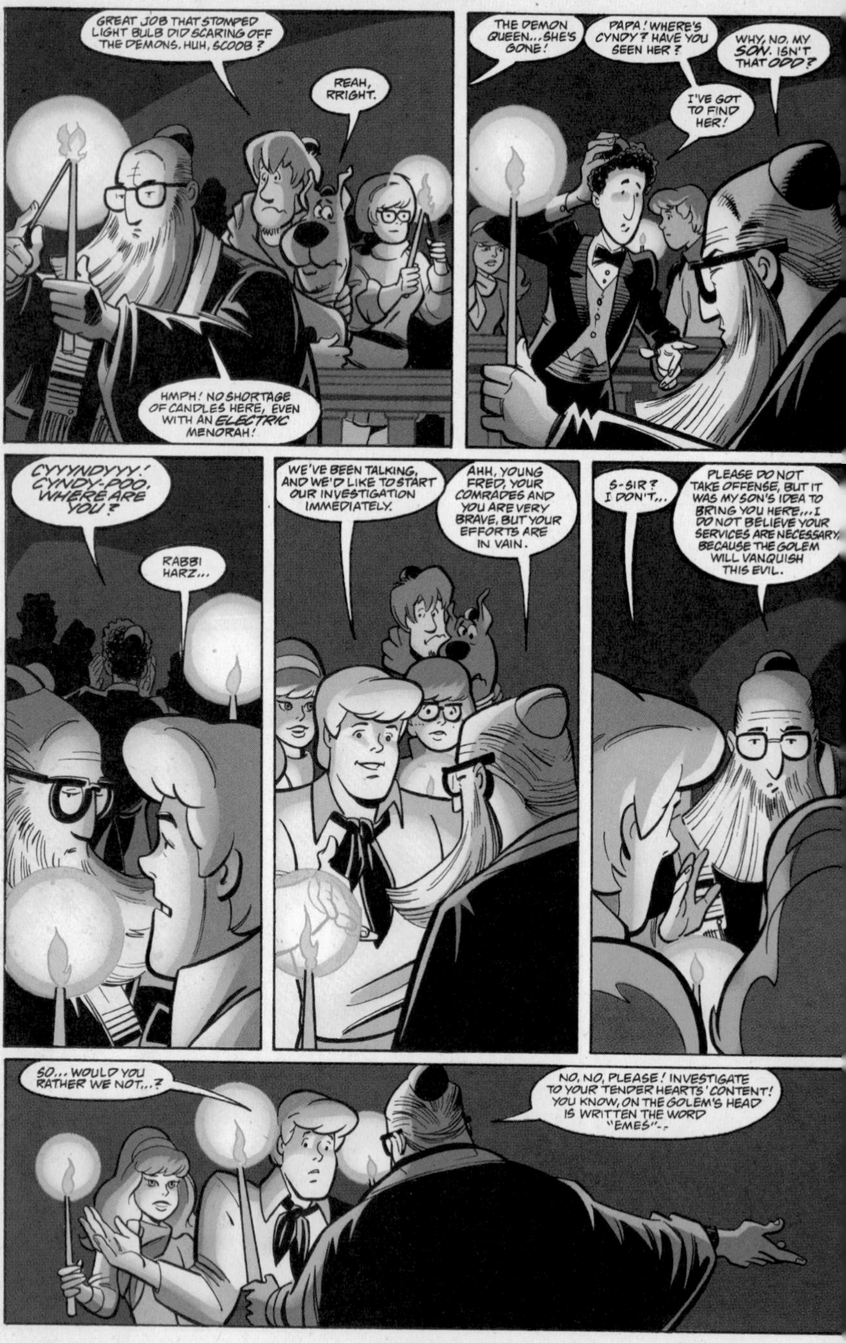
GREAT JOB THAT STOMPED LIGHT BULB DID SCARING OFF THE DEMONS. HUH, SCOOB?
REAH, RRIGHT.
HMPH! NO SHORTAGE OF CANDLES HERE, EVEN WITH AN ELECTRIC MENORAH!
THE DEMON QUEEN... SHE'S GONE!
PAPA! WHERE'S CYNDY? HAVE YOU SEEN HER?
I'VE GOT TO FIND HER!
WHY, NO, MY SON. ISN'T THAT ODD?
CYYYNDYYY! CYNDY-POO, WHERE ARE YOU?
RABBI HARZ...
WE'VE BEEN TALKING, AND WE'D LIKE TO START OUR INVESTIGATION IMMEDIATELY.
AHH, YOUNG FRED, YOUR COMRADES AND YOU ARE VERY BRAVE, BUT YOUR EFFORTS ARE IN VAIN.
S-SIR? I DON'T...
PLEASE DO NOT TAKE OFFENSE, BUT IT WAS MY SON'S IDEA TO BRING YOU HERE... I DO NOT BELIEVE YOUR SERVICES ARE NECESSARY, BECAUSE THE GOLEM WILL VANQUISH THIS EVIL.
SO... WOULD YOU RATHER WE NOT...?
NO, NO, PLEASE! INVESTIGATE TO YOUR TENDER HEARTS' CONTENT! YOU KNOW, ON THE GOLEM'S HEAD IS WRITTEN THE WORD "EMES"--

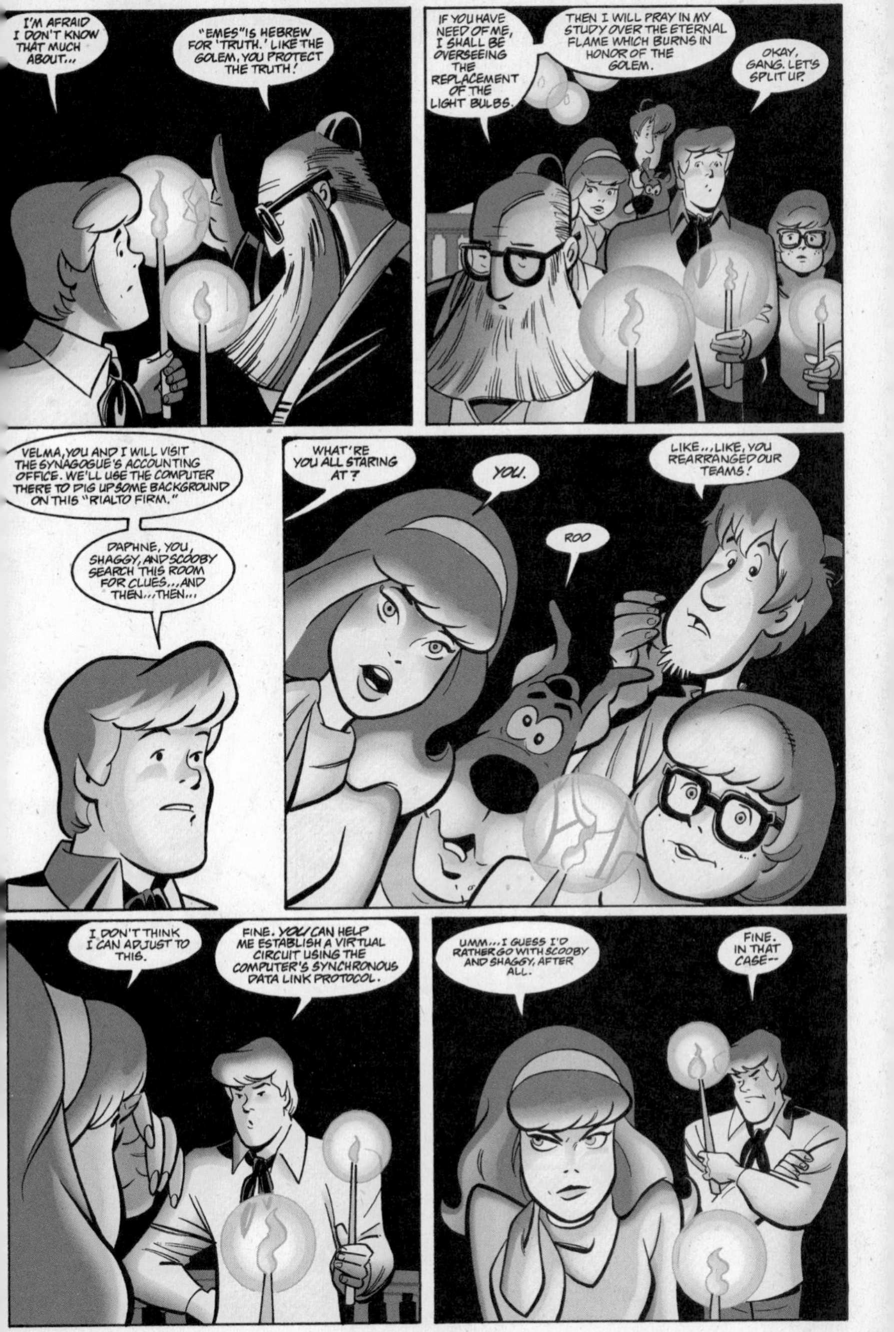
I'M AFRAID I DON'T KNOW THAT MUCH ABOUT...
"EMES" IS HEBREW FOR 'TRUTH.' LIKE THE GOLEM, YOU PROTECT THE TRUTH!
IF YOU HAVE NEED OF ME, I SHALL BE OVERSEEING THE REPLACEMENT OF THE LIGHT BULBS.
THEN I WILL PRAY IN MY STUDY OVER THE ETERNAL FLAME WHICH BURNS IN HONOR OF THE GOLEM.
OKAY, GANG. LET'S SPLIT UP.
VELMA, YOU AND I WILL VISIT THE SYNAGOGUE'S ACCOUNTING OFFICE. WE'LL USE THE COMPUTER THERE TO DIG UP SOME BACKGROUND ON THIS "RIALTO FIRM."
DAPHNE, YOU, SHAGGY, AND SCOOBY SEARCH THIS ROOM FOR CLUES... AND THEN... THEN...
WHAT'RE YOU ALL STARING AT?
YOU.
LIKE... LIKE, YOU REARRANGED OUR TEAMS!
ROO
I DON'T THINK I CAN ADJUST TO THIS.
FINE. YOU CAN HELP ME ESTABLISH A VIRTUAL CIRCUIT USING THE COMPUTER'S SYNCHRONOUS DATA LINK PROTOCOL.
UMM... I GUESS I'D RATHER GO WITH SCOOBY AND SHAGGY, AFTER ALL.
FINE. IN THAT CASE--

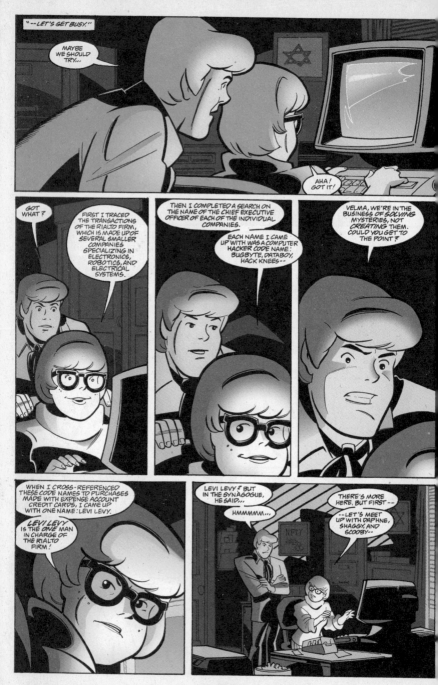

"--LET'S GET BUSY."

MAYBE WE SHOULD TRY...

AHA! GOT IT!

GOT WHAT?

FIRST I TRACED THE TRANSACTIONS OF THE RIALTO FIRM, WHICH IS MADE UP OF SEVERAL SMALLER COMPANIES SPECIALIZING IN ELECTRONICS, ROBOTICS, AND ELECTRICAL SYSTEMS.

THEN I COMPLETED A SEARCH ON THE NAME OF THE CHIEF EXECUTIVE OFFICER OF EACH OF THE INDIVIDUAL COMPANIES.

EACH NAME I CAME UP WITH WAS A COMPUTER HACKER CODE NAME: BUGBYTE, DATABOY, HACK KNEES--

VELMA, WE'RE IN THE BUSINESS OF SOLVING MYSTERIES, NOT CREATING THEM. COULD YOU GET TO THE POINT?

WHEN I CROSS-REFERENCED THESE CODE NAMES TO PURCHASES MADE WITH EXPENSE ACCOUNT CREDIT CARDS, I CAME UP WITH ONE NAME: LEVI LEVY.

LEVI LEVY IS THE ONE MAN IN CHARGE OF THE RIALTO FIRM!

LEVI LEVY? BUT IN THE SYNAGOGUE, HE SAID...

HMMMMM...

THERE'S MORE HERE, BUT FIRST--

--LET'S MEET UP WITH DAPHNE, SHAGGY, AND SCOOBY--

54

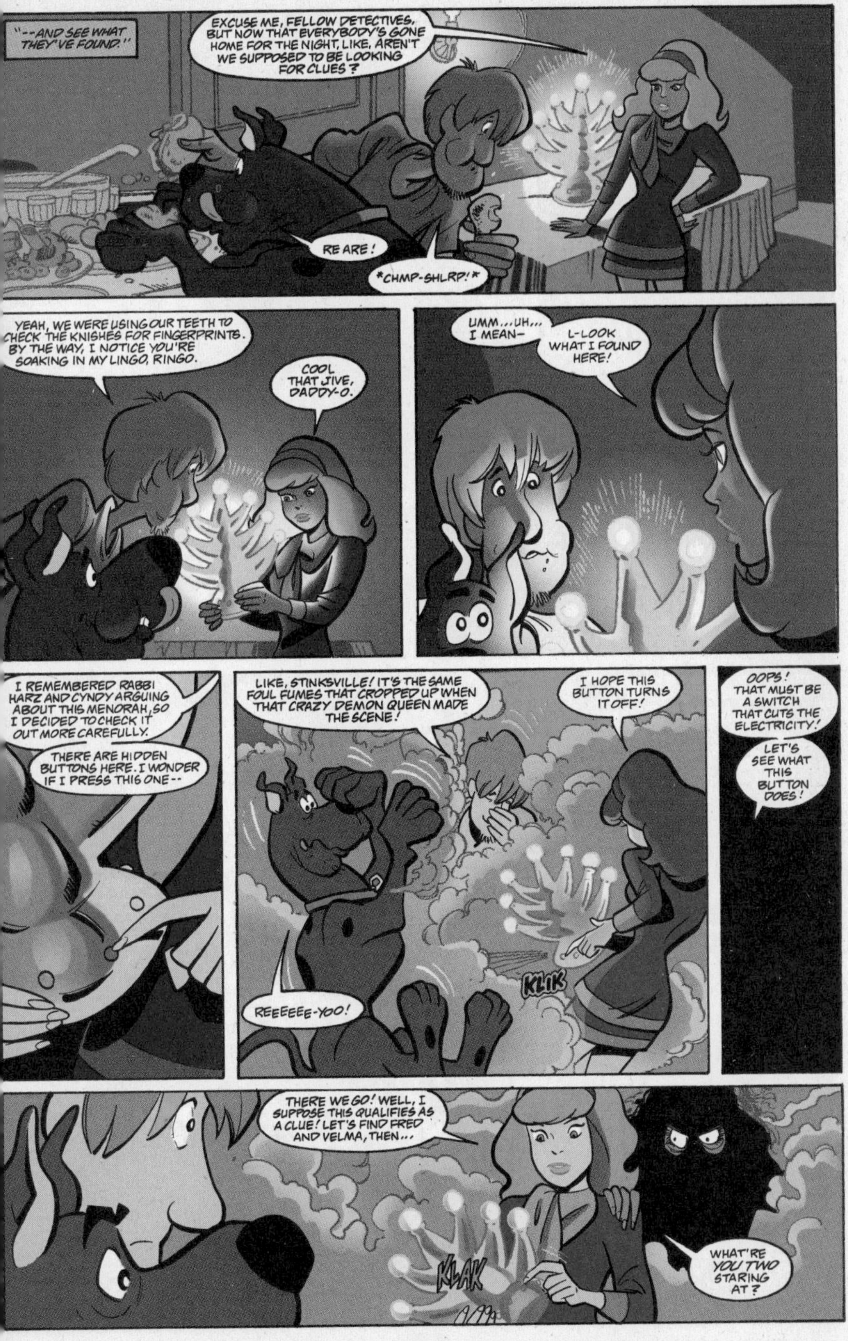
"--AND SEE WHAT THEY'VE FOUND."
EXCUSE ME, FELLOW DETECTIVES, BUT NOW THAT EVERYBODY'S GONE HOME FOR THE NIGHT, LIKE, AREN'T WE SUPPOSED TO BE LOOKING FOR CLUES?
RE ARE!
CHMP-SHLRP!
YEAH, WE WERE USING OUR TEETH TO CHECK THE KNISHES FOR FINGERPRINTS. BY THE WAY, I NOTICE YOU'RE SOAKING IN MY LINGO, RINGO.
COOL THAT JIVE, DADDY-O.
UMM...UH... I MEAN--
L-LOOK WHAT I FOUND HERE!
I REMEMBERED RABBI HARZ AND CYNDY ARGUING ABOUT THIS MENORAH, SO I DECIDED TO CHECK IT OUT MORE CAREFULLY.
THERE ARE HIDDEN BUTTONS HERE. I WONDER IF I PRESS THIS ONE--
LIKE, STINKSVILLE! IT'S THE SAME FOUL FUMES THAT CROPPED UP WHEN THAT CRAZY DEMON QUEEN MADE THE SCENE!
I HOPE THIS BUTTON TURNS IT OFF!
KLIK
REEEEEE-YOO!
OOPS! THAT MUST BE A SWITCH THAT CUTS THE ELECTRICITY!
LET'S SEE WHAT THIS BUTTON DOES!
THERE WE GO! WELL, I SUPPOSE THIS QUALIFIES AS A CLUE! LET'S FIND FRED AND VELMA, THEN...
KLAK
WHAT'RE YOU TWO STARING AT?

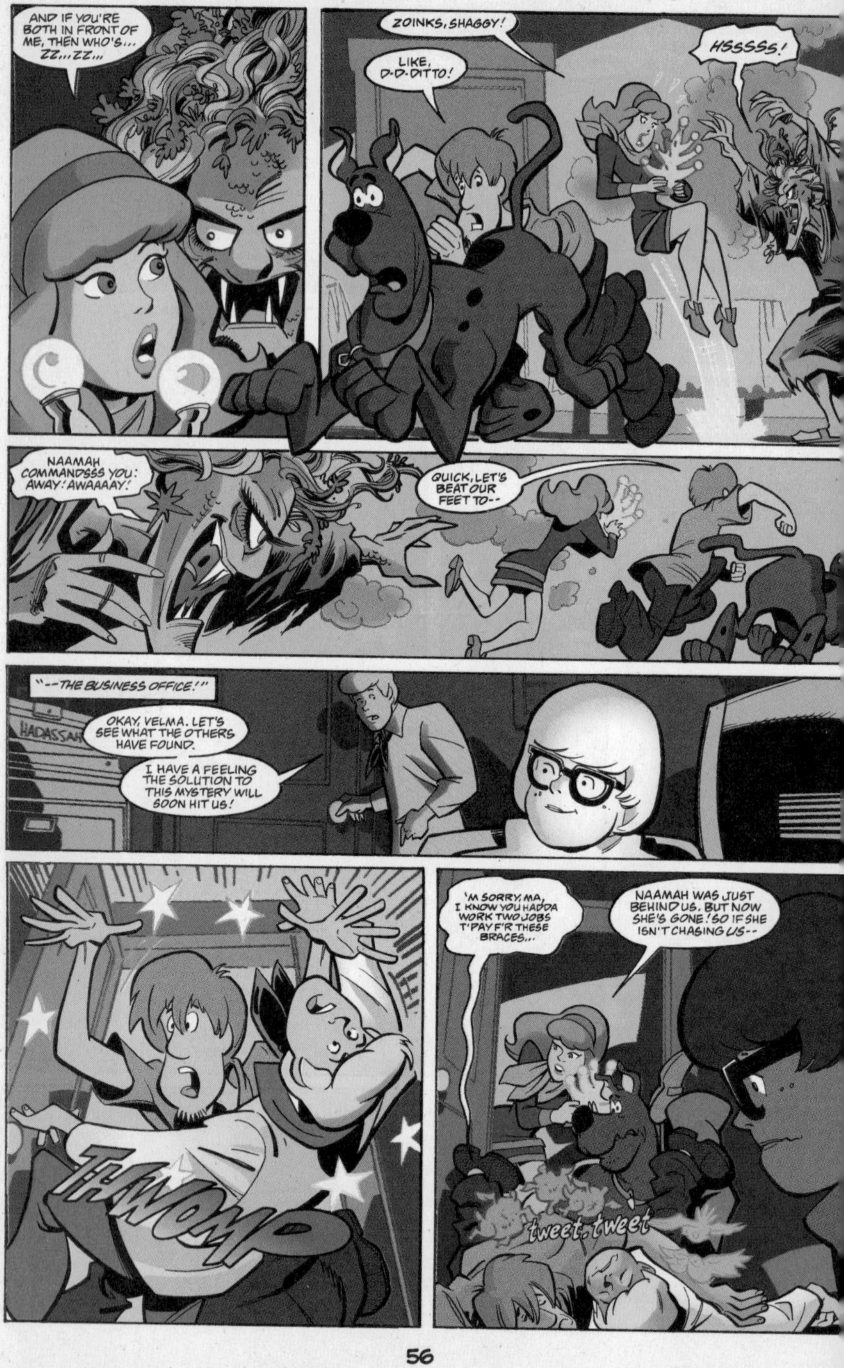

AND IF YOU'RE BOTH IN FRONT OF ME, THEN WHO'S... ZZ...ZZ...
ZOINKS, SHAGGY!
LIKE, D-D-DITTO!
HSSSSS!
NAAMAH COMMANDSSS YOU: AWAY! AWAAAAY!
QUICK, LET'S BEAT OUR FEET TO--
"--THE BUSINESS OFFICE!"
HADASSAH
OKAY, VELMA. LET'S SEE WHAT THE OTHERS HAVE FOUND.
I HAVE A FEELING THE SOLUTION TO THIS MYSTERY WILL SOON HIT US!
THWOMP
'M SORRY, MA, I KNOW YOU HADDA WORK TWO JOBS T'PAY F'R THESE BRACES...
NAAMAH WAS JUST BEHIND US. BUT NOW SHE'S GONE! SO IF SHE ISN'T CHASING US--
tweet. tweet

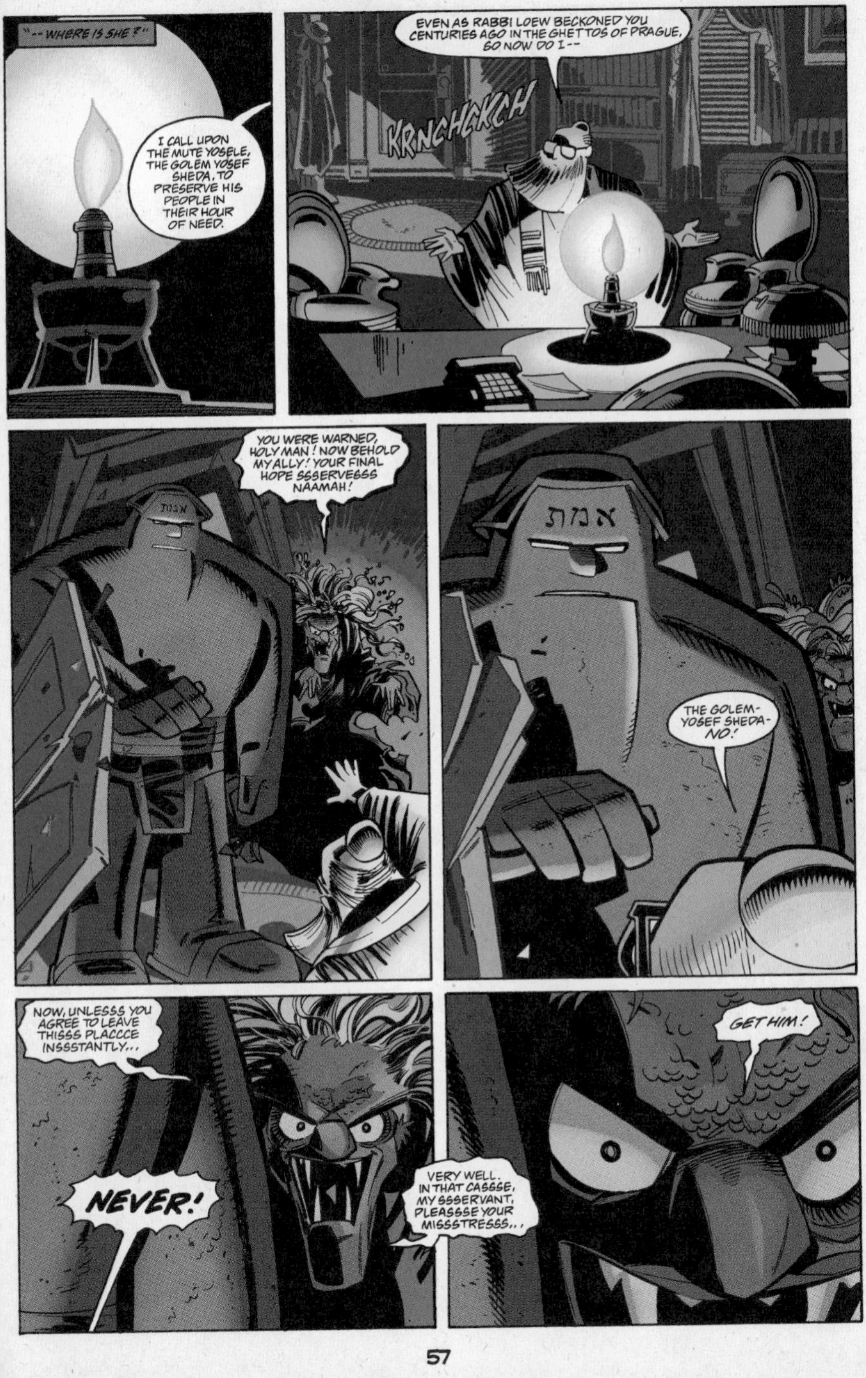
"--WHERE IS SHE?"
I CALL UPON THE MUTE YOSELE, THE GOLEM YOSEF SHEDA, TO PRESERVE HIS PEOPLE IN THEIR HOUR OF NEED.
EVEN AS RABBI LOEW BECKONED YOU CENTURIES AGO IN THE GHETTOS OF PRAGUE, SO NOW DO I--
KRNCHCKCH
YOU WERE WARNED, HOLY MAN! NOW BEHOLD MY ALLY! YOUR FINAL HOPE SSSERVESSS NAAMAH!
אמת
אמת
THE GOLEM-YOSEF SHEDA-NO!
NOW, UNLESSS YOU AGREE TO LEAVE THISSS PLACCCE INSSSTANTLY...
NEVER!
VERY WELL. IN THAT CASSSE, MY SSSERVANT, PLEASSSE YOUR MISSSTRESSS...
GET HIM!

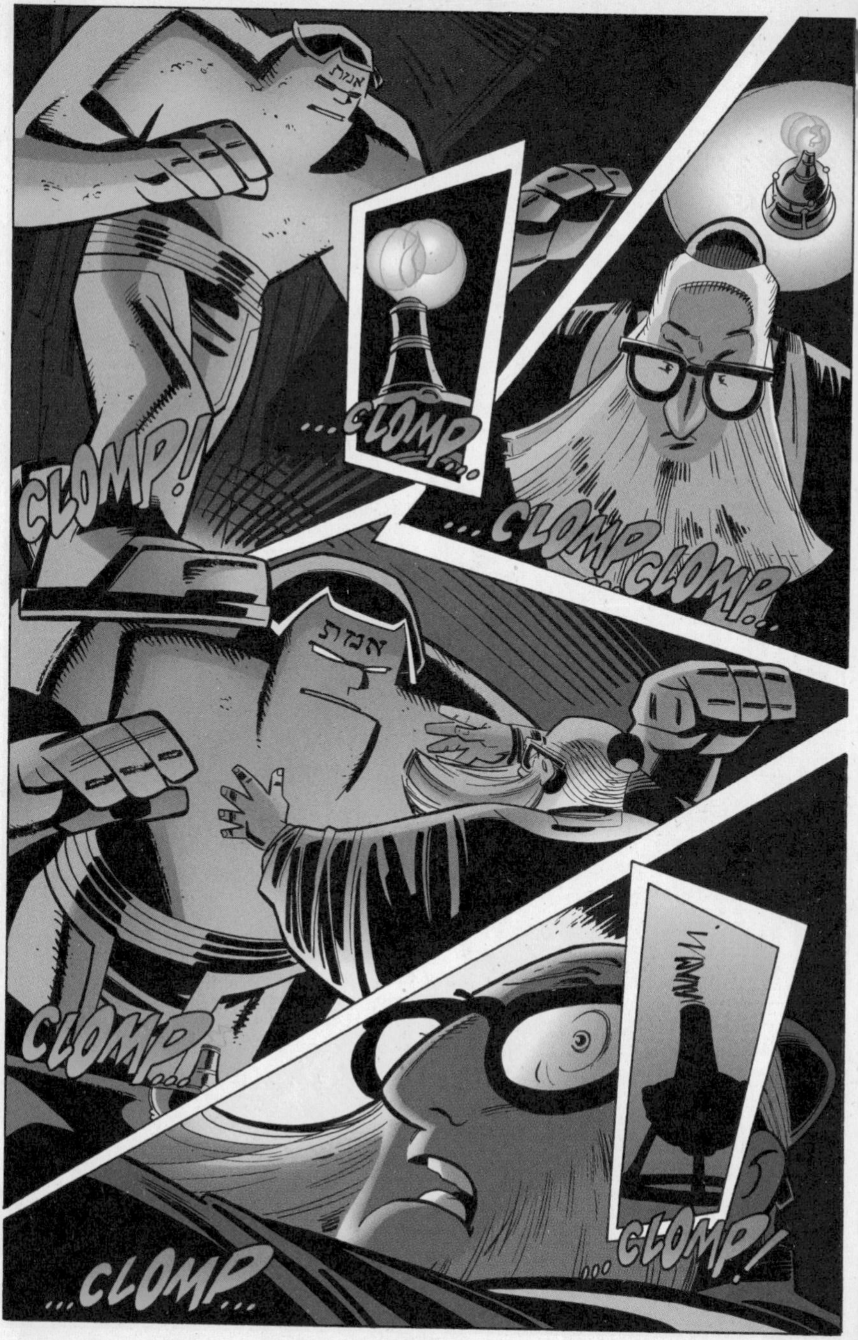
אמת
CLOMP!
...CLOMP...
...CLOMP
...CLOMP...
אמת
CLOMP...
...CLOMP...
...CLOMP!

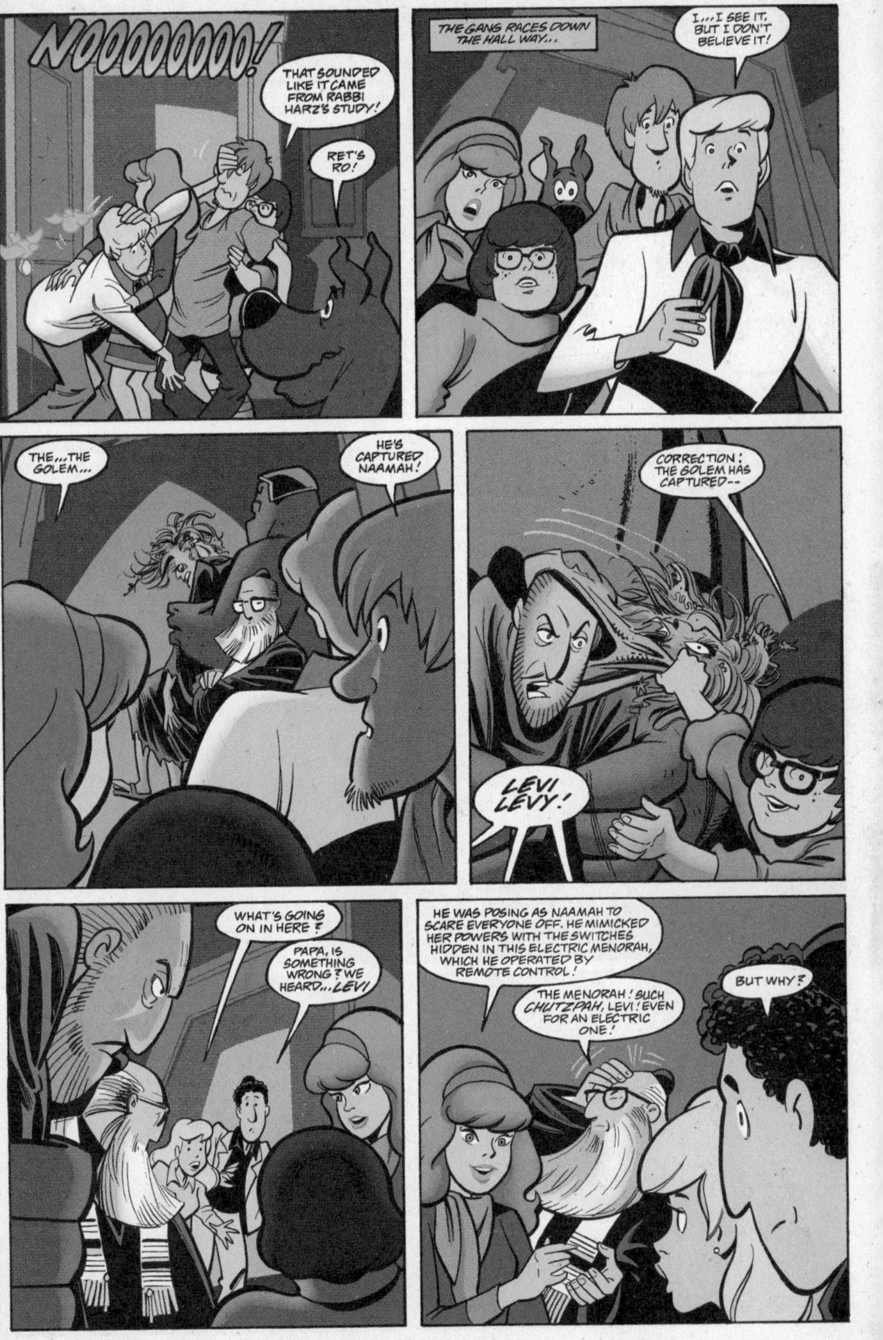
NOOOOOOOO!
THAT SOUNDED LIKE IT CAME FROM RABBI HARZ'S STUDY!
RET'S RO!
THE GANG RACES DOWN THE HALL WAY...
I... I SEE IT, BUT I DON'T BELIEVE IT!
THE... THE GOLEM...
HE'S CAPTURED NAAMAH!
CORRECTION: THE GOLEM HAS CAPTURED--
LEVI LEVY!
WHAT'S GOING ON IN HERE?
PAPA, IS SOMETHING WRONG? WE HEARD... LEVI
HE WAS POSING AS NAAMAH TO SCARE EVERYONE OFF. HE MIMICKED HER POWERS WITH THE SWITCHES HIDDEN IN THIS ELECTRIC MENORAH, WHICH HE OPERATED BY REMOTE CONTROL!
THE MENORAH! SUCH CHUTZPAH, LEVI! EVEN FOR AN ELECTRIC ONE!
BUT WHY?

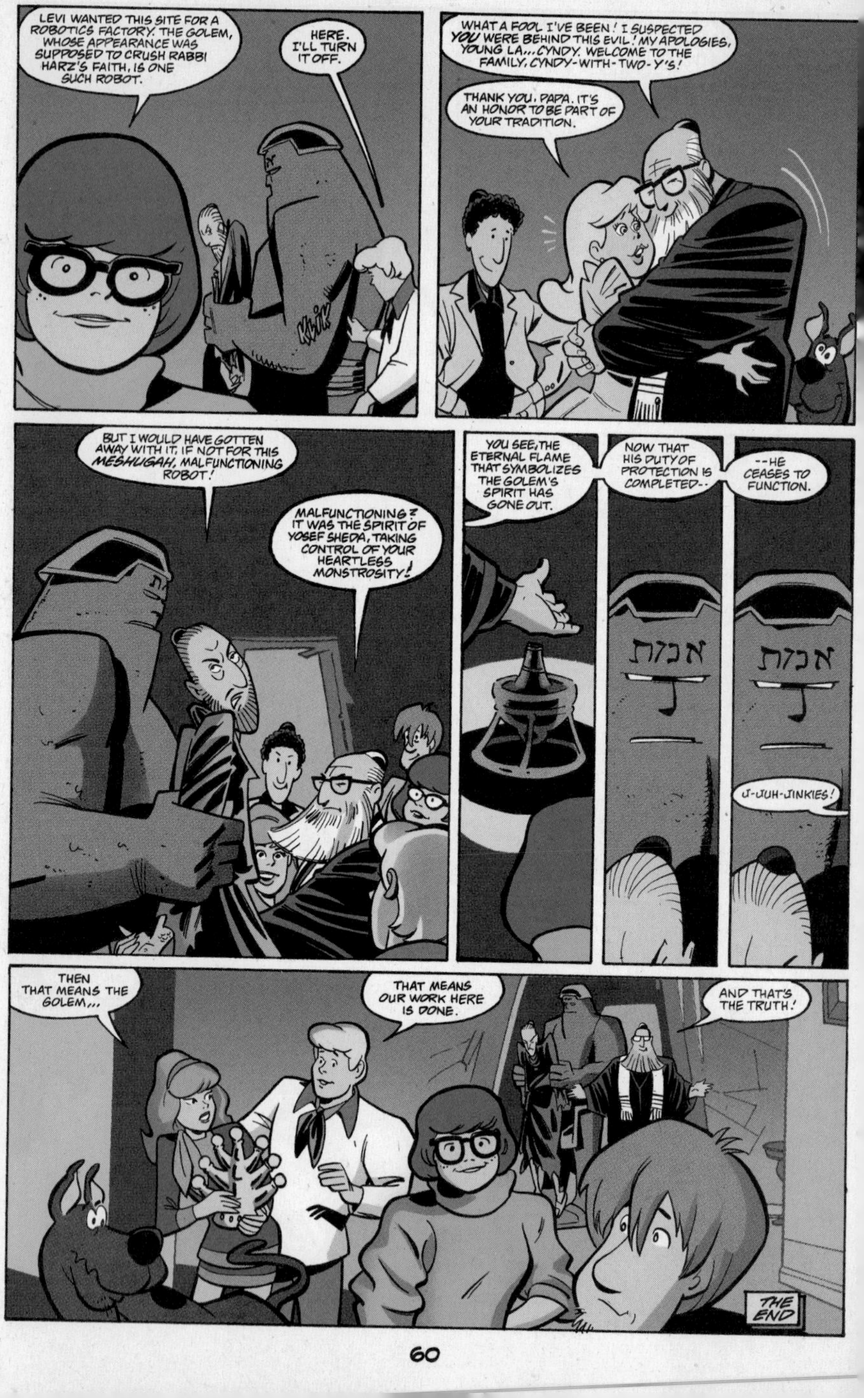
LEVI WANTED THIS SITE FOR A ROBOTICS FACTORY. THE GOLEM, WHOSE APPEARANCE WAS SUPPOSED TO CRUSH RABBI HARZ'S FAITH, IS ONE SUCH ROBOT.
HERE. I'LL TURN IT OFF.
KWIK
WHAT A FOOL I'VE BEEN! I SUSPECTED YOU WERE BEHIND THIS EVIL! MY APOLOGIES, YOUNG LA... CYNDY. WELCOME TO THE FAMILY, CYNDY-WITH-TWO-Y'S!
THANK YOU, PAPA. IT'S AN HONOR TO BE PART OF YOUR TRADITION.
BUT I WOULD HAVE GOTTEN AWAY WITH IT, IF NOT FOR THIS MESHUGAH, MALFUNCTIONING ROBOT!
MALFUNCTIONING? IT WAS THE SPIRIT OF YOSEF SHEDA, TAKING CONTROL OF YOUR HEARTLESS MONSTROSITY!
YOU SEE, THE ETERNAL FLAME THAT SYMBOLIZES THE GOLEM'S SPIRIT HAS GONE OUT.
NOW THAT HIS DUTY OF PROTECTION IS COMPLETED--
--HE CEASES TO FUNCTION.
J-JUH-JINKIES!
THEN THAT MEANS THE GOLEM...
THAT MEANS OUR WORK HERE IS DONE.
AND THAT'S THE TRUTH!
THE END

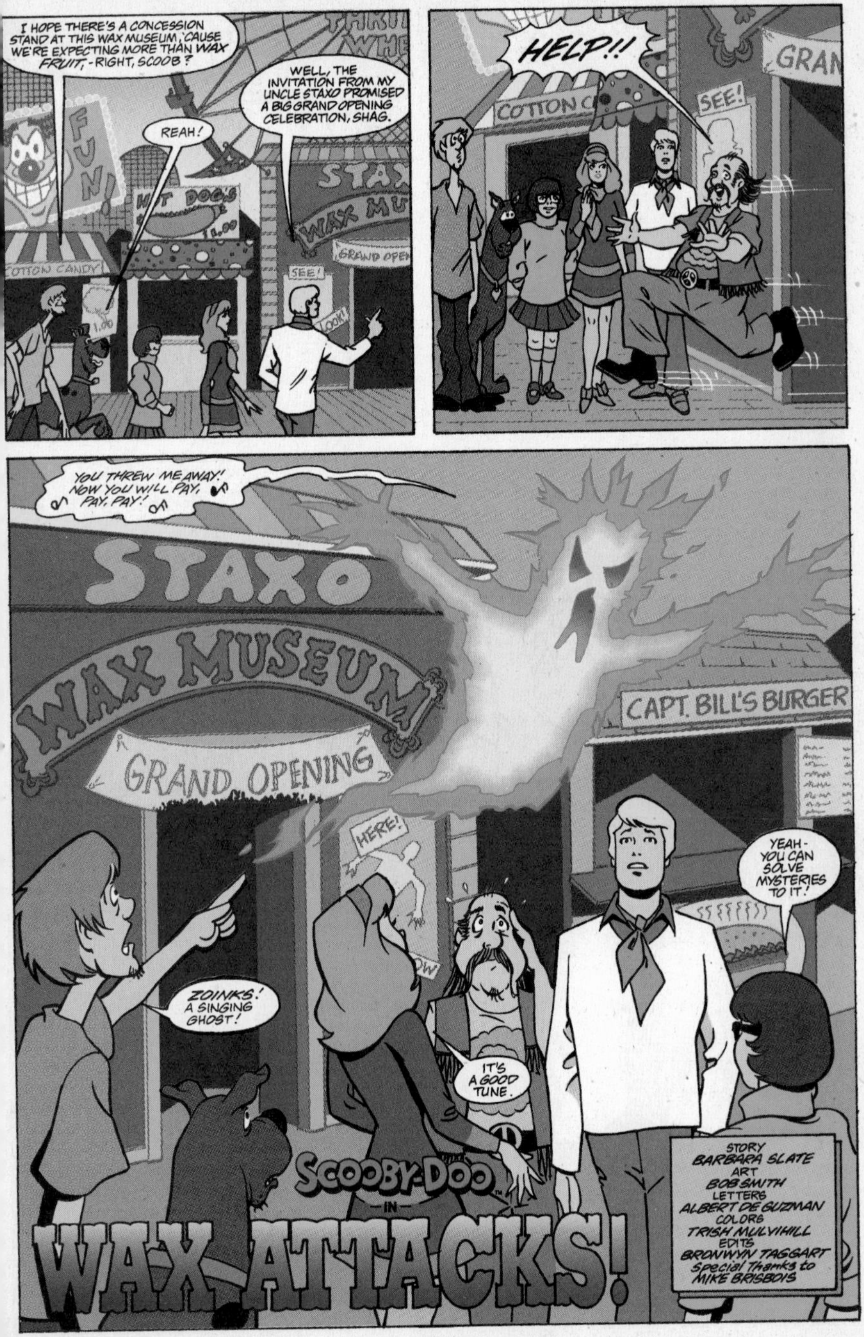
I HOPE THERE'S A CONCESSION STAND AT THIS WAX MUSEUM, 'CAUSE WE'RE EXPECTING MORE THAN WAX FRUIT, - RIGHT, SCOOB?
REAH!
WELL, THE INVITATION FROM MY UNCLE STAXO PROMISED A BIG GRAND OPENING CELEBRATION, SHAG.
FUN!
HOT DOGS
COTTON CANDY
STAXO WAX MU
GRAND OPEN
SEE!
LOOK!
HELP!!
COTTON C
SEE!
GRAN
YOU THREW ME AWAY! NOW YOU WILL PAY, PAY, PAY!
STAXO
WAX MUSEUM
GRAND OPENING
CAPT. BILL'S BURGER
HERE!
YEAH - YOU CAN SOLVE MYSTERIES TO IT!
ZOINKS! A SINGING GHOST!
IT'S A GOOD TUNE.
SCOOBY-DOO IN
WAX ATTACKS!
STORY BARBARA SLATE
ART BOB SMITH
LETTERS ALBERT DE GUZMAN
COLORS TRISH MULVIHILL
EDITS BRONWYN TAGGART
Special Thanks to MIKE BRISBOIS

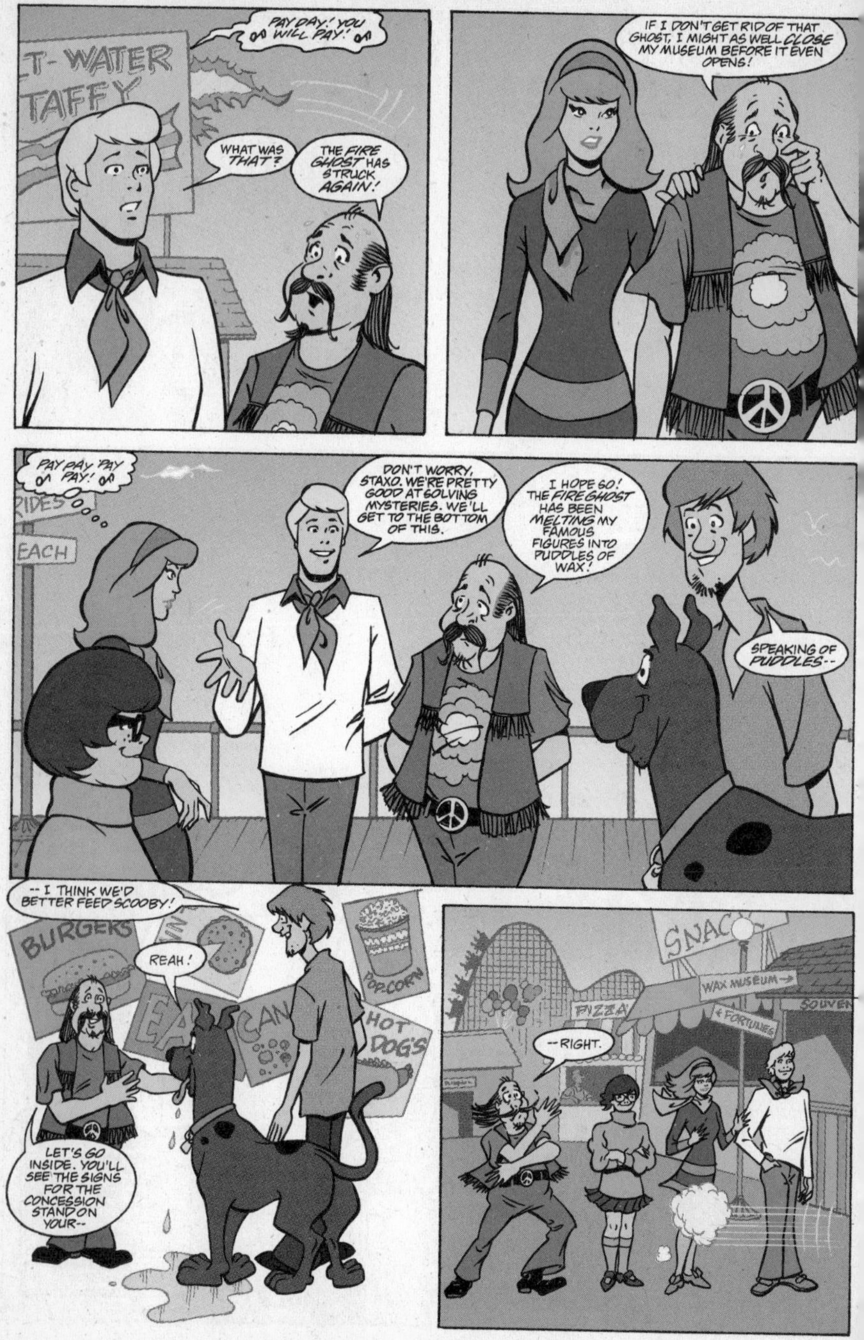
PAY DAY! YOU WILL PAY!
LT-WATER TAFFY
WHAT WAS THAT?
THE FIRE GHOST HAS STRUCK AGAIN!
IF I DON'T GET RID OF THAT GHOST, I MIGHT AS WELL CLOSE MY MUSEUM BEFORE IT EVEN OPENS!
PAY PAY PAY PAY!
RIDES
EACH
DON'T WORRY, STAXO. WE'RE PRETTY GOOD AT SOLVING MYSTERIES. WE'LL GET TO THE BOTTOM OF THIS.
I HOPE SO! THE FIRE GHOST HAS BEEN MELTING MY FAMOUS FIGURES INTO PUDDLES OF WAX!
SPEAKING OF PUDDLES--
--I THINK WE'D BETTER FEED SCOOBY!
BURGERS
REAH!
POP-CORN
HOT DOG'S
LET'S GO INSIDE. YOU'LL SEE THE SIGNS FOR THE CONCESSION STAND ON YOUR--
SNAC
WAX MUSEUM
PIZZA
FORTUNES
SOUVEN
--RIGHT.

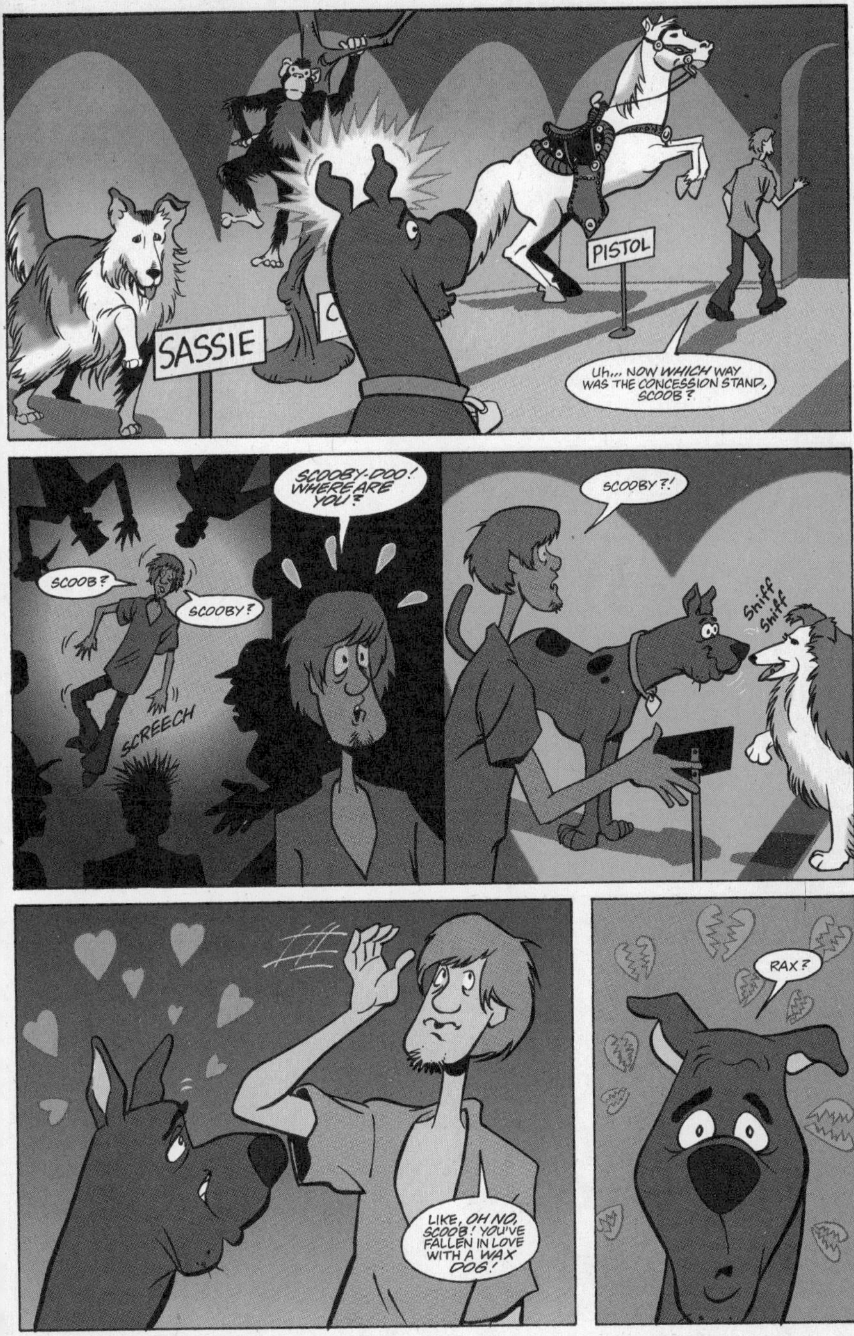
SASSIE
PISTOL
Uh... NOW WHICH WAY WAS THE CONCESSION STAND, SCOOB?
SCOOB?
SCOOBY?
SCREECH
SCOOBY-DOO! WHERE ARE YOU?
SCOOBY?!
Sniff Sniff
LIKE, OH NO, SCOOB! YOU'VE FALLEN IN LOVE WITH A WAX DOG!
RAX?

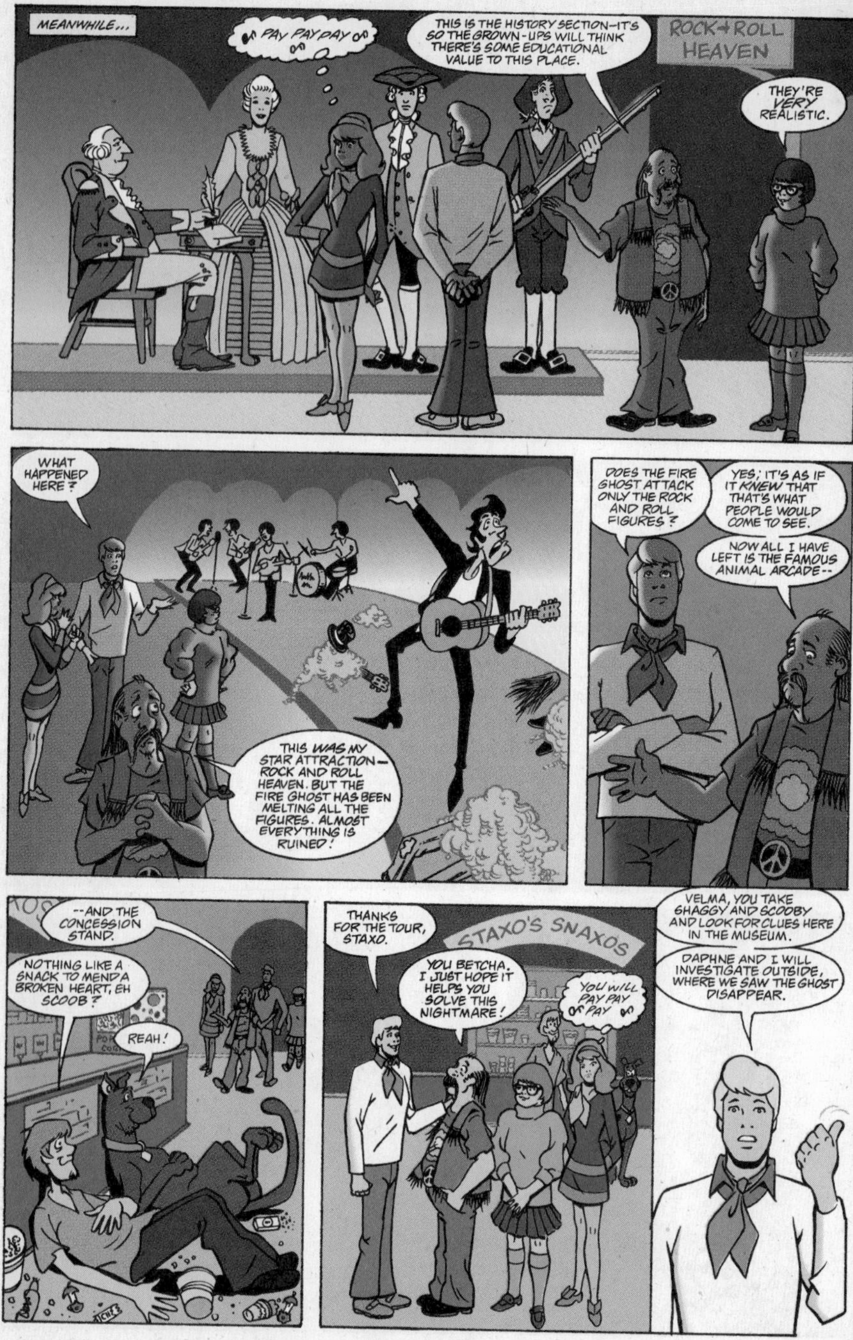
MEANWHILE...
PAY PAY PAY
THIS IS THE HISTORY SECTION—IT'S SO THE GROWN-UPS WILL THINK THERE'S SOME EDUCATIONAL VALUE TO THIS PLACE.
ROCK + ROLL HEAVEN
THEY'RE VERY REALISTIC.
WHAT HAPPENED HERE?
THIS WAS MY STAR ATTRACTION—ROCK AND ROLL HEAVEN. BUT THE FIRE GHOST HAS BEEN MELTING ALL THE FIGURES. ALMOST EVERYTHING IS RUINED!
DOES THE FIRE GHOST ATTACK ONLY THE ROCK AND ROLL FIGURES?
YES; IT'S AS IF IT KNEW THAT THAT'S WHAT PEOPLE WOULD COME TO SEE.
NOW ALL I HAVE LEFT IS THE FAMOUS ANIMAL ARCADE--
--AND THE CONCESSION STAND.
NOTHING LIKE A SNACK TO MEND A BROKEN HEART, EH SCOOB?
REAH!
THANKS FOR THE TOUR, STAXO.
STAXO'S SNAXOS
YOU BETCHA. I JUST HOPE IT HELPS YOU SOLVE THIS NIGHTMARE!
YOU WILL PAY PAY PAY
VELMA, YOU TAKE SHAGGY AND SCOOBY AND LOOK FOR CLUES HERE IN THE MUSEUM.
DAPHNE AND I WILL INVESTIGATE OUTSIDE, WHERE WE SAW THE GHOST DISAPPEAR.

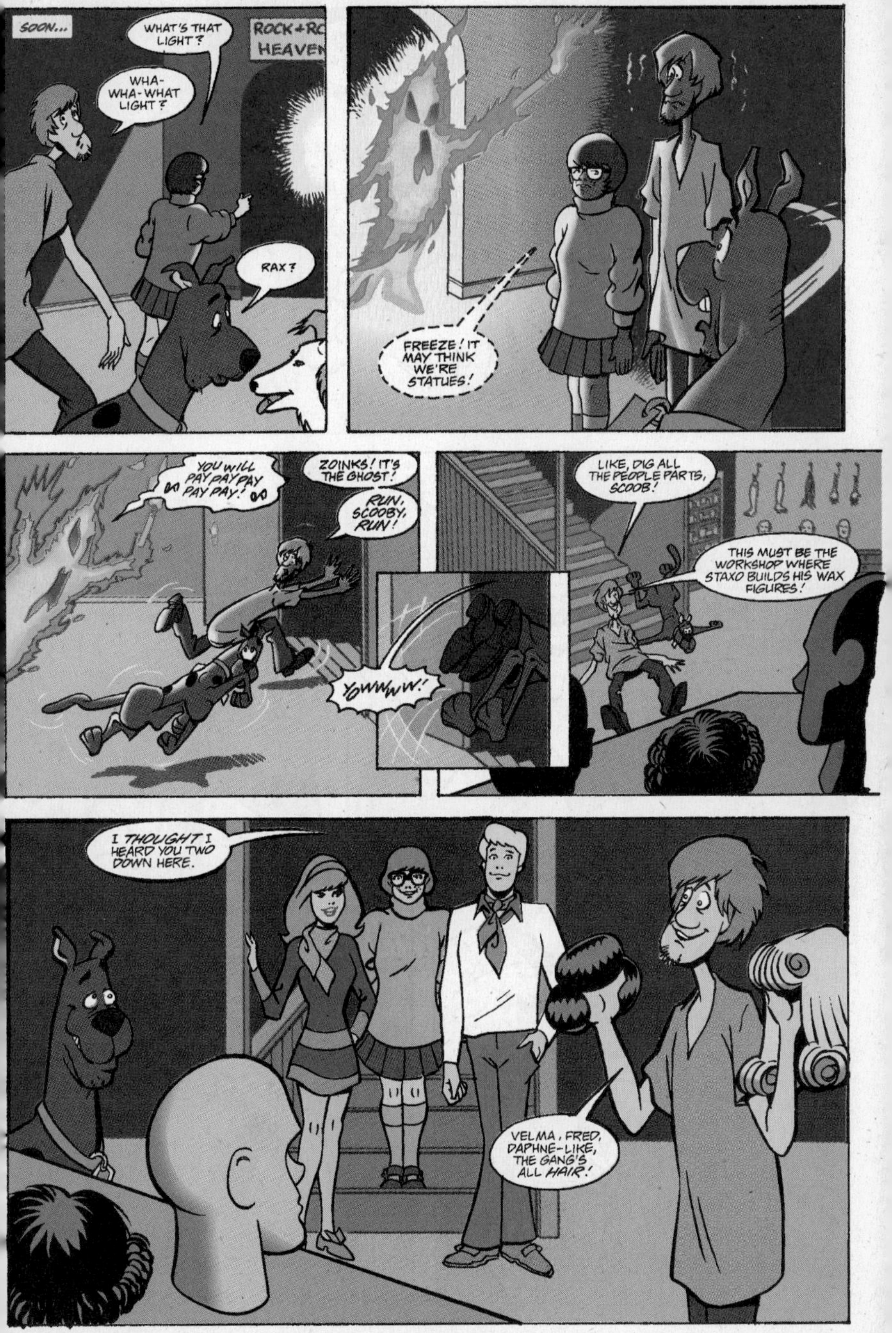
SOON...
WHAT'S THAT LIGHT?
WHA-WHA-WHAT LIGHT?
ROCK+RO HEAVEN
RAX?
FREEZE! IT MAY THINK WE'RE STATUES!
YOU WILL PAY PAY PAY PAY PAY!
ZOINKS! IT'S THE GHOST!
RUN, SCOOBY, RUN!
YOWWWW!
LIKE, DIG ALL THE PEOPLE PARTS, SCOOB!
THIS MUST BE THE WORKSHOP WHERE STAXO BUILDS HIS WAX FIGURES!
I THOUGHT I HEARD YOU TWO DOWN HERE.
VELMA, FRED, DAPHNE-LIKE, THE GANG'S ALL HAIR!

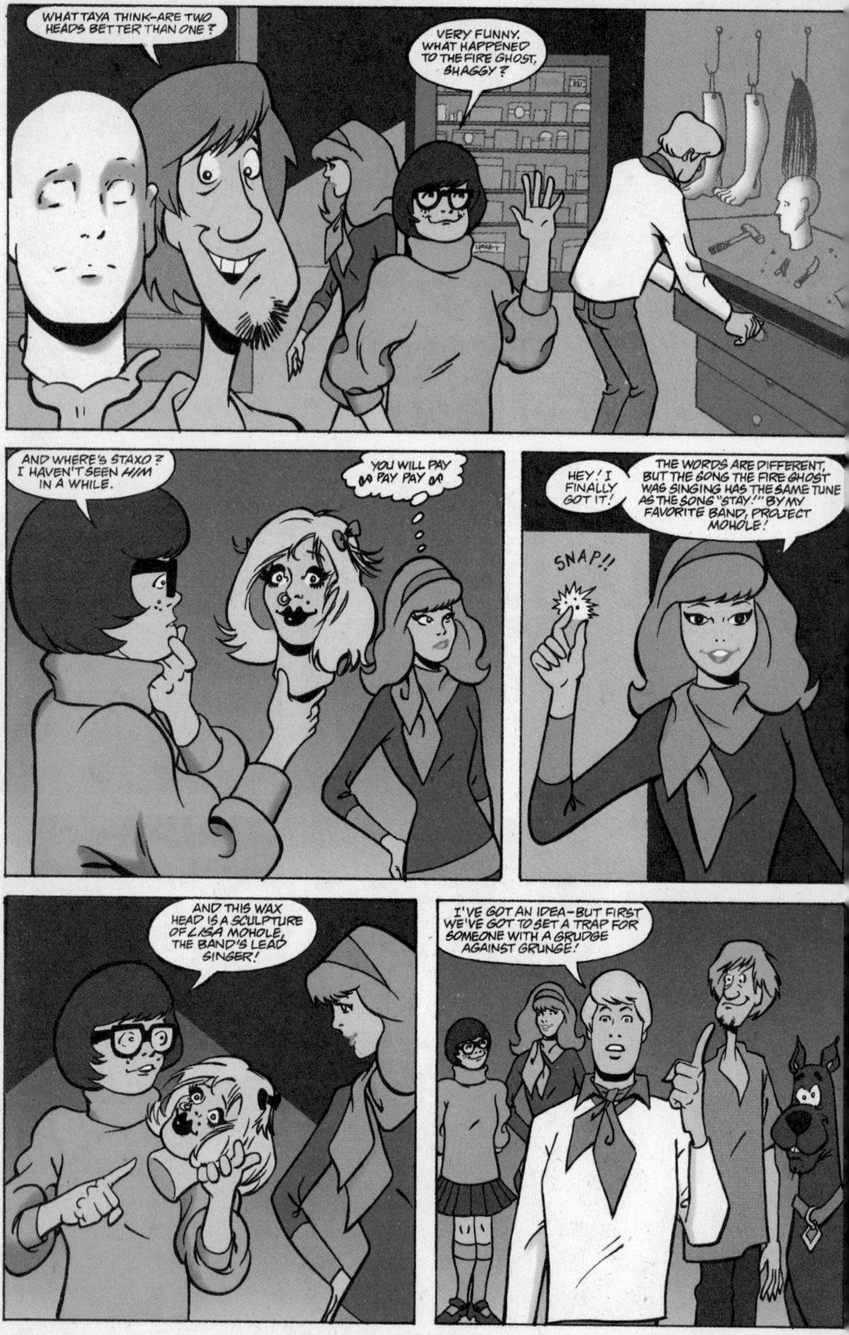
WHATTAYA THINK–ARE TWO HEADS BETTER THAN ONE?
VERY FUNNY. WHAT HAPPENED TO THE FIRE GHOST, SHAGGY?
AND WHERE'S STAXO? I HAVEN'T SEEN HIM IN A WHILE.
YOU WILL PAY PAY PAY
HEY! I FINALLY GOT IT!
SNAP!!
THE WORDS ARE DIFFERENT, BUT THE SONG THE FIRE GHOST WAS SINGING HAS THE SAME TUNE AS THE SONG "STAY!" BY MY FAVORITE BAND, PROJECT MOHOLE!
AND THIS WAX HEAD IS A SCULPTURE OF LISA MOHOLE, THE BAND'S LEAD SINGER!
I'VE GOT AN IDEA–BUT FIRST WE'VE GOT TO SET A TRAP FOR SOMEONE WITH A GRUDGE AGAINST GRUNGE!

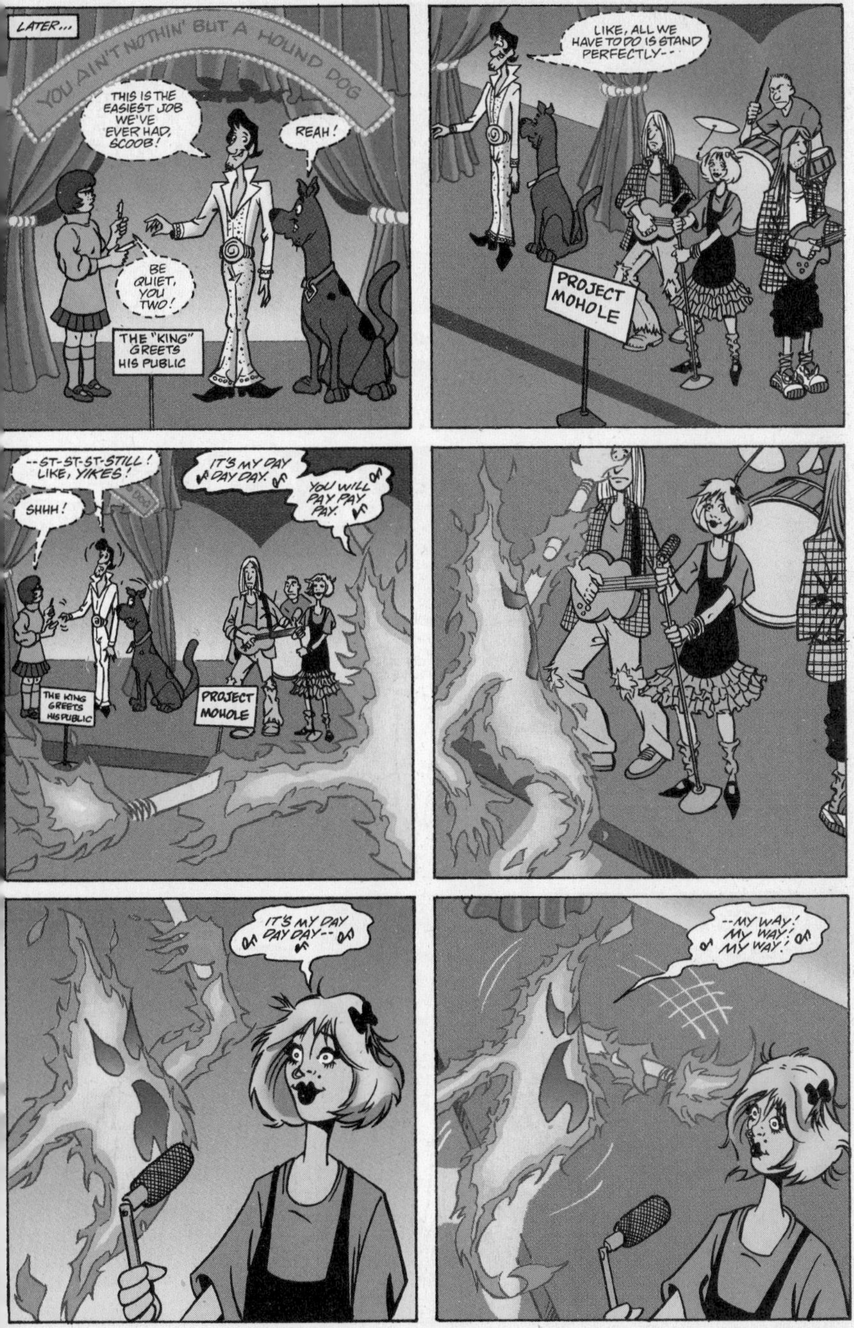

LATER...
YOU AIN'T NOTHIN' BUT A HOUND DOG
THIS IS THE EASIEST JOB WE'VE EVER HAD, SCOOB!
REAH!
BE QUIET, YOU TWO!
THE "KING" GREETS HIS PUBLIC
LIKE, ALL WE HAVE TO DO IS STAND PERFECTLY--
PROJECT MOHOLE
--ST-ST-ST-STILL! LIKE, YIKES!
SHHH!
IT'S MY DAY DAY DAY.
YOU WILL PAY PAY PAY.
THE KING GREETS HIS PUBLIC
PROJECT MOHOLE
IT'S MY DAY DAY DAY--
--MY WAY! MY WAY! MY WAY!

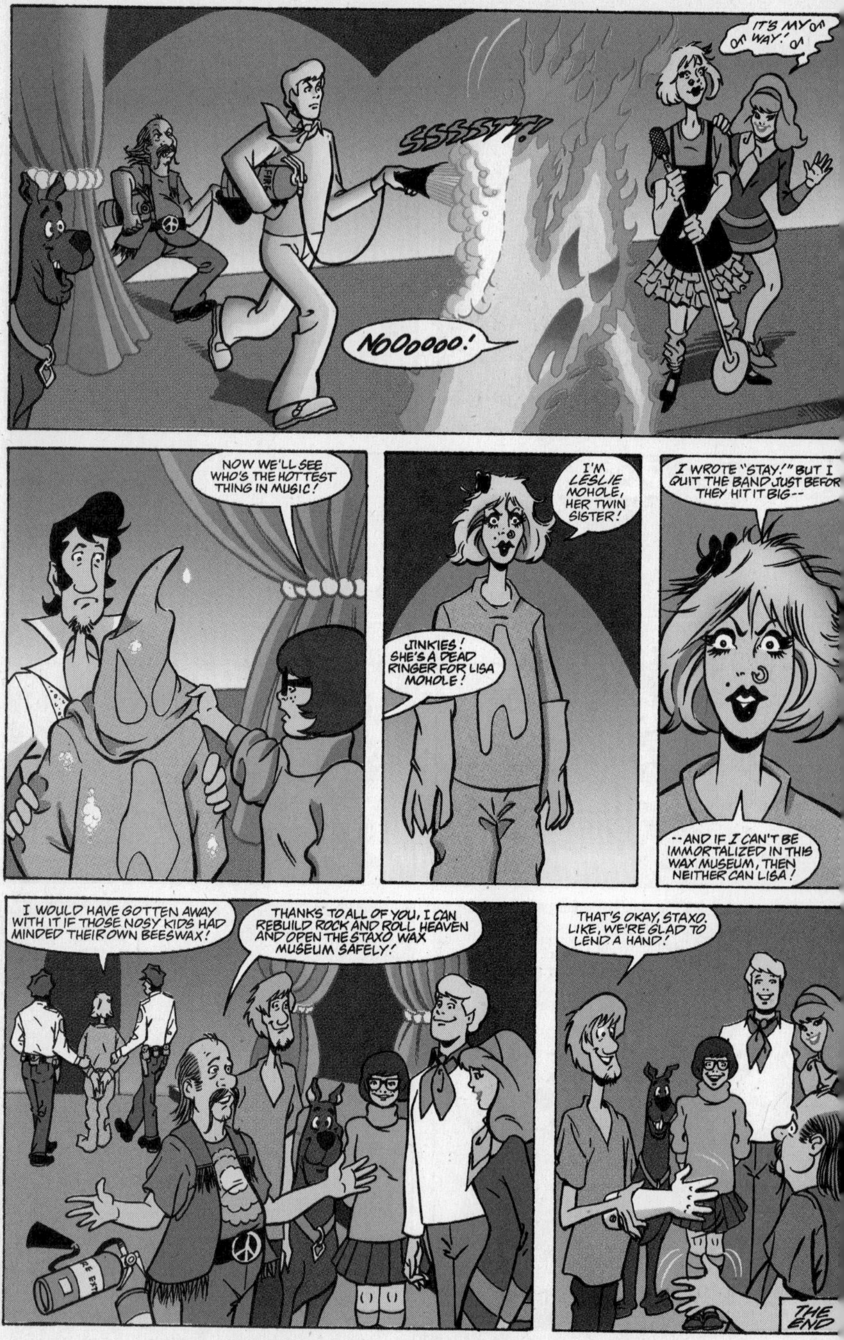
IT'S MY WAY!
SSSSSTT!
NOOoooo!
NOW WE'LL SEE WHO'S THE HOTTEST THING IN MUSIC!
JINKIES! SHE'S A DEAD RINGER FOR LISA MOHOLE!
I'M LESLIE MOHOLE, HER TWIN SISTER!
I WROTE "STAY!" BUT I QUIT THE BAND JUST BEFOR THEY HIT IT BIG--
--AND IF I CAN'T BE IMMORTALIZED IN THIS WAX MUSEUM, THEN NEITHER CAN LISA!
I WOULD HAVE GOTTEN AWAY WITH IT IF THOSE NOSY KIDS HAD MINDED THEIR OWN BEESWAX!
THANKS TO ALL OF YOU, I CAN REBUILD ROCK AND ROLL HEAVEN AND OPEN THE STAXO WAX MUSEUM SAFELY!
THAT'S OKAY, STAXO. LIKE, WE'RE GLAD TO LEND A HAND!
THE END

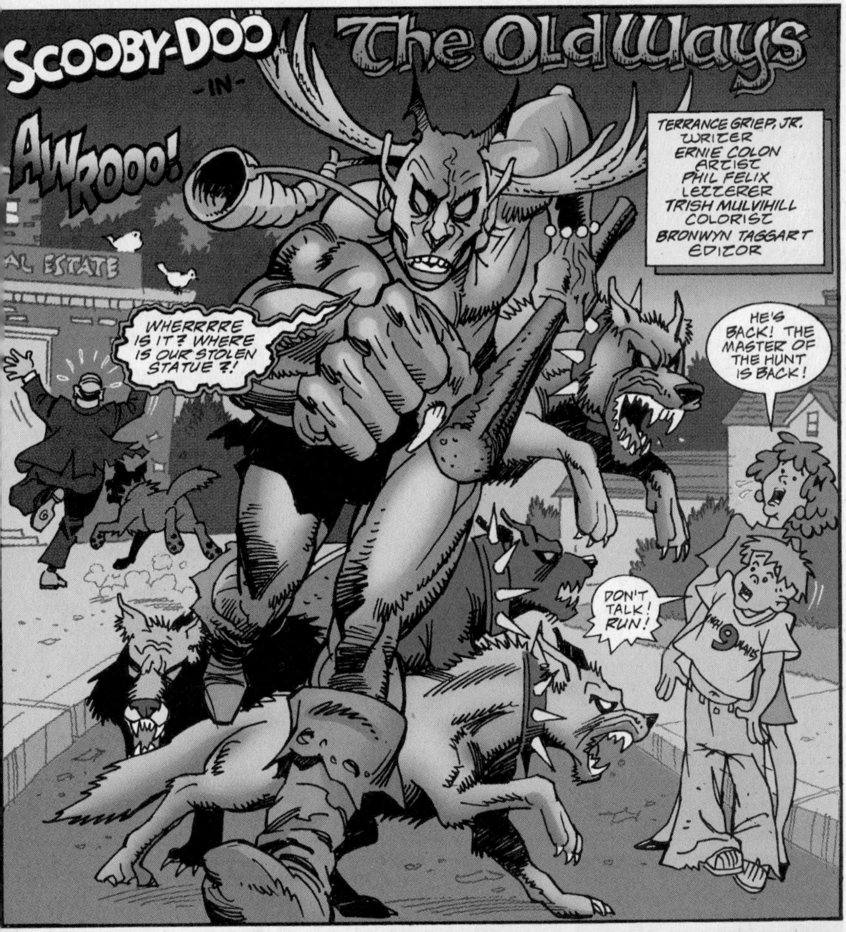
SCOOBY-DOO
-IN-
The Old Ways
AWROOO!
TERRANCE GRIEP, JR. WRITER
ERNIE COLON ARTIST
PHIL FELIX LETTERER
TRISH MULVIHILL COLORIST
BRONWYN TAGGART EDITOR
AL ESTATE
WHERRRRE IS IT? WHERE IS OUR STOLEN STATUE ?!
HE'S BACK! THE MASTER OF THE HUNT IS BACK!
DON'T TALK! RUN!

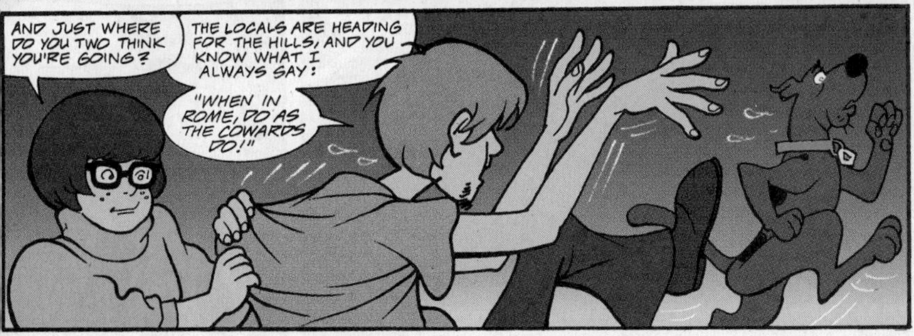
AND JUST WHERE DO YOU TWO THINK YOU'RE GOING?
THE LOCALS ARE HEADING FOR THE HILLS, AND YOU KNOW WHAT I ALWAYS SAY:
"WHEN IN ROME, DO AS THE COWARDS DO!"

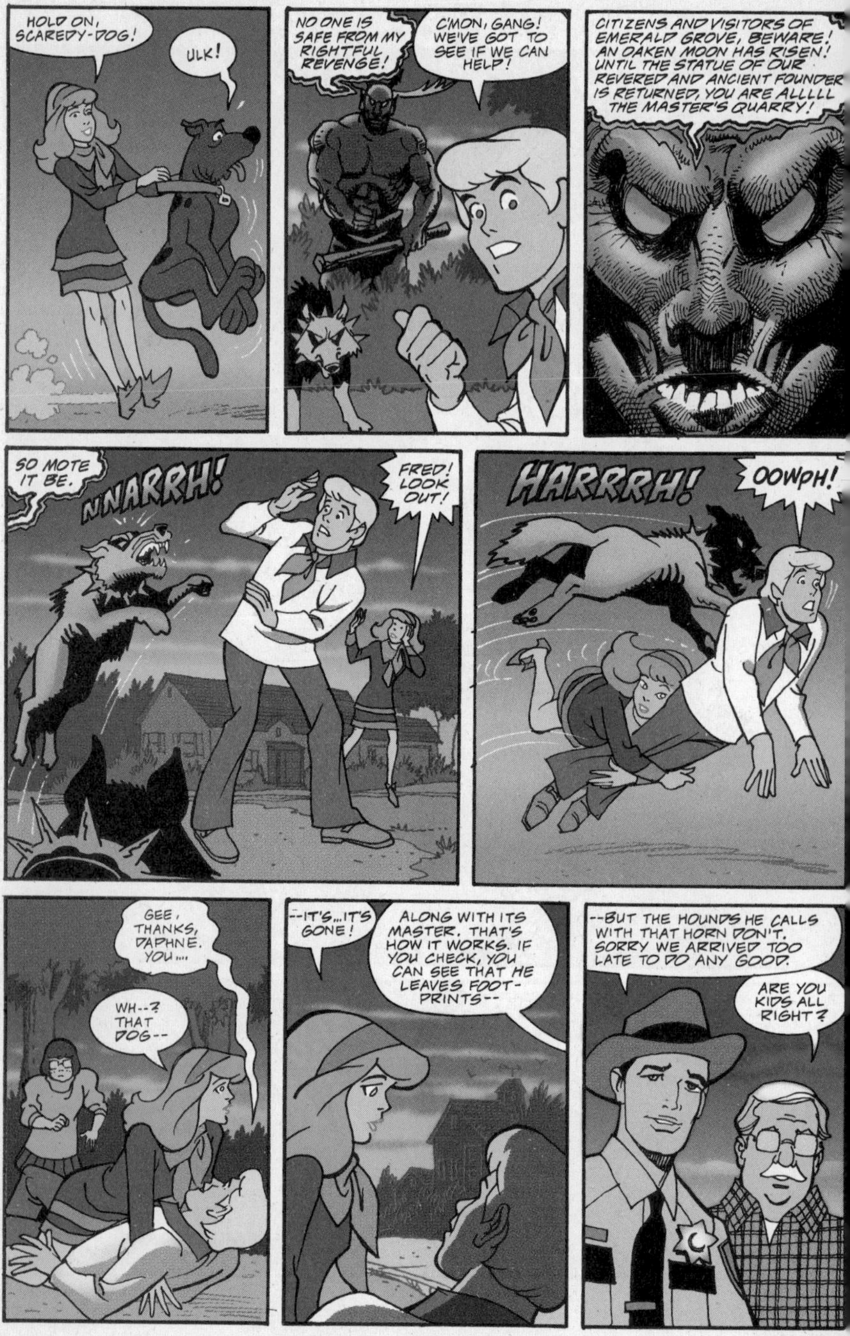
HOLD ON, SCAREDY-DOG!
ULK!
NO ONE IS SAFE FROM MY RIGHTFUL REVENGE!
C'MON, GANG! WE'VE GOT TO SEE IF WE CAN HELP!
CITIZENS AND VISITORS OF EMERALD GROVE, BEWARE! AN OAKEN MOON HAS RISEN! UNTIL THE STATUE OF OUR REVERED AND ANCIENT FOUNDER IS RETURNED, YOU ARE ALLLLL THE MASTER'S QUARRY!
SO MOTE IT BE.
NNARRH!
FRED! LOOK OUT!
HARRRH!
OOWPH!
GEE, THANKS, DAPHNE. YOU....
WH--? THAT DOG--
--IT'S...IT'S GONE!
ALONG WITH ITS MASTER. THAT'S HOW IT WORKS. IF YOU CHECK, YOU CAN SEE THAT HE LEAVES FOOT-PRINTS--
--BUT THE HOUNDS HE CALLS WITH THAT HORN DON'T. SORRY WE ARRIVED TOO LATE TO DO ANY GOOD.
ARE YOU KIDS ALL RIGHT?

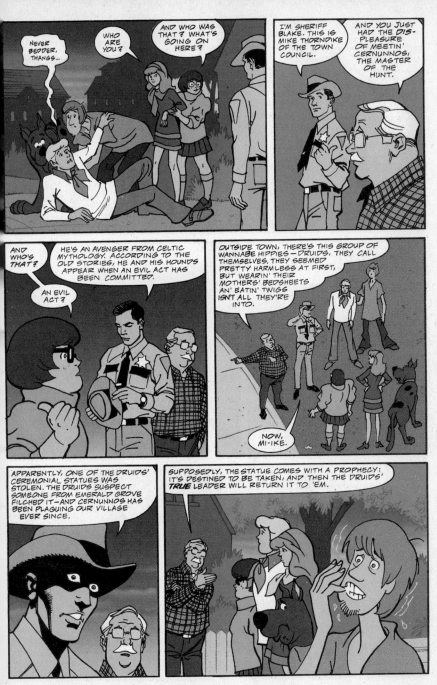

NEVER BEDDER, THANGS...

WHO ARE YOU?

AND WHO WAS THAT? WHAT'S GOING ON HERE?

I'M SHERIFF BLAKE. THIS IS MIKE THORNDIKE OF THE TOWN COUNCIL.

AND YOU JUST HAD THE *DIS-PLEASURE* OF MEETIN' CERNUNNOS, THE MASTER OF THE HUNT.

AND WHO'S *THAT?*

HE'S AN AVENGER FROM CELTIC MYTHOLOGY. ACCORDING TO THE OLD STORIES, HE AND HIS HOUNDS APPEAR WHEN AN EVIL ACT HAS BEEN COMMITTED.

AN EVIL ACT?

OUTSIDE TOWN, THERE'S THIS GROUP OF WANNABE HIPPIES—DRUIDS, THEY CALL THEMSELVES. THEY SEEMED PRETTY HARMLESS AT FIRST, BUT WEARIN' THEIR MOTHERS' BEDSHEETS AN' EATIN' TWIGS ISN'T ALL THEY'RE INTO.

NOW, MI-IKE.

APPARENTLY, ONE OF THE DRUIDS' CEREMONIAL STATUES WAS STOLEN. THE DRUIDS SUSPECT SOMEONE FROM EMERALD GROVE HAS FILCHED IT—AND CERNUNNOS HAS BEEN PLAGUING OUR VILLAGE EVER SINCE.

SUPPOSEDLY, THE STATUE COMES WITH A PROPHECY: IT'S DESTINED TO BE TAKEN, AND THEN THE DRUIDS' *TRUE* LEADER WILL RETURN IT TO 'EM.

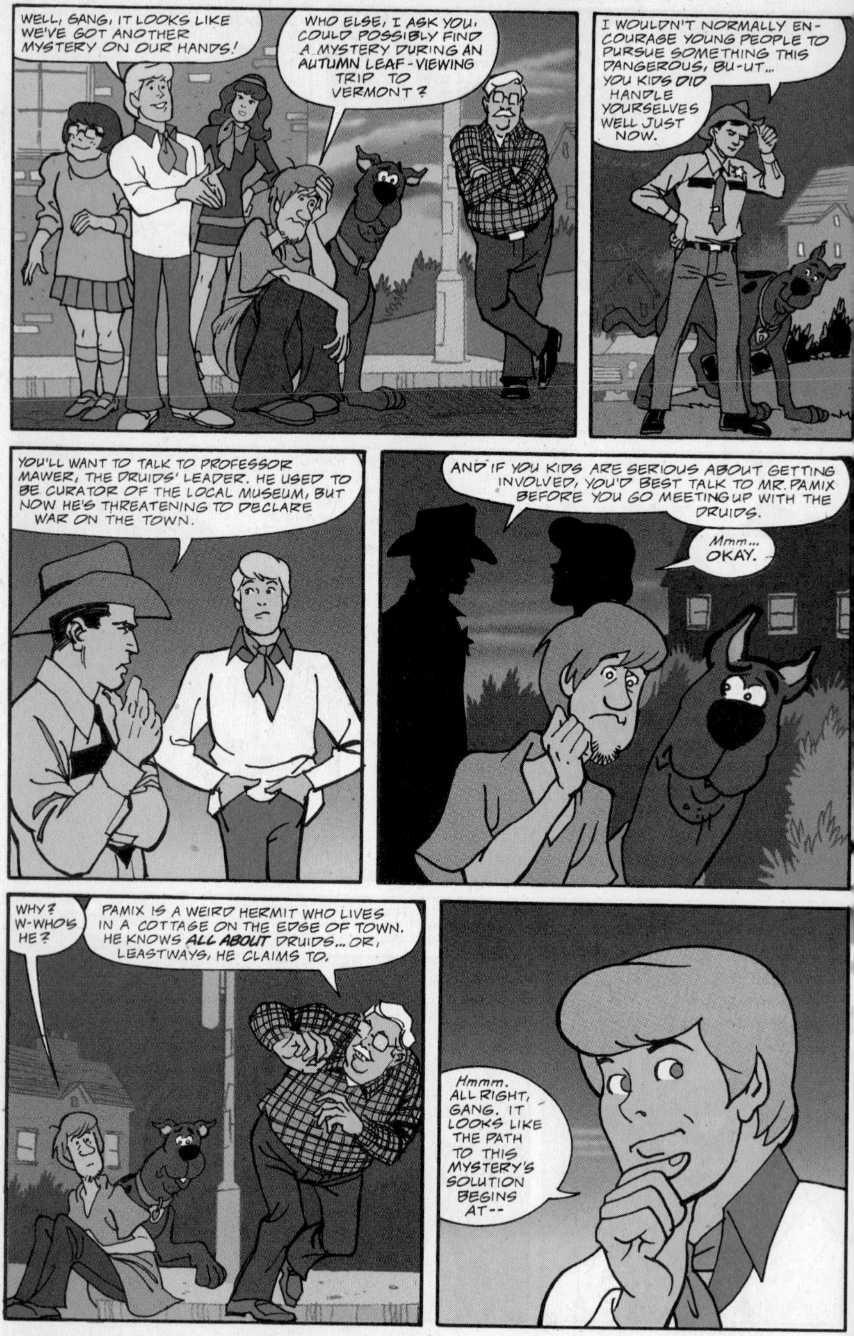
WELL, GANG, IT LOOKS LIKE WE'VE GOT ANOTHER MYSTERY ON OUR HANDS!
WHO ELSE, I ASK YOU, COULD POSSIBLY FIND A MYSTERY DURING AN AUTUMN LEAF-VIEWING TRIP TO VERMONT?
I WOULDN'T NORMALLY ENCOURAGE YOUNG PEOPLE TO PURSUE SOMETHING THIS DANGEROUS, BU-UT... YOU KIDS DID HANDLE YOURSELVES WELL JUST NOW.
YOU'LL WANT TO TALK TO PROFESSOR MAWER, THE DRUIDS' LEADER. HE USED TO BE CURATOR OF THE LOCAL MUSEUM, BUT NOW HE'S THREATENING TO DECLARE WAR ON THE TOWN.
AND IF YOU KIDS ARE SERIOUS ABOUT GETTING INVOLVED, YOU'D BEST TALK TO MR. PAMIX BEFORE YOU GO MEETING UP WITH THE DRUIDS.
Mmm... OKAY.
WHY? W-WHO'S HE?
PAMIX IS A WEIRD HERMIT WHO LIVES IN A COTTAGE ON THE EDGE OF TOWN. HE KNOWS ALL ABOUT DRUIDS... OR, LEASTWAYS, HE CLAIMS TO.
Hmmm. ALL RIGHT, GANG. IT LOOKS LIKE THE PATH TO THIS MYSTERY'S SOLUTION BEGINS AT--

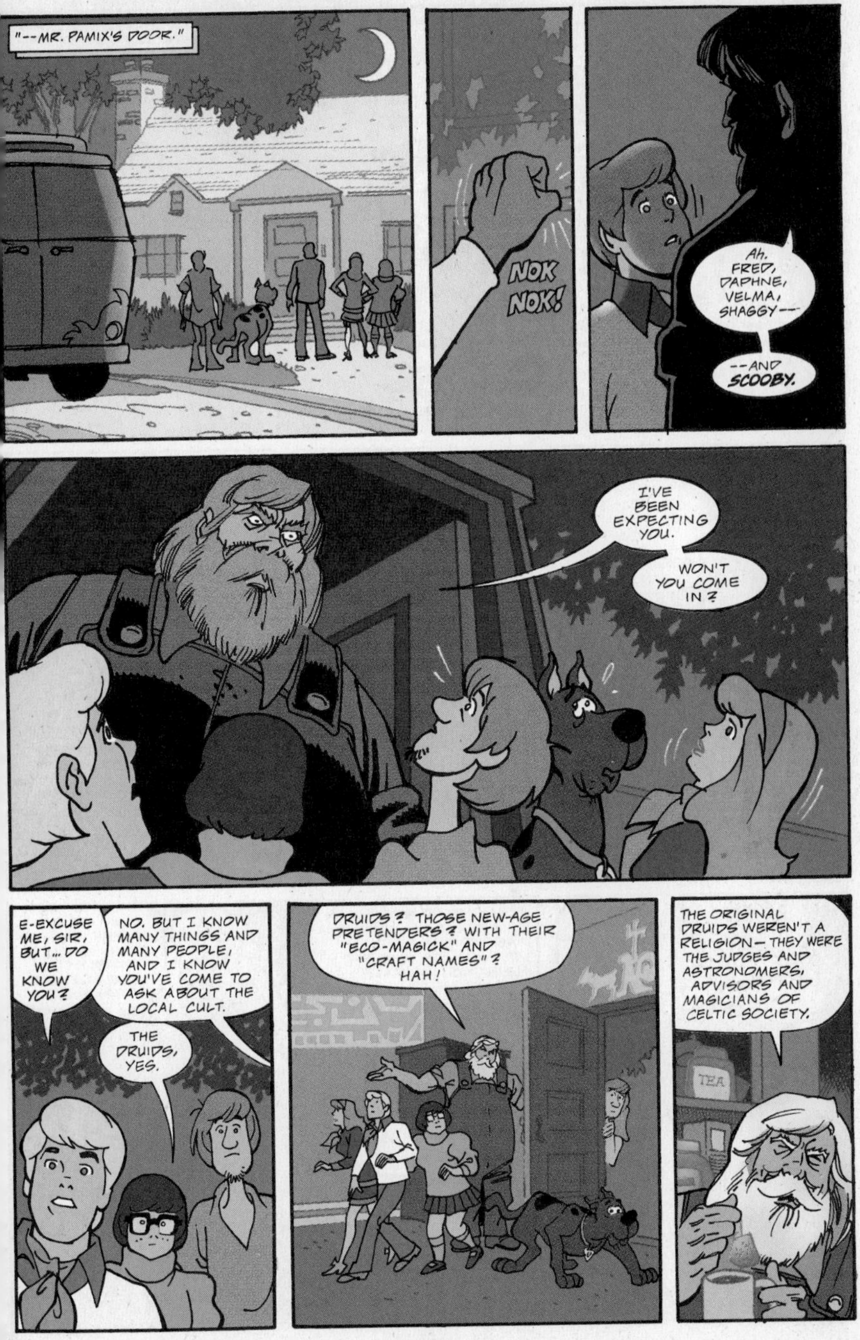
"--MR. PAMIX'S DOOR."
NOK NOK!
Ah. FRED, DAPHNE, VELMA, SHAGGY---
--AND SCOOBY.
I'VE BEEN EXPECTING YOU.
WON'T YOU COME IN?
E-EXCUSE ME, SIR, BUT... DO WE KNOW YOU?
NO. BUT I KNOW MANY THINGS AND MANY PEOPLE, AND I KNOW YOU'VE COME TO ASK ABOUT THE LOCAL CULT.
THE DRUIDS, YES.
DRUIDS? THOSE NEW-AGE PRETENDERS? WITH THEIR "ECO-MAGICK" AND "CRAFT NAMES"? HAH!
THE ORIGINAL DRUIDS WEREN'T A RELIGION— THEY WERE THE JUDGES AND ASTRONOMERS, ADVISORS AND MAGICIANS OF CELTIC SOCIETY.
TEA

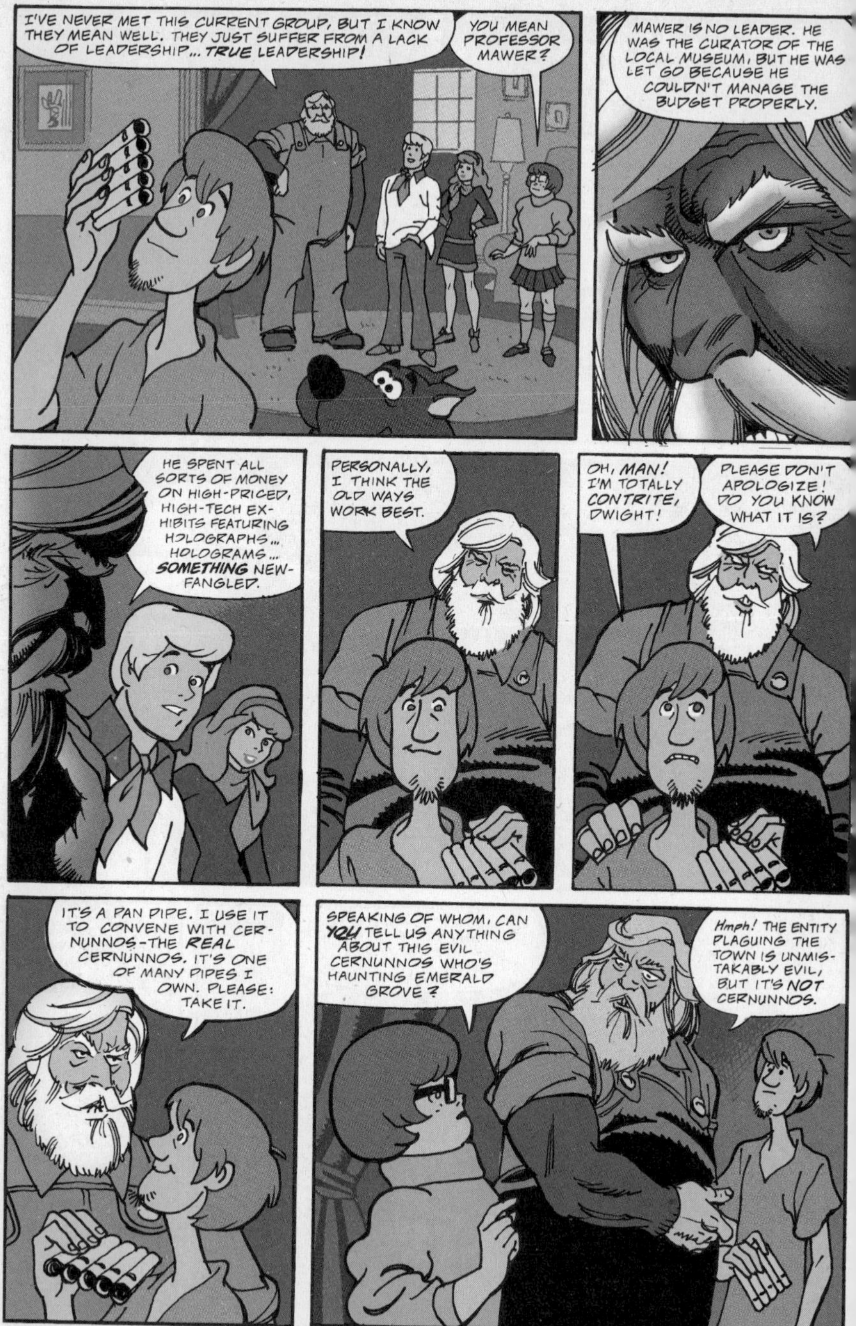

I'VE NEVER MET THIS CURRENT GROUP, BUT I KNOW THEY MEAN WELL. THEY JUST SUFFER FROM A LACK OF LEADERSHIP... TRUE LEADERSHIP!
YOU MEAN PROFESSOR MAWER?
MAWER IS NO LEADER. HE WAS THE CURATOR OF THE LOCAL MUSEUM, BUT HE WAS LET GO BECAUSE HE COULDN'T MANAGE THE BUDGET PROPERLY.
HE SPENT ALL SORTS OF MONEY ON HIGH-PRICED, HIGH-TECH EXHIBITS FEATURING HOLOGRAPHS... HOLOGRAMS... SOMETHING NEW-FANGLED.
PERSONALLY, I THINK THE OLD WAYS WORK BEST.
OH, MAN! I'M TOTALLY CONTRITE, DWIGHT!
PLEASE DON'T APOLOGIZE! DO YOU KNOW WHAT IT IS?
IT'S A PAN PIPE. I USE IT TO CONVENE WITH CERNUNNOS-THE REAL CERNUNNOS. IT'S ONE OF MANY PIPES I OWN. PLEASE: TAKE IT.
SPEAKING OF WHOM, CAN YOU TELL US ANYTHING ABOUT THIS EVIL CERNUNNOS WHO'S HAUNTING EMERALD GROVE?
Hmph! THE ENTITY PLAGUING THE TOWN IS UNMISTAKABLY EVIL, BUT IT'S NOT CERNUNNOS.

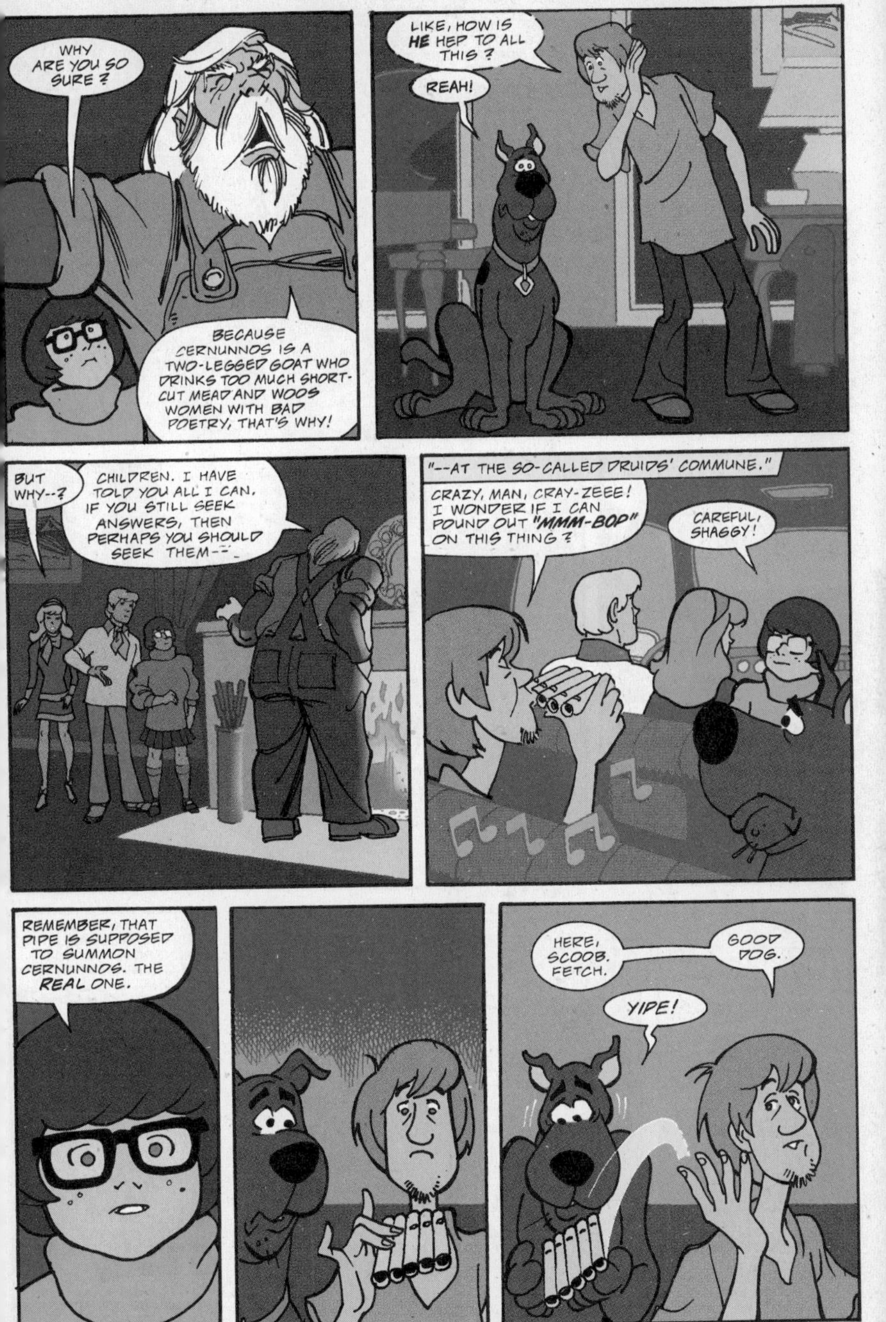
WHY ARE YOU SO SURE?
BECAUSE CERNUNNOS IS A TWO-LEGGED GOAT WHO DRINKS TOO MUCH SHORT-CUT MEAD AND WOOS WOMEN WITH BAD POETRY, THAT'S WHY!
LIKE, HOW IS HE HEP TO ALL THIS?
REAH!
BUT WHY--?
CHILDREN. I HAVE TOLD YOU ALL I CAN. IF YOU STILL SEEK ANSWERS, THEN PERHAPS YOU SHOULD SEEK THEM--
"--AT THE SO-CALLED DRUIDS' COMMUNE."
CRAZY, MAN, CRAY-ZEEE! I WONDER IF I CAN POUND OUT "MMM-BOP" ON THIS THING?
CAREFUL, SHAGGY!
REMEMBER, THAT PIPE IS SUPPOSED TO SUMMON CERNUNNOS. THE REAL ONE.
HERE, SCOOB. FETCH.
GOOD DOG.
YIPE!

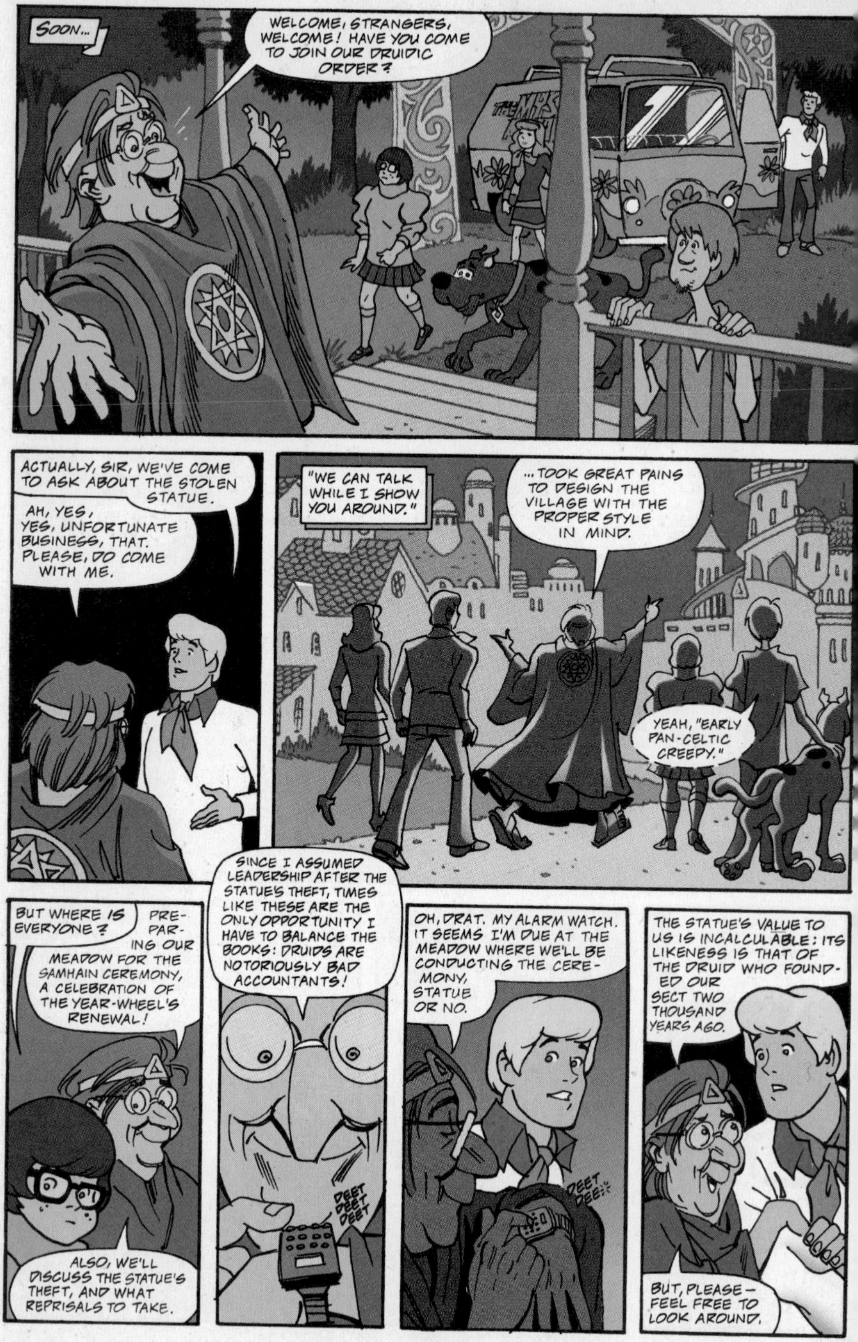

SOON...
WELCOME, STRANGERS, WELCOME! HAVE YOU COME TO JOIN OUR DRUIDIC ORDER?
ACTUALLY, SIR, WE'VE COME TO ASK ABOUT THE STOLEN STATUE.
AH, YES, YES, UNFORTUNATE BUSINESS, THAT. PLEASE, DO COME WITH ME.
"WE CAN TALK WHILE I SHOW YOU AROUND."
...TOOK GREAT PAINS TO DESIGN THE VILLAGE WITH THE PROPER STYLE IN MIND.
YEAH, "EARLY PAN-CELTIC CREEPY."
BUT WHERE IS EVERYONE?
PREPARING OUR MEADOW FOR THE SAMHAIN CEREMONY, A CELEBRATION OF THE YEAR-WHEEL'S RENEWAL!
ALSO, WE'LL DISCUSS THE STATUE'S THEFT, AND WHAT REPRISALS TO TAKE.
SINCE I ASSUMED LEADERSHIP AFTER THE STATUE'S THEFT, TIMES LIKE THESE ARE THE ONLY OPPORTUNITY I HAVE TO BALANCE THE BOOKS: DRUIDS ARE NOTORIOUSLY BAD ACCOUNTANTS!
DEET DEET DEET
OH, DRAT. MY ALARM WATCH. IT SEEMS I'M DUE AT THE MEADOW WHERE WE'LL BE CONDUCTING THE CEREMONY, STATUE OR NO.
DEET DEE
THE STATUE'S VALUE TO US IS INCALCULABLE: ITS LIKENESS IS THAT OF THE DRUID WHO FOUNDED OUR SECT TWO THOUSAND YEARS AGO.
BUT, PLEASE — FEEL FREE TO LOOK AROUND.

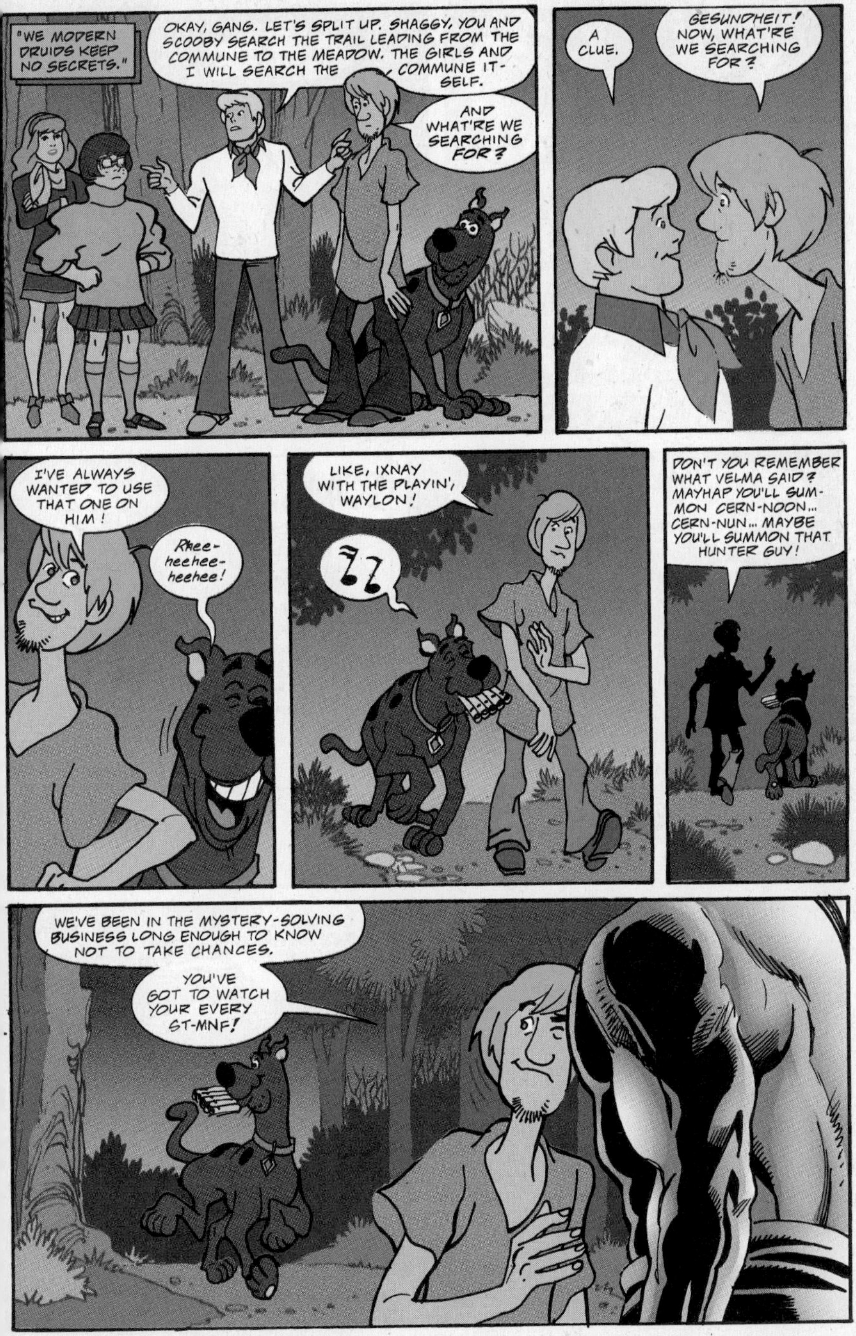
"WE MODERN DRUIDS KEEP NO SECRETS."
OKAY, GANG. LET'S SPLIT UP. SHAGGY, YOU AND SCOOBY SEARCH THE TRAIL LEADING FROM THE COMMUNE TO THE MEADOW. THE GIRLS AND I WILL SEARCH THE COMMUNE IT-SELF.
AND WHAT'RE WE SEARCHING FOR?
A CLUE.
GESUNDHEIT! NOW, WHAT'RE WE SEARCHING FOR?
I'VE ALWAYS WANTED TO USE THAT ONE ON HIM!
Rhee-heehee-heehee!
LIKE, IXNAY WITH THE PLAYIN', WAYLON!
DON'T YOU REMEMBER WHAT VELMA SAID? MAYHAP YOU'LL SUM-MON CERN-NOON... CERN-NUN... MAYBE YOU'LL SUMMON THAT HUNTER GUY!
WE'VE BEEN IN THE MYSTERY-SOLVING BUSINESS LONG ENOUGH TO KNOW NOT TO TAKE CHANCES.
YOU'VE GOT TO WATCH YOUR EVERY ST-MNF!

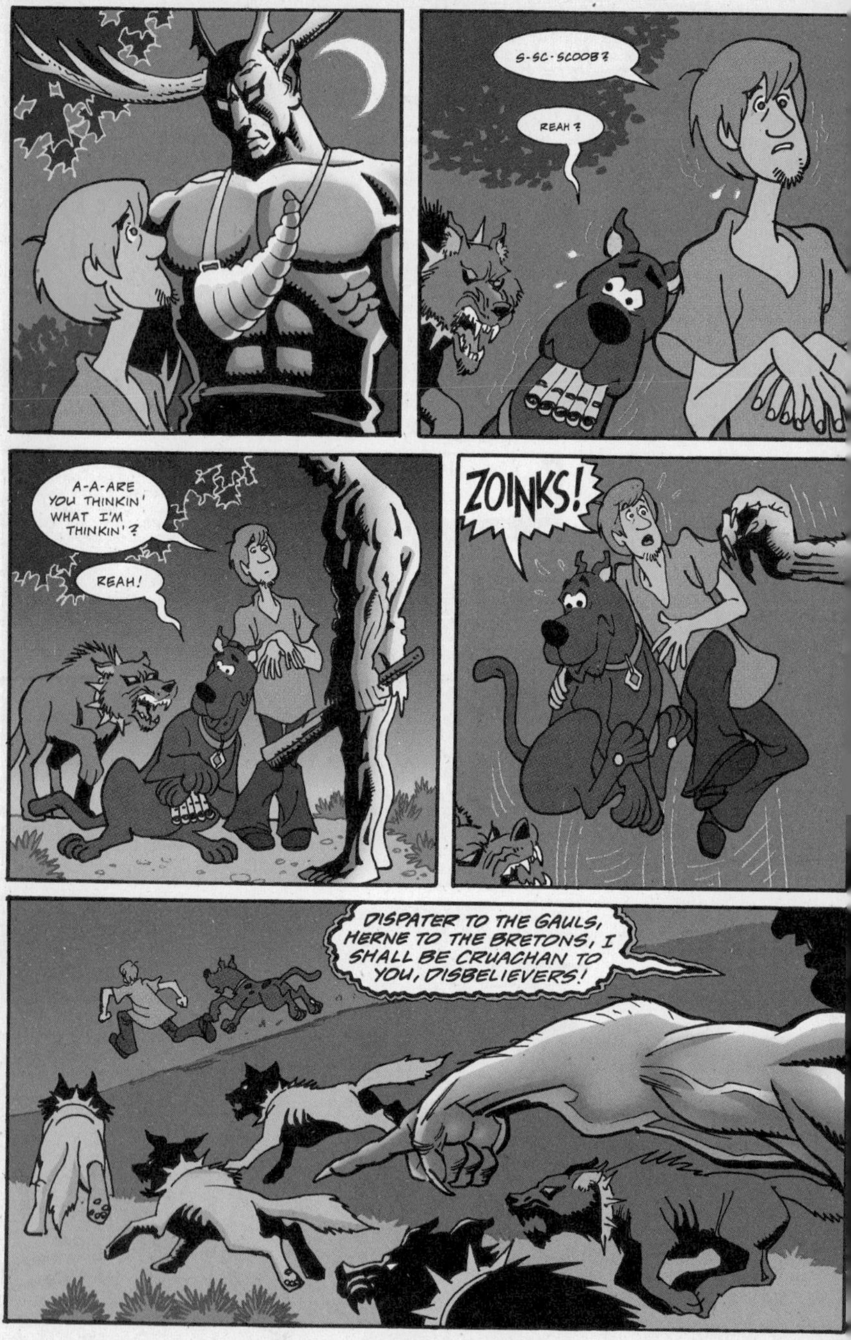

S-SC-SCOOB?
REAH?
A-A-ARE YOU THINKIN' WHAT I'M THINKIN'?
REAH!
ZOINKS!
DISPATER TO THE GAULS, HERNE TO THE BRETONS, I SHALL BE CRUACHAN TO YOU, DISBELIEVERS!

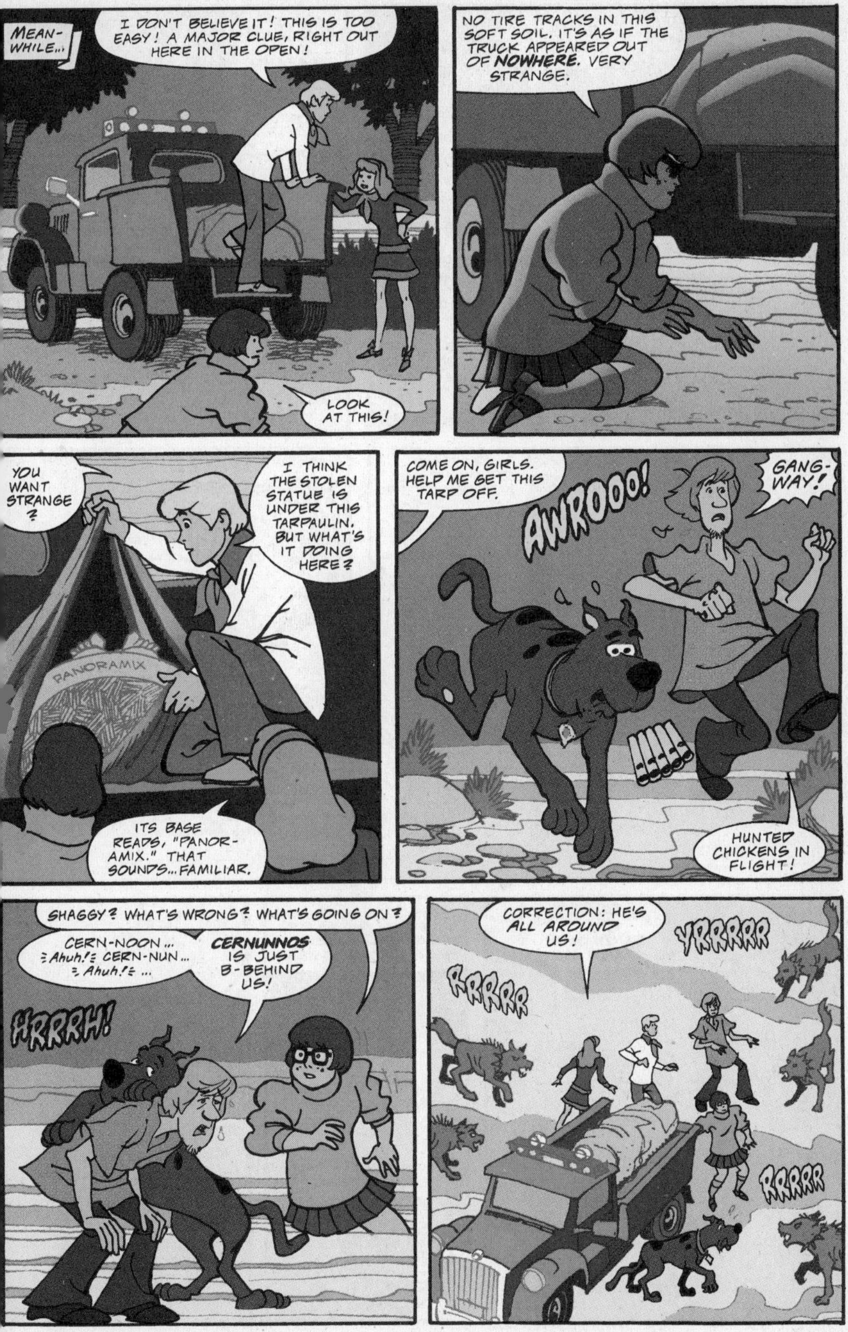

MEAN-WHILE...
I DON'T BELIEVE IT! THIS IS TOO EASY! A MAJOR CLUE, RIGHT OUT HERE IN THE OPEN!
LOOK AT THIS!
NO TIRE TRACKS IN THIS SOFT SOIL. IT'S AS IF THE TRUCK APPEARED OUT OF **NOWHERE**. VERY STRANGE.
YOU WANT STRANGE?
I THINK THE STOLEN STATUE IS UNDER THIS TARPAULIN. BUT WHAT'S IT DOING HERE?
PANORAMIX
ITS BASE READS, "PANOR-AMIX." THAT SOUNDS... FAMILIAR.
COME ON, GIRLS. HELP ME GET THIS TARP OFF.
AWROOO!
GANG-WAY!
HUNTED CHICKENS IN FLIGHT!
SHAGGY? WHAT'S WRONG? WHAT'S GOING ON?
CERN-NOON ... *Ahuh!* CERN-NUN ... *Ahuh!* ...
CERNUNNOS IS JUST B-BEHIND US!
HRRRH!
CORRECTION: HE'S *ALL AROUND* US!
YRRRRR
RRRRR
RRRRR

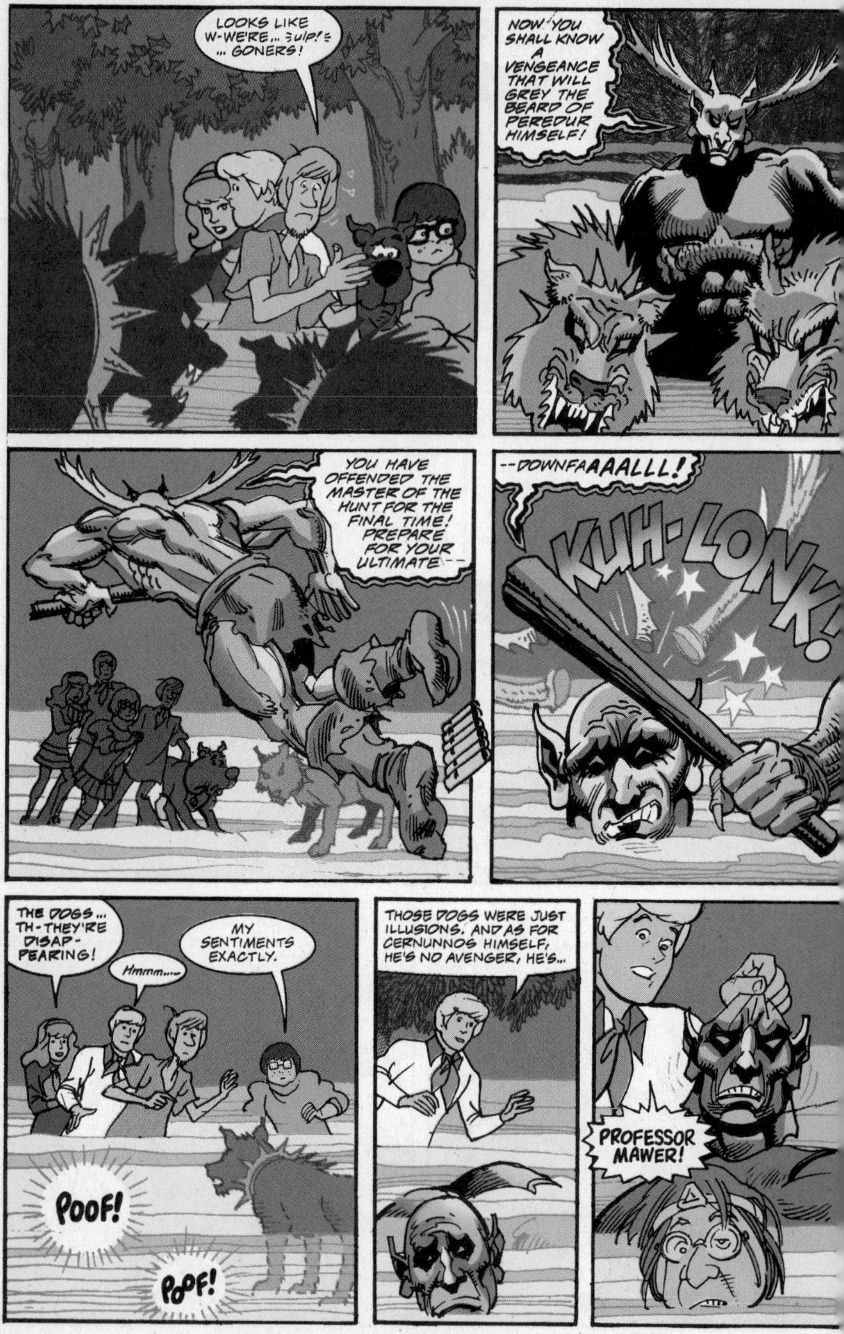
LOOKS LIKE W-WE'RE... GULP! ...GONERS!
NOW YOU SHALL KNOW A VENGEANCE THAT WILL GREY THE BEARD OF PEREDUR HIMSELF!
YOU HAVE OFFENDED THE MASTER OF THE HUNT FOR THE FINAL TIME! PREPARE FOR YOUR ULTIMATE--
--DOWNFAAAALLL!
KUH-LONK!
THE DOGS... TH-THEY'RE DISAP-PEARING!
Hmmm....
MY SENTIMENTS EXACTLY.
POOF!
POOF!
THOSE DOGS WERE JUST ILLUSIONS. AND AS FOR CERNUNNOS HIMSELF, HE'S NO AVENGER, HE'S...
PROFESSOR MAWER!

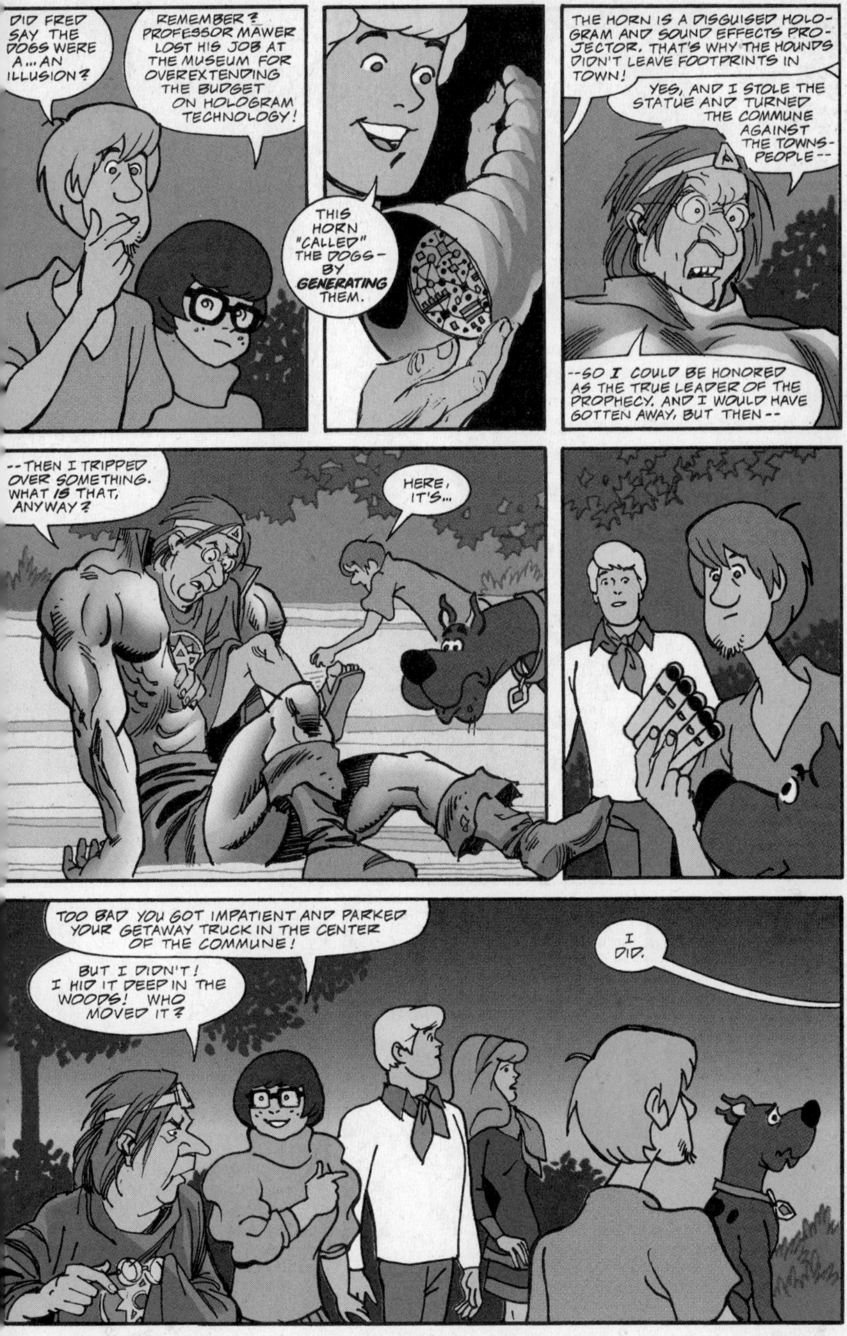
DID FRED SAY THE DOGS WERE A... AN ILLUSION?
REMEMBER? PROFESSOR MAWER LOST HIS JOB AT THE MUSEUM FOR OVEREXTENDING THE BUDGET ON HOLOGRAM TECHNOLOGY!
THIS HORN "CALLED" THE DOGS -- BY GENERATING THEM.
THE HORN IS A DISGUISED HOLOGRAM AND SOUND EFFECTS PROJECTOR. THAT'S WHY THE HOUNDS DIDN'T LEAVE FOOTPRINTS IN TOWN!
YES, AND I STOLE THE STATUE AND TURNED THE COMMUNE AGAINST THE TOWNSPEOPLE --
--SO I COULD BE HONORED AS THE TRUE LEADER OF THE PROPHECY. AND I WOULD HAVE GOTTEN AWAY, BUT THEN --
-- THEN I TRIPPED OVER SOMETHING. WHAT IS THAT, ANYWAY?
HERE, IT'S...
TOO BAD YOU GOT IMPATIENT AND PARKED YOUR GETAWAY TRUCK IN THE CENTER OF THE COMMUNE!
BUT I DIDN'T! I HID IT DEEP IN THE WOODS! WHO MOVED IT?
I DID.

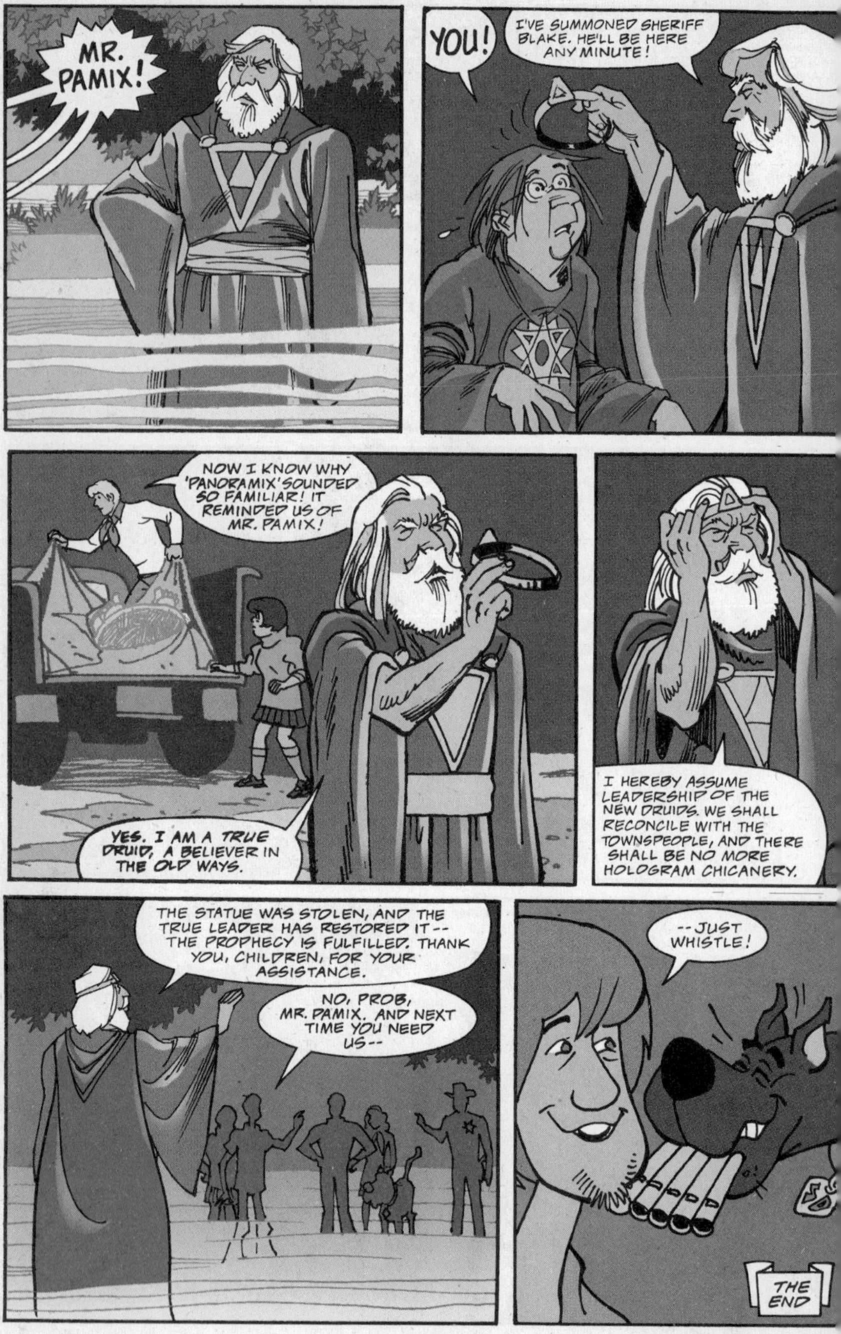
MR. PAMIX!
YOU!
I'VE SUMMONED SHERIFF BLAKE. HE'LL BE HERE ANY MINUTE!
NOW I KNOW WHY 'PANORAMIX' SOUNDED SO FAMILIAR! IT REMINDED US OF MR. PAMIX!
YES. I AM A TRUE DRUID, A BELIEVER IN THE OLD WAYS.
I HEREBY ASSUME LEADERSHIP OF THE NEW DRUIDS. WE SHALL RECONCILE WITH THE TOWNSPEOPLE, AND THERE SHALL BE NO MORE HOLOGRAM CHICANERY.
THE STATUE WAS STOLEN, AND THE TRUE LEADER HAS RESTORED IT -- THE PROPHECY IS FULFILLED. THANK YOU, CHILDREN, FOR YOUR ASSISTANCE.
NO, PROB, MR. PAMIX. AND NEXT TIME YOU NEED US --
-- JUST WHISTLE!
THE END

SCOOBY-DOO™ in HOW I SPENT MY WINTER BREAK

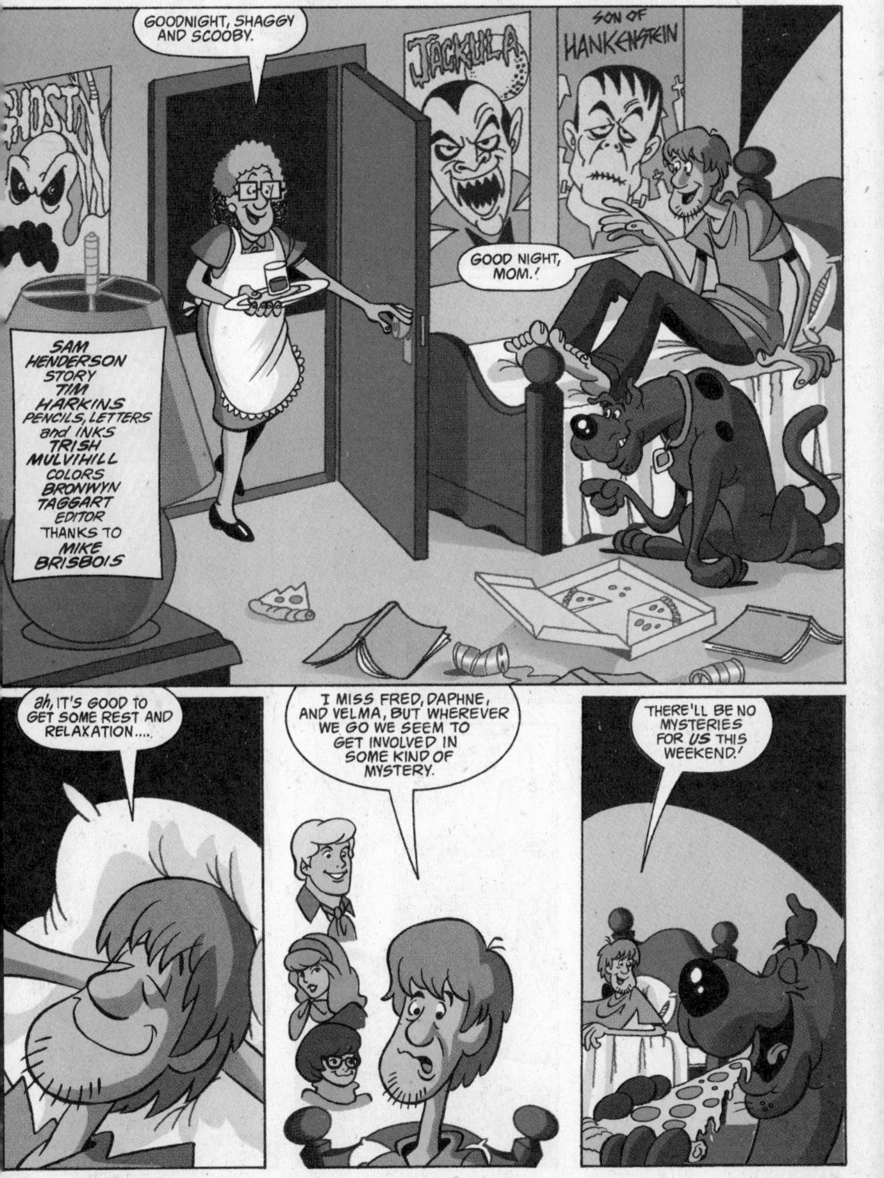
GOODNIGHT, SHAGGY AND SCOOBY.
JACKULA
SON OF HANKENSTEIN
GOOD NIGHT, MOM.!
SAM HENDERSON STORY TIM HARKINS PENCILS, LETTERS and INKS TRISH MULVIHILL COLORS BRONWYN TAGGART EDITOR THANKS TO MIKE BRISBOIS
ah, IT'S GOOD TO GET SOME REST AND RELAXATION....
I MISS FRED, DAPHNE, AND VELMA, BUT WHEREVER WE GO WE SEEM TO GET INVOLVED IN SOME KIND OF MYSTERY.
THERE'LL BE NO MYSTERIES FOR US THIS WEEKEND!

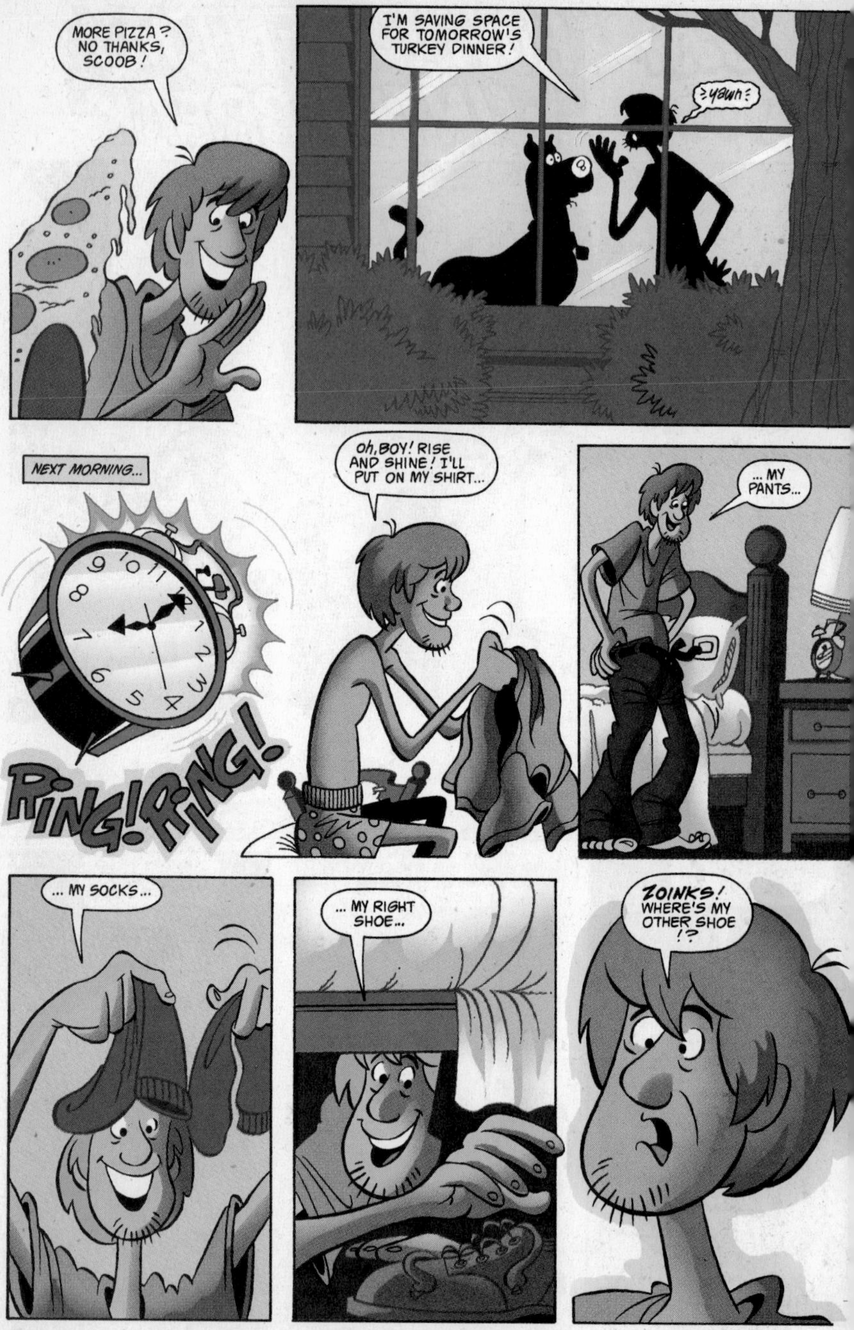
MORE PIZZA? NO THANKS, SCOOB!
I'M SAVING SPACE FOR TOMORROW'S TURKEY DINNER!
yawn
NEXT MORNING...
RING! RING!
Oh, BOY! RISE AND SHINE! I'LL PUT ON MY SHIRT...
... MY PANTS...
... MY SOCKS...
... MY RIGHT SHOE...
ZOINKS! WHERE'S MY OTHER SHOE !?

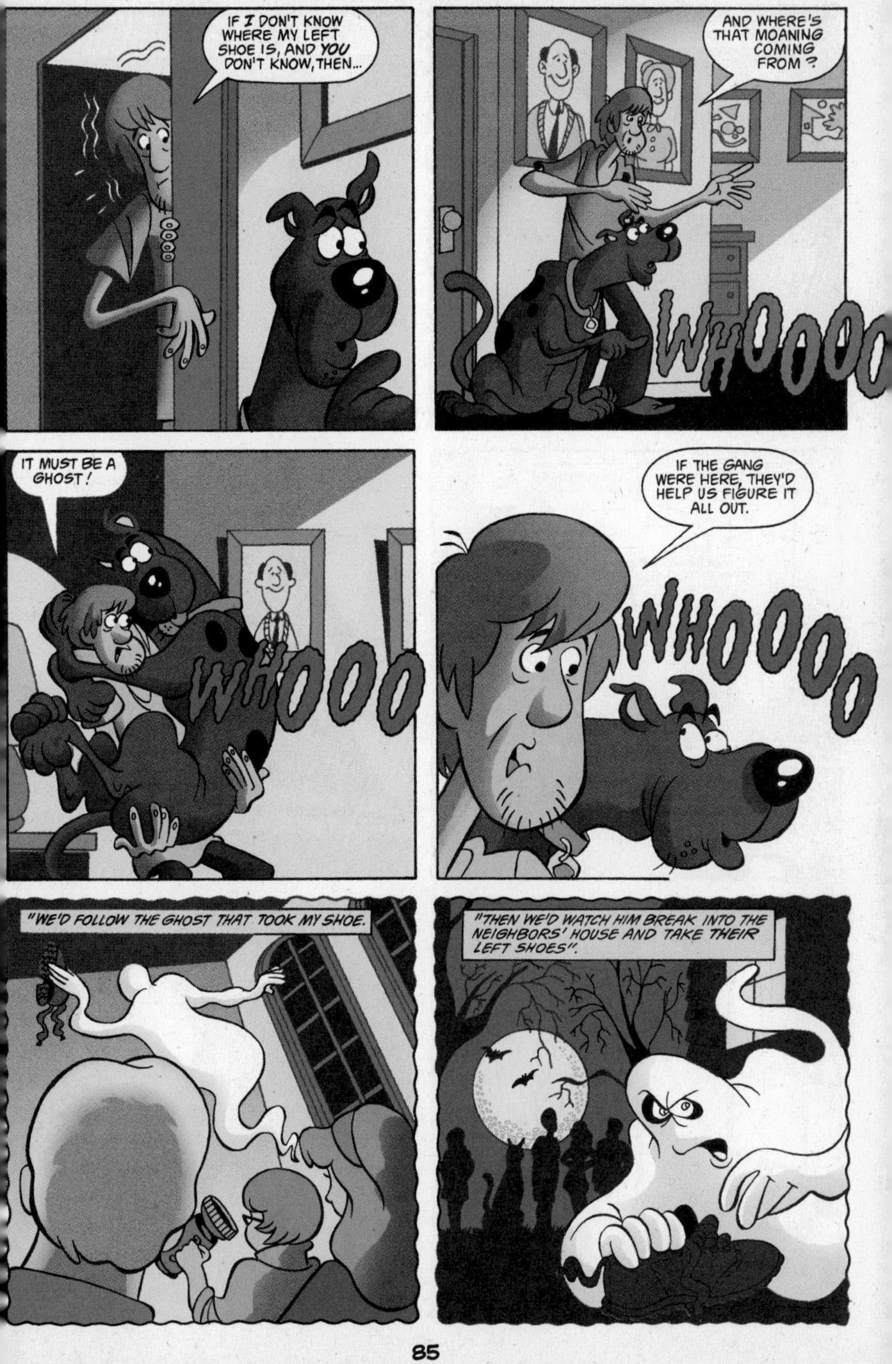
IF I DON'T KNOW WHERE MY LEFT SHOE IS, AND YOU DON'T KNOW, THEN...
AND WHERE'S THAT MOANING COMING FROM ?
WHOOOO
IT MUST BE A GHOST !
WHOOO
IF THE GANG WERE HERE, THEY'D HELP US FIGURE IT ALL OUT.
WHOOOO
"WE'D FOLLOW THE GHOST THAT TOOK MY SHOE.
"THEN WE'D WATCH HIM BREAK INTO THE NEIGHBORS' HOUSE AND TAKE THEIR LEFT SHOES".

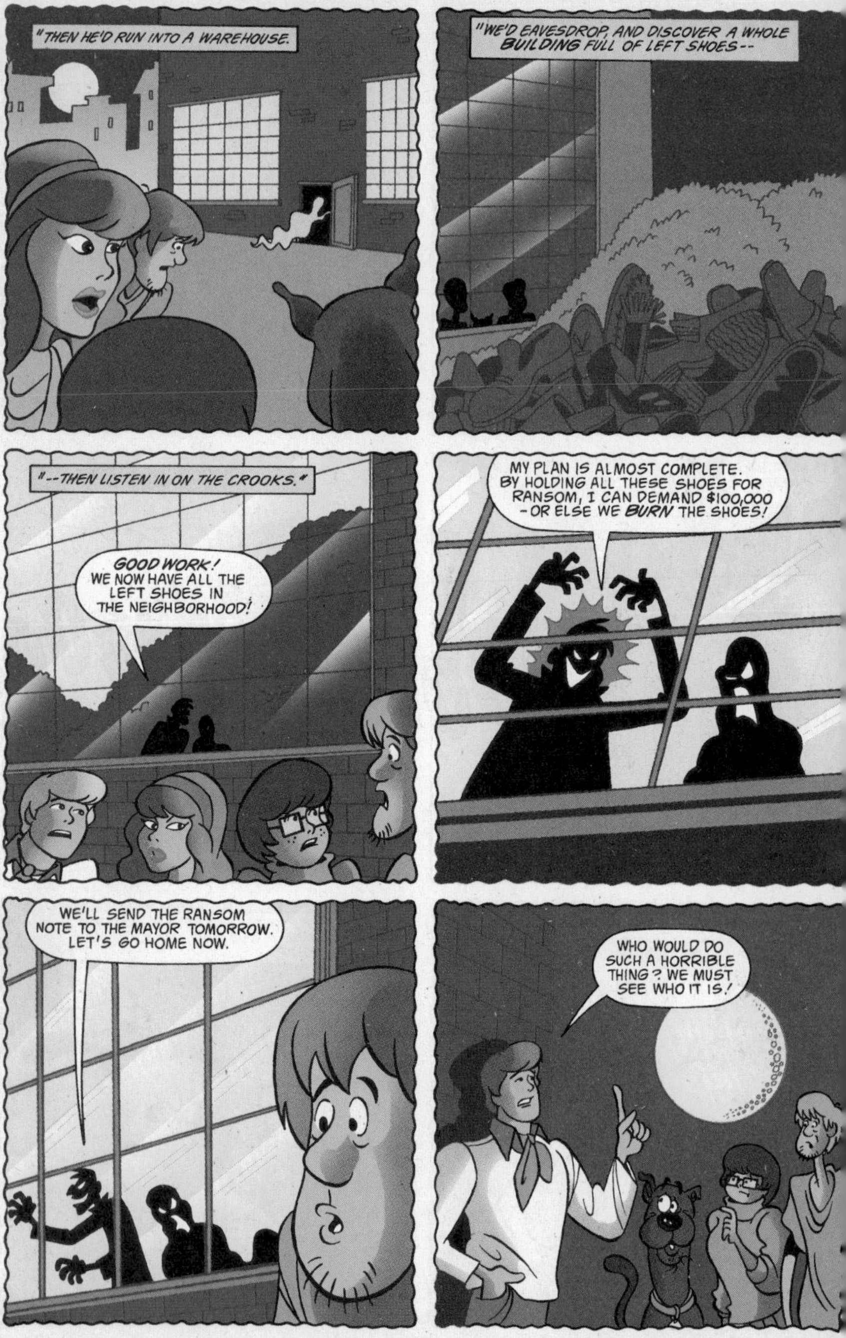
"THEN HE'D RUN INTO A WAREHOUSE.
"WE'D EAVESDROP, AND DISCOVER A WHOLE BUILDING FULL OF LEFT SHOES--
"--THEN LISTEN IN ON THE CROOKS."
GOOD WORK! WE NOW HAVE ALL THE LEFT SHOES IN THE NEIGHBORHOOD!
MY PLAN IS ALMOST COMPLETE. BY HOLDING ALL THESE SHOES FOR RANSOM, I CAN DEMAND $100,000 - OR ELSE WE BURN THE SHOES!
WE'LL SEND THE RANSOM NOTE TO THE MAYOR TOMORROW. LET'S GO HOME NOW.
WHO WOULD DO SUCH A HORRIBLE THING? WE MUST SEE WHO IT IS!

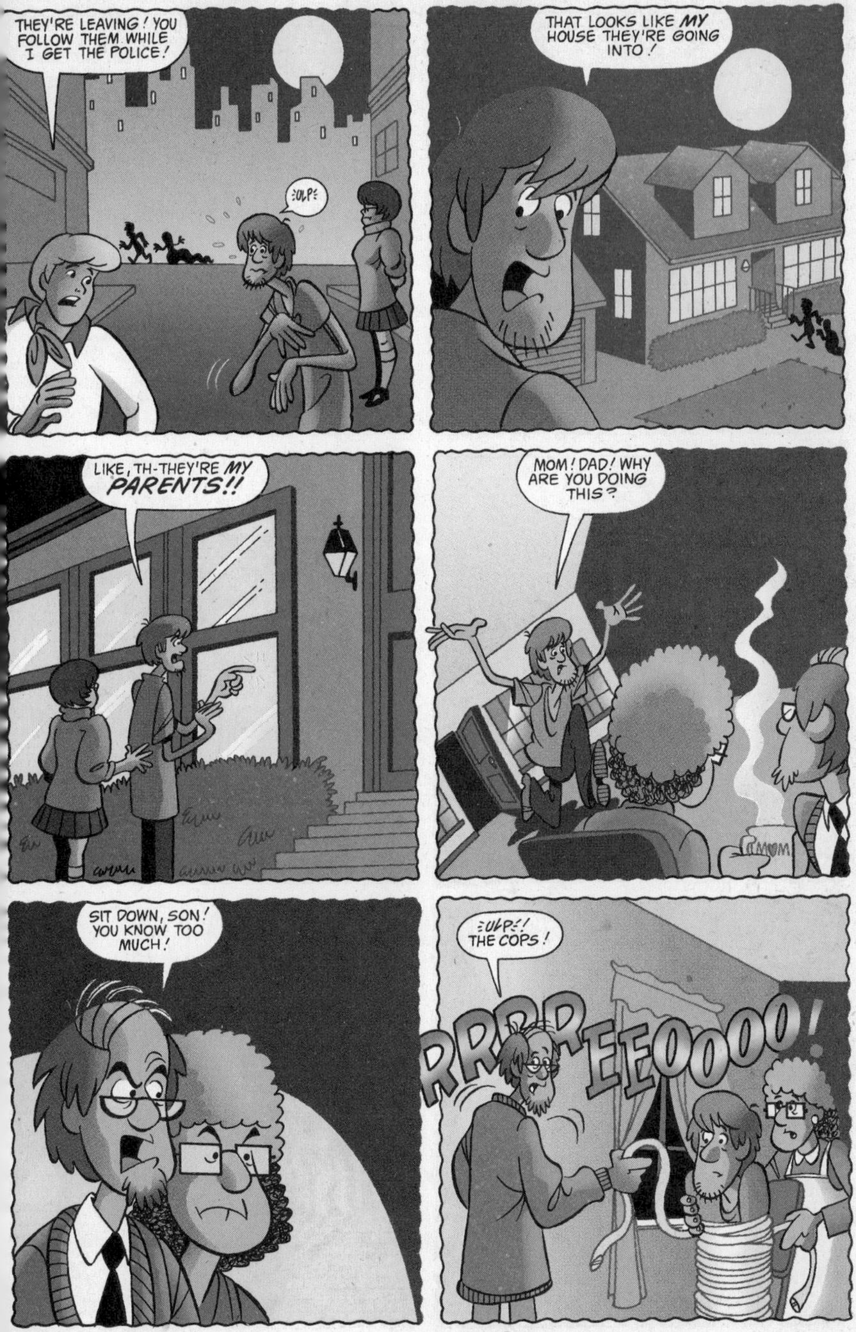
THEY'RE LEAVING! YOU FOLLOW THEM WHILE I GET THE POLICE!
ULP
THAT LOOKS LIKE MY HOUSE THEY'RE GOING INTO!
LIKE, TH-THEY'RE MY PARENTS!!
MOM! DAD! WHY ARE YOU DOING THIS?
MOM
SIT DOWN, SON! YOU KNOW TOO MUCH!
ULP! THE COPS!
RRRREEOOOO!

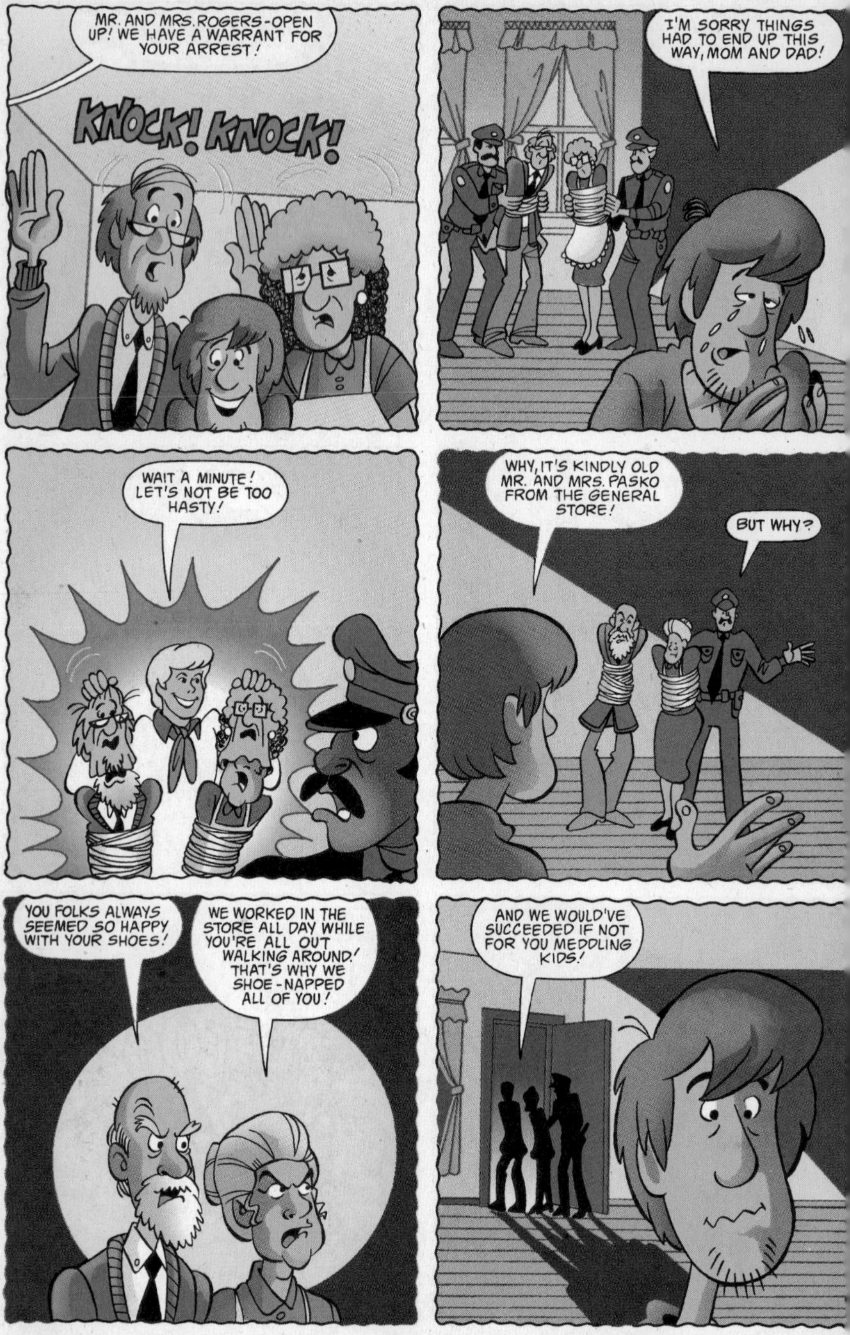
MR. AND MRS. ROGERS-OPEN UP! WE HAVE A WARRANT FOR YOUR ARREST!
KNOCK! KNOCK!
I'M SORRY THINGS HAD TO END UP THIS WAY, MOM AND DAD!
WAIT A MINUTE! LET'S NOT BE TOO HASTY!
WHY, IT'S KINDLY OLD MR. AND MRS. PASKO FROM THE GENERAL STORE!
BUT WHY?
YOU FOLKS ALWAYS SEEMED SO HAPPY WITH YOUR SHOES!
WE WORKED IN THE STORE ALL DAY WHILE YOU'RE ALL OUT WALKING AROUND! THAT'S WHY WE SHOE-NAPPED ALL OF YOU!
AND WE WOULD'VE SUCCEEDED IF NOT FOR YOU MEDDLING KIDS!

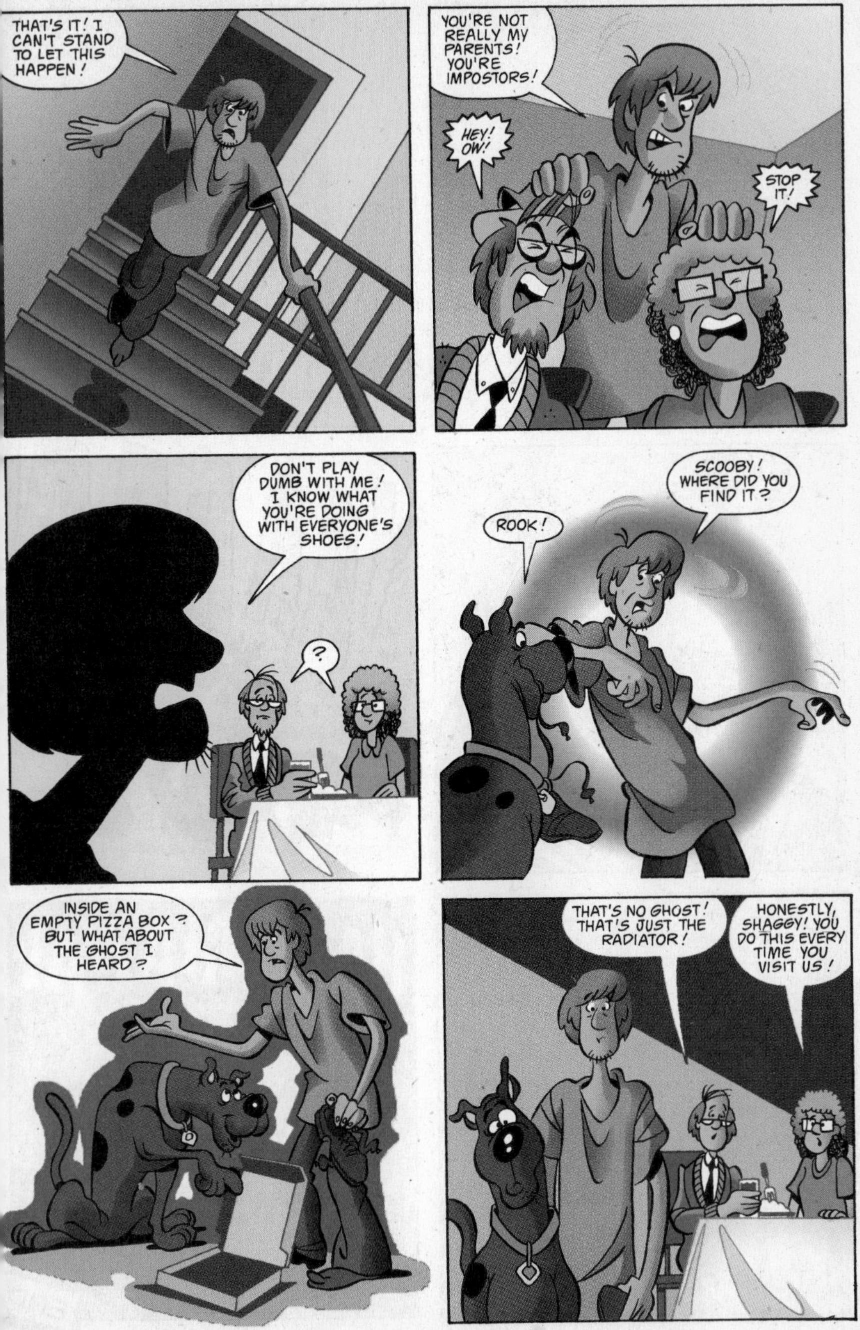
THAT'S IT! I CAN'T STAND TO LET THIS HAPPEN!
YOU'RE NOT REALLY MY PARENTS! YOU'RE IMPOSTORS!
HEY! OW!
STOP IT!
DON'T PLAY DUMB WITH ME! I KNOW WHAT YOU'RE DOING WITH EVERYONE'S SHOES!
?
ROOK!
SCOOBY! WHERE DID YOU FIND IT?
INSIDE AN EMPTY PIZZA BOX? BUT WHAT ABOUT THE GHOST I HEARD?
THAT'S NO GHOST! THAT'S JUST THE RADIATOR!
HONESTLY, SHAGGY! YOU DO THIS EVERY TIME YOU VISIT US!

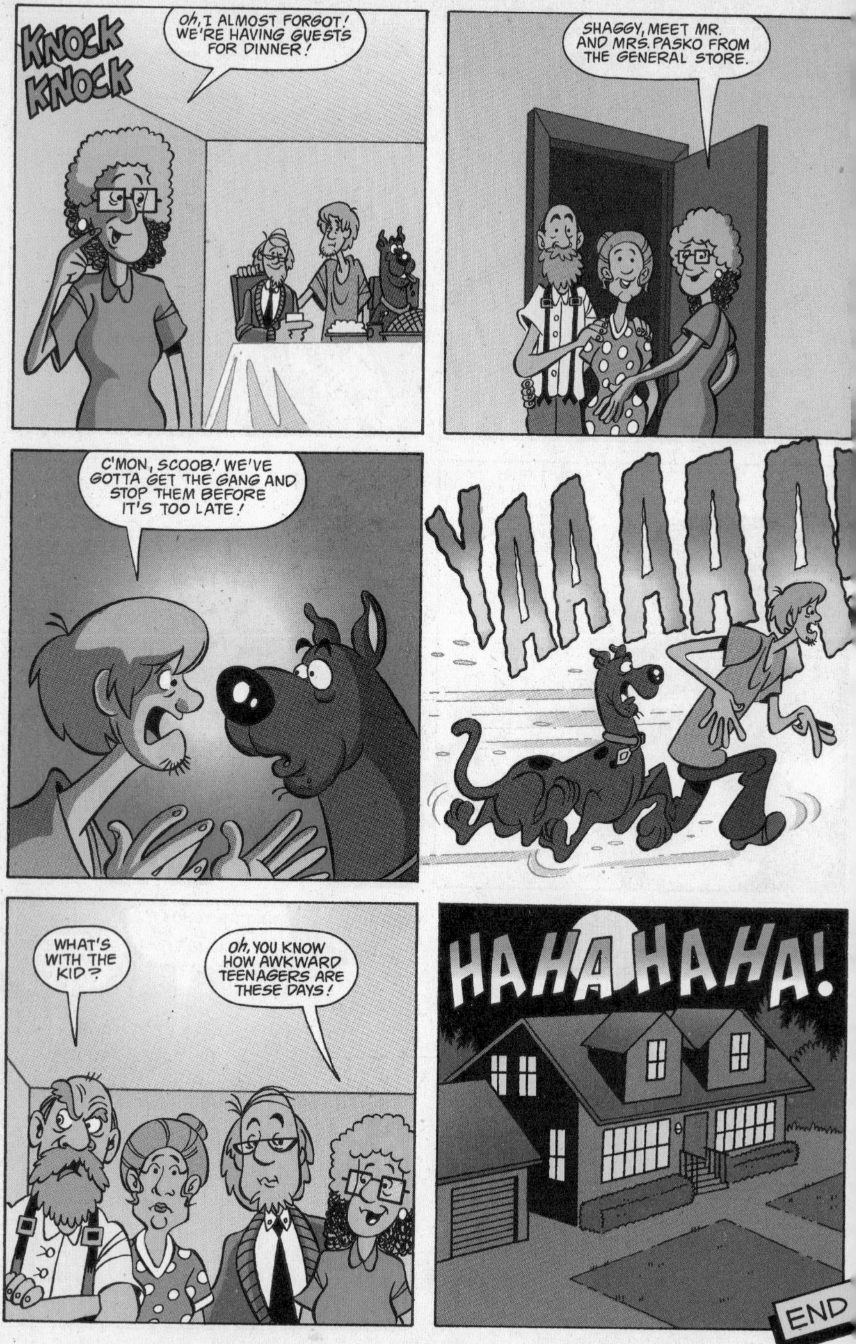
KNOCK KNOCK
OH, I ALMOST FORGOT! WE'RE HAVING GUESTS FOR DINNER!
SHAGGY, MEET MR. AND MRS. PASKO FROM THE GENERAL STORE.
C'MON, SCOOB! WE'VE GOTTA GET THE GANG AND STOP THEM BEFORE IT'S TOO LATE!
YAAAAA
WHAT'S WITH THE KID?
OH, YOU KNOW HOW AWKWARD TEENAGERS ARE THESE DAYS!
HAHAHAHAHA!
END

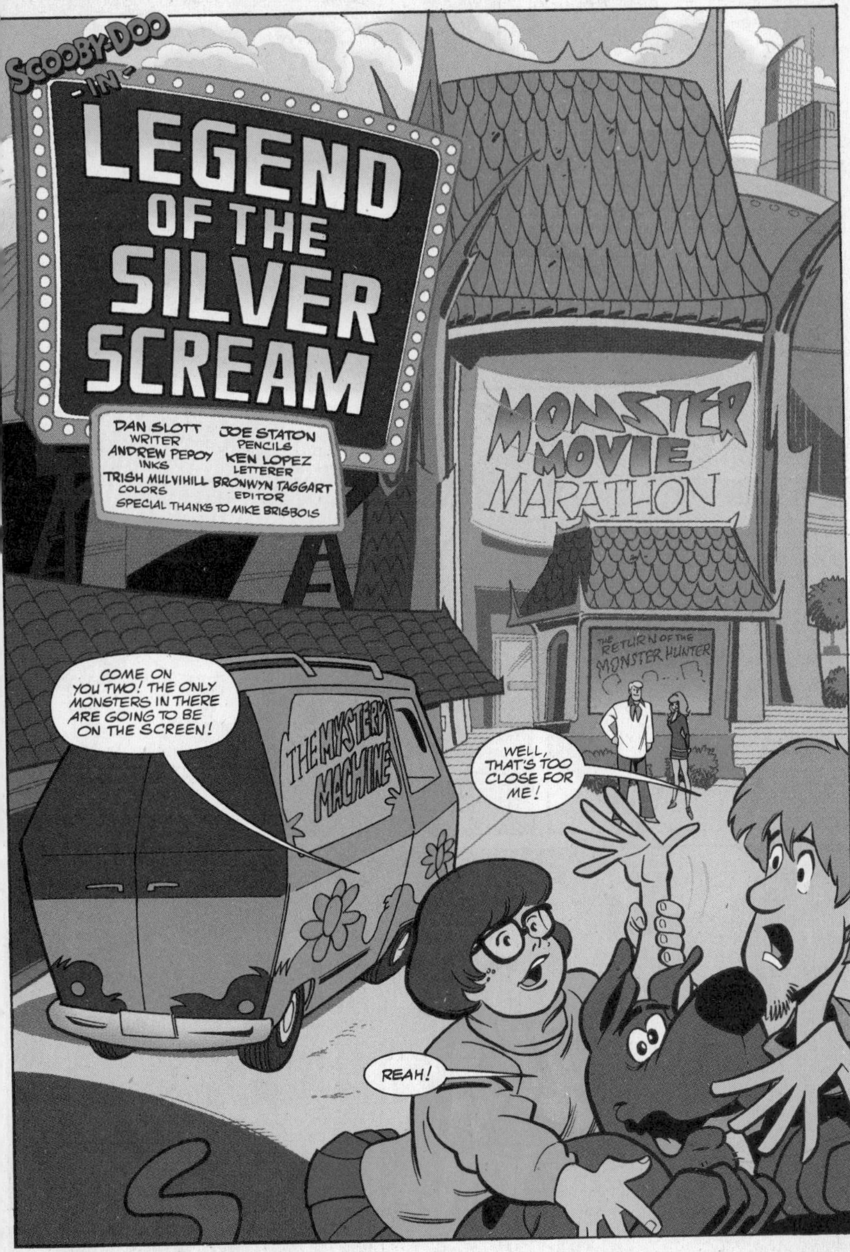
SCOOBY-DOO
-IN-
LEGEND OF THE SILVER SCREAM
DAN SLOTT WRITER
JOE STATON PENCILS
ANDREW PEPOY INKS
KEN LOPEZ LETTERER
TRISH MULVIHILL COLORS
BRONWYN TAGGART EDITOR
SPECIAL THANKS TO MIKE BRISBOIS
MONSTER MOVIE MARATHON
THE RETURN OF THE MONSTER HUNTER
THE MYSTERY MACHINE
COME ON YOU TWO! THE ONLY MONSTERS IN THERE ARE GOING TO BE ON THE SCREEN!
WELL, THAT'S TOO CLOSE FOR ME!
REAH!

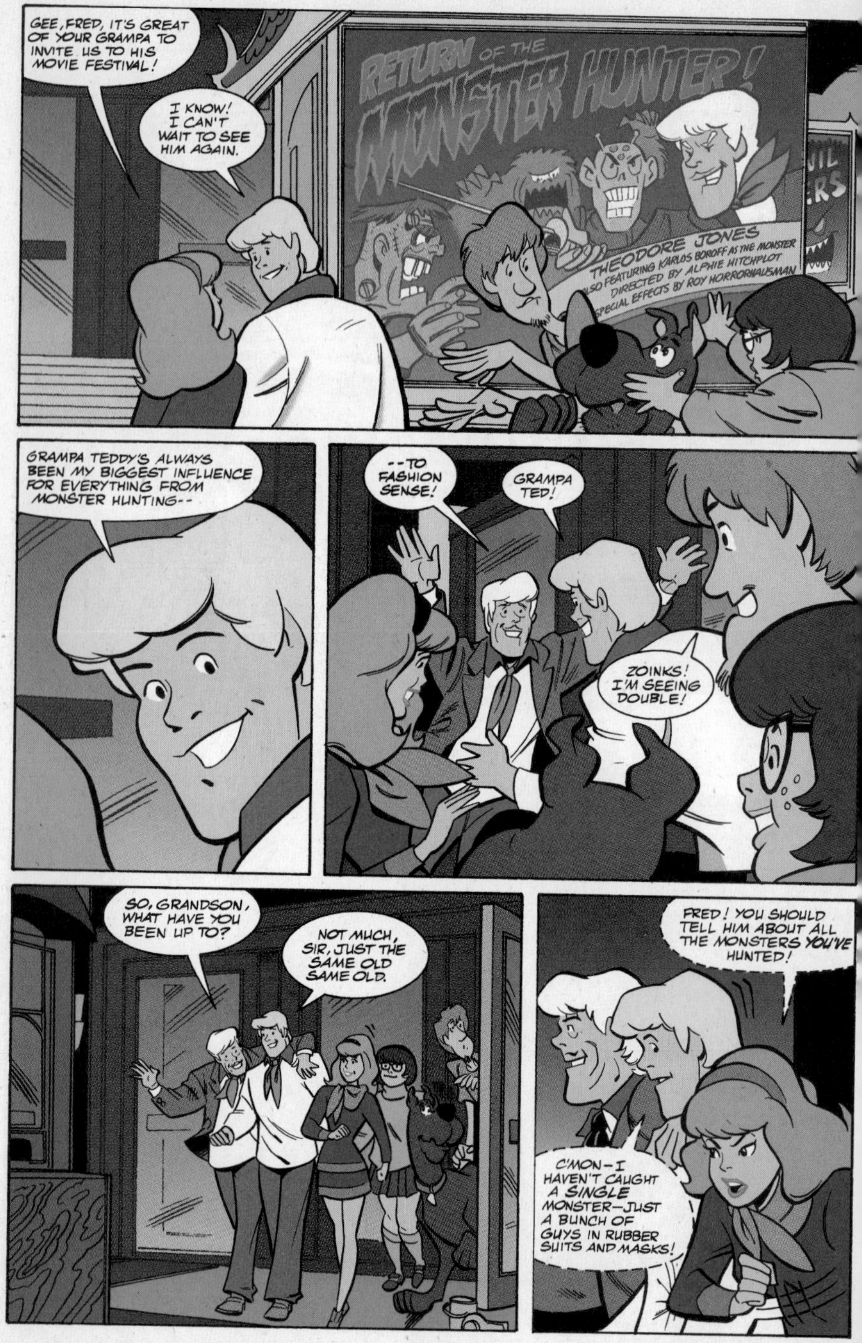
GEE, FRED, IT'S GREAT OF YOUR GRAMPA TO INVITE US TO HIS MOVIE FESTIVAL!
I KNOW! I CAN'T WAIT TO SEE HIM AGAIN.
RETURN OF THE MONSTER HUNTER!
THEODORE JONES
ALSO FEATURING KARLOS BOROFF AS THE MONSTER
DIRECTED BY ALPHIE HITCHPLOT
SPECIAL EFFECTS BY ROY HORRORHAUSMAN
GRAMPA TEDDY'S ALWAYS BEEN MY BIGGEST INFLUENCE FOR EVERYTHING FROM MONSTER HUNTING--
--TO FASHION SENSE!
GRAMPA TED!
ZOINKS! I'M SEEING DOUBLE!
SO, GRANDSON, WHAT HAVE YOU BEEN UP TO?
NOT MUCH, SIR, JUST THE SAME OLD SAME OLD.
FRED! YOU SHOULD TELL HIM ABOUT ALL THE MONSTERS YOU'VE HUNTED!
C'MON—I HAVEN'T CAUGHT A SINGLE MONSTER—JUST A BUNCH OF GUYS IN RUBBER SUITS AND MASKS!

WELL, FREDERICK, AREN'T YOU GOING TO INTRODUCE ME TO YOUR FRIENDS?

YES, SIR! THIS IS VELMA, AND DAPHNE, AND--

A PLEASURE!

--HEY?! WHERE'D SHAGGY AND SCOOBY GET TO?

WHAT THOUGHTFUL FRIENDS YOU HAVE, FREDDY, GETTING SNACKS FOR EVERYONE!

UMM...

THIS OUGHTA LAST ME AND SCOOB UNTIL INTERMISSION!

I THOUGHT I'D SEEN ALL YOUR MOVIES, MR. JONES, BUT I'VE NEVER HEARD OF RETURN OF THE MONSTER HUNTER.

THAT'S BECAUSE IT WAS NEVER RELEASED! THE MASTER PRINT WENT MISSING FOR YEARS--

--UNTIL ONE OF MY FANS FOUND IT IN AN OLD ATTIC AND SENT IT TO ME AS A GIFT!

GEE, IT MUST BE SUPER VALUABLE!

PRICELESS!

RETURN OF THE MONSTER HUNTER

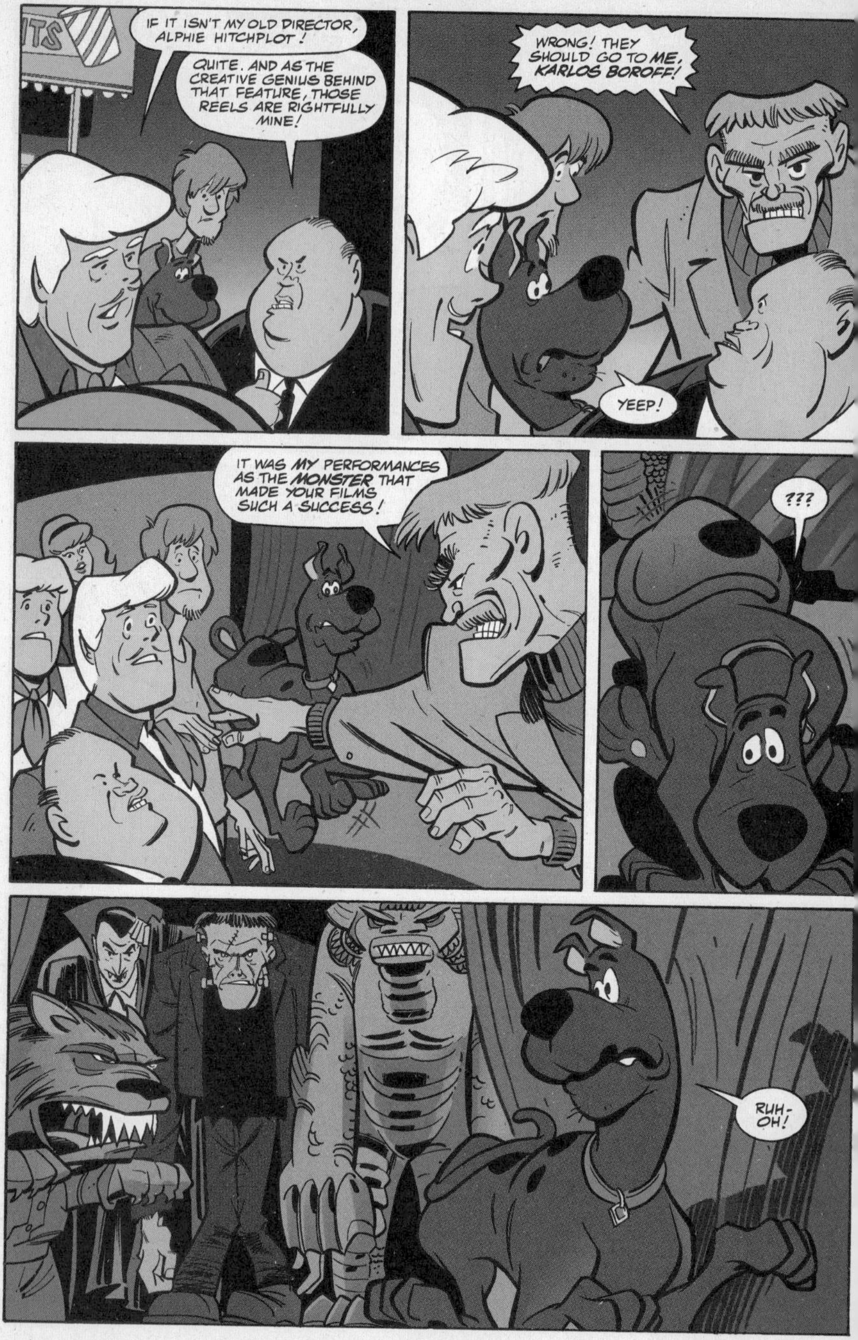

ITS
IF IT ISN'T MY OLD DIRECTOR, ALPHIE HITCHPLOT!
QUITE. AND AS THE CREATIVE GENIUS BEHIND THAT FEATURE, THOSE REELS ARE RIGHTFULLY MINE!
WRONG! THEY SHOULD GO TO ME, KARLOS BOROFF!
YEEP!
IT WAS MY PERFORMANCES AS THE MONSTER THAT MADE YOUR FILMS SUCH A SUCCESS!
???
RUH-OH!

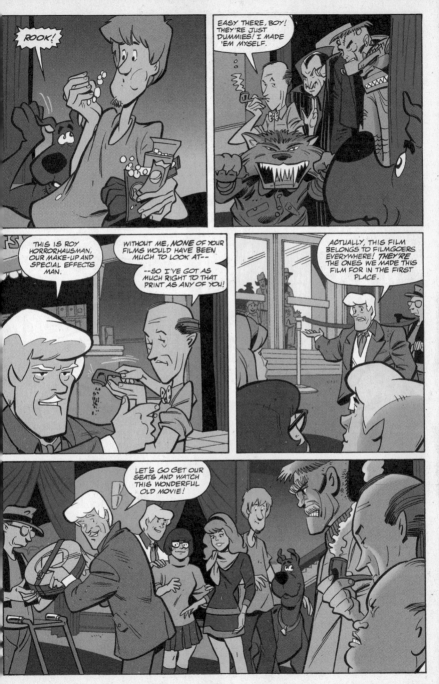

ROOK!

EASY THERE, BOY! THEY'RE JUST DUMMIES! I MADE 'EM MYSELF.

THIS IS ROY HORRORHAUSMAN, OUR MAKE-UP AND SPECIAL EFFECTS MAN.

WITHOUT ME, *NONE* OF YOUR FILMS WOULD HAVE BEEN MUCH TO LOOK AT--

--SO I'VE GOT AS MUCH RIGHT TO THAT PRINT AS ANY OF YOU!

ACTUALLY, THIS FILM BELONGS TO FILMGOERS EVERYWHERE! *THEY'RE* THE ONES WE MADE THIS FILM FOR IN THE FIRST PLACE.

LET'S GO GET OUR SEATS AND WATCH THIS WONDERFUL OLD MOVIE!

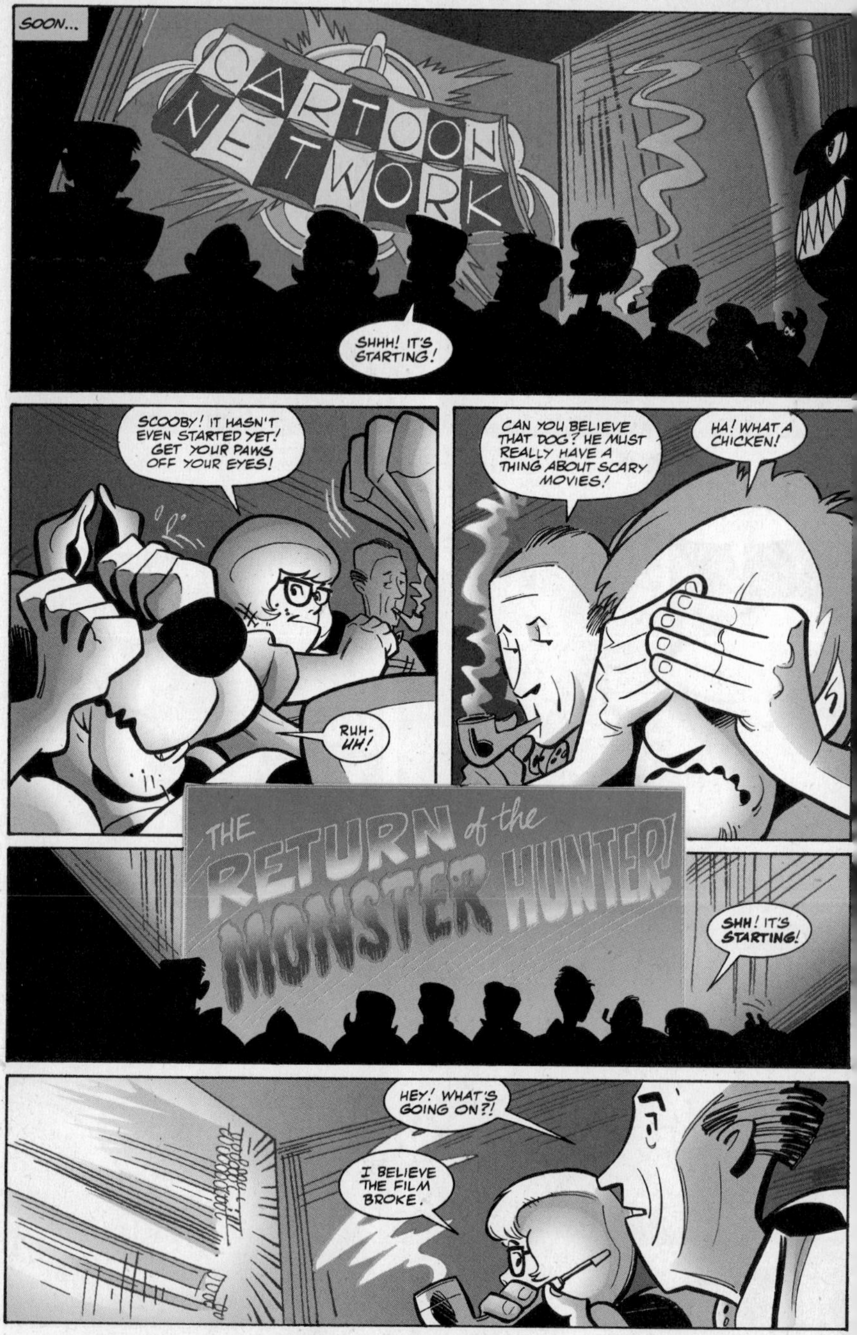
SOON...
CARTOON NETWORK
SHHH! IT'S STARTING!
SCOOBY! IT HASN'T EVEN STARTED YET! GET YOUR PAWS OFF YOUR EYES!
RUH-UH!
CAN YOU BELIEVE THAT DOG? HE MUST REALLY HAVE A THING ABOUT SCARY MOVIES!
HA! WHAT A CHICKEN!
THE RETURN of the MONSTER HUNTER!
SHH! IT'S STARTING!
HEY! WHAT'S GOING ON?!
I BELIEVE THE FILM BROKE.

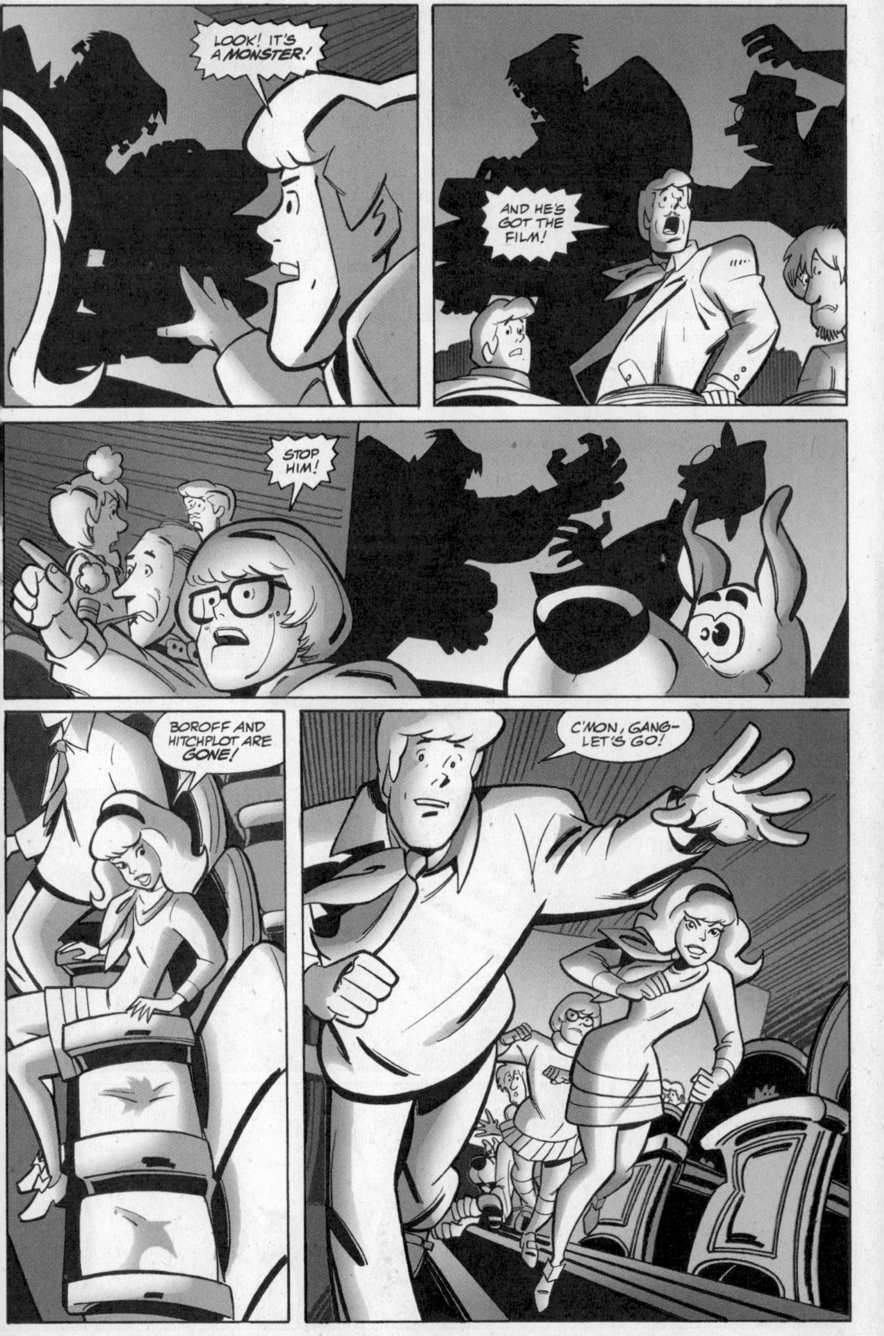
LOOK! IT'S A MONSTER!
AND HE'S GOT THE FILM!
STOP HIM!
BOROFF AND HITCHPLOT ARE GONE!
C'MON, GANG-LET'S GO!

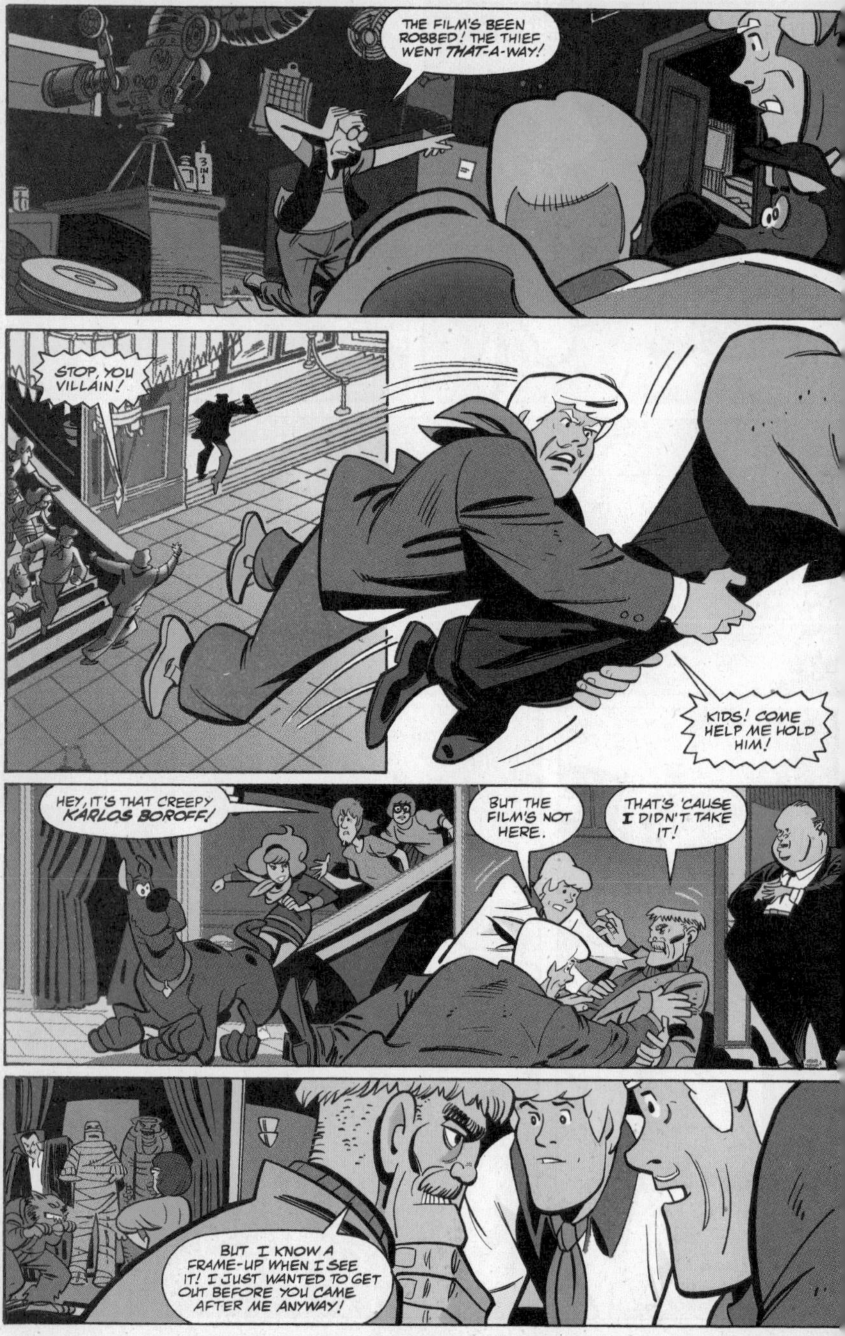
THE FILM'S BEEN ROBBED! THE THIEF WENT THAT-A-WAY!
STOP, YOU VILLAIN!
KIDS! COME HELP ME HOLD HIM!
HEY, IT'S THAT CREEPY KARLOS BOROFF!
BUT THE FILM'S NOT HERE.
THAT'S 'CAUSE I DIDN'T TAKE IT!
BUT I KNOW A FRAME-UP WHEN I SEE IT! I JUST WANTED TO GET OUT BEFORE YOU CAME AFTER ME ANYWAY!

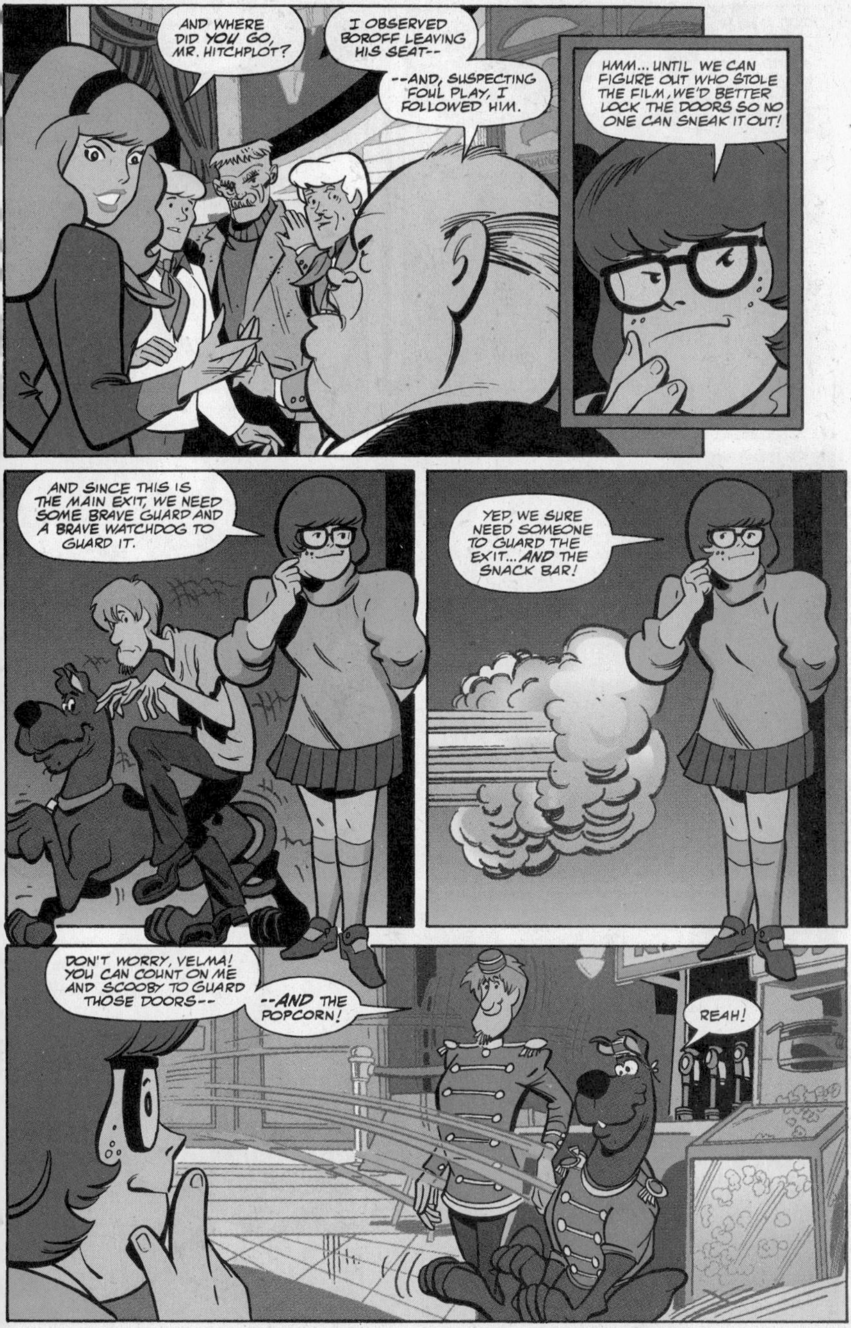
AND WHERE DID *YOU* GO, MR. HITCHPLOT?
I OBSERVED BOROFF LEAVING HIS SEAT--
--AND, SUSPECTING FOUL PLAY, I FOLLOWED HIM.
HMM... UNTIL WE CAN FIGURE OUT WHO STOLE THE FILM, WE'D BETTER LOCK THE DOORS SO NO ONE CAN SNEAK IT OUT!
AND SINCE THIS IS THE MAIN EXIT, WE NEED SOME BRAVE GUARD AND A BRAVE WATCHDOG TO GUARD IT.
YEP, WE SURE NEED SOMEONE TO GUARD THE EXIT... *AND* THE SNACK BAR!
DON'T WORRY, VELMA! YOU CAN COUNT ON ME AND SCOOBY TO GUARD THOSE DOORS--
--*AND* THE POPCORN!
REAH!

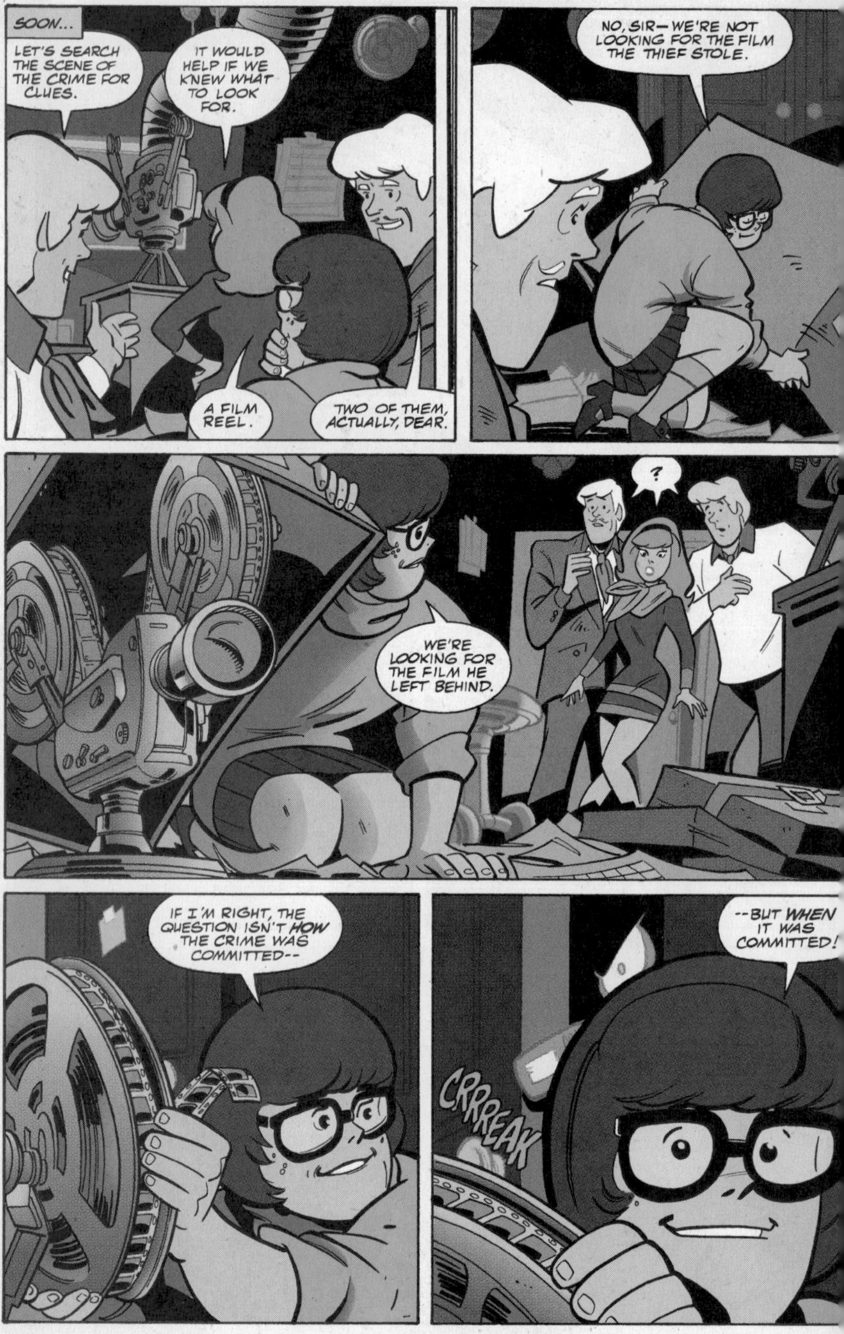
SOON...
LET'S SEARCH THE SCENE OF THE CRIME FOR CLUES.
IT WOULD HELP IF WE KNEW WHAT TO LOOK FOR.
A FILM REEL.
TWO OF THEM, ACTUALLY, DEAR.
NO, SIR— WE'RE NOT LOOKING FOR THE FILM THE THIEF STOLE.
?
WE'RE LOOKING FOR THE FILM HE LEFT BEHIND.
IF I'M RIGHT, THE QUESTION ISN'T HOW THE CRIME WAS COMMITTED--
--BUT WHEN IT WAS COMMITTED!
CRRREAK

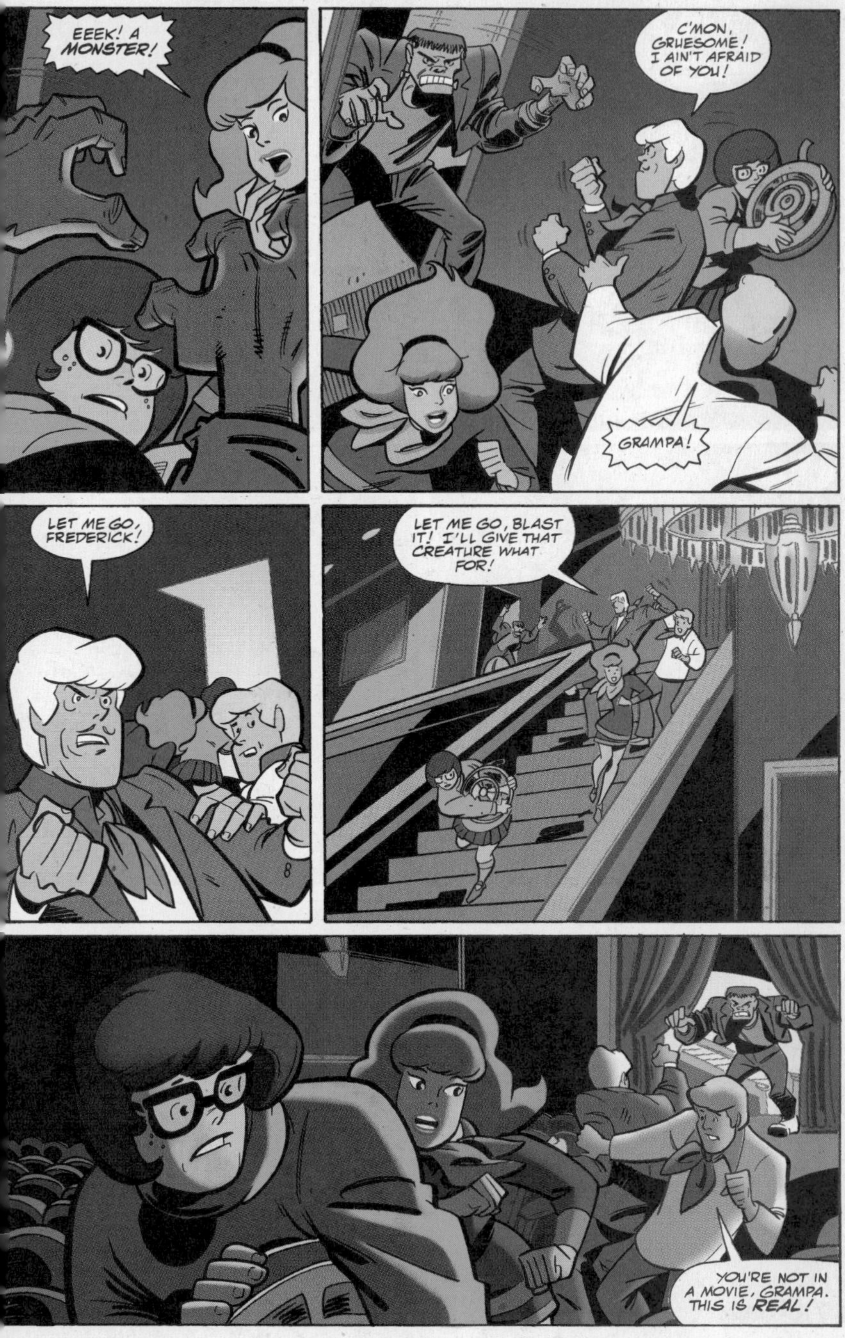

EEEK! A MONSTER!
C'MON, GRUESOME! I AIN'T AFRAID OF YOU!
GRAMPA!
LET ME GO, FREDERICK!
LET ME GO, BLAST IT! I'LL GIVE THAT CREATURE WHAT FOR!
YOU'RE NOT IN A MOVIE, GRAMPA. THIS IS REAL!

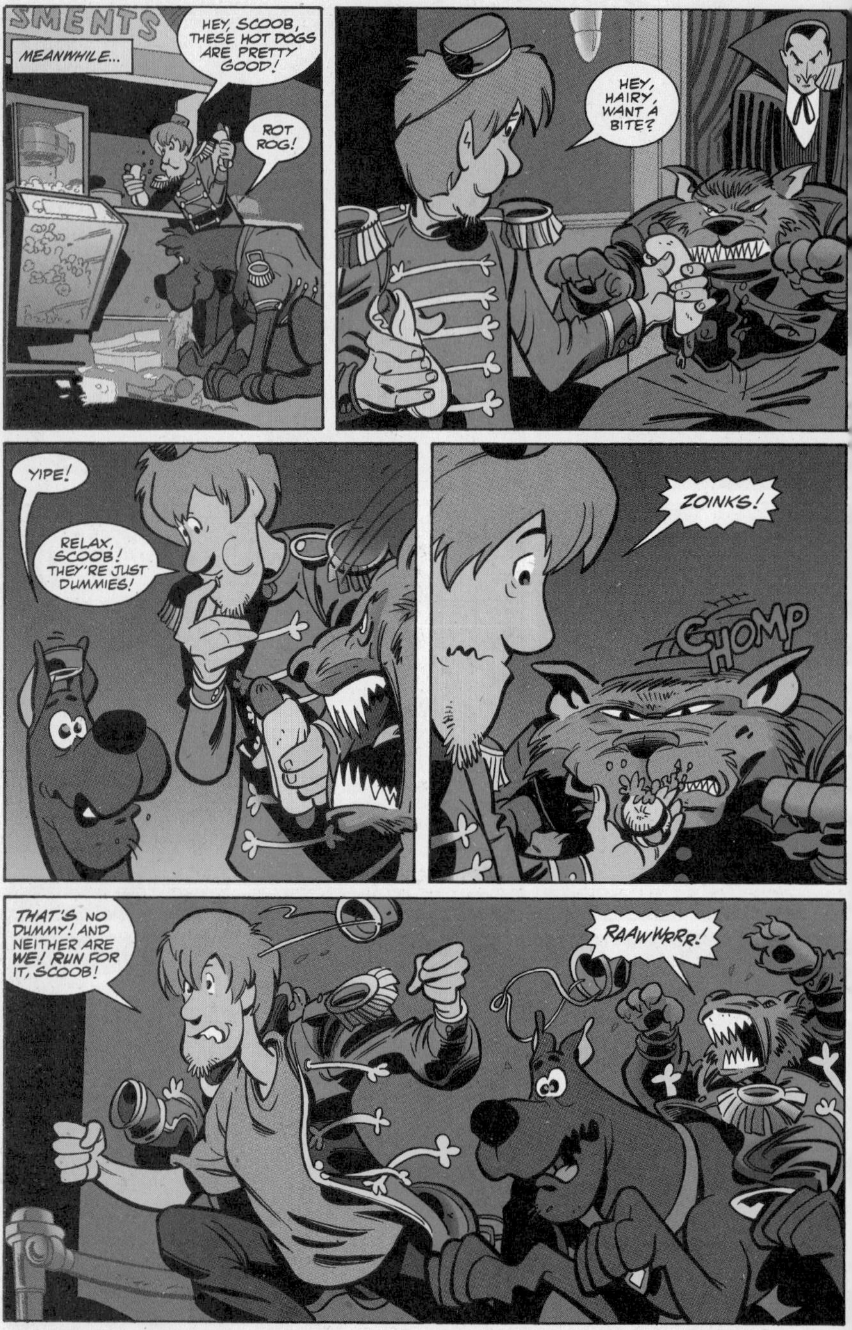
SMENTS
MEANWHILE...
HEY, SCOOB, THESE HOT DOGS ARE PRETTY GOOD!
ROT ROG!
HEY, HAIRY, WANT A BITE?
YIPE!
RELAX, SCOOB! THEY'RE JUST DUMMIES!
ZOINKS!
CHOMP
THAT'S NO DUMMY! AND NEITHER ARE WE! RUN FOR IT, SCOOB!
RAAWWRRR!

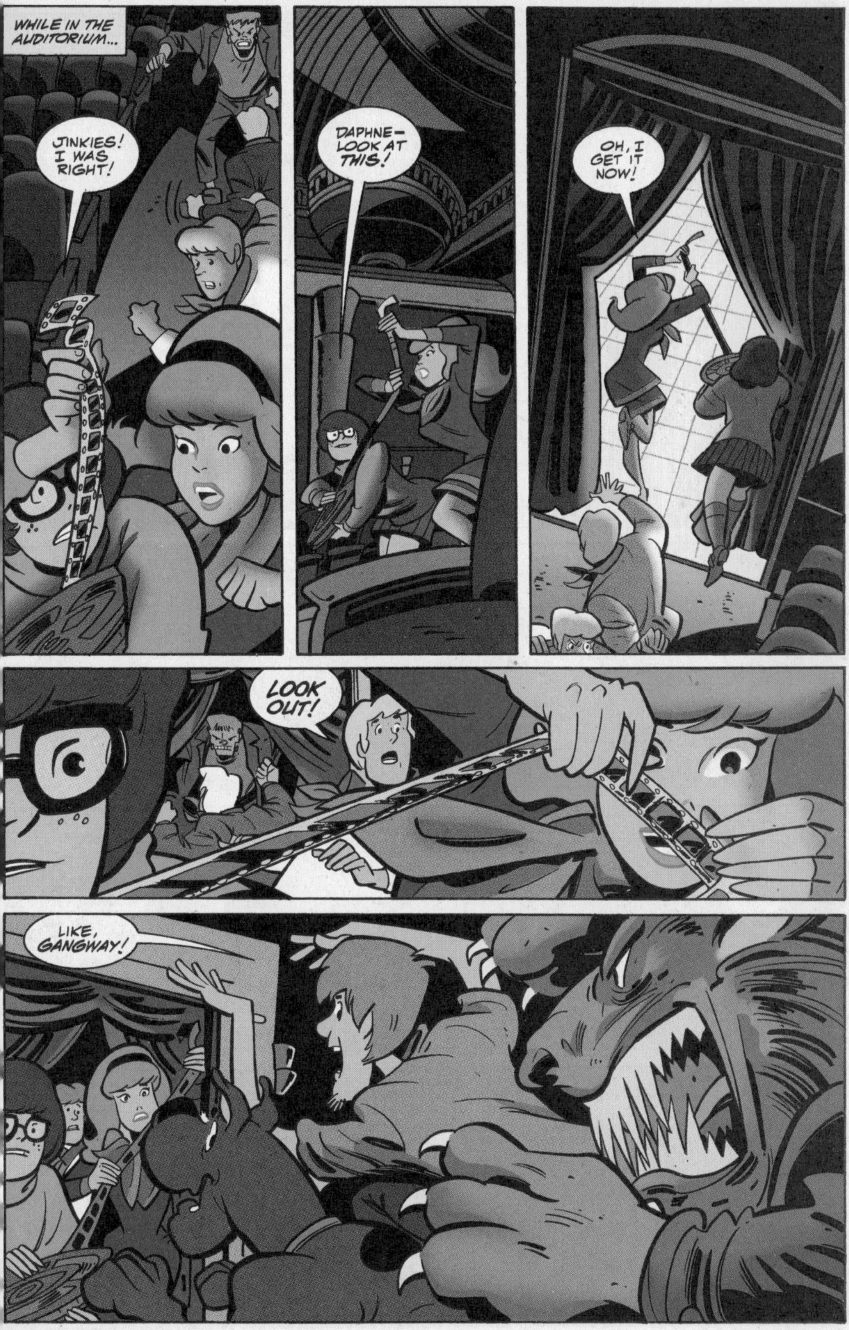
WHILE IN THE AUDITORIUM...
JINKIES! I WAS RIGHT!
DAPHNE— LOOK AT THIS!
OH, I GET IT NOW!
LOOK OUT!
LIKE, GANGWAY!

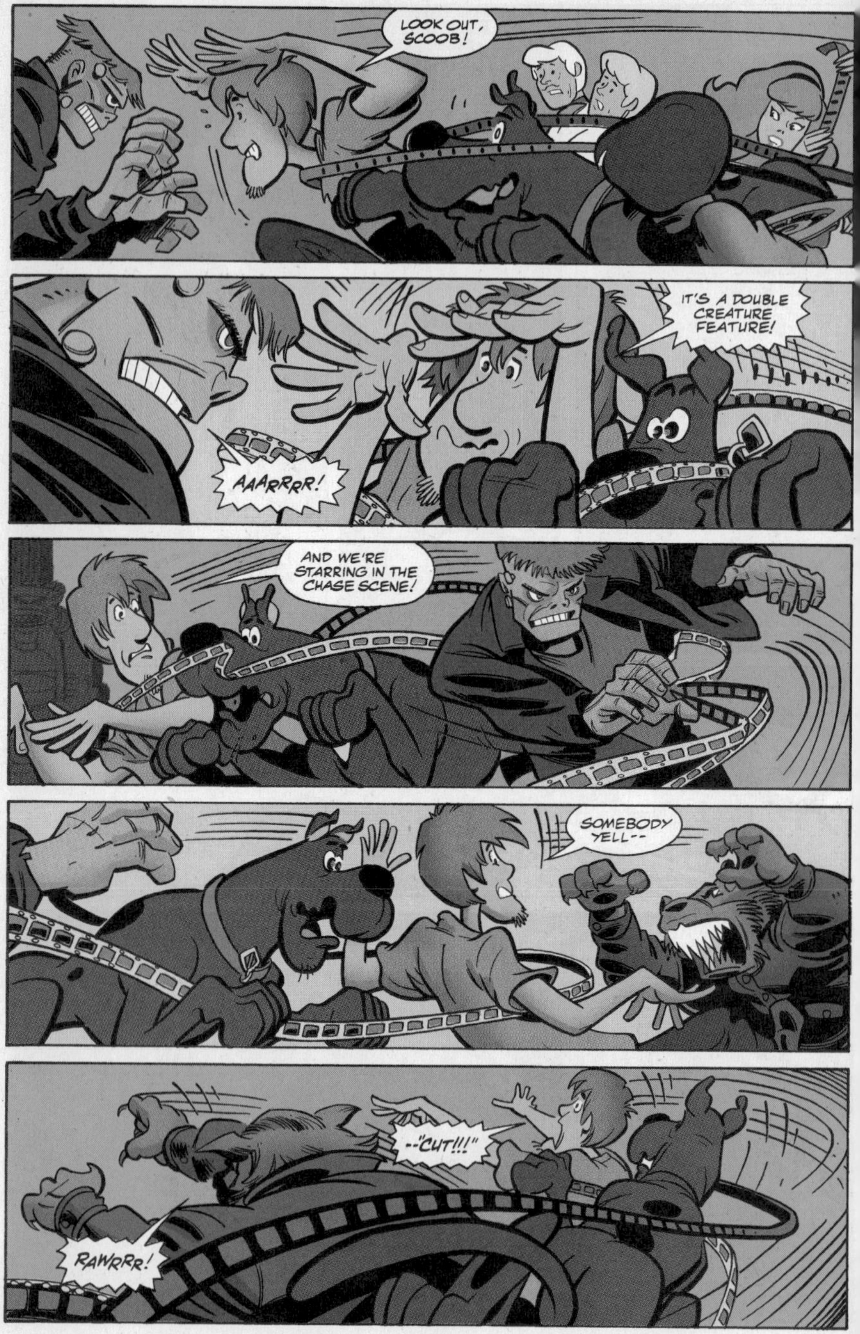

LOOK OUT, SCOOB!
IT'S A DOUBLE CREATURE FEATURE!
AAARRRR!
AND WE'RE STARRING IN THE CHASE SCENE!
SOMEBODY YELL--
--"CUT!!!"
RAWRRR!

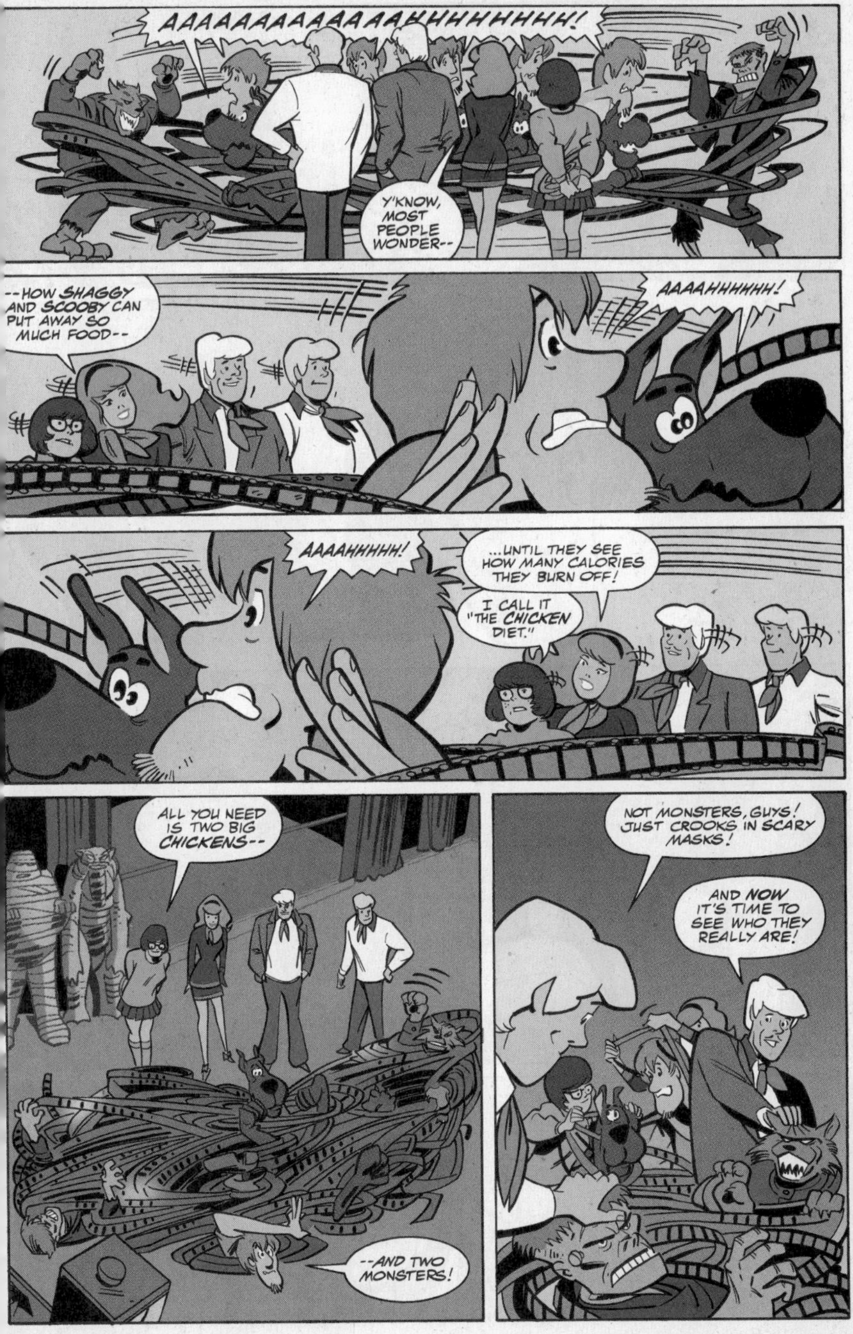
AAAAAAAAAAAAAHHHHHHHH!
Y'KNOW, MOST PEOPLE WONDER--
--HOW SHAGGY AND SCOOBY CAN PUT AWAY SO MUCH FOOD--
AAAAHHHHHH!
AAAAHHHHH!
...UNTIL THEY SEE HOW MANY CALORIES THEY BURN OFF!
I CALL IT "THE CHICKEN DIET."
ALL YOU NEED IS TWO BIG CHICKENS--
--AND TWO MONSTERS!
NOT MONSTERS, GUYS! JUST CROOKS IN SCARY MASKS!
AND NOW IT'S TIME TO SEE WHO THEY REALLY ARE!

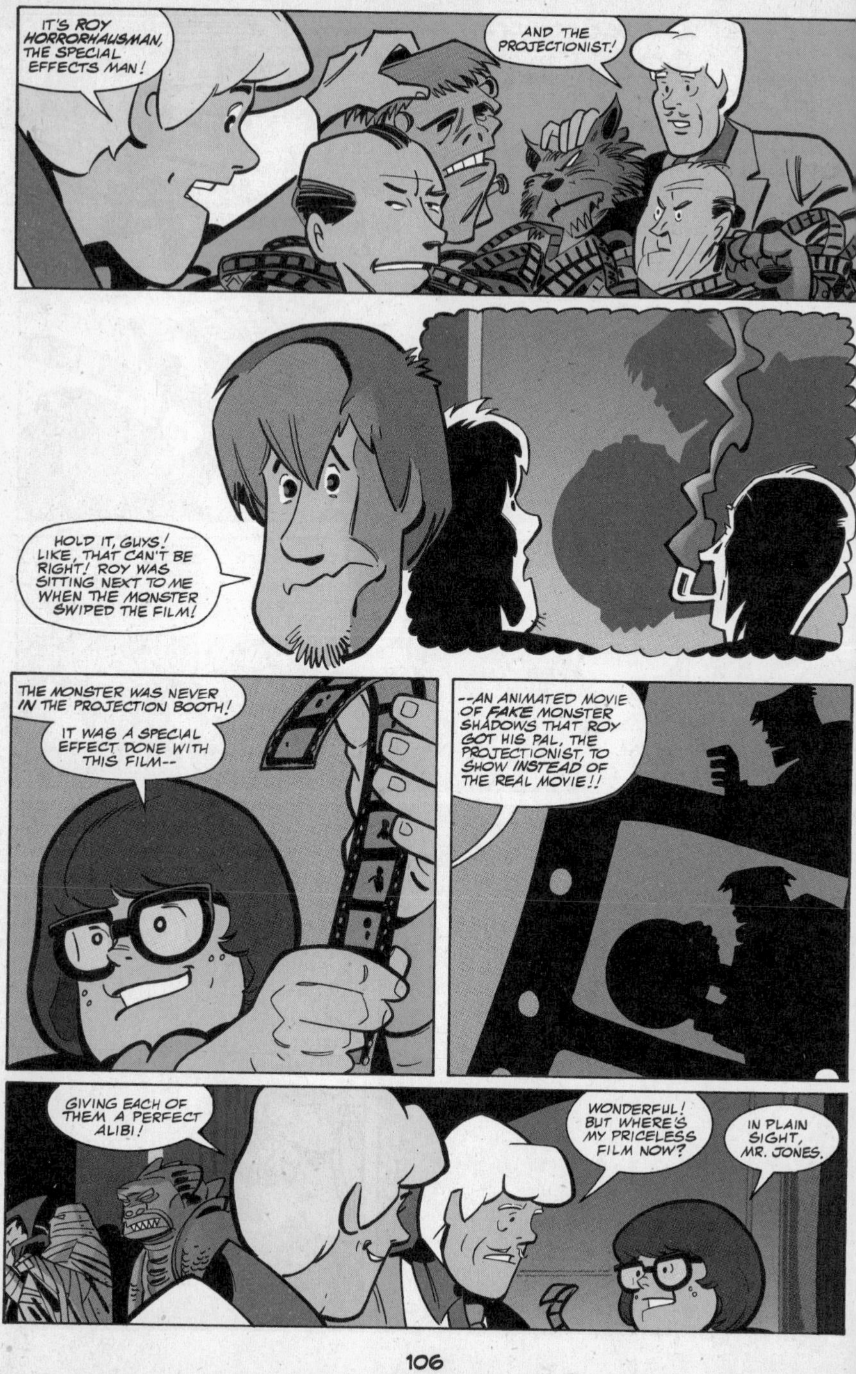
IT'S ROY HORRORHAUSMAN, THE SPECIAL EFFECTS MAN!
AND THE PROJECTIONIST!
HOLD IT, GUYS! LIKE, THAT CAN'T BE RIGHT! ROY WAS SITTING NEXT TO ME WHEN THE MONSTER SWIPED THE FILM!
THE MONSTER WAS NEVER IN THE PROJECTION BOOTH!
IT WAS A SPECIAL EFFECT DONE WITH THIS FILM--
--AN ANIMATED MOVIE OF FAKE MONSTER SHADOWS THAT ROY GOT HIS PAL, THE PROJECTIONIST, TO SHOW INSTEAD OF THE REAL MOVIE!!
GIVING EACH OF THEM A PERFECT ALIBI!
WONDERFUL! BUT WHERE'S MY PRICELESS FILM NOW?
IN PLAIN SIGHT, MR. JONES.

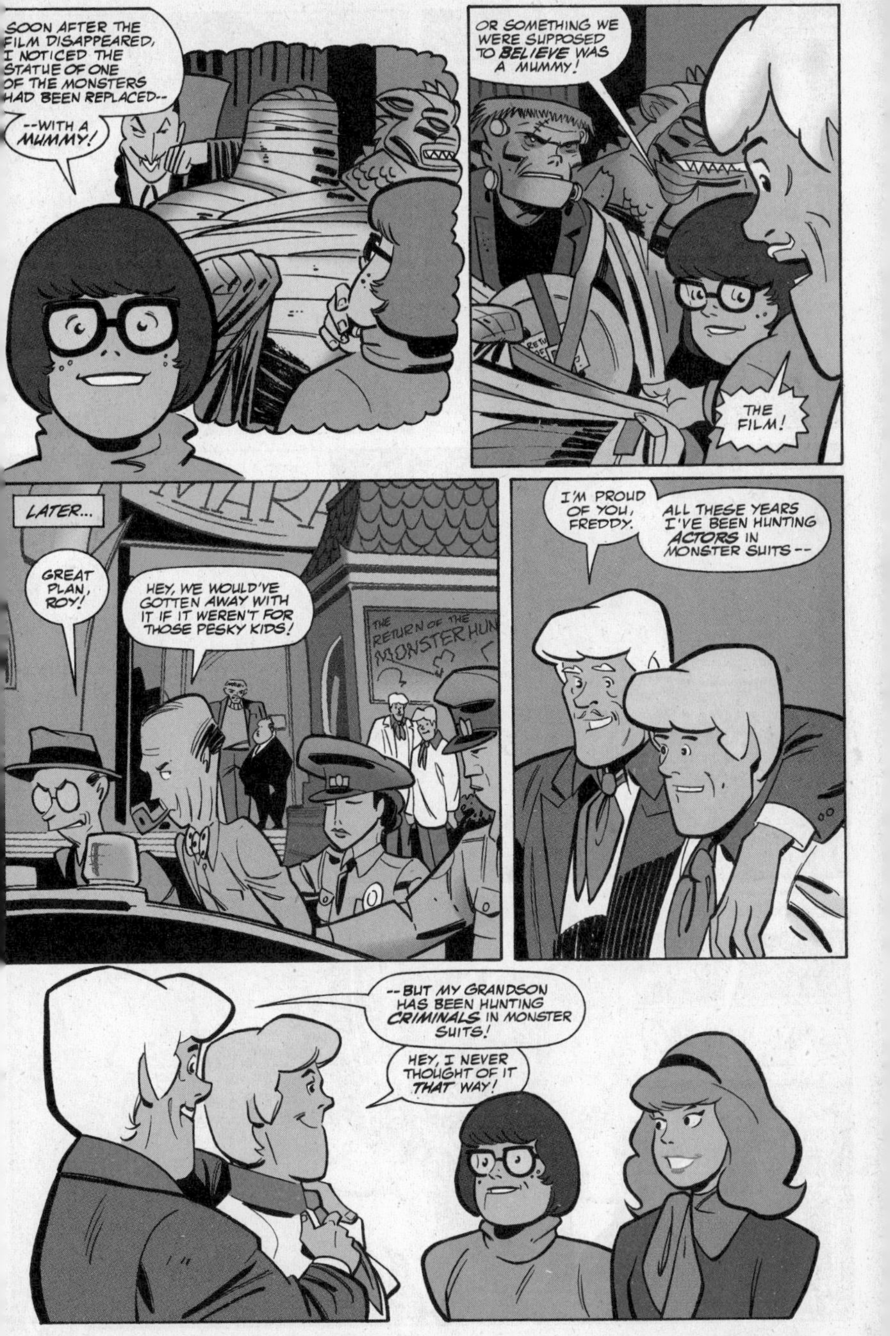
SOON AFTER THE FILM DISAPPEARED, I NOTICED THE STATUE OF ONE OF THE MONSTERS HAD BEEN REPLACED--
--WITH A MUMMY!
OR SOMETHING WE WERE SUPPOSED TO BELIEVE WAS A MUMMY!
THE FILM!
LATER...
GREAT PLAN, ROY!
HEY, WE WOULD'VE GOTTEN AWAY WITH IT IF IT WEREN'T FOR THOSE PESKY KIDS!
THE RETURN OF THE MONSTER HUN
I'M PROUD OF YOU, FREDDY.
ALL THESE YEARS I'VE BEEN HUNTING ACTORS IN MONSTER SUITS--
--BUT MY GRANDSON HAS BEEN HUNTING CRIMINALS IN MONSTER SUITS!
HEY, I NEVER THOUGHT OF IT THAT WAY!

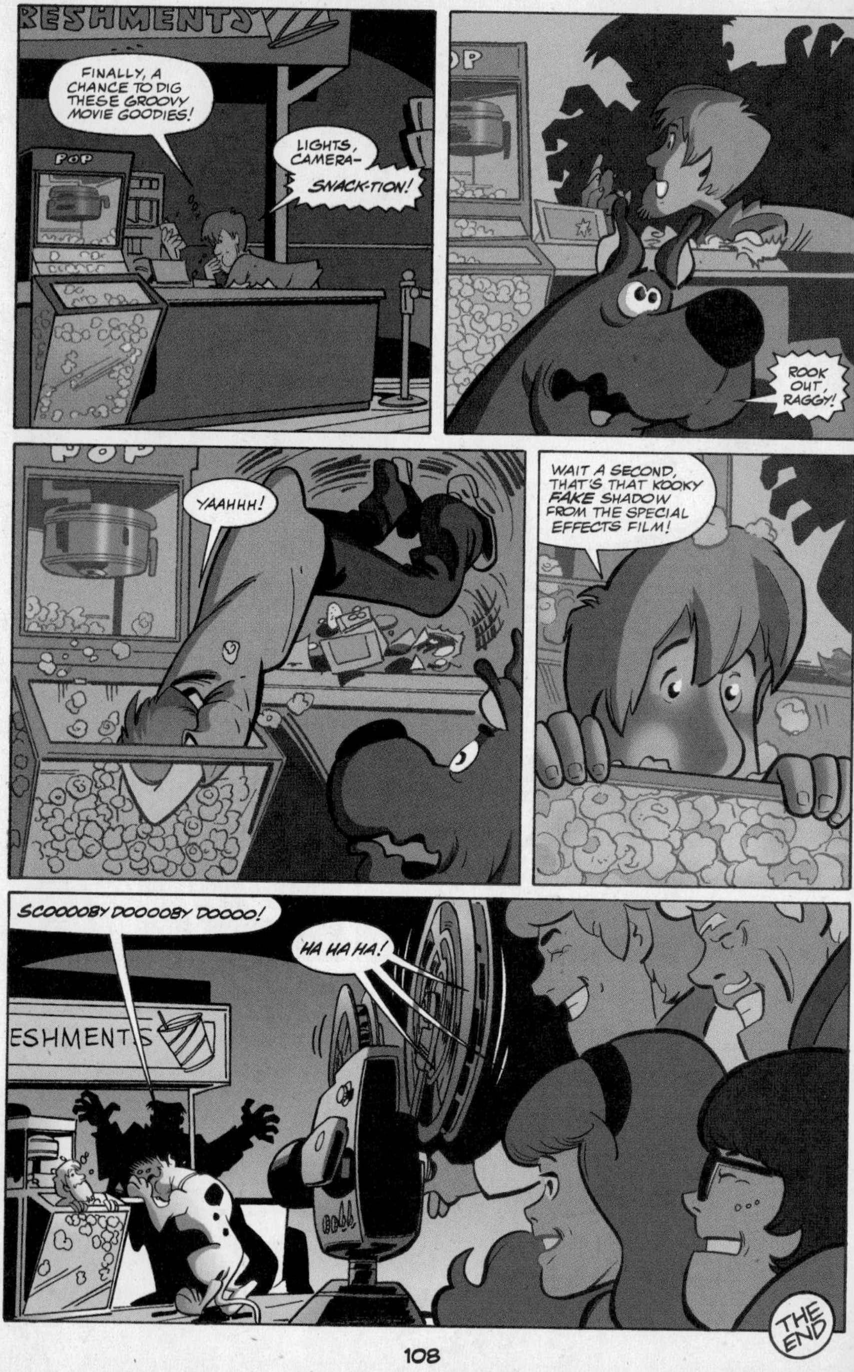
RESHMENTS
FINALLY, A CHANCE TO DIG THESE GROOVY MOVIE GOODIES!
LIGHTS, CAMERA-
SNACK-TION!
POP
ROOK OUT, RAGGY!
YAAHHH!
WAIT A SECOND, THAT'S THAT KOOKY FAKE SHADOW FROM THE SPECIAL EFFECTS FILM!
SCOOOOBY DOOOOBY DOOOO!
HA HA HA!
ESHMENTS
THE END

SCOOBY-DOO -IN-

THE BEST LAID PLANS...

STORY: CHRIS DUFFY ART and LETTERING: TIM HARKINS
COLORING: PATRICIA MULVIHILL EDITING: BRONWYN TAGGART

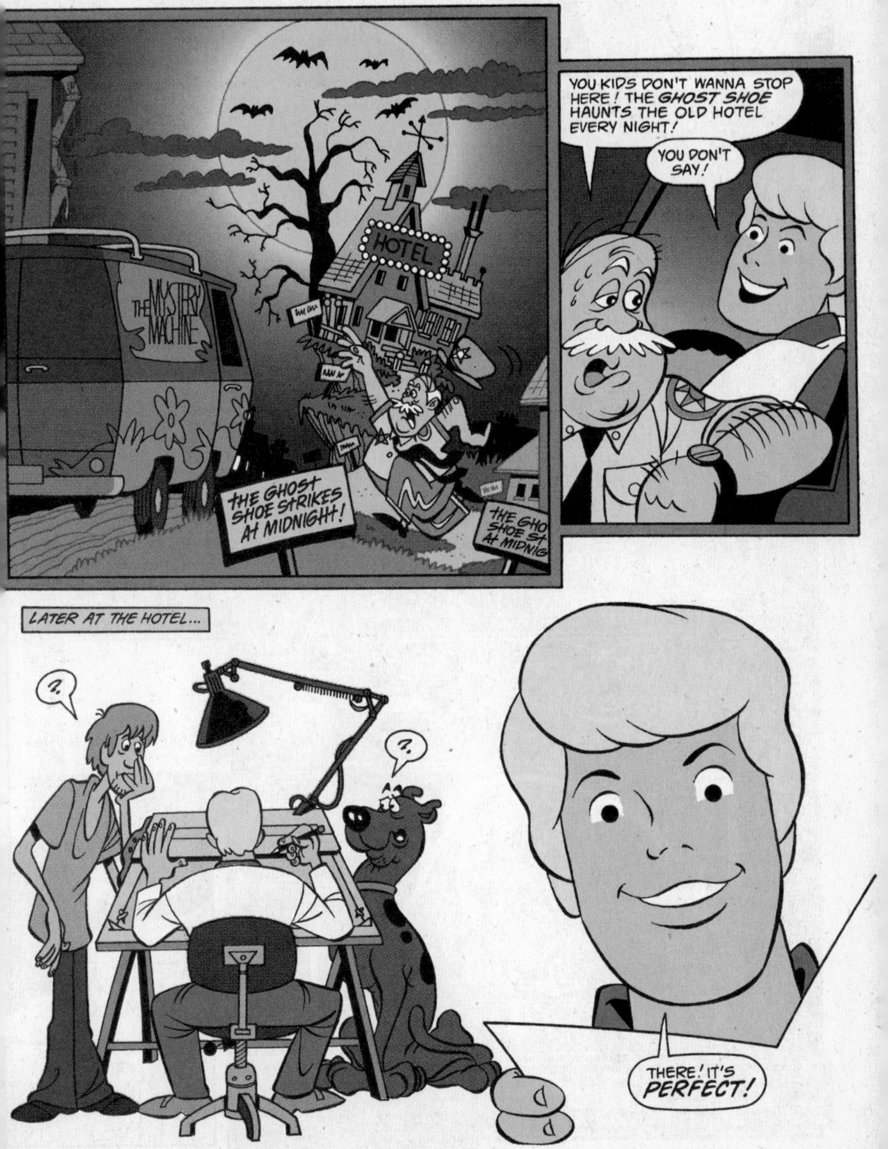

HOTEL
THE MYSTERY MACHINE
THE GHOST SHOE STRIKES AT MIDNIGHT!
YOU KIDS DON'T WANNA STOP HERE! THE *GHOST SHOE* HAUNTS THE OLD HOTEL EVERY NIGHT!
YOU DON'T SAY!
LATER AT THE HOTEL...
?
?
THERE! IT'S *PERFECT!*

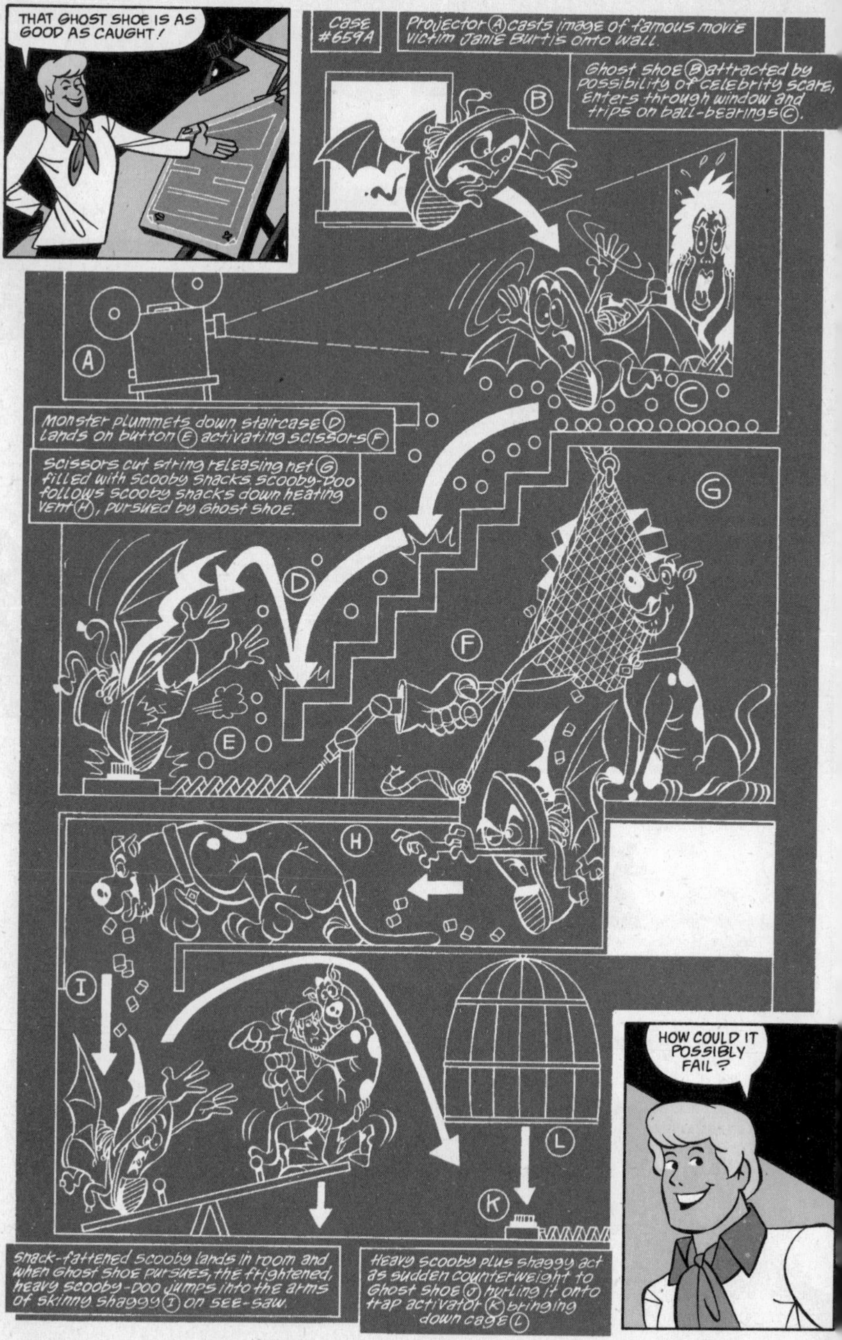

THAT GHOST SHOE IS AS GOOD AS CAUGHT!
Case #659A
Projector Ⓐ casts image of famous movie victim Janie Burtis onto wall.
Ghost shoe Ⓑ attracted by possibility of celebrity scare, enters through window and trips on ball-bearings Ⓒ.
B
A
C
Monster plummets down staircase Ⓓ lands on button Ⓔ activating scissors Ⓕ
Scissors cut string releasing net Ⓖ filled with scooby snacks. Scooby-Doo follows scooby snacks down heating vent Ⓗ, pursued by Ghost shoe.
G
D
F
E
H
I
L
K
HOW COULD IT POSSIBLY FAIL?
Snack-fattened scooby lands in room and when Ghost shoe pursues, the frightened, heavy scooby-Doo jumps into the arms of skinny shaggy Ⓘ on see-saw.
Heavy scooby plus shaggy act as sudden counterweight to Ghost shoe Ⓙ hurling it onto trap activator Ⓚ bringing down cage Ⓛ

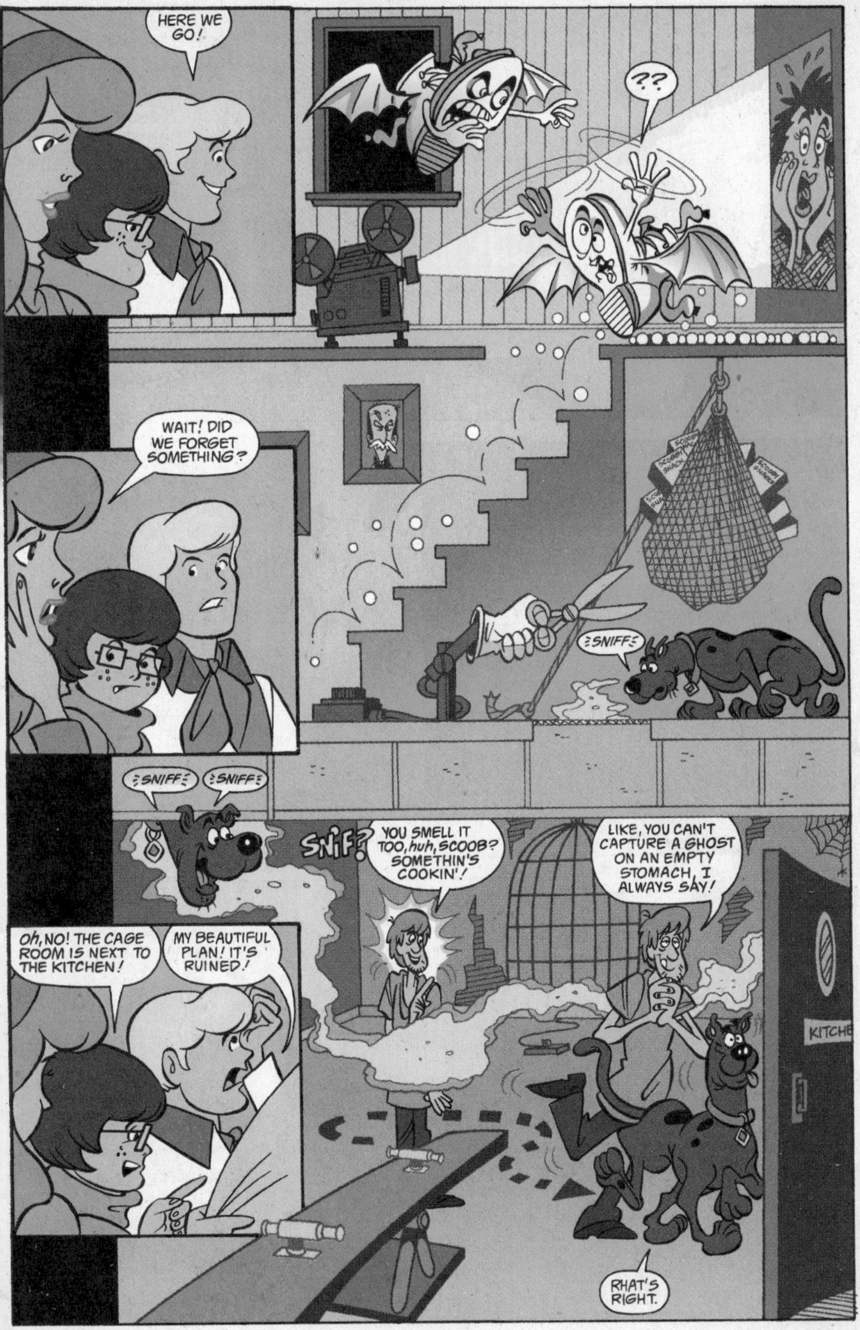
HERE WE GO!
??
WAIT! DID WE FORGET SOMETHING?
SNIFF
SNIFF
SNIFF
SNIF?
YOU SMELL IT TOO, huh, SCOOB? SOMETHIN'S COOKIN'!
LIKE, YOU CAN'T CAPTURE A GHOST ON AN EMPTY STOMACH, I ALWAYS SAY!
RHAT'S RIGHT.
Oh, NO! THE CAGE ROOM IS NEXT TO THE KITCHEN!
MY BEAUTIFUL PLAN! IT'S RUINED!
KITCHE

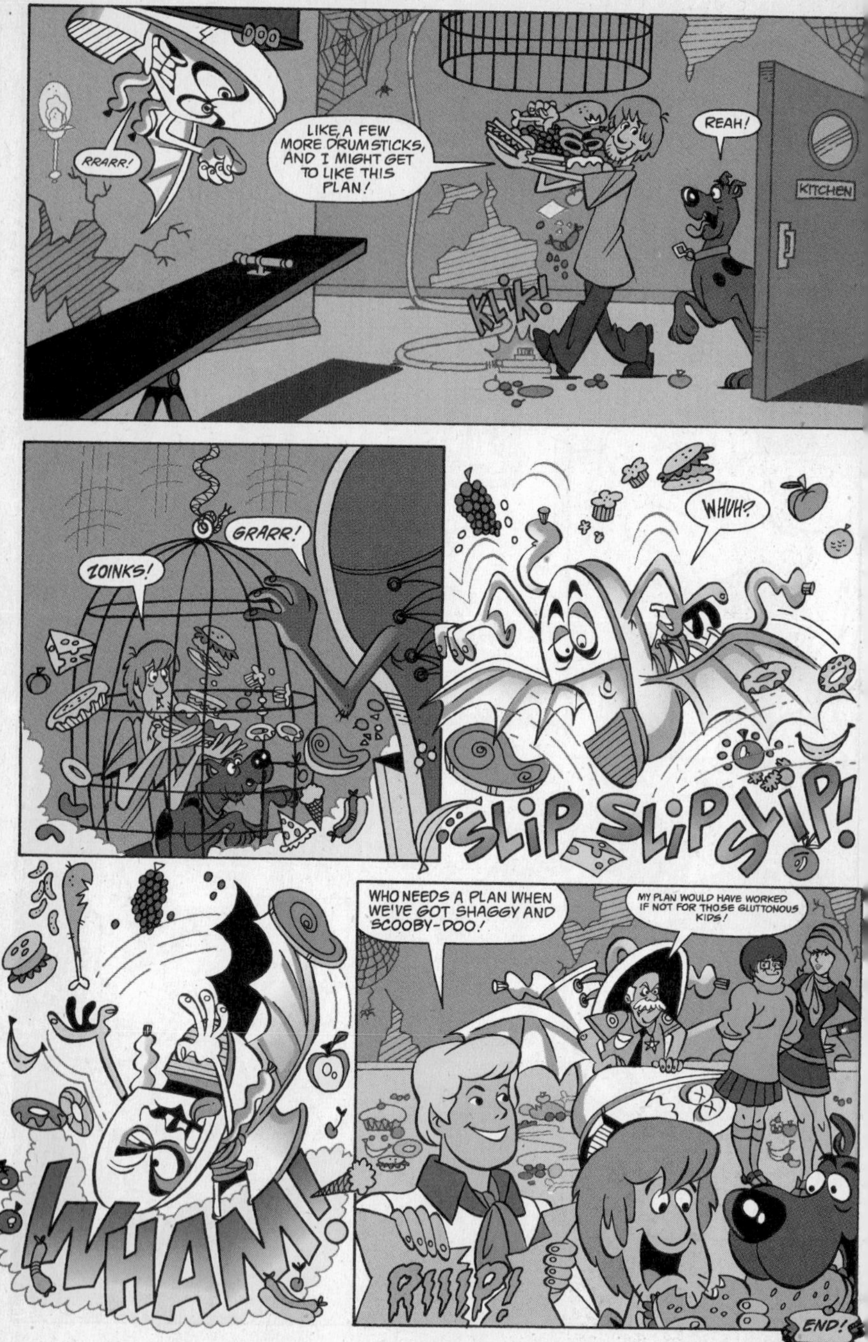
RRARR!
LIKE, A FEW MORE DRUMSTICKS, AND I MIGHT GET TO LIKE THIS PLAN!
REAH!
KITCHEN
KLIK!
ZOINKS!
GRARR!
WHUH?
SLIP SLIP SLIP!
WHAM!
WHO NEEDS A PLAN WHEN WE'VE GOT SHAGGY AND SCOOBY-DOO!
MY PLAN WOULD HAVE WORKED IF NOT FOR THOSE GLUTTONOUS KIDS!
RIIIP!
END!